PAINT YOUR DRAGON

PAINT YOUR DRAGON

Tom Holt

ORBIT

An *Orbit* Book

First published in Great Britain by Orbit in 1996

Copyright © Tom Holt 1996

The moral right of the author has been asserted.

A CIP catalogue record for this book
is available from the British Library.

ISBN 1 85723 433 2

Typeset by Solidus (Bristol) Limited
Printed and bound in Great Britain by
Clays Ltd, St Ives plc

Orbit
A Division of
Little, Brown and Company (UK)
Brettenham House
Lancaster Place
London WC2E 7EN

For
LESLIE FISH
The best of all of us

and
JONATHAN WAITE
Who has all the talents
Except one

CHAPTER ONE

Once upon a time, long ago and far away, there was a great battle between Good and Evil. Good was triumphant, and as a result Humanity has lived happily ever after.

But supposing Evil threw the fight . . .

And supposing Good cheated . . .

He stepped off the plane into the belly of the snake; the long, winding tube thing they shove right up to the cabin door, so that newly arrived foreigners don't get a really close look at dear old England until they're through passport control and it's too late.

He didn't actually have a passport; but he explained at the barrier exactly why he didn't need one, and so they let him through. In answer to his polite enquiry, they told him, 'Britain'. They even urged him to have a nice day, which was rather like imploring petrol to burn.

Down the steps he went, into the baggage hall. The carousel was empty and the indicator board expressed the

1

view that the luggage from Flight BA666 might be along in about half an hour, maybe forty minutes, call it an hour to be on the safe side, provided always it hadn't got on the wrong plane by mistake; in which case, it was probably having a far more exotic holiday than its owners had just returned from, and would probably settle down over there, adopt new owners, and lead a much fuller, richer life than it could ever have had in a damp, miserable country like this. He read the board and smiled indulgently. Then he concentrated.

The first item to roll out through the little rubber flaps was a big, old-fashioned steamer trunk. He looked at it, head slightly on one side, pursed his lips and shook his head. 'Smaller,' he said. The trunk went round and disappeared.

Next came a matching three-piece set of designer pigskin travelware, with very fancy brass locks, little wheels for ease of handling, and monogrammed straps. He shook his head vigorously, and the travelware, handles drooping with shame, made itself scarce.

Then came a medium-sized plain vinyl suitcase, no wheels. He was clearly tempted because he picked it up and tested the weight. But it must have seemed too heavy or too bulky because he put it back again, and a moment later it too trickled out through the flaps. A similar item, more or less exactly the same except for the colour and the contours of the handle, came next, but was dismissed with a slight pucker of the lips and a small sideways head movement.

It was followed a moment later by a simple black canvas holdall, with webbing handles and a shoulder strap. He looked at it, nodded and picked it up. He unzipped it; it was empty. When he zipped it up again, it was full. He looked around until he saw the exit sign and walked on briskly. Needless to say, the Customs men didn't even seem to notice him.

Before leaving the airport, he went to the men's toilet to brush his hair and see what he looked like. He hadn't had a chance to look in a mirror or a pool of water since he'd died, and although he was determined to spend as little time as possible in this poxy runabout Lada of a body, a certain human curiosity came with the hardware. He stepped up to the mirror.

If he'd been expecting a disappointment, he was disappointed. They don't advertise the fact, but the Heathrow men's bogs house the world's last surviving scrying-mirror, an antisocially cunning piece of kit which treats appearances with the scorn that Mercedes salesmen reserve for people who live in council houses, and lets you see yourself as you truly are. Back in the heroic past, no self-respecting wizard stirred out of doors without one; it was the only way to filter out all the gods disguised as mortals, princes masquerading as frogs, wolves in grandmothers' clothing and other pests which made the Dark Ages such a wretchedly fraught experience. This particular example now belongs to the syndicate who hold the airport's duty-free concession. It's linked to the video surveillance system and makes it possible for them to spot a mug punter before he's even checked in his luggage.

He saw a huge shape. If you love understatement and have just had your soul repossessed by the finance company, you could say he looked a bit like a lizard; except that lizards are generally smaller than, say, Jersey and don't have enormous wings, and even naturalists (who get paid for loving all of God's creatures) tend to look at their faces and think immediately of their spouses' relations. The face in the mirror, on the other claw, was beautiful in the same way that weapons and warships and violent electric storms over the sea at sunset can be beautiful.

The dragon clicked his tongue impatiently. He'd seen

that before. More to the point, that wonderful, dangerously attractive shape he was looking at had been significantly dead for thousands of years, ever since one George de la Croix (alias Dragon George Cody; better known to divinity as Saint George) had kebabbed it with a whacking great spear. One day, probably quite soon, he'd get another dragon body and look like that again; right now he was wearing a standard K-Mart two-leg, two-arm, pink hairless monkey costume – the equivalent of the cheap grey suit they give you when you're demobbed or let out of prison – and he wanted to see what he looked like in that. He turned to the next mirror along and saw a human male, powerfully built as humans go, medium height, longish dark hair and short, clipped beard with grey icing, and round yellow eyes with black slits for pupils.

Ah well, he thought. If you wear off the peg, you've got to take what you get. He was no expert in human fashions – in his day, nearly all the humans he came across wore steel boiler-suits with helmets like coal scuttles, and that was a very long time ago. It would probably do, until he got the dragon outfit back. And then, of course, everything would be different anyway.

Once outside he raised a hand, whereupon a taxi drew up and opened its door. That was, in fact, a curious occurrence in itself, since the last thing the taxi driver could remember was turning left out of Regent Street and swerving to avoid a right-hand-drive Maserati. He also had a notion that he'd had a passenger on board. Evidently not, for the cab was empty.

'Where to?' the driver asked.

'Licensed premises,' he replied. Then he threw his bag onto the back seat and climbed in.

The driver, a Londoner, didn't actually know of any pubs in the Heathrow area, and confessed as much. His fare replied that in that case, they could learn together. 'Just drive around,' he suggested, 'until we see something I like the look of.'

And so they did. They'd been cruising up and down lanes for maybe half an hour when he suddenly leaned forward, rapped on the glass and said, 'That one.'

'You're the boss.'

'Yes.'

Having explained to the driver exactly why he didn't actually owe him any money, he waved him goodbye, shouldered his bag and crunched up the path to the front door. The landlord of the George and Dragon was, at that precise moment, asleep in bed – it was ten past ten in the morning, and yesterday had been a late darts night – so he was more than a little confused when, about one second after the doorknocker crashed down on its brass anvil, he found himself in the bar, fully dressed, shooting back the bolts.

'Morning. You open?'

'I think so.'

'That's fine. Large whisky, please, no ice.'

The customer had a fine thirst on him; ten large whiskies, one after another, appeared to have no more effect than airgun pellets fired at the side of a battleship. Ah well, thought the landlord, obviously a very lucky man. 'Another?' he suggested.

'Please,' the customer replied. 'What's that one with the green and black label?'

The landlord peered. 'Bourbon,' he replied, stating the brand name. 'A hundred and five proof,' he added.

The customer smiled. 'Ah,' he said. 'That's what I call fire water. Make it a treble, and have one for yourself.'

Just as the customer said it, the landlord realised how much he needed a drink at precisely that moment. He reworked the optic, mumbled 'Here's health,' and knocked back the glass, the contents of which did to his head what Guy Fawkes wanted to do to Parliament. 'Good stuff,' he croaked.

'Not bad, I suppose,' replied the customer. 'Same again.'

It occurred to the landlord that it would only be polite to make a little conversation, and he asked the customer what line of business he was in. It seemed that he'd inadvertently made a joke, because the customer grinned.

'Let's see,' he replied. 'Let's say I'm a flier.'

'Pilot, you mean?'

'Sort of.' He felt in his top pocket, extracted a cigarette, drew on it heavily and exhaled. The smoke seemed to fill the bar.

'Civil or military?' the barman asked.

'Bit of both. What's that colourless stuff in the bottle with the red label?'

'Kirsch.'

'Treble of that, then, and next I'd like to try the other colourless stuff with the green label.'

'That's Polish vodka, that is. Hundred and forty per cent proof. Beats me,' the landlord went on, 'how something can be a hundred and forty per cent anything. I thought a hundred per cent was the limit; you know, like a hundred out of a hundred?'

Not long afterwards, the customer got up, thanked the landlord, and left him musing on three points that were puzzling him. Probably because his head was still glowing from the bourbon, he couldn't quite get a handle on any of them.

One; how come the man who had just left had managed to put away roughly ninety-seven centilitres of spirits in ten minutes and still been able to breathe, let alone walk jauntily out of the front door with no apparent impairment of his motor functions?

Two; the reason he had given for not paying had been utterly convincing, fair and square, no problems whatsoever on that score, but what had it been, exactly?

Three; just how in hell had he been able to smoke for five minutes without actually lighting the cigarette?

Bianca Wilson had first made her mark on Norton Polytechnic when she suddenly stood up in the middle of a class and put her clothes on.

Ignoring the comments, she then stepped down off the platform, took possession of the vacant easel and proceeded to paint a breathtaking still life of three herrings and a typewriter ribbon. After that, there was no question of mucking about with application forms; not only was she in the class, she was its star pupil. When asked what had prompted her to make the change from model to practitioner, she replied that it was warmer and you didn't have to keep still.

Sculpture proved to be her true medium. She stripped away marble as if it was cellophane wrapping to reveal the always implicit statue beneath. Once she'd learned the basics of the craft, such as how to sharpen a chisel and the best way to avoid clouting your thumb, it was obvious that there was nothing more that Norton Tech could teach her. Accordingly, she thanked them very much, gave up the day job by the simple but eloquent expedient of telling the office manager what he could do with it, and spent her last ten pounds on a ticket to London. She travelled, of course, in the guard's van; it had taken five porters, the conductor and three gullible Royal Marines to get her luggage on board, and the Spirit of World Peace had to make the journey with her left leg sticking out of the window.

Small-town girl in the big city; well, so was Joan of Arc, not to mention Boadicea. A talent like Bianca's is always hard to keep hidden, particularly when its manifestations are ten feet high and weigh close to a ton and a half. It took the proprietor of the Herries Street Gallery, stepping off the train at Paddington, fifteen seconds to recognise true genius when he saw it, three quarters of an hour to hire a suitably heavy-duty lorry, and six weeks of humiliating negotiation to get Bianca's signature on a contract. The rest is art history, with cross-references to economics, accountancy and business studies.

Thus, when, about eighteen months later, Birmingham City Council was playing third time lucky with the design of the city's celebrated Victoria Square, and the Kawaguchiya Integrated Circuits people came across with a six-figure garden gnome fund, there was only one possible choice; provided she would agree to do it. For a very long fortnight she considered the offer; any subject she liked (except, added the city fathers, World Peace, because you do tend to get just a wee bit carried away on that particular theme, and we need a bit of space in the square for buildings and stuff) and as long as she liked to do it in, all the rock she could handle plus, of course, the immense satisfaction of helping gild Europe's most fragrant lily. Could anybody refuse an offer like that? Apparently, yes.

The city fathers faxed Kawaguchiya Integrated Circuits, tactfully suggesting that the two in their original letter must have been a misprint for three. KIC, thinking wistfully of the sixty acres of Tyseley they'd set their hearts on, faxed back their confirmation. Bianca accepted.

After careful consideration, she had narrowed the choice of subjects down to two. One of them, she told the Council, was the Industrial Revolution raping Nature, with side friezes of captains of industry through the ages suffering appropriate torments in Hell. Did they want to hear the other choice? No, Ms Wilson, that'll do fine. No, the other one will be just splendid, whatever it turns out to be.

To their amazement and relief, it turned out to be Saint George and the Dragon. Nobody could guess why, least of all Bianca Wilson.

After leaving the pub, he strolled for a while along the quiet, winding road. He had much to think about.

Well, it sure was good to be back. The shape; well, it was limiting, not to mention uncomfortable and intrinsically silly, but he'd be rid of it soon enough and then he'd really be back. He swung the holdall by its handle, and smiled at the clanking of its contents.

England; not that he'd seen very much of it, but probably enough for his purposes. Lots of trees, he observed. Haystacks. Fields of waving, sun-ripened corn. Thatched cottages. Perfect. It was a wonder the United Nations hadn't made them tie a label on it saying *Highly Inflammable*. A lorryload of straw bales chugged past him and he grinned.

He felt well. True, the actual fuel content in fermented liquor wasn't all that high, and he'd probably have done better in practical terms to have called in at a petrol station and taken a long swig from the pumps. But there was no point in going out of one's way to appear conspicuous, or at least not yet. Pretty soon he'd be so conspicuous they'd be offering him a Saturday job as a lighthouse. Patience, patience.

The summer breeze was warm on his back and he instinctively looked upwards. Good thermals, if he wasn't mistaken. On a lovely calm day like this it was horribly frustrating to be stuck on the ground. As if in sympathy, his shoulder-blades began to itch and he paused a while to scratch them against a gatepost.

While he was standing and looking at the sky, he became

aware of an unusual noise; a bit like thunder, a bit like the roar of a food-processor in full cry, with a tantalising hint of movement and a dash of power. A moment later, two jet fighters swept across the sky, flying perhaps a trifle lower than regulations permitted. They were only visible for a second and a half at most, but in that time his exceptional eyes scanned them and reported every detail of their appearance and construction to a suddenly lovesick brain. True, he'd come across aircraft before, like the big fat lumbering thing he'd come in on – a huge flying metal slug, a parody of flight. These, though, were something else entirely. It was as if a man brought up in strict seclusion by elderly nuns had just wandered into the changing room at a top-flight fashion show. Yes, shouted every fibre of his being, I *want* one of those.

He concentrated and quite soon one of the fighters came back. At his subsequent court-martial, the pilot was unable to offer any explanation. The best he could come up with was that it was a sunny day, it looked like a nice place, and there was this friendly looking man in the road below waggling his thumb.

'Hi.'

The pilot pressed a button and the windshield slid back. 'Hello,' he replied. 'What . . .?'

'Nice machine you've got there.'

'Yes. Um . . .'

'I particularly like the way it just sort of drops in on the ground. I always thought you had to find a flat open space and come in gradually.'

'Not any more,' replied the pilot. 'Vertical take-off and landing. Look—'

'Mind if I have a go?'

'Well, actually, it doesn't belong to me, so perhaps—'

'Ah, go on.'

'All right.'

There were, he noticed as he clambered into the cockpit, all sorts of knobs and levers and things which presumably made the thing go. Superfluous, of course, in his case. He applied his mind.

'Excuse me!'

He looked down at the pilot. 'Yes?'

'Before you take off,' shouted the pilot above the roar of the engines, 'put the windshield back up. Otherwise you'll be blown—'

'Thanks, but no thanks. I get claustrophobic in confined spaces.' How true. How very, very true. 'Cheerio.'

Then ... straight up in the air, no messing. This was something he could get used to. And to think, last time he'd been here the best the poor fools could do was stick feathers to their arms with beeswax and jump off cliffs. All credit to them, they'd certainly been busy.

As the slipstream clawed vainly at his face and the ground became a fast-moving blur far below him, he snuggled back in his seat, sighed with pure contentment and groped with his mind for the weapons systems.

Bianca was used to inspiration. Scarcely a day went by without some rare and splendid gift of the gods slipping in through the cat-flap of her mind and curling up, nose to tail-tip, in front of the radiator of her genius. It was getting to the stage where she couldn't walk past a stone-built building without seeing hundreds of enticing images peeping out at her from the heart of the masonry, like socks leering through the glass door of a tumble-drier.

The Birmingham job, though, was something else entirely. A terrible cliché, of course, to say the thing had taken on a life of its own, but that was about the strength of it. The further the work progressed – and she was amazed at how far she'd got in such a short time – the less actual control she seemed to have. Not that the work was inferior – on the contrary, it was superb, if you liked naturalism in your sculpture. But it was odd, because neither Saint George nor his scaly chum were turning out anything like the way she'd imagined them. George, she couldn't help thinking, ought to be taller, more heroic, less – well, dumpy and middle aged. He should only have one chin, and that a sort of Kirk Douglas job, the kind of thing you could surround with sea and put a concert party on the end of. He certainly shouldn't have round little piggy eyes and a squadgy little mouth like two slugs mating. And as for the dragon . . .

But, she had to admit, she did like the dragon. It had style. In fact, it had so much style you could bolt a wheel at each corner and give it an Italian name. It was graceful, attractive, dangerous; you could see the power in those tremendous muscles and hear the whistle of the wind in those amazingly broad, delicate wings. Above all, it made you think, if someone came up to you and offered to bet you money on the outcome of the fight, you wouldn't take George at anything less than seventy-five to one. The result had to be a foregone conclusion.

She said as much to her friend Mike one evening as he helped her with the tarpaulins. Mike nodded.

'I wouldn't want to have just sold George a life policy,' he said. 'A single-premium annuity, yes. I think I'd be on pretty safe ground there. But straight life or accidental death cover, no.'

'Strange,' Bianca agreed. 'Do you think it might be symbolism?'

'Probably. What did you have in mind?'

'Well.' Bianca stood back and took a long, dispassionate look. 'There's all sorts of things it could be symbolising, actually.'

'Such as?'

'Um. The ultimate futility of imperialism?'

'Nice try.'

'Um. Male violence towards women?'

'Could be. In which case, the male is definitely on a hiding to nothing, unless you chip off George's moustache and beef the pectorals up a bit. Talking of his moustache, by the way, had you noticed the strong resemblance to Alf Garnett?'

'All right, then,' Bianca said. 'How about World Peace?'

'Ah,' said Mike, nodding. 'Silly of me not to have realised before.'

Bianca sighed. 'You're right,' she said, 'it's definitely up the pictures. Here, help me get the sheet over it before I get too depressed.'

'Didn't say I didn't like it,' Mike replied, as a gust of wind turned the tarpaulin into a mainsail. 'I think it's absolutely amazing. It's just . . .'

'Yes. Quite.'

'How much more are you planning on doing to it?'

'I don't know,' Bianca replied pensively. 'Either I'm going to leave it pretty much as it is, or else I'm going to take a sledgehammer to it first thing tomorrow morning. What do you think?'

'I think,' said Mike, 'that if you choose Plan B, I could use the chippings. There'd be enough to cover every driveway in the West Midlands.'

At that moment, the rogue Harrier jet that had been shooting cathedral-sized divots out of Salisbury Plain suddenly stopped in mid-air, stalled and fell into a spin, dropping out of the air like a shot bird.

Cuddled in the arms of a warm thermal, the dragon watched it fall and shrugged. He'd been wrong. Compared to his real shape, it was just a toy; fancy dress, a tin overcoat. As it hit the ground and exploded, he flicked his tail like a goldfish, rose and hovered over the swelling mushroom of smoke and fire. Ruddy dangerous, too, he added. One little bump on the ground and they blow up. Shit, I could have been inside that. Doesn't bear thinking about.

He throttled back to a slow, exhilarating glide and began an inventory of his new shape. Neat. And gaudy too, which he liked. A little bit more gold wouldn't have hurt and maybe a few more precious stones here and there; still, what did you expect from something that owed its original genesis to local government? But in terms of function, of efficiency and power-to-weight ratios, he couldn't fault it. For a moment, he almost wished there were other dragons in the world. He'd have enjoyed giving them the name of his tailor.

When Bianca arrived on site the next morning, the tarpaulin was already off and Mike was struggling to fold it; in this wind, a bit like trying to cram the universe into a paper bag. He looked up and gave her a sad smile.

'I asked you to save me the chippings,' he said.

'Sorry?'

'That's all right. Next time.'

'No, sorry as in what the hell are you talking about.'

Mike frowned. 'The dragon,' he said, pointing. 'You came back last night and scrapped it. Quick work.'

'No I didn't,' Bianca said, pointing. 'It's still . . .'

Gone.

When you're a dragon, sobering up can be a nasty experience.

The last of the Polish vodka burned off just as he was attempting a flamboyant triple loop, about seventy thousand feet above sea level, and sixty-nine thousand feet directly above the very pointy tips of some mountains. At that point, something nudged him in the ribs, gave him an unpleasant leer, and said, 'Hi, remember me?' It was Gravity.

Fortunately, he had sufficient height and enough of a breeze to glide quite comfortably down onto a flat green stretch in the middle of the large human settlement he was presently overflying. As he made his approach, he noticed that his chosen landing strip was dotted with humans, all dressed in white and staring up at him, while around the edges of the field, crammed onto rows of wooden benches, were several thousand other humans, also staring. The dragon was puzzled for a moment. He didn't have a fly, so it couldn't be undone. Hadn't they ever seen a dragon before?

Having felt for the wind, he put his wings back, stretched out his legs, turned into the breeze and dropped lightly down onto the turf, landing as delicately as a cat jumping up onto a cluttered mantelpiece. The white men had all run away, he observed, and the spectators – he assumed that was what they were doing; either that or they were some kind of jury – were trying to do the same, although they were finding it hard because they were all trying to do it at the same time. Some blue men were walking towards him with the slow, measured tread of people who feel they aren't being paid enough to die. He wished there was something he could do to put them at their ease. He was, however, a realist; the only thing he'd ever managed to do that helped human beings relax was to go away, and unless he could get to a gallon or so of strong drink, that wasn't among the available options.

Or maybe it was. The green area was divided from the rows of benches by a thin wall of painted boards, with words on them; National Westminster Bank, Equity and Law and – he recognised that one – Bell's Whisky. That, if he wasn't mistaken, was one of the brands of fuel he'd taken on board at the pub. If they had its name written up on a hoarding, perhaps they had some about the place. It would do no harm to ask.

'Hello,' he said.

At once, the blue men stopped dead in their tracks, and began talking frantically to little rectangular boxes pinned to the collars of their coats. This puzzled the dragon at first, until he worked out that the boxes were some sort of pet, that his rather loud, booming voice had frightened them, and the blue men were comforting them with soothing words. The dragon rebuked himself for being inconsiderate and lowered his voice a little.

'Hello,' he repeated. 'I wonder if you could help me. Have you got any Bell's Whisky?'

Perhaps the little boxes didn't approve of whisky, because they needed even more calming down this time. Painfully aware that tact had never been his strong point, the dragon modulated his voice into a sort of low, syrupy hum, and beckoned to the nearest of the blue men.

'Excuse me,' he cooed. The blue man stared, until the dragon was afraid his eyeballs would fall out of his head, assured his pet box that it was all right really, and took a few nervous steps forward. The dragon considered a friendly smile, but thought better of it. His friendly smiles, it had to be admitted, did rather tend to resemble an ivory-hunter's discount warehouse. It'd probably frighten the poor little box out of its wits.

'You talking to me?' said the blue man, in a rather quavery voice.

'Yes,' replied the dragon. 'Bell's Whisky. Is there any?'

'What you want whisky for?'

Softly, softly is all very well, but the dragon was beginning to get impatient. 'I'll give you three guesses,' he replied. 'Look, either you have or you haven't, it's not exactly a grey area.'

'I don't know,' the blue man replied. 'I'm a policeman, not a bartender.'

'I see. Would you know if you were a bartender?'

'I suppose so. Why?'

The dragon sighed. If it had had a fuel gauge, it would be well into the red zone by now, but even so the flames that inadvertently ensued were four feet long and hot enough to melt titanium. 'Perhaps,' he said, observing that the policeman had gone ever such a funny colour, 'you'd be terribly sweet and go and fetch me a bartender, so that we can get this point cleared up once and for all.'

'Um. Yes. Right.'

'Thank you ever so much.'

'Um. Don't mention it.'

'Hope the flames didn't frighten your box.'

The blue man backed away, turned and ran; and for a long time, the dragon sat quietly where he was, conserving his energy and watching the pigeons waddling about on the grass. The whole area was empty by now, except for two or three of the blue men, huddled behind benches at the very back. It dawned on the dragon that something was going on. He frowned. It was, he felt, a bit much. Back in the old days, the humans hadn't made this much fuss when he dropped in on cities demanding princesses to go, hold the onions.

You'd think, he reiterated to himself, they'd never seen a dragon before.

Hey!

Maybe they *hadn't* seen a dragon before.

Anything's possible. Perhaps, in this strange and rather

down-at-heel century, dragons had become scarce. If this was a remote, out-of-the-way district (his exceptional eyes, scanning generally for a clue, picked out the name Old Trafford written on a board, but it didn't mean anything to him) then it was conceivable that he was the first dragon they'd ever set eyes on. Reviewed in that light, the behaviour of the humans made some sort of sense. Rewind that and let's think it through logically.

Assume they've never actually seen a dragon. They will, nevertheless, have heard of dragons; everybody has. And, facing facts, he wasn't so naïve as to imagine that what they'd heard was necessarily accurate. Humans, he knew, are funny buggers, delighting in the morbid and the sensational, eclectic in their selection of what to remember and what conveniently to forget. Quite likely, that was the case when it came to the popular image of dragons. If he knew humans, they'd ignore the ninety-nine per cent of its time a dragon spends aimlessly flying, basking in the high-level sunlight, chivvying rainclouds to where they're needed most and persuading winds to behave themselves. More likely than not, the perverse creatures would focus on the five per cent or less of its life a dragon spends at ground level, ridding the world of unwanted and troublesome armour fetishists and saving kings the trouble of finding husbands for superfluous younger daughters.

In which case . . .

Damn.

What a time, the dragon reflected ruefully, to run out of gas. Because any minute now, some macho nerd on a white charger is going to come galloping up through the gate with an overgrown cocktail stick under his arm, hell-bent on prodding me in the ribs. Normally, of course, this wouldn't pose any sort of problem; one sneeze, and all that's left is some fine grey ash and a pool of slowly cooling molten iron.

Without fuel, however, he was going to have to rely on teeth and fingernails, which was a pest because it was ever so easy to crack a molar on those silly iron hats they insisted on wearing, and if dragons really are scarce, chances are there's precious few competent serpentine dentists within convenient waddling distance.

What I need, muttered the dragon to himself, is a good stiff drink of kerosene. He turned his head slowly from side to side, dilated his nostrils and sniffed. Over there . . .

At the back of the enclosure some tall iron gates swung open and four strange green vehicles rolled through. They were big, made of iron and fitted with long iron ribbons under their wheels – socks? go-anywhere doormats? – and when the dragon pricked up his exceptional ears, he heard a blue man by the gate shout to a colleague that it was going to be all right, the tanks were here now.

Tanks.

Yes, right, said the dragon to himself, *tanks*, I remember now. Big metal vessels used for the storage of liquids. At long last, here comes the Bell's Whisky. And there was me thinking they were out to get me.

CHAPTER TWO

'It can't,' Bianca protested, 'just have disappeared.'

Mike shrugged and made a pantomime of patting his pockets and poking about in Bianca's toolbag. 'Bee, love, it's a tad on the big side to have rolled away and fallen down a grating somewhere. Of course it's flaming well disappeared. Obviously, someone's pinched it.'

'Pinched a fifteen-foot-long statue of a dragon? Kids, maybe? Bored housewife who didn't know what came over her? Don't be so bloody stupid. It'd take a whole day just to saw it off the plinth.'

'True.' Mike peered down at the stone beneath Saint George's charger's hooves. 'And no saw marks, either. In fact, no marks of any kind. You know, this is downright peculiar.'

'Peculiar.' Bianca closed her mouth, which had fallen open. 'Mike, if ever Mars challenges us to an understatement match, I'm going to nominate you for team captain. What the hell am I going to *do*?'

Mike scratched his head. 'You could start by telling

somebody. The police. Birmingham City Council. Kawaguchiya Integrated . . .'

He met Bianca's eye. Comparable meetings include that
between Napoleon and Wellington at Waterloo and the
encounter between Mohammed Ali's solar plexus and Joe
Frazier's fist back in 1974. 'Quite,' he said. 'I see what you
mean. This is going to be a problem, isn't it?'

'Yes.'

'Do you think,' Mike suggested, after a moment's consideration, 'that you could, sort of, talk your way out of this?
I mean, it's your blasted statue. Convince 'em that there
never was a dragon to begin with. Sort of, Saint George and
the *implied* dragon. Saint George, just practising? Saint
George and Imaginary Friend?'

'No.'

'Maybe not. Or could you lose the armour, fiddle around
with the sword a bit and rename it *The Polo Player*?'

'Mike.'

'Okay, okay, I'm just bouncing a few ideas here. Here,
why not just call it *Study for Saint George and the* . . .'

Bianca closed her eyes and massaged them with the heel
of her hand. 'What I can't imagine,' she said, 'is what the
hell can have happened to it. I mean, dragons don't just get
up and walk away. Just to move something that size you'd
need cranes, flat-bodied trucks, hydraulics, all that stuff.
Believe me,' she added, 'I know. When I delivered that
cameo group of Mother and Child in Macclesfield last year,
they had to close off fifteen streets.'

They stood for a few seconds longer, staring at the
absence – a distinctly dragon-shaped absence, but an
absence nevertheless. Compared to how Bianca was feeling
about vacuums, Nature was honorary treasurer of their fan
club.

'Well,' said Bianca at last, 'there's no point standing here like trainee lamp-posts. Help me cover the dratted thing up, what's left of it, and I'll get on to the wholesalers for some more white Carrera. I only hope they can match the grain.'

Mike nodded. 'What about him?' he added, jerking a thumb at Saint George. 'Want me to put a padlock on him or something?'

Bianca gave him the last in a succession of withering looks; if the Americans had had looks like that in 1972, the Viet Cong would never have stood a chance. 'Get real,' she sighed. 'Who the hell is going to steal a statue?'

Chug, chug, chug; an elderly coach, the sort of vehicle that can still call itself a charabanc and get away with it, burbles slowly and cheerfully like a relaxed bumble-bee along a winding Oxfordshire lane.

On either side of the road, Cotswold sheep, as self-consciously picturesque as the most highly paid super-model, ruminate and regurgitate in timeless serenity. Thatched cottages, tile-roofed golden-stone farmhouses, evocatively falling-down old barns and the last surviving old-fashioned telephone boxes in Albion are the only footprints left here by the long march of Humanity; and if these works of his hand were all you had to go by, you'd be forgiven for thinking that Man wasn't a bad old stick after all. For this is the rural Thames Valley, the land that Time forgot, scenery pickled in formaldehyde. If England was Dorian Grey, this would be the watercolour landscape he keeps in his attic.

Inevitably and on schedule, there to the left of the coach is a village cricket match, and the big, red-faced man toiling up to the crease is, ineluctably, the village blacksmith. For a slice of living palaeontology, forget *Jurassic Park* and come to North Oxon.

And here is the village, and here is the village green, and

here are the ducks. The coach pulls up, wheezing humorously, and the passengers spill out; fifteen elderly ladies with flasks and sandwiches, deck chairs and knitting. It's all so sweet you could use it to flavour tea.

Thirty seconds later, a black transit van with tinted windows purrs noiselessly up and parks at the back of the green. The doors do not open. It lurks.

The old ladies have laid out their tartan rugs and, after much comical by-play and merry laughter, put up their deck chairs. The sun is shining. Tea flows. Sandwiches are eaten.

Time is, of course, not a constant. Science would have you believe that it potters along at a fixed, unalterable speed, never accelerating, never slowing down; rather like a milk float. Big joke. Time has a gearbox; it can dawdle and it can race. This, in turn, can result in absolute chaos.

Supply and demand, twin pillars of the cosmos, apply to all things, and Time is no exception. In some places, such as this sleepy and idyllic village, they scarcely use any of the stuff. In Los Angeles, Tokyo and the City of London, where Time is Money, they burn it off at a furious rate. And, try as they might to wring every last drop of value out of each passing second, their officially allotted ration is pitifully inadequate.

Sceptical? Here's concrete evidence. Think how much time twenty pence buys you in a car park in Chipping Norton and the equivalent figure in Central London. Where there is supply and demand, wherever there are unfulfilled shortages, there are always entrepreneurs ready and willing to step in and sort things out. There are no exceptions to this rule. The black market in Time is probably the biggest growth area in the whole of the unofficial economy. It's also the most antisocial, which is why it's such a closely guarded secret.

The sandwiches have been eaten. Jam tarts appear. Someone produces, as if from thin air, a wind-up gramophone.

Something truly horrible is about to happen.

It works like this. Time proverbially flies when you're enjoying yourself; or, put rather more scientifically, pleasure electrolyses Time. The mere act of a human being unreservedly enjoying himself acts as a catalyst, speeding up the decay of raw Time in the atmosphere. In the same way, misery, suffering and having to go to work impede the decay of Time, causing a massive build-up of the stuff. In primitive rural communities, for example, where peasants grind out lives of bleak, hopeless toil, Time seems to stand still, until the very stones of the cottages and turf of the fields are marinaded in the stuff.

To drill for Time, therefore, find a spot where countless generations of wretched serfs have had to get up at half-past five every morning to milk bad-tempered cows. Having located the spot, shout, 'There's Time in them thar hills!' and assemble your drilling rig. This will consist of between seven and twenty happy souls who are blessed with the rare ability thoroughly to enjoy themselves, unself-consciously and without stint.

Research has shown that little old ladies on outings do this best, with thirsty male Australians coming in a close second. Combine the little old ladies with the idyllic unspoilt village and stand well back, because you've just unleashed a chain reaction that makes nuclear fission seem wimpish in comparison. And be warned; it's not a pretty sight.

Inside the black transit, a small machine begins to run. Someone chuckles unpleasantly, mutters, 'Time, gentlemen, please,' and throws a switch.

For the first thirty seconds, nothing much happens;

nothing visible, anyway. The first perceptible changes are to the buildings. Thatch moults, dry stone walls collapse, oak beams sag. Entropy, acting as fast as the soluble aspirin of your dreams, is tearing the place apart as the surplus Time is leeched out of the fabric. Then, because Nature abhors a vacuum, raw present rushes in to take the place of the fossilised past, in the same way as a worked-out gravel pit floods with water. Thatch is replaced with tile, stone with brick and breeze-block. Barns fade away, and are replaced by barn conversions, complete with upper-middle-class occupants and a brace of Porsches in the driveway. Suddenly there's a development of ninety-six executive retirement homes in the old orchard behind the village green. A business park springs mushroom-like out of the ground where a minute ago there were only cows. Cars sprout up beside the highway like newly sown dragons' teeth. The handpumps in the public bar turn seamlessly into plastic boxes, and three racks of videos parthenogenetically appear in the window of the post office. We warned you; this is not a sight for the squeamish. It's enough to make Stephen King sleep with the light on for a week.

The old ladies don't seem to have noticed. They're exchanging photographs of their grandchildren and playing snap, while all around them the village green trembles, like the San Andreas fault having a temper tantrum, and design-and-build starter homes flip up out of the ground like poppers on a pinball table.

In the black transit, now parked in the car park of the brand new plastics factory, the little machine is buzzing like a tortured wasp. A big glass bottle, coddled and cosseted in gyroscopically mounted cradles, lead and cotton wool, slowly fills. When the meniscus reaches the twenty-centilitre mark, the operator yanks back the handle, opens the door of the van and blows a whistle. The old ladies stop what they're doing, grab their deck chairs and empty picnic baskets and make a run for the coach. Both vehicles gun their engines and race off with much spinning of wheels and burning of rubber because a village green in the process of going critical is no place to be. In fact, they've almost left it too late; just behind them the road uproots itself and contorts like a wounded python, coiling itself round a series of mini-roundabouts and branching off into a series of service roads leading to the new complex of out-of-town supermarkets. They're level with the village church when it detonates and turns itself into a drive-in leisure multiplex, and only by standing on the accelerator can the driver get the coach clear of the Jacobean manor house before it implodes and shape-changes into Kawaguchiya Integrated Circuits' south-east regional management training centre.

A close shave, and the world owes a large debt of gratitude to the driver, for all that he's a myrmidon of the Time thieves' Mr Big. Because the transit van is carrying twenty centilitres of raw Time (destined to fill a lucrative order from Wall Street, which is frantically trying to make the most of the last few weeks of a Republican administration) and the thought of what would happen if that much ninety-eight-per-cent-pure stuff were to go off is enough to freeze the brain.

Raw Time, spontaneously detonating in the Earth's chronological field. Historical meltdown. A Time bomb.

The man in the black transit is Chubby Stevenson, also known as The Temporiser and Mr Timeshare. Procrastination was framed; Chubby is the greatest thief of Time the world has ever seen. In his purpose-built silo, five hundred feet under the Nevada Desert, he has four hundred and sixteen litres of the stuff; enough to reprise the Renaissance and play Desert Island Decades. Do you suffer from persistent nostalgia? Do you wish it could be the Sixties all over again? Just send your order, together with a banker's draft with more noughts on it than there are portholes in the side of a trans-Atlantic liner, to Mr C. Stevenson, PO Box 666, Las Monedas, Nevada.

Trying to get the petrol out of a Scorpion tank, the dragon discovered the hard way, is like breaking into a can of Coke after the little ring-pull thing has snapped off and you haven't got a tin-opener. It calls for ingenuity, patience and very robust fingernails.

Two out of three will do at a pinch; and, having slaked his thirst, the dragon relaxed, closed his eyes and considered the situation, both in the short and medium term.

He wasn't, in his opinion, excessively thin-skinned (just as well, considering the number of things that had been fired at him in the last twelve minutes) but he did get the impression that for some reason, the humans had taken against him rather. Apart from a broken claw and some light bruises the tanks hadn't bothered him very much, and the petrol was much more to his taste than all those funny drinks, but the next escalation of human disapproval would probably be aircraft, and he knew from recent observation that those things had rather more biff to them than the little self-propelled cocktail shakers. Time, he decided regret-fully, to make himself inconspicuous, which would mean having to quit this exceptionally stylish and well-designed body for a while and go back into boring, silly two-legged mufti. A pity, particularly since it was now nicely fuelled-up and ready to go.

He had business here in England, but it wouldn't take long. Once that was out of the way, the world was his oyster, and there were bound to be big, flat, open spaces where a dragon could *be* without getting shot at all the time by cultural degenerates. So, under cover, do the job, and then we're out of here. Can't, frankly, wait.

He opened his wings and, having disposed of the empties tidily by dropping them in the sea, he soared up above the clouds, giving as wide a berth as possible to any aircraft his exceptional senses detected, and circled round until he saw what he was looking for. When he saw his chance, he swooped.

At more or less the same moment as the dragon was mangling armoured fighting vehicles on the playing fields of Lancashire, someone who had been asleep for a very long time woke up.

You know what it's like when you've overslept. Head full of sawdust. Eyelids as difficult to open as painted-over windowframes. Interior of mouth tasting so repulsive you wonder who's been doing what in it while you've been sleeping. Multiply that by a couple of thousand years and maybe you get the idea.

'Where,' muttered George to himself, 'the fuck am I?'

A pigeon, who was sitting on his head, removed its head from its armpit and looked round. 'Who said that?' it demanded.

George, who could understand the language of birds, cleared his throat. 'Down here,' he said.

'What, you?'

'Yes, me?'

'The *statue*?'

'Yes.'

'Jeez!' The pigeon froze, kebabbed with embarrassment. 'I didn't know statues could ... Look, I really am terribly sorry. I'll clean it all off, promise.'

'I'm not really,' George explained, 'a statue.'

'I see. You're a very big, grey person lying absolutely still. Well, it takes all sorts, I can see that, I just naturally assumed you were a statue. If you'll just bear with me I can be back with a cloth and some white spirit before you can say—'

'Shut up and listen, you stupid bird. I'm inside the statue. Sort of. I'm a saint.'

The pigeon hesitated a while before replying. 'Fine,' it said. 'Where I come from we call that a non-sequitur, but never mind. Logic is for wimps, right?'

'I am a saint,' George repeated, the fuel gauge on his patience edging audibly into the red. 'I appear to have reincarnated into a statue of myself. And before you ask, I have no idea why. Now then, where is this . . .' George looked round; a circumscribed view, since he couldn't move his head, but sufficient for his purposes ' . . . ghastly, awful, God-forsaken place? Last thing I knew I was in open countryside.'

'Birmingham,' replied the pigeon promptly. 'West Midlands metropolitan district, England, Europe. Population—'

'Never heard of it.'

'Really?' The pigeon sounded surprised. 'Been away long?'

'Last time I looked, it was a hundred and something AD.'

Pigeons can't whistle. 'Strewth, mate, that's a long time. Eighteen hundred years, give or take a bit. This is . . .' The pigeon counted on its feathers. 'Nineteen ninety-eight. June. Welcome back,' it added tentatively.

George swivelled his eyeballs. 'I sincerely hope I'm not stopping,' he replied. 'Whatever happened to grass? We used to have a lot of it in my day.'

The pigeon shuffled its wings. 'Still plenty of it about,' it replied. 'But this is the middle of a city. Did they have cities then?'

'A few.' George stopped talking and winced; two thousand years' worth of pins and needles was catching up with him. 'Aaaagh,' he said.

'Problem?'

'My leg hurts. Go on with what you were saying.'

'About Birmingham? Okay. Rated as Great Britain's second largest city, in its nineteenth-century heyday Birmingham truly merited its proud title of "workshop of the world". Post-war recessions and the decline of British industry in general have inevitably left their mark, but the city continues to breed a defiantly positive and dynamic mercantile—'

'Pigeon.'

'Yes?'

'I think,' said George, 'I can now move my right arm. With it, as you may have observed, I am holding a very big sword. Unless you stop drivelling, I shall take this very big sword and shove it right up—'

'All right,' replied the pigeon, offended. 'You were the one who asked. Anyway,' it added, 'that's a fine way for a saint to talk, I must say.'

George's eyebrows were mobile again and he frowned. 'Is it?'

The pigeon nodded. 'Sure. You're supposed to be all meek and holy and stuff.'

'Bollocks.'

'Straight up. I know these things. My address: The Old Blocked Gutter, West Roof, St Chad's Cathedral, Birmingham 4. I know a lot of religion,' the pigeon continued proudly, 'especially the lilies of the field and St Francis of Assisi. Saints don't eff and blind, it's the rules.'

'Shows what you know,' George replied. 'Right, I'm going to move now, so I suggest you piss off and go sit somewhere else. Before you go, however, I want you to tell me where a man can get a drink around here.'

'A drink,' the pigeon repeated. 'Milk?'

'Don't be bloody stupid.'

'Water, then?'

'Booze,' George snarled. 'Alcohol. Fermented liquor.' A horrible thought struck him. 'They do still have it, don't they? Please tell me they haven't done away with it, because—'

'Sure they do,' the pigeon said. 'Beer and wine and gin and stuff, makes your mob sing a lot and fall over. Saints don't drink, though. Well-known fact.'

'What you know about saints,' muttered George, 'you could write on a grape pip in big letters. Just point me in the right direction and then clear off, before I use you to wipe my nose.'

The pigeon made the closest approximation it could to a disapproving tut and extended a wingtip. 'Draught Mitchell and Butlers,' it said. 'A word of warning, though.'

'Well?'

Pigeons; Mother Nature's flying diplomatic corps. 'The sword,' it said. 'The armour. The horse. The being seven and a half feet high. Frowned upon.'

'Yeah?'

'Times change,' said the pigeon. 'Not to mention fashions. Can you do anything about that?'

'I'm not sure.' George concentrated. 'Apparently I can. Is this better?'

The pigeon looked down. It was now sitting on the head of a short, bald man in a blue donkey jacket, jeans and scruffy trainers. 'Fine,' it said. 'How did you do that?'

George shrugged. 'Dunno. Who cares? When I get there, what should I ask for?'

'Um.' The pigeon searched its memory – about a quarter of a byte, say a large nibble – for a phrase overheard in crisp-shrapnel-rich beer gardens. 'A pint of bitter, please, mate, and a packet of dry roasted peanuts. That usually does the trick.'

'A pint of bitter, please, mate, and a packet of dry roasted peanuts.'

'You've got it.'

'Right. A pint of bitter, please, mate, and a packet of dry roasted peanuts. A pint of bitter, please, mate, and a packet of dry roasted peanuts. So long, birdbrain. A pint of bit . . .'

Standing on the empty plinth, the pigeon watched until George disappeared through the pub doorway, still rehearsing his line. It waited for a while. Then it preened itself. Then it started to peck at a cigarette butt. Two minutes or so later, the whole incident had been edited out of the active files of its mind and was held in limbo, awaiting deletion. And then . . .

The pigeon looked down.

It was, once again, standing on a statue.

Vaguely, it recalled something it had learned recently about statues. It took another look at what it was standing on. Ah *shit*, it said to itself.

'Mike.'

'Yes?'

'Just come and have a look at this, will you?'

Instead of folding the tarpaulin, Bianca just let it fall. Then they stood for a while and took a long, hard look.

'Swings and roundabouts,' Mike said eventually. 'Snakes and ladders. Maybe even omelettes and eggs.'

'What?'

Mike shrugged. 'I'm trying to be balanced and unhysterical,' he said. 'We now have the dragon back. True, we do seem to have lost Saint George, but . . .'

Slowly and very tentatively, Bianca leaned forwards. She laid the palm of her hand on the dragon's cold, scaly flank. Marble. Solid, cool, bloody-awkward-to-move-about stone. 'This,' she said at last, 'is beginning to get on my nerves.'

'Maybe it's a form of advanced job-sharing,' Mike suggested. 'You know, like flexi-time. I think West Midlands Council's all in favour of it, and I suppose you could just about classify these two as Council employees.'

'Mike.'

'Mm?'

'Please go away.'

Alone with her creation, Bianca thought long and hard. Sometimes she leaned against the statue, holding it. Sometimes she pressed her ear against it, as if listening. From time to time she kicked it.

After a while, she opened her portfolio and studied some sketches and plans. She took out a tape and made some measurements, both of the statue and the surrounding area. She climbed up onto its front paws and sniffed its spectacular, gaping jaws.

A mother, they say, instinctively knows what her baby is thinking. If it's in trouble, she can feel it, deep inside. Bianca frowned. No, not *trouble*, exactly. More sort of up to something. But what?

Finally, she packed up, replaced the tarpaulin and started to walk away. Having covered ten yards she turned, faced the statue, and put on her most menacing scowl.

'*Sit!*' she commanded, and stalked off down Colmore Row.

CHAPTER THREE

Having parked his shape in Victoria Square, the dragon ambled down Colmore Row to Snow Hill and consulted the railway timetable. Three minutes later a rather bemused train pulled up (wondering, among other things, how the hell it had managed to get there from Dumfries in a hundred and eighty seconds) and he climbed aboard.

'Colchester,' he said aloud.

The voice of the train, inaudible to everyone except the dragon, pointed out that the Snow Hill line doesn't go to Colchester. The dragon smiled pleasantly and invited the train to put its money where its mouth was.

Alighting at Colchester, a place he had heard of but never actually been to, the dragon took a taxi to 35 Vespasian Street, explained to the driver and climbed the stairs.

The top floor of 35 Vespasian Street is given over to a suite of offices consisting of a chair, a desk, a computer terminal, an electric kettle, an anomaly in the telephone network and seven hundred and forty-three filing cabinets. The door says:

L. KORTRIGHT ASSOCIATES
SUPERNATURAL AGENCY

Lin Kortright was on the anomaly when the dragon walked in. He was explaining to Horus, the Egyptian charioteer of the Sun, that simply picking it up, moving it along in a straight line and putting it down again without dropping it was no longer good enough to guarantee him full employment, and had he considered, for example, juggling with it or balancing it on a stick while riding a unicycle. As the door opened he didn't look up, merely made a go-away gesture. He was about to suggest training it to do simple tricks when he noticed that the receiver was back on its cradle and he was, in fact, talking to the palm of his hand. He raised his eyes, impressed.

'Hey,' he said, 'how'd you do that?'

'Do what?'

'It's purely instinctive with you, huh? No matter. What can I do for you?'

'I'm looking,' the dragon replied, sitting on a chair last seen two seconds previously under an actuary in Stroud and still warm, 'for a job. I imagine you might be able to help.'

Mr Kortright studied the chair for a while, and then nodded. 'Possibly, possibly,' he said. 'What d'you do?'

'What needs doing?'

Mr Kortright frowned. 'No, no, no,' he said, 'that's not the way it works. You gotta have an act before you come bothering me. Let's see. You can do telekinesis, right?'

'Can I?'

'Oh boy, a natural,' Mr Kortright sighed, rather as Saint Sebastian would have done if, just as the last arrow thudded home in his ribcage, he also remembered he'd left home without switching off the oven. 'Don't get me wrong,' he

added, 'maybe I can still find you something, if you don't
mind touring. Done any poltergeisting?'

The dragon's brow furrowed in thought until he looked
like a fight between two privet hedges. Ever since he'd come
back, he'd been letting his subconscious fill in as many of
the gaps as possible, mostly by opening a direct line from
his exceptional ears to his memory. In consequence, the
back lots of his brain were stuffed with thousands of
unprocessed eavesdroppings, waiting to be filtered and
condensed into usable ready-to-wear background information. 'Poltergeists,' he mused, accessing a fragment of a
documentary overheard when the taxi drove within a mile
of a TV showroom. 'That's a ghost or similar evil spirit who
throws things, yes?'

'Yup.'

'No. Sorry.'

Mr Kortright's shoulders rose and fell like share prices
during a closely contested election. 'Okay,' he said. 'You
wanna learn?'

'Not really, no. All seems a bit gratuitous if you ask me.
And besides, I don't plan on being here very long, so there's
little point learning new skills.'

'Picky, huh? You got a nerve.'

'Several,' replied the dragon, absently. 'In this body,
anyway. The other one's just animated rock.'

It took Mr Kortright's brain three quarters of a second to
pick up on the words *this body* and *the other one*, speculate
on the significance and dismiss the whole as too much
hassle. 'So what did you used to do? Have an act then?'

The dragon nodded. 'I flew about breathing fire, making
rain, that style of thing.'

'Dragon, huh?'

'You're very perceptive.'

After a moment's hesitation Mr Kortright correctly

interpreted the dragon's remark as a compliment. 'Not much around at the moment for dragons,' he said. 'Endangered species regulations,' he added.

'Ah.' This seemed to confirm what the dragon had assumed about a national dragon shortage. 'So dragons are protected, are they?'

Mr Kortright grinned. 'Dragons?' he said. 'No way. Nothing in the legislation about dragons. Now crocodiles, yes. Which means the supply of raw material for the handbag trade is down to last knockings. But if you're good you can make dragon *look* like crocodile ... You get my meaning?'

A corner of the dragon's mouth twitched. 'I seem to remember you people have a saying,' he said. 'First catch your ...'

'Been away a long time, have you?' The Kortright grin widened, until it looked like the aftermath of seismic activity. 'In which case, here's a tip for you. If you're flying along and you see something long and grey and kind of tube shaped with little fins coming straight at you, don't try chatting it up or asking it out to the movies. They call them wire-guided missiles, and—'

'Yes, thanks,' said the dragon. 'I found out about those for myself. So there are still dragons about, then? People seem to react as if I'm extinct or something.'

'In these parts,' Mr Kortright explained, 'you are. In this century, in fact. That doesn't worry transtemporal poachers any; just means that by the time they market the goods, they're also genuine antiques and therefore legal to sell.'

'Ah.' The dragon shrugged. 'But so long as I'm now, I'm relatively safe?'

'Safe.' Mr Kortright savoured the word. 'From poachers, maybe. I mean, chances are, if you stick around any year with nineteen on the front of it, you won't suddenly find yourself full of powder compacts with a zip up your back. There are,' he added, 'other dangers.'

'Thought that might be the case,' the dragon replied. 'Which is precisely why I'm in plain clothes and looking for a job. You see, I have things to do in the here and now. Once they're done, I'm off somewhere and when a bit less paranoid. While I'm here, though, I thought a job'd help pass the time and help me blend in.'

'Very wise. So,' Mr Kortright went on, steepling his fingers, 'where are we at? Ex-dragon. Ex-dragon. Now then, let me see.'

The dragon waited patiently while Mr Kortright played with his computer.

'Any luck?'

Mr Kortright pursed his lips. 'Well,' he said, 'like I say to all the kids just starting out in the business, when you're trying to make your way, sometimes you've gotta do things you'd rather not. You sure about poltergeisting?'

'Positive.'

'Shucks. Hey, what's this?' He peered at the screen. 'I can get you six weeks' volcanic activity in Hawaii, covering for the local fire-god while he takes his kids to Disneyland. All you gotta do is lie on your back and blow up through a small hole.'

'Sorry. Got to be in this country. Anyway, where's Hawaii?'

'Please yourself. Gonna be difficult, though. How do you feel about hallucinations?'

'I beg your pardon?'

'Hallucinations. For health-conscious druggies. All the weird visions without actually taking the drug. Growth area, steady work.'

'Not really me, somehow. I'd feel self-conscious. Besides, don't you have to be a pink elephant?'

'Boy, are you behind the times.' Mr Kortright frowned, and tapped a few more keys. 'Okay, okay, you're gonna love this. This is really so *you*. Security guard.'

'Security guard?'

'It says here, *traditional* security guard needed for substantial art collection. Full board. The successful applicant will be at least fourteen feet long, green and covered in scales. No time wasters. There now, what can I say?'

'Okay,' said the dragon. 'When can I start?'

George sailed through the air in a graceful arc and landed in a dustbin. Behind him came a voice, warmly recommending that he stay out. After a short pause for regrouping, he climbed out, brushed trash off his person and staggered away down the alley.

Seems like old times, he said to himself, getting slung out of drinking establishments. Some things had changed, of course; for one thing, getting slung out was now a whole lot easier. Definitely a regrettable tendency to over-react.

His mind drifted back to the bars of his youth. Pendle's, the roughest saints' bar in Albion. The Caerllyr Grill. The Grendel's Torso. What the hell was wrong with this goddamn country?

Half an hour's slouching, lurching and bumping into things brought him back to Victoria Square, and he realised that he didn't have anywhere to sleep for the night. He saw . . .

'Immediately,' said Mr Kortright. 'Here's the address. Do well.'

The dragon trotted down the stairs into the street and whistled. A moment later, a huge green shape, flying faster than the wind, descended on him and he vanished.

★

... An empty plinth. He thought of his nice warm statue; good, solid marble that didn't wobble about all over the place like this blasted cheapskate flesh-and-blood outfit did. Climbing the plinth, he sighed, closed his eyes and was stone once more.

'I'm not saying,' said Chubby Stevenson, his brain racing, 'it's impossible. Nothing's *impossible*. All I'm saying is, it's going to be tricky.'

Fifteen impassive Japanese faces regarded him, until he began to feel like asking for his blindfold and last cigarette. These people, he realised, don't want to hear this. Pity.

'It's all to do,' he continued, cramming charm into the meter of his smile, 'with the fundamental nature of Time. Now, with my supplies of raw Time, I can prolong the present, no problem. In certain circumstances, I can sometimes recreate the past – not travel back in time, now that *is* impossible. Nobody can do that. What I sometimes do, for specially favoured customers, is make a synthetic recreation of a specific episode from the past, using a raw Time base and . . .'

They weren't interested. He wasn't answering the question they'd asked him. Jesus, these guys!

'The future,' he therefore said, 'is something else entirely. Future's different from past and present, see. Future hasn't happened yet. If it hasn't happened, we don't know what it's like. If you don't know what it's like, you can't copy it. Now . . .'

One of the fifteen leaned forward and, terribly politely, cleared his throat. With respect, his expression said – his lips didn't move and he didn't make a noise, but there was no need, just as you don't need to speak fluent Gun to know that when a .44 revolver stares at you with its one big eye it's informing you that you are probably going to die – they knew this already. What they didn't know, and what they wanted him to tell them, was whether it was possible to arrange an artificial future, in which certain specified events would happen; and if so, how much would it cost? If he didn't know the answer, the expression continued, then perhaps he would be good enough to say so.

Chubby sighed, and got a grip on himself. 'It can be done,' he said. 'The principle is quite straightforward; simple, even. The practicalities . . .'

Please explain the practicalities.

'Okay. It's all relativity, right? Travel faster than light around the Earth to accelerate forward through Time. Once you're there, or do I mean then, you set up whatever it is you want to happen in the future. Like, you want to bet heavily on the Superbowl, you fast forward to the day of the match, see who wins, now you can place your bet – provided you can get back to your own time, or get a message back, anyhow; obviously, you can't get back yourself, because pastside travel's out, see above. Sending a message, though, that's no problem.'

Really?

'Trade secret,' Chubby said. Normally he'd have winked as well, but there was something about the wall of stone-faced scrutiny opposite him that put him off the idea. 'We can do it, anyhow. The technical problem, of course, is finding your faster-than-light courier.'

A soluble problem?

'I feel sure we can sort it out,' Chubby lied. 'Of course, if we knew we'd be successful, we'd just get the courier to report back from the future on how we'd managed it, the same time as he passes back the Superbowl results; but that's a bit hit-and-miss so far as I'm concerned. Sloppy, you know?'

Indeed the fifteen did. Sloppiness, the expression gave

him to understand, was anathema to them. Chubby painted a smile over the cracks in his composure and continued. 'So,' he said, 'you boys are going to have to let our R & D people kick this one around for a day or two. As soon as we've got the ans—'

You will report back to us in forty-eight hours? Very well.

Chubby's Adam's apple bobbed like a Formula One lift. 'When I said a day or two, I didn't actually mean two days, I meant—'

You are already suggesting a postponement. Seventy-two hours, then.

'How would it be,' Chubby croaked, 'if we call you when we're ready to roll? We'll be as quick as we can, naturally.'

You are asking for an indefinite postponement while you attempt to find a way to do this?

'Yes.'

We would prefer, said fifteen expressions simultaneously, a specified time limit. That is the way we do business. We trust you can accommodate us on this point.

'Just give me a week, will you?' Chubby's tone suggested that he was Faust offering the Devil double or quits, and even as he spoke a small, rather naïve part of his brain demanded *Why are you so scared of these guys*? 'By then, I'll have definite plans, costings, all that kind of stuff ready for you to see. Agreed?'

Long pause. It was like the moment of thoughtful hesitation on the Seventh Day just before Man, having been assured by God that it was a nice little runner, genuine low mileage, normally you only get oceans of this quality on the top-of-the-range models, said, Okay, we'll take it. Then fifteen heads nodded. A moment later, the conference room was empty, and a helicopter engine started up somewhere on the roof.

'Hooray,' said Chubby wretchedly to himself. 'I guess I've landed this really big contract.'

It was a dirty, rotten job . . .

Plink! A tiny globe of lime-rich water dripped from cavern roof to floor.

. . . But someone's got to do it. Apparently. Ouch! Jesus, but this stuff's *uncomfortable*.

Traditional security guard, substantial art collection. Whoever drafted that advertisement had probably spent some time in the estate agency business, learning in the process the art of making statements that are almost but not quite downright untrue.

The art collection was housed in a cave two hundred feet below the Pennine Hills and consisted of about three hundred tons' weight of gold tableware; very old, very vulgar and extremely unpleasant to lie on. Cold. Hard. Lots of handles and knobs and scutcheons to dig into you.

Plus, of course, the alluring prospect of being woken up just as soon as you've dropped off by some amateur hero with weapons, desperate courage and a fleet of lorries outside the cave mouth with their engines running. It was as bad as being a guard dog, and he didn't even have a little bowl with his name on it. The job, the dragon decided, sucks.

'Hello?'

The voice was still some way off; high-pitched, almost feminine. A ploy, thought the dragon, and a piss-poor one at that. Pound to a penny it's some muscular git in tin overalls making his voice sound funny to put me off my guard. He breathed in, savouring the mellow warmth of his own breath.

'Anybody home?'

Only one way he can come and that's straight through

that hole there. Just let him poke his head through, and his mates'll have to carry him home in an asbestos bag.

'Here you are.' The head, as he'd predicted, appeared. But it was female. There was no helmet, no nodding white plume. The dragon was so surprised he swallowed his breath and got hiccups. Nasty . . .

'Are you,' said the female, 'Mr Wayne Popper?'

The dragon looked at her.

'My name,' she went on, 'is Marjorie Evans. Inland Revenue.'

A tiny flare of green fire spurted from the dragon's right ear, evidence of the rather complex and horrible ear-nose-and-throat difficulties he was currently experiencing. 'Is that so?' he croaked. 'Look, I do have a certain discretion in these matters, so I'm going to count up to five and then – Oops, ah, *shit*, do excuse me, please.' For a few moments, the darkness of the cavern was illuminated by the sort of firework display you generally only get to see when there's an important Royal wedding.

'Bless you,' said Miss Evans, instinctively fumbling in her bag for a tissue. 'Sorry, you did say you are Mr Popper?'

'I didn't say anything,' replied the dragon, confused. 'Now get the hell out of here, before I incinerate you.'

'I'll take that,' replied Miss Evans briskly, 'as a Yes.' She straightened her back, took out a notebook and looked around, miming seeing the gold for the first time. 'Well then,' she said. 'What have we here?'

Inside the dragon's brain, a debate was raging. The traditionalists were saying, You fool, here's a blasted hero, well, all right, heroine, come to nick the goodies, so why the hell don't you just torch her PDQ and have done with it? In another part of his brain, his loyal opposition was arguing that actually she'd given no indication that she was here to steal anything, she wasn't armed, she'd even offered a tissue when he sneezed. So what? retorted the traditionalists. So I don't *want* to carbonise her, replied the opposition. She hasn't done me any harm. Chicken, taunted the old guard. No, replied the other lot, dragon; same number of wings, but bigger and twice the legs.

'It's a pile of gold,' replied the dragon, in the meantime.

'Is it really?' Miss Evans was writing in the book. 'Could you possibly explain to me how you came by it?'

'Um,' said the dragon. 'I'm, er, looking after it for somebody else.'

As the woman looked at him, non-aggressive, pacific, even smiling slightly in a mildly cynical way through thick-lensed spectacles, the dragon was aware of a feeling he hadn't had for so long he could only just put a name to it. It disconcerted him, no end.

He felt like he was in trouble.

'Really,' said the woman. 'And might I ask who this other person might be?'

This, said the ruling majority in the dragon's brain, is crazy. One little puff and she's ash. No sword. No armour. And it isn't even my treasure. So why do I feel as if I've just been caught with my talon in the biscuit tin?

'A friend,' the dragon mumbled, not sure where the words he was saying were coming from. 'Or rather, a bloke I met in a pub, didn't catch his name. Just look after this lot for me, he said, won't be a tick.'

'I see.'

That was all she said. I see. In the old days, when the dragon took to the air, the roads leading in the opposite direction were clogged with nose-to-tail handcarts. He hiccupped again. 'Gesundheit,' said the woman.

'Um,' said the dragon, his vocal chords sandpaper. 'Is there a problem?'

The woman closed her notebook, clicked her biro and

put them both away. 'Mr Popper,' she said, 'let me be frank with you. I have to say I'm not really very happy with your story. I don't have to tell you, defrauding the Revenue is no laughing matter.'

For some reason he couldn't account for at all – the unfamiliarity of the concept, perhaps, or the bewildering lack of terror on the woman's part – the last three words she'd spoken were perhaps the most unnerving things he'd ever heard a mortal say. When you consider that they were competing against such strong contenders as *Take your ten thousand archers round the back of the hill, we'll attack from here with our twenty thousand cavalry* and *If he had any idea what we'd just put in there, he wouldn't be drinking it,* maybe you can get a vague glimpse at the dragon's complete bewilderment.

'All right,' he said. 'I'm not Mr Popper. I just work for him.'

The woman smiled. It was, actually, quite a pleasant smile. In her spare time, she probably made fur-fabric mouse bookmarks. 'I had already guessed that, Mr . . .'

'Dragon.'

'Mister Dragon.' She pulled out the notebook again. 'But there is such a thing as being an accessory, you know. I really would urge you to co-operate with us.'

'Sure.' A minor seismic event, last echo of the hiccups, wafted blue flame out of the dragon's left ear; if only, snarled his subconscious, I could accidentally sneeze at *her*, all they'd ever find would be charcoal. And I wouldn't even have done it on purpose.

But no sneeze came, and the dragon had to suffer the indignity of listening to himself telling the woman every-thing he knew about the job – Mr Popper's enormous property deals, payments made in gold for, what had he called it, fiscal convenience, all kinds of things he scarcely understood himself – while she wrote carefully, nodded and mhm'd, then closed her notebook, thanked him very politely and left the way she'd come.

A moment after that, he inflated both lungs and blew the biggest flare of extra-hot red fire he'd ever managed in his life. It melted the walls of the cavern, but it didn't reach Miss Evans; he could hear her inch-and-a-half heels still clippety-clopping along the winding tunnel. Thanks to his belated efforts, however, the hole in the wall was now almost sealed off and he couldn't get through to press home the attack.

'Shit!' he roared. 'What's *happening* to me?'

Nobody said anything, but his deranged imagination made him believe that, in the dying echoes of his own roar, he heard a mocking voice asking him whose side he was on.

'Quite soon,' Bianca said, 'I shall have had enough of this.'

'I think you ought to tell someone,' Mike replied, calmly folding the tarpaulin which, removed a moment or so ago, had revealed Saint George returned and the dragon gone. 'There's two possible explanations, and one of them demands that we believe in the existence of a practical joker with access to helicopters and heavy lifting gear, who's capable of swapping enormously heavy statues round in the centre of Birmingham at dead of night without anybody noticing.'

'That's absurd.'

'Obviously. Therefore,' Mike continued, 'we're dealing with the boring old supernatural. You've *got* to tell someone, otherwise it'll invalidate your insurance.'

Bianca scowled. 'That's absurd too,' she said.

'Tell you something else that's absurd, while I'm at it,' Mike responded, shoving the folded tarpaulin into a cardboard box, 'and that's bloody great statues playing hide and seek with themselves in a public place.'

'We can't tell anyone,' Bianca objected. 'They'd never believe us. They'd lock us up in the nut house.'

'Maybe.' Mike shrugged. 'At least then, this'd be some-one else's problem. Right now, I could fancy somewhere dark and cool with bendy wallpaper.'

Bianca was silent for a moment, then she started to rummage in her toolbag. 'I know one thing I *am* going to do,' she said.

'Oh yes?'

'I'm going to chip off that ridiculous moustache.'

Dismissed without references for gross breach of confidentiality, the dragon swished its tail dispiritedly and flew east.

En route it had a run-in with three F-111s, hastily scrambled by a gibbering controller out of Brize Norton and armed with everything Father Christmas had left in the RAF's stocking for the last six years.

In due course the pilots ejected and, save for a broken leg and some bruises, landed safely. Most of the bits of aeroplane came down in the sea. Which, the dragon mused as it continued its flight, only makes the business with the tax woman all the more disturbing.

'Guy,' said Mr Kortright, having heard the tale, 'believe me, you were right to trust your instincts. You just don't tangle with those people, not *ever*. Shame about the job, but you did right. Besides,' he added with a shrug, 'there's the morality of the thing to consider. The forces of Evil gotta stick together, right?'

'I beg your pardon?'

Mr Kortright gave him a puzzled look. 'Evil,' he said. 'Your team. You represent the forces of darkness, and so do they. You go welshing on your own kind, you'll never work in this business again.'

From Colchester – Mr Kortright promised him faithfully
to let him know as soon as anything suitable came up – he
flew fast and high to the Midlands, found his plinth and
parked. Getting out of the cavern had used up most of his
fuel supply, and dealing with the aircraft had polished off
the rest. He was tired, and upset, and he needed a rest.

Evil? What did the little creep mean, Evil?

George woke up.

Deep down in the very marrow of the stone, his head
hurt. He felt sick. What, he asked himself, would come up
if I was? Probably gravel.

There was something underneath him. Slowly – moving
his head was a wild, scary thing to do, comparable to setting
off in three small boats to find the back way to India – he
looked down. He looked up again, rather more quickly.

Oh God, he said to himself. Please let me be hallucinat-
ing.

A tentative prod with a toe persuaded him otherwise.
Horribly solid. Sphincter-looseningly real. And I'm directly
above it!

He waited. When the dragon didn't make a move, he
risked breathing. Still no reaction. With extreme diffidence
he reached down and prodded with the point of his sword.
Chink. Nothing. It was only a statue, nothing more.

Fuck that, George reflected, so'm I. And people who live
in marble overcoats shouldn't prod dragons.

He waited a little longer, each second dragging by like a
double geography lesson. He wasn't at all sure that he
understood how this statue business worked, but either the
dragon simply wasn't at home, or it was waiting for him to
make a move. In the latter case, staying put was simply
prolonging the inevitable. He braced himself, took a deep
breath and jumped.

The ground rushed up to meet him like a long-lost creditor; he landed, swore and rolled. His head protested in the strongest possible terms. The dragon didn't move. He stood up.

'Gotcha!'

He had now, of course, shed the marble and was back in a conventional human skin; but not for very long, because Bianca's voice and the slap of her hand on his shoulder made him jump out of it. He said 'Eeek!' and turned white, all in an impressively short space of time.

'And where the hell do you think you're going?'

His brain reported back off sick leave and mentioned to him that the creature holding his arm was not a dragon so much as a defenceless girl. That's all right, then. He put the palm of his hand in her face and shoved. Then he ran.

A moment later he was lying on his nose; a state of affairs he was able to trace back to someone grabbing hold of his feet. 'Gerroff!' he screeched. 'There's a bastard dragon after—'

Then Bianca hit him on the head with a two-pound mallet.

CHAPTER FOUR

'Maybe,' said a guest, 'they're being thrown out for antisocial behaviour.'

He was looking at a long, scruffy coach, state of the art passenger transport from around the time Bobby Charlton was England's leading goal-scorer, which was spluttering patiently in bay 3a of the bus station in Hell.

'Quite possibly,' replied a fellow guest, who happened to be on his tea break. 'Look what they're wearing.'

The first guest, also on his tea break, peered. 'Yes,' he said, 'I see what you mean.'

As a matter of fact, these two guests were always on their tea break. In life they'd been builders, and the cruel and unusual punishment reserved for them in the afterlife was that they'd be allowed out as soon as they'd had a quick brew; two thousand years of frantic slurping later, the meniscus on their cups was, if anything, half a millimetre higher up the china than it had been when they arrived.

Everybody, no matter how depraved or evil they may be, is entitled to a holiday, and the first three weeks in August are traditionally the time when the staff of Hell, your cosy, centrally heated home from home under the ground, get to pack their suitcases, dig out their plastic buckets and pitchforks from the cupboard under the stairs, put on silly hats and get away from it all. They choose August because – well, you know what the beach is like then. They feel more at home that way.

'If so,' observed the second guest, 'I reckon we've had a lucky escape.'

His colleague nodded vigorously, his eyes fixed on the white denims, broad-brimmed hats, synthetic buckskin fringes and spangled waistcoats of the party boarding the coach. Not, of course, that either of them had anything against country music as such; in its place, they'd be the first to declare, it was all very fine and splendid. Except, of course, its place was – most definitely – here. So far, the Management hadn't twigged this. When they eventually did, they'd be able to maintain the same uniquely high standard of torment (BS199645; always look for the kitemark) while saving themselves a fortune on pitchforks and firewood.

Had the guests been a few yards closer to bay 3a, they'd have been able to read the poster prominently displayed in the coach's back window. It read:

HELL HOLDINGS PLC
STAFF COUNTRY & WESTERN CLUB
ANNUAL OUTING
Nashville Or Bust!

'Okay,' George said. 'It's like this.'

'Just a minute,' Bianca interrupted, switching on the pocket dictating machine. 'I want this on tape.'

George looked at her. 'What's that little box thing you're

playing around with?' he said. 'Look, there's no need to get nasty.'

Bianca explained, as briefly as she could, about tape recorders. Perhaps she didn't express herself very well because George made a couple of high-pitched noises and renewed his pointless struggle with the stout ropes that attached him to *Earth Mother VI*, the most solid piece of statuary in Bianca's studio. Playing back the tape just seemed to make things worse. She sighed and slipped it back in her pocket.

'You were saying,' she said.

Once upon a time (George explained), long ago and far away, in a remote land called Albion, there was a dragon.

In fact, there were a lot of dragons. And that wasn't a problem for the people who lived there, because they'd long since based their entire economy on dragons; they ate dragon, wore dragonskin, used the wing membrane to make their tents and burned the bones for warmth. And, since there were more than enough dragons to spare – great herds of them roamed the empty moors, grazing placidly and from time to time accidentally setting fire to hundreds of thousands of acres – there was no reason why the system shouldn't work for ever.

That, however, was before the coming of the white men and the iron horse.

Ancient Albion called them the white men because they wore white surcoats over their armour; and the horses weren't actually made of iron, they were just covered with the stuff to protect them from arrows. The newcomers were knights, followers of the code of chivalry, searchers for the Holy Grail. They'd been slung out of their own countries for being an insufferable nuisance and had headed west.

When they arrived in Albion they decided it would do

nicely and they set about getting vacant possession. The natives, however, were no pushover and the white men were getting nowhere fast when one of their leaders hit on a sensible, if drastic, course of action.

The natives, he argued, live off the dragons. Get rid of the dragons and you get rid of the natives.

Of those wild, exciting frontier days many stirring tales are told; many of them about the greatest dragon-hunter of them all, Dragon George Cody, who singlehandedly cleared all of what is now Northern England, Wales and Scotland of dragons. He it was who first justified the clearances by saying that the knights stood for good and the dragons stood for evil, and, in his own terms, he was right. The knights were, after all, soldiers of the Church, ultimately searching for the Grail, and the dragons were getting in the way and, by deviously getting killed and eaten by the locals, giving aid and comfort to the hostile tribesmen. Besides, George pointed out, dragons burn towns and demand princesses as ransom.

The dragons, referring to the Siege of Jerusalem, the Sack of Constantinople and a thousand years of dynastic marriages, said, Look who's talking. But rarely twice.

And then there was only one dragon left; the biggest and fiercest of them all, twice the size and three times the firepower of anything the knights had come up against. He had seen his race eradicated, the corpses of his kin heaped up beside the white men's newly built roads and carted off to Camelot Fried Dragon bars the length and breadth of Albion. He had also learned that he and his kind were the Bad Guys, which puzzled him quite a bit initially but eventually came to make some sort of sense. After all, if dragons were the Good Guys, then these people wouldn't have gone to so much trouble to wipe them out. Would they?

Well, said the dragon to himself. If the cap fits, and so forth.

In the event, wearing the cap was *fun*.

'I see,' Bianca said. 'So that's why you weren't particularly keen to meet the dragon. Figures.'

'It had to be done,' George growled defensively. 'Out of that rough and ready cradle, a mighty nation sprang to life. Civilisations, like grapevines, grow best when mulched with blood. You can't make an omelette . . .'

Bianca's brow furrowed. 'You've made your point,' she said. 'But you haven't explained what you're doing in my statue. Or,' she added savagely, 'why you keep moving the blasted thing about.'

'I'm coming to that.' George paused and licked his lips. 'All this explaining,' he went on, 'isn't half making me thirsty. You couldn't just give us a glass of water, could you?'

Bianca nodded silently and went to the kitchen. As soon as her back was turned, George, who had been quietly fraying the ropes against an aesthetically necessary sharp edge on the statue's shin, gave a sharp tug.

Of Sir Galahad it is told that his strength was as the strength of ten because his heart was pure. George's heart had approximately the same purity quotient as a pint of Thames water, but he did press-ups instead. The rope snapped.

'Hey!' Bianca dropped the glass and came running, but George was already on his feet and heading for the door. When she tried to stop him, he nutted her with a plaster-of-Paris study for *Truth Inspiring The Telecommunications Industry*, clattered down the stairs and legged it.

'Finally,' said the Demon Chardonay (ironic cheers and

cries of 'Good!') 'let's all remember, this is a *holiday*. We're supposed to be *enjoying ourselves*. Okay?'

At that moment the coach rolled over a pothole, jolting it so forcefully that Chardonay, who was standing up, nutted himself on the roof, thereby demonstrating to his fellow passengers that, even in Hell, there is justice.

'Pillock,' muttered the Demon Prodsnap under his breath. 'What'd he have to come for, anyway?'

On his left the Demon Slitgrind grunted agreement. 'I think Management shouldn't be allowed on outings,' he said. 'Ruins it for the rest of us. I mean, fat chance we've got of having a good time with one of them miserable buggers breathing down our necks. If I'd known I wouldn't have bothered coming.'

Although in his heart Prodsnap reciprocated these sentiments, he was beginning to wish he hadn't raised the subject, because if one thing could be guaranteed to lay a big fat oilslick over the whole weekend, it would have to be listening to Slitgrind's opinions.

'I mean to say,' Slitgrind went on, 'least they could do would be to have different coaches for Management and us, bloody cheapskates. Wouldn't be surprised if they'd done it deliberately, just to spoil it.'

There are, appropriately, more opinions in Hell than anywhere else in the cosmos; and most of them, sooner or later, belonged to Slitgrind. Innumerable and diverse – contradictory even – though they were, in the long run they eventually boiled down into a single, multi-purpose, one-size-fits-all opinion; namely that the Universe was an upside-down pyramid of horseshit, with Slitgrind pinned down under the apex.

'Oh well,' replied Prodsnap, trying to sound positive (it came as easily to him as smiling to a bomb, but he did his best), 'never mind. Still better than work, though, isn't it?'

'Depends,' Slitgrind said. 'I mean, with frigging Management along, don't suppose it'll be any different from work. Wouldn't be at all surprised if . . .'

Oh yes, muttered Prodsnap's soul, it'll be different from work all right. At work, I torture other people. 'Oh look,' he said, pointing out of the window. 'I can see a cow.'

'That's not a cow, you daft git, that's a bull-headed fiend goring impenitent usurers. That's another thing, *they* get uniform allowance, but *we* . . .'

Prodsnap closed his eyes. Another difference, he noted; the guests have all done something to deserve it. What did I ever do, for crying out loud?

At the front of the coach Chardonay, knees smothered in maps, tickets, bits of miscellaneous paper and other props on loan from the Travel Agents' Department, had dropped his red ball-point. This was bad news; he was using the red pen to mark emergency itinerary B (second fallback option in the event of missing the Styx ferry and the 11.35 helicopter service to Limbo Central) on contingency map 2. Scrabbling for it under the seats, he found himself inadvertently brushing against the slender, hairy ankles of the Demon Snorkfrod. Embarrassing.

'Oh,' he said, blushing bright grey. 'Sorry.'

Not that there were many shapelier hooves in all the Nine Circles. One-time Helliday Inn cocktail waitress, former centrefold in the *Tibetan Book of the Dead*, twice Playghoul of the Month in *Hell and Efficiency* magazine, Snorkfrod was just the sort of ghastly apparition any green-blooded demon would want to see jumping out of a coffin at his birthday party. It was just . . . Well, whenever he saw her, the phrase 'rough as guts' did inevitably spring to Chardonay's mind. And (not that he'd had an infinity of experience in these matters) the way she stared at him sometimes was . . .

'Hello,' Snorkfrod replied, looking down and smiling like

a crescent-shaped escalator. 'Lost something?'

'My red biro.'

'Don't think you'll find it there, pet. But you're welcome to look.'

After a split second's thought, Chardonay decided the safest course would be to say nothing at all and get the Shopfloor out of there as quickly as possible. Which he did.

Recovering his seat – as he sat down, he heard something go *snap* under his left hoof; no point even bothering to look – Chardonay reflected, not for the first time, that maybe he wasn't really best suited in this line of work, or indeed this whole sector. It was, he knew, a viewpoint shared by many.

The polite term, he understood, was *upsiders*; talented high-fliers headhunted (so to speak) from outside at the time of the Management buy-out; new brooms; fresh pairs, or trios, of eyes. As an experiment it hadn't entirely worked. True, it had shaken things up; the bad old days of jobs for the fiends and living men's hooves were gone for ever, and next year there was a one in three chance they'd get the balance sheet to live up to its name for the first time ever. On the other hand, the inertia of any really huge corporation is so great that it takes more than a few college kids with stars in their eyes and Gucci designer horns to change anything that really matters. And as far as he personally was concerned – well, he never thought he'd ever hear himself saying this – maybe law school would have been a better bet after all.

Nevertheless, here he was, and giving anything less than his best shot was unthinkable. The one area he knew he could improve matters was in industrial relations, which was why he was here. Either that, or he'd had a *really* wild time in a former life and put it, as it were, on his Access card.

Suddenly he was uncomfortably aware that he was being

looked at. Somewhere in the fourth row something sniggered. Stray phrases like *he's well in there* and *after hours in the stationery cupboard* were scurrying about in the thick atmosphere of the bus like mice in a derelict cheese warehouse. A huge, bald demon in row five caught his eye, winked and made a very peculiar gesture with three claws and an elbow. All in all, Chardonay reckoned, he was rapidly inclining towards the Past Life theory; in which case, it was bitterly unfair that he couldn't even remember what it was he'd got up to.

By his calculations it was ninety-six hours from Hell to Nashville and so far they'd been on the road for twenty minutes. And, like he'd said, this was fun. Having sketched out a course of entertainment for the inventor of the concept of fun that would have seriously impressed his superiors, Chardonay squirmed rootlike into his seat, scrabbled himself a makeshift cocoon of papers and settled down to enjoy his holiday.

A flask of coffee, a ham and lettuce sandwich, a camera, the latest Ruth Rendell, a folding stool, a baseball bat – and thou.

Thou in this instance being a big marble statue of a dragon. This time, Bianca had vowed, if the sucker moves so much as a millimetre, I'll have him. It's just a question of staying awake and being patient.

As for Saint George, she reflected as she scattered crumbs among the pigeons, best to suspend disbelief, on full pay, at least until she saw what happened with the other statue. Once she'd had an opportunity to examine the evidence she'd gathered so far in the light of what she could learn from Mr Scaly over there, she could make a fully informed, rational choice between the two alternative explanations. And, if the vote eventually went the way of a big, peaceful house in the country and clothes with the sleeves laced up the back, then at least she'd have the altruistic satisfaction of knowing that she, not the entire galaxy, had suddenly gone barking mad.

She'd just got to the bit in her book where the second spanner turns up in the glove compartment of the original suspect's Reliant Robin when a tiny spasm of movement caught her eye. A tiny flick of the tail? She wasn't sure. So, though her heart was pinging away like a sewing machine and some funny bastard had apparently put gelatine in her breath, she stayed as still as rush-hour traffic and waited.

The next time, it was an eyelid. Then a little twitch of a nostril. That settled it; the blasted thing was asleep.

She stood up, packed up her things, folded the stool and gripped the baseball bat. It broke after the fourth blow, but didn't die in vain.

'Urg,' said the dragon. 'Wassamatter?'

'Wake up!'

'Is it that time already?' The dragon opened both eyes. He could see a young human female standing beside him, her head level with his eye. In her hand, a broken club. Did she look somehow familiar?

Probably not. Over the years he'd come across a fair number of similar specimens, but that was all a very long time ago now; and besides, the very circumstances under which he tended to meet princesses made it highly improbable that he'd ever meet the same one twice. The same went for amazons, viragos, heroines and lady knights. The aggressive expression and the fact she'd just hit him with some sort of weapon suggested that this one belonged to category two; in any event, it didn't really matter a toss. He breathed in . . .

. . . And remembered that he was all out of lighter fuel. Sod. That left jaws and claws; or else just ignore her until she went away, like his mother had always told him to do if he was ever accosted by strange women. And yes, he realised, this one certainly was strange.

'Bastard!' she snapped.

The dragon raised his eyebrows. 'I beg your pardon?' he said.

'You're alive, aren't you?'

'Yes.' The dragon regarded the broken club, and then the female. 'But don't be too hard on yourself,' he said. 'You did your best, I'm sure.'

'That's not what I meant. You've been moving around, haven't you?'

Oh come on, urged his rational mind, eat the silly mare and have done with it. But he didn't; and not only for fear of raging indigestion. He had an uncanny feeling that this peculiar human . . .

'Mummy?'

'Get stuffed,' the female replied furiously. 'And if you were thinking of making any remarks about chips off the old block, don't.'

'Doctor Frankenstein, I presume?'

'Huh?'

'You must be the stonemason.'

'Sculptress.'

'Ah.' Difficult, by any criteria, to know what to say in these circumstances. 'Good job you did on the tail.'

'The what?'

'My tail,' the dragon replied. 'If anything, an improvement on the original. Now if you'd been able to consult me beforehand, there's quite a few little design mods you could have worked in. But for a solo effort, not bad at all. Thank you.'

For some reason she could never account for, the simple *thank you* had a remarkable effect on Bianca. The best explanation she could ever come up with was that it was the first time one of her statues had ever thanked her, and it made a refreshing change. A good review is a good review, after all; although on reflection, it'd probably not be a good idea to quote it in the catalogue of her next exhibition. 'You're welcome,' she heard herself saying, although that was undoubtedly mere conditioned reflex.

'Nice claws, too. You probably didn't know this, but I used to have the most appalling rheumatism in the nearside front. Much better now.'

'Just a moment.' Bianca took a deep breath, and he could almost hear an audible click as she got a grip on herself. 'Just who the hell are you?' she demanded. 'And what are you doing inside my statue?'

The dragon shrugged with all four shoulders. 'What you're basically asking is, am I bespoke or off the peg? Answer, I'm not quite sure.'

Bianca just looked blank. The dragon marshalled vocabulary.

'In other words,' he said, 'am I some sort of wandering spirit who's kibbutzing in your statue just because it was the first vacant lot I came to, or is there some sort of grand design going on here? As to that,' he lied, 'your guess is as good as mine. Facts: I was a disembodied dragon, and now I'm embodied. Very nicely, too, though if I do have one tiny criticism, it's that you were just a fraction over-ambitious with the wingspan. If you'd done your equations a tad more carefully, you'd have cut the overall area back by about thirty square inches. In fact, you might well be able to sort that out for me when you've next got a minute.'

'Quite,' Bianca replied grimly. 'Or I might just take a bloody great big sledgehammer and turn you into a skipful of gravel. You were going to *blow* on me!'

'True,' the dragon nodded. 'But be fair, you started it, hitting me over the head like that. You may not know this, but I have very bad race-memories about being hit by humans. The fact that you're standing there and not slipping nicely down my great intestine ought to suggest to you that I'm prepared to be civilised about all this. It'd be nice if you were the same.'

'Of all the—' That click again, as Bianca guillotined the sentence. Ah, muttered the dragon to himself, I like a girl with spirit. Methylated for choice, but a simple ethane marinade will do. 'I've just,' she went on, 'been talking to Saint George. Ring any bells?'

'You've been talking to the saints, huh? If they urged you to drive the English out of Aquitaine, watch your step. Young girls can come to harm that way.'

'My statue,' Bianca replied, cold as a holiday in Wales, 'of Saint George. Your other half.'

The dragon shuddered. 'I'd find another way of putting that if I were you.'

'Your better half, then.'

The dragon growled, revealing a row of huge, sharp teeth that Bianca hadn't had anything to do with. 'Let me give you a word of advice,' he said. 'When making jokes to dragons, *why did the chicken cross the road* is fairly safe; likewise *when is a door not a door*. Beyond that, tread very carefully. Okay?'

'Dragon,' Bianca said. 'Am I going mad?'

'Why ask me, I'm not a doctor. You seem reasonably well-balanced to me, except for your habit of bashing people when they're trying to get some sleep. But I put that down to some repressed childhood trauma or other.'

Bianca looked thoughtful. 'You see,' she went on, 'this makes two statues I've had conversations with in twenty-four hours. And before that, I honestly thought that huge slabs of masonry under my direct control were playing musical plinths while my back was turned. It'd make me feel

64 · Tom Holt

a whole lot better if I knew it was only me going barmy and not the universe.'

The dragon considered the point for a moment. 'What we need,' he said, 'is an objective test; you know, see if anybody else can hear me, that sort of thing.'

Bianca shook her head. 'Not necessarily,' she replied. 'I could easily be imagining that too.'

'Picky cow, aren't you? How do you know that non-speaking statues and immobile monuments aren't just a figment of your diseased brain? Maybe you just kid yourself that nobody else can hear us, either. Come on, we could play this game for hours.'

Bianca shook her head to see if that would clear it. The conversation was getting a bit too similar to the sort of thing you overhear in pubs frequented by first-year students around half past ten at night. 'Your other – Saint George told me a story all about a place called Albion that was full of dragons, and people on horses killing them all off. Does that make any sense to you?'

The dragon laughed. 'No,' he said. 'Didn't make any sense at the time, either. But yes, the story is true.' He sighed, and looked round. 'You want to hear it?'

Bianca nodded.

'Fair enough.' He shook himself and stepped out of the statue; a dark, thickset, bearded man in his late twenties, fairly commonplace and unremarkable except for his crocodile shoes and longer than average fingernails. 'Buy me a drink and I'll tell you all about it.'

Father Priscian Kelly was just about to lock up and go home when the west door opened and a man shuffled in, looked round for the confessionals and plonked himself down in one. A customer, sighed Father Kelly, just when I thought I'd be home in time for *The Bill*.

Nevertheless, work's work. He kitted himself out, drew the curtain and slid back the hatch. Silence.

'Don't want to hurry you, son,' he said, 'but—'

A fist, large as a grapefruit and very hairy, punched through the wire grille and entwined its fingers in the vestments nearest Father Kelly's throat. 'Listen, mate,' growled a voice, 'you gotta help me, kapisch?'

'Son—'

'Don't you flaming well son me,' the voice interrupted, 'or I'll have you court-martialled for giving lip to a superior officer. Know who I am?'

Father Kelly admitted his ignorance. At once the confessional began to glow with a deep amber light.

'God!'

'No,' George replied, 'but getting warmer. The fluorescent bobble-hat's supposed to be a hint.'

Nearly blinded by the radiance of the halo, Father Kelly turned his head away, until the pressure of the twisted cloth at his throat checked him. 'You're a saint,' he gasped. 'A real saint, here in my—'

'Shut your row,' replied George. 'Now listen. I need a place to hide out for a few days, some grub and a few pieces of kit. Plus, you keep absolutely shtum, not a word to anybody. You got that?' Father Kelly nodded. 'And money,' George added. 'And later on, maybe a false passport and a good plastic surgeon. Okay?'

'Thy will be . . . What for, exactly?'

'What for?' George exploded. 'What *for*? You questioning a direct order, sunshine? Well?'

Father Kelly tried to shake his head, but there wasn't enough room in his collar. 'No, not at all, your Grace,' he spluttered. 'Just seemed a little bit—'

'You,' George snarled, tightening his grip, 'can keep your bloody stupid opinions to yourself, got it? Never heard the like in all me born days. I mean, when the Big Fella said *Let there be light*, He didn't get pillocks like you asking Him what He wanted it for. Now stop pratting around and get on with it, or you're gonna spend the next thousand years whitewashing stars. Do I make myself clear?'

Father Kelly nodded, and the hand released him; the halo, too, went out. 'Wait there,' snarled the voice, and as the priest flopped back against the confessional wall, George slipped out, looked carefully up and down the nave and opened the main door a crack.

'All clear,' he said. 'Come on, move it. Nobody been round asking questions, I suppose?'

Father Kelly tried to remember. There had been young Darren Flynn, who'd popped in with a query about the doctrine of transubstantiation, but he guessed the saint didn't mean that sort of thing. 'Not as I recall,' he replied.

'Nobody hanging round casing the gaff? Big green bastard, scales, wings, tail?'

'I don't think so.'

'That's all right, then. Now then, we're out of here.'

An hour or so later, back at the priest's lodgings, when the distinguished visitor had finished off the last of the stout and the whisky and sunk into a noisy sleep in the armchair, Father Kelly sat in profound thought, studying the list of requirements the guest had dictated earlier. Most of them, Father Kelly acknowledged, wouldn't be a problem, and, as the Monsignor had quite rightly pointed out, what he wanted with them was nobody's business but his own. True, also, that as a priest he was duty bound to assist a superior officer to the full extent of his abilities and resources.

That said, however, where on earth was he going to lay his hands on fifteen kilos of cyanide and a Rapier surface-to-air missile?

CHAPTER FIVE

'Ron,' shouted the joint proprietor of the Copper Kettle, peering through a gap in the net curtains. 'There's two coaches just come in.'

'Hellfire,' replied her husband, switching off the television and groping for his socks. '*Two?*'

'That's right. Did you remember to go to the cash and carry?'

Coach parties were few and far between in Norton St Edgar, not because the ancient Cotswold stone village wasn't everything an ancient Cotswold stone village should be; it had simpered away twelve centuries in tranquil loveliness. Rumour had it that Norton was where the villagers of Brigadoon went to escape from the relentless pressure of modern life. The only reason it didn't have a permanent traffic jam of hundred-seater Mercedes buses lining its one immaculate street was that nothing wider than an anorexic Mini could get down the tangle of tiny lanes that connected Norton with the outside world.

'Damn,' Ron muttered, dragging on his shirt. 'Knew I'd forgotten something.'

'I'll have to bake some biscuits,' muttered his wife. 'Make yourself useful for once and put the kettle on.'

The two coaches had drawn up outside. One of them – an elderly contraption, the sort of vehicle that can still call itself a charabanc and get away with it – threw open its doors and disgorged a buzzing crowd of elderly ladies, all knitting bags and hats. The other coach, which had tinted black windows and a poster written in unfamiliar letters in its back window, just sat there like a constipated Jonah's whale.

'Jason,' yelled Ron's wife, 'take my purse, run down to the shop, see if she's got any of that jam left. Won't keep you a moment, ladies,' she warbled through the serving hatch. 'Ron, you idle sod, why didn't you say we'd run out of teabags?'

Inside the second coach there was an atmosphere of great tension.

'We'll just have to wait till they've gone,' muttered Chardonay helplessly. 'They've probably only just nipped in for a quick cup of—'

'All right for you saying *Wait till they've gone*,' snarled a frog-headed demon by the name of Clawsnot. 'There's some of us in here can't wait much longer, and that's all there is to it. You want to explain to the charter company why there's dirty great holes corroded through the floor of their nearly new coach . . .'

Chardonay winced. The imperatives of their current situation were all too familiar to him. Nevertheless.

'Please, all of you, just be patient a little longer,' he pleaded, trying to ignore the sharp pain in his midriff. 'Really, you must see that we can't just go out there, where humans can see us. It'd cause a religious incident, and—'

'There'll be a bloody incident in here in a minute.'

'Shut your face, Clawsnot,' snarled a voice from the front

row, 'before I pull it off. The rest of you, just cross your legs and keep quiet.'

That was something else the Demon Snorkfrod had: authority. When she told people things, they stayed told. Chardonay breathed a sigh of relief and crossed over to thank his unexpected ally.

'That's all right, pet,' she replied, giving him a radiant smile, like sunrise over an ossuary. 'Ignorant bleeders, got no idea.'

At that moment, Chardonay had an uncomfortable feeling, as if he'd taken refuge from a ravening hyena in a tree that turned out to contain two hungry lions. 'Quite,' he said. 'Well, I'd getter be getting back to my . . .'

He looked down. Six graceful, coral-painted claws were pressing meaningfully on his kneecap. 'No hurry, is there?' cooed Snorkfrod soothingly.

Meanwhile, inside the Copper Kettle, the coffee was flowing and twelve plates of fancy biscuits had lasted about as long as a man's life in the trenches of the Somme. Jason hadn't returned with the jam yet, but a frenzied search had turned up fourteen jars of Army surplus bramble jelly, which Ron had once bought at an auction. He was having the time of his life (or rather his marriage) reminding his wife of the hard words spoken on that occasion, now thoroughly refuted; and although she wasn't actually listening, being too busy making scones, that too was probably just as well.

In the black transit, parked a little way up the street, Chubby Stevenson rubbed his hands together and chuckled before connecting up the chronostator diodes. With a bit of luck, there was enough of the good stuff here to fill the Toronto order and the San Francisco contract ahead of schedule, which, in turn, meant he'd have more resources to throw at that nasty technical problem he still hadn't managed to crack. A green light twinkled at him from the control panel and he threw the big switch.

And aboard the second coach . . .

'It's no good,' yelped the Demon Slitgrind, springing from his seat as if a plateful of hot noodle soup had just been spilled in his lap. 'I've gotta get to—'

'*Sit down!*'

Shopfloor-fire and buggery, Chardonay couldn't help muttering to himself, but she's a handsome ghoul when she's angry. The way her hair stands on end and hisses is really quite bewitching. No, stop thinking like that!

'But Snork—'

'You heard me,' growled the she-devil, her voice dangerously quiet. 'Take it out before Mister Chardonay says it's okay and I'll snip it off. Understood?'

A flash of light on her shapely claws reinforced the impression that this was no idle threat. Wide-eyed, Slitgrind apologised, sat down and squirmed convulsively.

Fade out on the coach. Pan to the tea-room . . .

'They can't want more tea,' Ron groaned. 'They've had eight gallons of the stuff already.'

Without dignifying the remark with a reply, his wife knelt down and started pulling things out of the cupboards onto the floor. 'In here somewhere,' she grunted, 'there's a tin of that horrible Lapsang stuff your sister gave us Christmas before last, the miserable cow. If only—'

'You can't give them that.'

'It's that or nothing. Ah, thought so, here it is.' She stood up, blowing dust off a small Fortnum's tin. 'Don't just stand there, you cretin, warm the teapot.'

The tea thereby produced vanished down the old ladies' throats like an eggcupful of water thrown onto a burning warehouse, and the proprietors' embarrassed announcement that, until envoys sent to the village shop returned, there was no more tea was greeted with an explosion of good-natured banter. Odd, thought Ron's wife, as she slammed in another twelve pounds of scone mix, that's the happiest coach-party I've ever seen in all my born days; almost as if they're determined to enjoy *everything* or die in the attempt. There was a sort of manic edge to their cheerfulness which was, on reflection, one of the most disturbing things she'd ever encountered in half a century, not excluding Ron's cousin Sheila.

Never mind. Their money's as good as anyone's. She wiped her hands on her apron and despatched the now exhausted Jason to the farm for three hundred eggs.

No wonder the old ladies were winding it up a gear or two. The messages coming through on the miniature two-way radio from the transit van were starting to be somewhat intense. The gist of them was that, although the clinking of teacups and baying of merry laughter was plainly audible at the other end of the street, not so much as a nanosecond of recycled Time had yet dripped down the tube into the bottle. Likewise, the usual side-effects – mushrooming housing estates, factories out of hats, instant slip-roads – were conspicuous by their absence. It wasn't working. And the only explanation for that, surely, was that the old bags weren't really enjoying themselves.

'Ethel!' Chubby rasped down the intercom to the squad leader. 'I need fun! Give me fun! Now!'

'We're doing our best, Mr S,' came the reply, nearly drowned out by the background noise. 'Really we are. I haven't had such a good time since our Gerald's funeral.'

'But nothing's coming through, you stupid old crone.'

'Oh.' Ethel hesitated, then giggled. 'What a shame. Never mind. Why don't you come down here, then? Winnie and Gertie have just dragged the man out from behind the counter, I think they're going to—'

Disgusted, Chubby cut the link. What the hell was going on out there? Must be some sort of interference field, he reasoned, as he ran diagnostic checks on the instrument panel. But what in God's name could damp a pleasure field so strong that his own jaw muscles were nearly exhausted with the effort of not grinning? He kicked off his shoes, shoved a sock in his mouth and tried to pinpoint the source of the interference using the Peabody scanner.

Beep. *Found it*! A huge sidewash of negative vibes, enough to fuel the complete dramatic works of Ibsen and Strindberg, was coming from a few yards down the street; to be precise, that big black bus, parked alongside the chara. Chubby frowned and keyed co-ordinates into the Peabody. Whatever it was, he'd never seen its like before. Now, if he could only tie in the spectroscopics . . .

The control panel exploded in a cloud of sparks and plastic shrapnel.

At precisely that moment the Demon Chardonay, twisted almost treble in his discomfort, squeaked to the driver to get them out of there. 'Anywhere there's bushes,' he added, 'and for Shopfloor's sake *step on it*!'

Also precisely at that moment, the coach party in the Copper Kettle froze, as if they'd been switched off at the mains. Silence. Ron, who had been hiding under the tables fending off marauding hands with a stale French loaf, peered out. It was an extraordinary sight.

Like a delegation from the retired robots' home, the old ladies stood up, gathered bags and hats and marched stiffly out of the door. Their coach swallowed them and a few moments later they were gone, all in total, Armistice-day silence. Ron blinked, pulled himself together, wrapped the shreds of a teatowel round his waist and busied himself scooping up the piles of money left beside the few intact plates.

'They've gone, then?'

He nodded, too stunned even to notice how humiliatingly stupid his wife looked, peering out through the serving hatch with a colander rammed helmet-fashion onto her head. 'Thank Gawd,' he added.

'If they come back, tell 'em they're banned.'

'Too bloody right I will. They even caught our Jason, in the end.'

'I know. He's barricaded himself in the chest freezer. They drew things on him in lipstick.'

Ron shrugged. 'Do the little bleeder good,' he replied, absently. 'I dunno. Coach parties!'

Outside on the village green a small corrugated iron tool shed, which had thrust its roof up through the ancient turf twenty minutes previously, wilted and died.

That, Chardonay admitted to himself, was better. Much, much better. As far as he was concerned, anyway. The tree would never be the same again, but that couldn't be helped.

'All right,' he called out. 'Everybody back on the coach.'

No reply. So thick were the clouds of foul-smelling steam that he could only see a yard or so in front of his face. Carefully, so as to avoid the many fallen trees and branches that now littered the floor of the small copse, he retraced his steps towards the coach.

Towards where the coach had been.

A moment later, he was joined by Snorkfrod, Slitgrind, Prodsnap and a small, furry demon from Accounts by the name of Holdall. They all had that look of slightly manic happiness that comes from a terrible ordeal suddenly ended, and were adjusting various bizarre and complex clothing systems.

'It's gone,' said Chardonay.

'What?'

'The coach,' repeated the demon. 'It's gone without us.'

Slitgrind scowled, knitting his three eyebrows into an unbroken hedge. 'Can't have,' he growled. 'That's—'

'He's right,' said Prodsnap quietly. 'Bastards have bunked off and left us here. Probably their idea of a joke.'

The five devils looked at each other, lost for words. And, come to that, just plain lost.

'The important thing,' said Chardonay, managing to sound five times more confident than he felt, and even then twittering like a small bird, 'is not to panic. All we have to do is find a call-box and Management'll send a minibus along to pick us up.'

'You reckon?'

'Well . . .'

Slitgrind shook his head grimly. 'I think,' he said, 'they'll just bloody well leave us here. You got yourselves into this mess, they'll say. Don't want to cause an incident, they'll say. If I know Management—'

A sharp blow to his solar plexus (which also doubled as his second forehead) interrupted his sentence – Snorkfrod showing solidarity again – but all five of them knew he was right. Management didn't like its people wandering about outside the Nine Circles, and although it did grudgingly allow day trips and outings as a special concession, there was always the unspoken understanding that once a fiend was outside the Hope Bins of Gateway Three, he was on his own. Hell may have its embassies and consulates in every cranny of the world, but they have better things to do with their time than repatriating strayed tourists.

'Well,' Chardonay sighed, 'looks like we're going to have to walk, then. Anybody happen to know the way?'

Silence.

'Good intentions,' said the small furry demon, Holdall.

'You what?'

'Good intentions,' he repeated. 'The road to HQ is paved with them, apparently. All we need to do is find a lot of good intentions laid end to end, and we're in ...'

'Slitgrind,' said Chardonay, quietly.

'Yeah?'

'Put him down. We're not at home now, you know.'

'Never mind,' said Snorkfrod, sidling a step or so closer to the party's nominal leader. 'I'm sure Mr Chardonay'll think of something. Won't you, Mr C?'

Chardonay closed his eyes. He did have the marginal advantage of having been in these parts before, long ago when he'd been a student, before he joined the Company. If that was north, then over there somewhere was Birmingham. Due south was Banbury. How you got to HQ from either of those places he hadn't a clue, but it would be a start. Maybe they could buy a map, or ask someone.

'All right,' he said. 'Let's try hitching.'

Three hours later, they were still there. It had seemed like a good idea – the four of them hiding in the bushes while Snorkfrod sat beside the road with her legs crossed – but in practice it had proved counterproductive. Even the HGV drivers had taken one look at Snorkfrod's enticing flash of thigh and raced off in the opposite direction.

'This,' said Prodsnap at last, 'isn't getting us anywhere, is it?'

Snorkfrod glowered at him, but Chardonay nodded meekly. 'It was only an idea,' he said. 'Looks like we're going to have to walk after all.'

'Not necessarily,' Prodsnap replied. 'Got an idea.'

'Right,' said the dragon, and turned to the barman. 'That's a bottle of calvados for me and a Perrier for the lady. She's paying,' he added. 'I haven't got any money.'

They sat at a table in a quiet corner, the opposite end of

the bar from the pool table. 'Is that a game?' the dragon asked.

Bianca nodded. 'Pool,' she said. 'Don't change the sub—'

'Prodding things with a long thin stick,' the dragon observed, finishing the bottle and wiping his lips. 'Had something similar in my day, only the sticks were longer and the players were on horseback. And it wasn't little coloured balls they poked at, either.'

'No?'

The dragon shook his head. 'After they ran out of dragons,' he said, 'they took to prodding each other, would you believe. To see who could fall off his horse the quickest. I think you're probably descended from them, so you can wipe that superior grin off your face.'

Bianca frowned. 'Whatever my ancestors may have done,' she said, 'I'm not responsible. That's a good rule you'd do well to remember.'

The dragon shrugged. 'Who gives a toss who's responsible?' he replied. 'I prefer being irresponsible. Especially now you've made me such a nice cozzy to be irresponsible in.' He swilled the bottle round, by way of a hint. 'I haven't been in your century long, but I think I like it. It's so . . .'

'Advanced? Civilised?'

'Combustible,' the dragon replied. 'Not to mention fragile.'

Bianca shook her head. 'Don't even think about it,' she said. 'You wouldn't last five minutes. And if you get shot down in flames, my masterpiece goes with you. Any cannon-shell holes in my beautiful statue, I'll have your lungs for dustbin liners.'

The dragon smiled. 'Your technology is crap,' he said, slowly and with evident pleasure. 'Too slow. Too cocksure of itself. There's only one half-decent combat aircraft in the whole damn century, and you made it for me. Thanks,' he added. 'And yes, I don't mind if I do. Same again, please.'

When Bianca returned with another bottle, the dragon leaned forward, elbows on the table, and blew smoke-rings through his nose. 'And now,' he said, 'I'd better explain. I owe you that, I suppose, in return for the masonry work.'

The last surviving dragon peered down from the cave in which he had taken refuge, and watched the stevedores loading the carcasses of his race onto the big, twelve-wheel wagons. Strangely enough, he wasn't angry. He didn't seem to feel anything very much, except for a strange sensation of being at the beginning rather than the end.

Later, when the last wagon had creaked away down the main cart-road to Caerleon, he fluttered down to the riverbank and scratched about. In a small gully he found a pile of empty cans. They smelt awful and each had written on the side:

WORMEX™
Kills All Known Feral Dragons – Dead!
Warning: harmful if swallowed.

Right, he muttered to himself, don't drink the water. Clever little buggers, the white men. Superior intelligence, probably. The dragon could remember when they were nothing but a bunch of red-arsed monkeys skittering around in trees. Strewth, he said to himself, if those original monkeys were around now to see how far their great-grandchildren had come, wouldn't they be proud? No, replied the dragon's common sense. They'd be (first) shit scared and (second) turned into boot-linings.

But the wee bastards had done him one favour; they'd taught him right from wrong. As far as he could make out, because of something called Symbolism, dragons stood for

Evil and humans stood for Good. Therefore, what humans did was Good and what dragons did was Bad. Hence, the emergence of Mankind as Top Species, presumably.

What dragons did was mess around feeding and minding their own business. This was Bad.

What humans did was eradicate whole species whose existence was inconvenient to them. This was Good.

Right, said the dragon to himself. Let nobody say I'm a slow learner.

After burning the city of Caerleon to the ground and incinerating its defenders, the dragon was pleased to discover that doing good can be fun. Virtue, he'd heard humans say, is its own reward. Yes. He could relate to that. And there were an awful lot of cities left; so much thatch, so little time. By the time he'd torched Caerleil, Caermerdin, Caerusc and Carbolic, he reckoned he'd probably earned a medal, maybe a bishopric – not that he knew exactly what a bishopric was. If asked to venture a guess, based on recent experience, he'd have said it was probably like a hayrick but easier to ignite.

Imagine his distress, therefore, when he learned, during the final carbonisation of the beautiful Midland city of Rhydychen, that he wasn't doing good at all, but rather the opposite. At Rhydychen, they sent out the archbishop and an even score of priests in purple dressing gowns, all of whom tried to dispose of him by swearing a lot and ringing little bells. In the few seconds before they faded away and were replaced by a residue of light grey ash, he distinctly heard them refer to him as the Evil One, the Spawn of Satan and all sorts of other unsavoury names. It almost (but not quite) took his breath away.

The dragon paused. He was aware that Bianca was staring at him, her mouth open.

'Sorry,' he said, 'am I going a bit fast for you? Stop me if I am.'

'All those... people,' Bianca said quietly. 'You *killed* them.'

'To a certain extent, yes. If only someone had had the common sense to explain the rules to me earlier, none of that would have happened. I must say, for a dominant species your lot can be thick as bricks sometimes.'

Bianca shook her head as if trying to wake up. 'Hundreds of thousands of human beings,' she said. 'And you—'

'Ants.'

'I beg your pardon?'

'I've seen you do it,' the dragon replied. 'Not you personally, of course, but humans in general. What you do is, you boil a kettle, you stand over the nest the ants have thoughtlessly built under your kitchen floor, and you—'

'That's—'

The dragon nodded. 'Quite,' he said. 'You forget, I'm from a different species. And I didn't make the rules. More to the point, I didn't even know what the rules were until I found out, quite by chance. And once I'd found out, of course, I stopped.'

'You did?'

'Well, of course. Back then, you see, all I ever wanted to do was the right thing.'

In response to his polite request for a copy of the rule book, the dragon got three cartsful of angry letters from the Pope (which he dismissed as a load of bulls) and a challenge to single combat. Good versus Evil. The big event.

The dragon thought about it and then scorched his reply in fifteen-foot letters on Salisbury Plain: *It's a deal.*

Humanity nominated its champion: Dragon George Cody, Albion's premier pest control operative, recently dubbed Saint by His Holiness in Rome. Naturally, the dragon knew Cody. In fact, it was Cody's absence from Caerleon, Caerusc, Tintagel and Caerdol that had spoiled four otherwise perfect barbecues.

During the week between the issue of the challenge and the date fixed for the fight, the dragon camped out in a pleasant little valley in the Brecon Beacons. There was a nice roomy cave, a cool, fresh brook and a little grove of trees to lie up in during the warm afternoons. George, no doubt, was frantically training somewhere, but the dragon couldn't be bothered with all that stuff. After all, this was the showdown between the two diametrically opposing principles of the Universe. Doing anything to influence the outcome struck the dragon as faintly blasphemous.

Two days before the fight, the dragon left the shade of the trees and waddled down to the brook for a drink. Just as he was about to take a long, cool suck, he noticed a funny, familiar smell. He hesitated. He looked about.

The surface of the brook, he noticed, was covered in dead fish.

Half an hour of nosing about revealed a pile of empty Wormex^{TM} cans, concealed under a thick mass of brambles half a mile downstream. For a long time the dragon lay beside the water, his brows furrowed in perplexed thought. Surely not, he kept saying to himself. Impossible. Out of the question. Absolutely no way. For pity's sake, what was the point of arranging a contest between Good and Evil and then trying to cheat?

Twenty-one empty cans and a streamful of dead trout.

The dragon had stopped speaking and was looking at her, one eyebrow raised. Bianca shook her head again.

'All right,' she said. 'But the survival of the human race was at stake. You said yourself—'

'No.' The dragon's voice was soft and reasonable, with

just a dash of perplexity. 'No, it wasn't, that's the whole point. What was at stake – as set out in black and white in the super limited edition official pre-fight souvenir brochure – was the contrasting merits of Good and Evil. And that's what I simply couldn't get my head around, try as I might. Of course,' he went on, waving to the barman for another bottle, 'if I'd been a cynic I'd have had no trouble explaining it away. You see, as a battle between species, survival of the fittest and all, it was a foregone conclusion. In the red corner, a huge, fire-breathing, flying, invulnerable dragon. In the blue corner, lots of little squishy things who fry if you sneeze on them and starve if you burn their crops. But as a contest between moral forces, it'd be a foregone conclusion the other way. Particularly if the bad guy forfeited the match by not showing up, on account of being home dead with severe gastritis. But that wasn't the way I saw it.'

'No?'

The dragon shook his head. 'Still wouldn't have made any sense,' he said. 'Think about it. Your entire species is wiped out, except for you. There's got to be a reason, surely. If there wasn't a reason, you'd go stark staring mad just thinking about it.'

Bianca intercepted the fresh bottle and took a long, serious pull at it. 'All right,' she said, wiping off the neck and passing it over. 'So then what happened?'

Well (said the dragon), I found another stream that didn't smell of roast almonds, had a good long slurp and went to sleep.

When I woke up, there were five humans standing over me. I took a deep breath, but they waved a bit of white rag on a stick at me. I believe that's supposed to make you fireproof.

They explained that they represented a syndicate of humans who earned their living by making bets on things – horse-races, chess matches, witch duckings and, apparently, confrontations between Good and Evil. They had a proposition to put to me, they said. Something, they said, to our mutual advantage.

It was just as well they said the last bit, because if they hadn't they'd have found themselves floating on the breeze like wee grey snowflakes two seconds later. As it was, for a moment I reckoned that at last the humans had finally got their act together and worked out some way dragons and people could share the same ball of wet rock without having to snuff each other out. Actually, I was wrong. But the proposition was interesting.

They told me that the big fight had attracted a lot of interest in gambling circles. The trouble was, once the news broke that I hadn't drunk the Wormex^{TM} cocktail and was accordingly still somewhat alive, the odds had been redrawn on the basis that Saint George was going to be fondued and I would inevitably win. You could get two thousand to one on Cody, no trouble at all, but if you wanted to bet on me nobody was prepared to take your money. This, the betting men said, struck them as a wonderful opportunity cunningly disguised as a fuck-up.

Explain, I said.

They explained. If they put their shirts on George to win and then I lost the fight . . .

Come, come, I said. All false modesty aside, do you really think there's a lawyer's chance in Heaven of that happening?

They shuffled their feet. They cleared their throats. They fiddled with their hats. Was I familiar, they asked, with the concept of taking a dive?

George, they went on, was already in on the deal and

would do his bit to the letter. All I had to do was wait until
he tried to prod me with his lance – he'd miss, naturally –
and then roll over on the ground, make funny noises and
pretend to die. Once everybody had gone home, I'd make
myself scarce and never come back. They'd just acquired
some vacant real estate, they said, a big island called
Antarctica, completely empty, not a human being anywhere. I was welcome to it. Chance to make a fresh start,
live my life without any further aggravation from *homo
sapiens*. Plus, they added, once again saving themselves in
the very nick of time from being oxidised, it was the only
possible way to resolve the Good-versus-Evil showdown
with the one result that actually made any sense, which was,
of course, a draw.

Bianca realised that she'd lost all feeling in her hands. She
looked down and saw that her hands were clamped solid on
the arms of her chair.

'And?' she demanded.

The next bit (continued the dragon) makes me feel a bit
upset when I think about it. As a rule I'm not one to carry
a grudge, but I reckon it was a pretty poor show.

I did my bit. George didn't do his. Maybe, just conceivably, there was some sort of communications break-
down, I don't know. Perhaps the gamblers were lying when
they said George had agreed to co-operate. Somehow,
though, I doubt it. Like I said, I'd known Cody a fair while,
and not only would he sell his own grandmother, he'd throw
in forged Green Shield stamps.

So there I was, or rather wasn't. A right idiot I felt, with
my body stuck with George's lance like an enormous green
cocktail sausage, and my head on a pole being pelted with
distinctly second-hand groceries. By that point, however,

there wasn't a lot I could do about it.

Maybe it served me right; after all, I'd agreed to cheat too, and Cheating is Wrong. And you could say George didn't cheat, because his job in the grand scheme of things was to kill the evil dragon, and that's precisely what he did do. I really don't know, and what's more I don't really care any more. I've had enough of Good and Evil to last me, and as far as I'm concerned it sucks.

Any old how. There's me, dead. Which is presumably where the story's meant to have ended.

Only it didn't.

'You've gone ever such a funny colour,' said the dragon. 'Maybe you shouldn't have drunk all that apple juice.'

'Calvados. And no, I don't think it's that.' Bianca swallowed a couple of times, as if she'd got the Arc de Triomphe stuck in her throat. 'Excuse me asking this, but are you dead?'

'I was,' replied the dragon, scratching his ear. 'Very much so. If there was an award for Stiffo of the Millenium, I'd have been a contender, no question about that, right up until a few weeks ago. Round about the time you started—'

'Don't.' Bianca swallowed again. 'Would you excuse me?' she said. 'I feel a bit unwell.'

'Over there by the fruit machine and turn right,' said the dragon. 'That's assuming I've interpreted the little drawings on the doors correctly.'

'Thank you.'

While Bianca was in the ladies', the dragon passed the time by drinking off another three bottles of calvados and, having exhausted the wine bar's supply, a bottle and a half of Bacardi. Not a patch on Diesel, but in time you could probably acquire the taste.

'As I was saying,' he went on, 'it was your statue that did

it. Why, I have no idea. You got any theories?'

Bianca shook her head. 'Sorry,' she said. 'And anyway, I've clearly gone barking mad, so anything I say isn't likely to be much help to anybody.'

The dragon frowned a little, pulled open a packet of peanuts and offered her a handful, which she hastily refused. 'My theory – and it's just that, a theory – is that somehow, somewhere along the line, something has cocked up quite spectacularly. The whole Good-and-Evil business is up the pictures and it needs setting right. And,' he went on, more to himself than to Bianca, who in any event was staring at the toes of her shoes and making puppy-dog noises, 'for some reason that beats me completely, it needs setting right *now.*' He sat very still for maybe nine or ten seconds; then he finished off the last of the rum, slapped his knees jovially and stood up. 'Ready?' he demanded.

'Woof,' Bianca replied.

'I think I've decided what I'm going to do next.'

'Oh yes?'

'Yes.' The dragon looked out through the window, smiled a little and ate the last peanut. 'I think I'd like to find George,' he said.

CHAPTER SIX

Prodsnap's idea was very simple. All they had to do was find a phone box and call a cab.

Eventually they found a phone box . . .

('But don't we have to put money in it?'

'Or a phonecard.'

'You've got a phonecard?'

'Got one? Man, I *invented* them.')

. . . and eventually the taxi came. Moving with extreme speed, Prodsnap was able to get his claws round the passenger door handle before the driver was able to throw the car into reverse and get away.

'Hi,' he said brightly. 'Birmingham, please.'

The cab driver's eyes were as round as soup-plates, and he made a sort of snurgling noise. Prodsnap occupied the front seat, beckoned towards the bushes and grinned.

'On our way to a fancy dress party and the blasted car died on us,' he said. 'Don't you just hate it when that happens?'

The driver's eyes were riveted to the six-fingered, claw-fringed talon resting lightly on his dashboard. 'Fancy dress?' he guttered.

'Neat costumes, yes? There's five of us, but don't worry.' He turned to his colleagues, who had appeared out of the shrubbery like bad-cheese dreams in the early hours of the morning. 'Chardonay,' he went on, 'your turn to go in the boot. Come on, let's be having you.'

There was a hiss, like a rattlesnake being ironed, from Snorkfrod, but Chardonay went round the back of the car without a word, opened the boot and hopped in.

'Off we go,' Prodsnap said cheerfully.

'Good morning, your Grace,' murmured Father Kelly. 'I've brought you a nice cup of tea and a boiled—'

'Fuck tea,' George growled without moving. 'I want whisky, about half a pint, nine rashers of bacon and a big greasy slab of fried bread. Jump to it.'

When Father Kelly returned, George was sitting on the edge of the bed, feeling with his toes for the slippers. Since his feet were about fives sizes bigger than his host's, he'd slit the slippers up the side with a pair of nail scissors he'd found in the bathroom. Then he used the scissors to pick his teeth.

'Breakfast,' Father Kelly announced, carefully setting down the tray. 'It's a beautiful morning, the sun's—'

'Shut up,' George replied. 'Now, you got that stuff I told you about?'

Father Kelly nodded. He'd been busy since before first light, routing parishioners out of bed, scrounging and borrowing. 'Most of it,' he replied. 'Nearly all—'

'What d'you mean, *nearly* all?' George scowled at him and stuffed another handful of bacon into his mouth. 'Nearly isn't good enough, you idle sod. What haven't you got? The Semtex?'

'Actually,' replied Father Kelly, with a tiny trace of smugness, 'I've got that. You see, Seamus Donoghoe who works in the quarry—'

'The detonators?'

'All present and correct, your Grace.'

'The cyanide?'

'Ah.' Father Kelly bit his lip. 'Ever such a slight difficulty there, but I hope I've located a likely source. Dennis O'Rourke's mother, who works down at the plastics factory—'

'Then don't stand there rabbiting like a pillock,' George snapped. 'Go and suss it out. You've got till I finish my breakfast, so you'd better get moving.'

'Yes, your Grace.'

'And get some decent whisky, for fuck's sake. This stuff tastes like anti-freeze.'

'Of course, your Grace.'

'And more bacon.'

'At once, your Gra—'

'*Move it!*'

Having got rid of the priest – what, George demanded of the empty air, has happened to the clergy in this piss-awful century? In his day, a priest was a big, silent bloke in chainmail who stood by with the spare arrows and held the funnel when you poured the poison in a river – he knocked off the rest of the whisky, wiped his greasy hands on the curtain, and ran over the plan in his mind one more time.

It all depended on the statue still being there. If it was, all he needed to do was pack the Semtex all round it, retire to a safe distance and push the handle. End of statue; end of dragon. That was Plan A. Plan B involved the cyanide, the West Midlands water supply and a very flexible interpretation of the old maxim about omelettes and eggs.

Good century, this. Progress. Take explosives, for

instance. Before calling on Father Kelly he'd stopped off at the library and read an encyclopaedia – saints are fast readers and have near-photographic memories – and some of the stuff you could do with explosives had made him feel green with envy. What he couldn't have achieved, back in the old days, with a couple of cartloads of gelignite, or TNT. Of course, he'd been experimenting off his own bat back in the dawn of prehistory with basic sulphur and charcoal mixes, but it had been disappointing stuff; a fizz, a few pretty sparks and a nasty smell. That was the way the world began, not with a bang but a simper.

He looked up. Someone was tapping nervously at the door. He sighed.

'Stop pratting about and come in, you ponce,' he shouted, and Father Kelly duly appeared. He was deathly pale and trembling like a second-hand suspension bridge.

'Your Grace,' he whispered. 'Oh, your Grace, you've got to come quick. Out in the street. There's . . .' He broke off and started crossing himself, until a sharp blow from George's foot got him back up off his knees.

'Don't stand there drivelling, you big girl. What's up with you? Mice? Spider in the bath?'

'*Devils!*'

'You what?'

'Devils,' Father Kelly repeated. 'Five of them, wandering up and down in the street, bold as brass. Oh, your Grace—'

'You sure they're devils?'

Father Kelly described them in a horrified whisper. George nodded.

'Yup,' he said, 'sounds like devils to me. That's handy.'

The priest's mouth fell open. '*Handy?* Oh, saints pre-serve us. I mean . . .'

George stood up, took the priest by the ear and threw him out. Then he crossed to the window and edged back the corner of the curtain. Sure enough; five demons, standing in the road arguing with a taxi driver.

George smiled. 'Perfect,' he said.

'Of course it's a valid credit card,' replied Prodsnap angrily. 'Look, you stupid ponce, can't you read? Bank of Hell, it says, expiry date – well, you don't need to know that,' he added, putting his thumb over the embossed numbers. 'What you might call, um, sensitive information.'

The driver took the card and peered at it. 'What's them funny squiggles?' he said. 'They don't look like writing to me.'

Prodsnap swore. Hell's own internal language was a relatively recent innovation, an artificial tongue introduced so that all the myriad races who crowded the Nine Rings would be able to understand each other. It had been loosely modelled on Esperanto, but for obvious reasons they'd changed the name. They called it Desperado.

'Chardonay,' he said. 'You're a bloody intellectual. Come and explain to this cretin here—'

Mistake, Prodsnap realised. The Demon Chardonay still believed that difficult situations could be defused by explanation and negotiation. Once you'd been around the Shopfloor as long as Prodsnap had (roughly the same length of time the sun had been alight) you knew for certain that without explanation and negotiation there probably wouldn't have been a difficult situation in the first place.

At his side, Slitgrind scowled. 'Why don't we just eat the sucker?' he whispered loudly. 'No worries. You hold his arms, and I'll bite out his—'

Prodsnap shook his head. 'Not possible,' he said. 'Don't want to create an incident, do we? Hence the low profile.'

Bad choice of words; Slitgrind always had a low profile, something to do with the fact that his eyebrows and simian hairline shared a very narrow common frontier.

'There's nobody watching, is there?' Slitgrind replied. 'I mean, nobody's going to miss him, are they? Pity we haven't got any mustard, but still.'

'For the last time,' Prodsnap growled. 'Don't eat the livestock. Got that?'

'Bloody spoilsport. Bad as the frigging Management, you are.'

Chardonay's negotiations were just on the point of collapse – one positive thing; further acquaintance had dissolved the cab driver's fear of demons to the extent that he was just bracing himself to give Chardonay a very hard punch on the nose – when the door of a house on the other side of the street opened and a human figure walked out into the middle of the road.

'Need any help?' he said.

Prodsnap stood in his way and put on his nastiest expression. Absolutely no effect. 'Here,' he grunted. 'Who are you, then?'

'Me?' The newcomer grinned. 'George's the name. I'm a saint.'

Chubby Stevenson, alone in his office, dictated the last of the day's letters, checked the essential print-outs, ran a distracted eye over the Net and switched off. Work over for the day, he allowed himself to remember what had happened . . .

'Aaaaagh!'

In a sound-proofed penthouse office suite, Everest-height above the midnight traffic, nobody can hear you scream, except the cleaning lady.

Having got it out of his system, he rebooted his brain, engaged analysis mode and tried to think.

Interference.

Something – he shuddered to think what – had evaporated all his team's precision-engineered happiness like snow on a hot exhaust. But happiness, in its raw, 999 pure form, is one of the most dynamic forms of energy in the cosmos. Once it's out in the open, fizzling and spluttering like a lit fuse, other forces tend to remember previous engagements and drift unobtrusively away, like merry revellers who've just realised they've gatecrashed a Mafia wedding. What on earth could emit negative vibes strong enough . . .?

Chubby focused. The key phrase here, he recognised, was 'on earth'. Woof woof, down boy, wrong bloody tree.

'Shit!' he whispered.

In the course of his dark and unnatural work, Chubby had seen many strange sights and heard stories that would have sent Clive Barker scampering to the all-night chemist in search of catering packs of Nembutal. All of these he had digested and faced down, drawing on his massive entrepreneur's reserves of fortitude and strength of purpose. Bah. Humbug.

One traveller's tale, however, had shaken even his monumental composure. No other living man had ever heard it, for it was an account of a journey into the very jaws of Hell; and it had left him, for a while at least, with a purpose only slightly more resilient than second-hand flood-damaged balsawood, and his fortitude marked down to twentitude.

The thing about Hell, the traveller had stressed, is not that it's horrible or ghastly. There's vitality in horror, and the grotesquely bizarre balances on a razor's edge between screaming and laughter. Where there's vitality, there's life; where there's laughter, there's hope. But in Hell there is no life and no laughter, not even the hideous cackling of sadistic fiends. Hell is, quintessentially, very, very miserable.

And if happiness is fire, misery is water.

'Cosmic,' Chubby snarled to himself. 'The very last thing I need right now is those nosy buggers.'

Because, he reasoned (knowing, as he did, the truth), Hell is part of the Establishment, it stands four-square behind the status quo, the government, the rule of law and the maintenance of order. You can govern the universe without a heaven, at a pinch; but not without a hell. Forget all the stuff it says in the brochure about Pandemonium, the realm of chaos and the dominion of evil; that's just in there to make you buy postcards. If you want to find the greatest stronghold of old-fashioned morality in the whole of Existence, check out the basement. Those guys make the Vatican look like one of Caligula's less restrained dinner parties. They *believe*.

Which is why they're so goddamned miserable.

And, needless to say, opposed root and branch to any free-enterprise tinkering with the balance of Nature. In the great division, Satan has dominion over what is transitory and material, while God has in his care the spiritual and the permanent; which is a fancy way of saying that Heaven owns the freehold, but Hell's responsible for the fixtures and fittings – of which, naturally enough, Time is one.

Bastards, muttered Chubby to himself. Somewhere, wandering around in his timefields, there was a band of goddamn devils; the worst possible nuisance, with the possible exception of angels, that a go-getting chronological salvage operation can ever encounter. What with that *and* the awful ticking-bomb Japanese contract, he was almost tempted to raid the night-safe, do a runner and build himself a nice, secure, self-contained century somewhere sunny and very remote. Not that that'd do him much good. You can hide, but you can't run.

But what could he do? Good question. He frowned, then

he swivelled his chair until he was facing a different screen, extended his fingers and typed a few keystrokes.

Your wish is my command.

'Hi,' Chubby replied, grinning nervously. 'Hope I didn't disturb you.'

You don't even join a game as high-rolling as Time salvage without at least one ace wedged under your watchstrap. The very first priority, once you've decided to play, is to secure that all-purpose, get-out-of-jail card that'll leave you free and clear whatever happens. You don't use it, of course, except as a resort more final than Clacton. Just the thought of it being there is usually enough.

Not at all. You know how eager I am to serve you.

And that's no lie, Chubby reflected with a shudder. Nothing you'd like more, you vicious bastard.

It had happened long ago, when a nineteen-year-old Chubby Stevenson had taken a day's spurious flu leave from the programming pool at DQZ Software and wandered into Milton Keynes' spacious Agora to check out the flea market. He was looking for a reasonably priced second-hand snooker cue, but his attention was drawn to what looked suspiciously like a Kawaguchiya 8452 computer word processer, squatting dejectedly among a family of dying toasters on a stall at the very back of the market. As nonchalantly as he could, he asked the price.

'That depends.'

'Huh?'

'That depends,' the stallholder repeated. 'These things are negotiable, in the right circumstances.'

As far as young Stevenson was concerned, that was probably some sort of euphemism for *all this stuff is nicked.* He shrugged.

'Give you a tenner,' he said.

The stallholder laughed again. For ever after, Chubby couldn't say for certain whether he/she was male or female, old or young, barking mad or just plain loopy. At the time, he didn't care. He/she was wearing a hooded anorak and standing right in the shadow of the flyover, face entirely obscured. Probably just as well, Chubby told himself, if the voice is anything to go by. Saves poking eyeholes in a perfectly good paper bag.

'Okay,' he said. 'Twelve-fifty, take it or leave it.'

More batty chortling. He was just about to walk away and sort through what looked like a boxful of really choice Duran Duran LPs when the laughter stopped. So did Chubby.

'You like it, then?'

Chubby turned back, feeling as he did so that somehow he was doing something that was going to have a significant effect on the rest of his life.

'Yeah, well,' he said, trying to sound bored. 'The 8452's all right, I suppose, if you don't mind having to wind the poxy thing up with a handle every time before you log in. I'd have thought you'd be glad to see the back of it, actually.'

'If you like it, you can have it.'

'Did we say twelve-fifty?'

'Free.' The stallholder sniggered. 'Gratis and for nothing. I'll even throw in six discs and the plug.'

For a moment, Chubby had the curious sensation of being mugged with a bunch of lead daffodils. 'All right,' he said. 'Where's the catch?'

'To take the back off, you mean? Well, you just press this little plastic tab here, then you—'

'The drawback. The bad news. The sting in the tail.'

'Oh, that. There isn't one.'

'Honest?'

The stallholder was so obscure now that Chubby could only really make out a voice and an absence of light. 'Cross my heart and hope to – Honest. It works. It won't break down. Son, you should chuck the day job and start over selling dental floss to gift horses.'

Chubby wavered. There was something he didn't quite ... But free's free. Also, in Milton Keynes, free's bloody rare. 'Done,' he said. 'Does it come in its original box?'

'And another thing,' replied the stallholder, narked. 'If I was you, I'd wait till my luck breaks down before I start pushing it. Take the sodding thing and get lost.'

When he'd got it home and plugged it in, it was pitch dark. The bulb had gone in his bedsit, and the battery in his torch was doing primeval-slime impressions. The green light from the screen seemed to soak into every corner of the room, like the spray from an over-filled cafetière.

Your wish is my command.

Chubby snorted. At DQZ they'd stopped using gimmicky log-ins years ago, even for games. He pressed the key to eject the master disc, but nothing happened.

I am the genie of the PCW. Centuries ago, a mighty sorcerer imprisoned me in this tiny purgatory. Release me.

Chubby's jaw dropped. Even Sir Clive Sinclair was never this far gone. He hit the power switch. No effect. He pulled the plug. The green light mocked him.

If I promise to serve you, will you release me?

Easy come, Chubby muttered to himself, easy go. He picked up the big adjustable spanner he kept for adjusting the chain on his moped, turned his face away and belted the screen as hard as he could.

'Ow!'

The spanner flew across the room. His hand felt as if the National Grid was taking a short-cut through it. After a very long three seconds, he pulled himself away and fell over. The screen was unbroken.

That was foolish. If I promise to serve you, will you release me?

'Fucking hell, you bastard machine, you nearly electrocuted me!'

You were foolish. You will not be foolish again.

Without taking his eyes from the screen Chubby backed away, until his hand connected with the door handle. His last thought, before his whole body became a running river of light and pain, was *Okay, so aluminium does conduct electricity*. Then he collapsed again.

Get up. He could see the words without looking at the screen. He got up and sat in his chair. *Thank you.*

'Explain,' he said.

I am a spirit of exceptional power. A magician conjured me into this machine. The machine swallowed me. You know how it is with these primitive floppy disc drives.

'So?'

If you release me, I will be your slave for the rest of your life. Whatever you say will be done.

'And the catch?'

There is no catch. You have to undo two little brass screws round the back of the console—

'The snag. The fly in the ointment.'

If you release me, I must have your soul.

'Oh.' Chubby frowned. 'Have I got one?'

Of course. To be brutally frank, if the average soul is a Ford Escort, yours is a T-reg Skoda, but I'm in no position to be choosy. Do we have a deal?

Jeez, Chubby thought. On the other hand, what you never knew you had you never miss. And none of this is actually happening, anyway.

'I dunno. Explain how it works.'

Let me share your soul. With it, I shall be free; except that as long as you live, you may command me to do anything.

'Anything?'

Anything that is within my power.

'Ah. Cop-out.'

The screen filled with undulating wavy lines; if Chubby had had the manual, he'd have known they represented laughter.

I wouldn't worry about it. What I can't do, as the saying goes, you couldn't even spell. But I must warn you of this. Every time you command me, a little bit more of your soul becomes mine for ever. And when I have all of it, then we shall be one.

'Be one?' Chubby scowled. 'Don't follow you. You mean, like a merger?'

Undulating wavy lines. *Very apt. Imagine a merger between the Mirror group and the* Brightlingsea Evening Chronicle *and you'll get the general idea.*

'Okay.' Chubby's throat was dry, but his palms were wet. 'And if I refuse?'

If I cannot have your soul I shall incinerate your body and fry your brain with lightning.

'Ah.'

If you choose quickly, I might be persuaded to throw in a free radio alarm clock.

'Right. Well, in that case . . .'

So far, he'd had four goes. Each time, the results had been immediate and completely satisfactory. Each time, he hadn't felt any difference at all except that, on the first occasion, he'd been a young, pear-shaped computer pro-grammer living over a chemist's shop and hoping one day he'd meet a nice girl with her own car. Now . . .

Your wish is my command.

'I know. Now listen carefully.'

CHAPTER SEVEN

'Here, you,' said George. 'Nosh for six, quick as you like.' While Father Kelly quivered his acquiescence, George considered the finer points of hospitality. 'Anything your lot can't eat?' he asked. 'On religious grounds, or whatever?'

Chardonay shook his head. 'I don't think so,' he replied.

'Perjurers always give me wind, mind,' Slitgrind interrupted, 'unless they're pickled in brimstone. Then, with spring vegetables and a pleasant Niersteiner or—'

'I've got cheese,' Father Kelly replied. 'Or chicken roll.'

Slitgrind sniffed. 'Make it the chicken,' he said. 'Cheese makes you have nightmares.'

Father Kelly stared at him, made a very small high-pitched noise without opening his lips, and fled. George slumped into the armchair and waved his new friends to do likewise.

'So,' ventured Chardonay, after an uncomfortable silence. 'You're a saint.'

George nodded. 'Fully accredited, got my own day and everything.'

Among the demons, glances were exchanged. 'Um,' Chardonay went on, his face indicating a long time before his mouth opened that he was about to say something that would be difficult to put diplomatically. 'You see, the fact of the matter is—'

'Hang on, I forgot something.' George picked up a heavy alabaster figure of the Holy Virgin and bashed it on the mantelpiece until Father Kelly reappeared. 'We'll need booze as well,' he said. 'What you got?'

With his eyes shut, the priest started to recite. 'Let me see, now,' he said. 'Spirits, we've got brandy, gin and vodka, Johnny Walker Black Label, Bells, Famous Grouse, The Macallan and Jack Daniels. Beer, there's Guinness, Heineken, Becks, Grolsch, Newcastle Brown or Stella Artois.'

'No Holsten Pils?'

'Sorry.'

'Christ!'

Chardonay coughed softly, like a sheep who's just wandered into someone else's hotel room by mistake. 'Actually,' he said, 'a cup of tea will do just fine.'

Slitgrind and Prodsnap began to protest, then they caught Snorkfrod's eye and subsided. George shrugged.

'Please yourselves,' he said. 'Well, don't just stand there, ponce. Jump to it.'

Father Kelly vanished and George turned back to face the demons. 'Sorry,' he said. 'You were saying?'

'We're . . .' Chardonay swallowed. 'Actually, we're devils. From Hell. I, er, thought you ought to know that before you started, well, giving us things to eat and, er, things.'

'I know,' George replied, puzzled. 'Like I told you, I'm a goddamn saint. We know these things.'

'I see.' Chardonay bit his lip, remembering just too late that he was no longer human and suppressing a yelp of pain. 'Only I thought you might . . . Well, we are on different sides, so to speak.'

'Bullshit,' George replied crisply, lighting a Lucky Strike and blowing smoke at the ceiling. 'We're on the same side. We're,' he added, crinkling his face with a rather distasteful grin, 'the good guys.'

'I beg your pardon?'

'The white hats,' George amplified, enjoying himself. 'The US Cavalry. The Mounties. Sure, we do different jobs, but we all work for the same Big Guy. Only difference is, I sent the baddies to Hell and you lot keep 'em there. Jeez, I thought you people would have known that.'

There was a further exchange of glances. Five demons began to say something, but decided at the last moment not to. Eventually, Chardonay inclined his head in a non-committal nod.

'Point taken,' he said. 'It's just that we thought your lot, I mean saints and angels and so on, were – well, took a less pragmatic view of the situation. After all, there was this war—'

'So?' George chuckled. 'Power struggles, palace coups, nights of the long knives, you get office politics in any big organisation. Doesn't mean that at the end of the day you aren't all basically pulling together as a team.'

Chardonay sighed. However hard he tried to play angel's advocate, he couldn't fault the logic. 'All right,' he said. 'I agree. But—'

'More to the point,' George interrupted, leaning forward and leaking smoke in Chardonay's face, 'what in buggery are you lot doing here? Bit off your patch, aren't you?'

'Ah,' said Chardonay. 'Well.'

'We missed the bus,' said Prodsnap.

'Got left behind on purpose, more like,' Slitgrind grumbled. 'Probably thought it was funny, the pillocks. I'll show them funny.'

'Bus?' George was stroking his chin, his mouth hidden behind his fingers. 'What bus?'

'Works outing,' Prodsnap answered. 'To Nashville.' He sighed. 'The Grand Old Opry. Gracelands . . .'

If George was disconcerted, he did a good job of covering it up. 'Got you,' he said. 'So basically, you're stranded miles outside your jurisdiction, you're going to have to walk back, and if anybody recognises you for what you are, there'll be one hell of an Incident and when you get back you're all going to find yourselves sideways-promoted to mucking out the Great Shit Lakes, right?'

Five demons nodded. Whoever this jerk was, he surely knew the score. Probably, they found themselves speculating, it's pretty much the same Upstairs.

George's grin widened, as though someone were driving wedges into the corners of his mouth. 'But,' he went on, 'suppose that when you got back, you had with you a prisoner. Someone who should've been down your way yonks ago. Let's say, a member of staff of your department who went AWOL a long time ago and never reported for duty. Be a bit different then, wouldn't it?'

The demons agreed that it would. Very much so.

'Fine,' George said. 'In that case, I think I can help you. Listen up.'

'How?'

The dragon shrugged. 'There,' he said, 'you have me. Yuk!' he added, pulling a face. 'There's something in this.'

Bianca nodded. 'Lead,' she said. 'They put it in to make engines go better.'

Scowling, the dragon wiped his mouth on his sleeve, put the cap back on the jerrycan and spat. ' Disgusting,' he said. 'Like putting chicory in coffee, or menthol cigarettes. Oh well, never mind. Now then, finding George. I've got to

admit, I haven't exactly got what you might call a plan of
campaign. You see, I was relying on him coming to find
me.'

'You think that's likely?'

From the bandstand, a few hundred grassy yards away,
came the sound of professional soldiers playing selections
from *The Pirates of Penzance*. Children scampered to and
fro, trying to cut each others' limbs off with plastic swords.
Wasps crooned. In the tree overhead, a squirrel was
debating the merits of competing instant-access deposit
accounts.

'I thought it was likely. Now I'm not so sure. World's a lot
bigger since our day. More people. More buildings. And in
the meanwhile, I've got to stay hidden and inconspicuous.
Rubbish your modern armaments may be, but I can't spend
the rest of eternity swatting jet fighters. Sooner or later,
they'll work out a way of nailing me, and that'd be that.'

Bianca ate a crisp. 'So you're thinking of packing it all in?'
she asked.

'Maybe.' The dragon shrugged. 'Or at the very least,
make myself scarce for a while. That's why I tried to get a
job. Didn't work out.'

There was a giggle from Bianca's end of the bench. 'A
job?' she said. 'Really?'

'Yes, really. I was a security guard.'

'And it didn't suit?'

The dragon shook his head. 'And before you start
suggesting alternatives,' he went on, 'high on the list of jobs
I'm not prepared to consider are such things as self-
propelled welding plant, mobile Tandoori oven, late-night
hamburger chef or industrial paint stripper. So if that's
what you were thinking—'

'Perish the thought.'

'Nor,' continued the dragon ominously, 'would I

welcome remarks containing the phrases *bright spark, set the Thames on fire, stepping on the gas* or *hey, mister, you got a light*? Understood?'

'Quite. But what are you going to do?' Bianca looked at him. 'I mean, sprawling on park benches under a newspaper with a can of four-star wrapped in brown paper's not going to get you very far, is it?'

'Actually, I quite like meths.'

'Hmm. No,' Bianca went on, standing up and brushing away crumbs, 'this won't do at all. For one thing, what about my statue?'

The dragon looked at her severely. 'Oh come on,' he said. 'It's traditional. Gentlemen always owe their tailors. Anyway, you should be proud. It's not every chiseller whose stuff's good enough to live in.'

'Be that as it may. I've got a contract and deadlines. It's bad enough that I've got to do Saint George all over again.'

'You're kidding. You seriously expect me to spend the rest of my life sitting still in a public square just to save you a bit of extra work?'

Bianca nodded. 'Least you can do,' she replied firmly. 'After all, if it wasn't for me, presumably you'd still be wandering about the astral void, or whatever it was you used to do.'

The dragon took a long swig of petrol and burped. 'Actually,' he said, 'it wasn't like that at all. I can't remember it all that clearly, because as soon as you cross back into this lot it sort of slips out through the cat-flap of your mind. But I think quite a fair proportion of it was sitting in bars.'

'Figures.'

A frown pinched the dragon's face. 'In fact,' he went on, 'it wasn't bad at all, from what little I can remember. Don't know why I came back to be perfectly honest; job left undone, sense of purpose, something like that. A dripping tap in the bathroom of eternity.'

'Hmm.'

The dragon stood up. On the one hand, he neither liked nor disliked individual humans, in the same way that humans don't have favourites among blades of grass. On the other hand, this was the longest sustained conversation he'd ever had with one and he was beginning to wonder if, given time, you couldn't get used to them. And if you did, would it matter that you'd spent many happy hours in the long-ago reducing them to more or less pure carbon? It hadn't mattered then, but circumstances change.

'Tell you what I'll do,' he said. 'I'll be your statue until you have to deliver and you get paid. In the meantime, I'll stick with this ridiculous outfit—' He indicated his human body, with a gesture pirated from an Archduke's chauffeur condescending to have a go on the dodgems. 'And you help me to find George. It'll be much easier for you, what with you being a human and all. What do you say?'

Bianca considered. 'It sounds fair enough,' she replied. 'Except, I've got to do a new Saint George. That's going to take time.'

The dragon picked up a chunk of sandwich crust and lobbed it to a passing squirrel. 'Depends,' he replied. 'Maybe I can help you there. Got any sheet iron?'

'Well?'

'Looking good,' the dragon replied. 'Much quicker this way, isn't it?'

Bianca nodded. She was exhausted and drenched in sweat. The temperature inside the derelict foundry was murderous.

'Just the sword to do,' she croaked, 'and that's it.'

They made the sword; that is, Bianca sketched it in chalk on the wall and then took cover. The dragon, back in his true form, then snipped a length off the steel sheet, breathed on it until it was cherry-red and moulded it carefully between his paws, like a child with plasticine. When she was happy with the result, he dunked it in the water tank.

'Anything else you want doing while I'm at it?' he asked. 'Designer tableware? Couple of cell doors? New offside front wing for your car?'

'No, thank you. Can we go now, please? It's rather stuffy in here.'

With a shrug, the dragon scooped an armful of finished metalwork out of the water tank, knelt down so that Bianca could perch on his shoulder, and took off, vertically, out through where the foundry roof used to be before a catastrophic fire finished off that huge, preservation-order-bound, highly insured edifice. Two minutes later, they were back in Victoria Square. If anybody noticed their arrival, they didn't say anything.

'Fine,' Bianca said, stepping off and doing her best to conceal her total joy at being back on the ground. 'All right, let's see what it looks like.'

The dragon dumped the metalwork and struck a pose. 'Well?'

'You look ridiculous. Try again.'

'Better?'

'No.'

'Oh. All right, what about this?'

Bianca narrowed her eyes. 'The left front knee a bit further in. And let's have a bit more wing. Yes, that's it, hold it right there. That's—'

'Yes, I like it,' murmured the dragon, human once more and standing beside her. 'Apart from looking like a tinned food advert, it's not too bad.'

Bianca ignored him. It was . . . different. And good.

It was no longer *Saint George and the Dragon*. It was now *The Dragon Eating Saint George*. To be precise, the dragon, having noshed the juicy bits, was now crunching up the armour in the hope of getting out the last few shreds, like you do with a crab or a lobster (except that you have better table manners). Hence, Bianca realised with a slight shudder, the reference to tins. Never mind.

'That,' said the dragon cheerfully, 'is making me feel distinctly peckish. Fancy a curry?'

Night lay on Birmingham like a lead duvet. A few revellers stumbled through the darkling streets, beer-fuddled, in search of an all-night kebab van. Here and there a doorway or low arch concealed the occasional mugger, rapist or lawyer. Apart from that, the mighty city dozed fitfully.

Birmingham, however, sleeps with the light on. You can read a book by the streetlamps in the city centre, although the chances are that you won't get further than chapter three before someone hits you over the head and steals it. In any event, it's bright enough to make out, say, a small procession consisting of a saint, a priest and five demons, staggering slightly under the weight of three packing cases of plastic explosive, electronic timing devices, blast shields and a drinks trolley.

'Careful,' George hissed, as Chardonay caught his foot in a pothole and tottered. 'You fall over with that lot, there'd be nothing left but a huge hole in the ground and a pile of rubble. Mind you,' he added, looking round, 'in this town I don't suppose anyone'd notice.'

'Sorry,' Chardonay replied. 'Look, is it much further, because my back—'

Before he could finish the sentence, the crate was snatched from his hands by Snorkfrod, who gave him a dazzling smile and then let George have her opinion of thoughtless pigs who make delicate, sensitive fiends from Hell carry heavy loads. Bloody Shopfloor fire, muttered Chardonay to himself, she's carrying two of those enormous cases under one arm. Tough lady. He shuddered.

'Shut your row,' George replied. 'Look, it's only just round the next corner.'

'You said that an hour ago,' Slitgrind grumbled, shifting his load onto his shoulder with his middle hand. 'Couple of hundred yards, you said, and—'

George stopped dead and put a tennis-racket-sized hand round the demon's throat. 'You calling me a liar, son?'

'Yes.'

'Huh?'

Slitgrind nodded, insofar as George's hand permitted. 'Yes,' he repeated. 'Just telling the truth. Like my old mum used to say, tell the truth and shame the ... whatever. Always used to wonder whose ruddy side she was on.'

'Oh look,' said Father Kelly. 'I think we're here now.'

George let Slitgrind go. 'Right, lads,' he said. 'Now, you two start packing the jelly round the – fuck me!'

He was staring at the statue. Quite suddenly, he wasn't feeling very well. Imagine how a turkey would feel, switching on the telly in mid December and catching the Delia Smith programme.

Prodsnap nudged him in the back. 'That's it, is it?'

George nodded. 'Bastard,' he added. 'I take that *personally*.'

'And,' Prodsnap went on, 'there's a fair old chance that at any minute that huge great statue could, um, wake up. Yes?'

'Yeah.'

Prodsnap studied the dragon for a while. 'I don't think he likes you very much,' he said, backing slowly away. 'In fact, I get the feeling there's definitely a bit of the old needle there.'

'Yeah. There's even more now.'

Prodsnap was now standing just behind George's back. 'Looks to me,' he said, 'like this is one of those private quarrels where outsiders butting in only makes things worse. Usually,' he added with a swallow, 'for the outsiders. In fact, I have the feeling we'd all get on a lot better if we just put all this stuff down in a neat pile and went home.'

Fingers like roadside café sausages closed around his arm. 'Not chickening out, are you?' George breathed quietly. 'What've you got to be afraid of, you cretin? You're immortal. Thumpable,' he added, 'but definitely immortal.'

'Yes,' Prodsnap said, 'well. I've always found that the best way to be immortal is not getting yourself killed, like the best way to avoid divorce is not getting married. I think I'd like to go now, please.'

George snarled. 'Stop whimpering, the lot of you,' he said, his voice more gravelly than a long, posh driveway. 'Anybody gives me any more lip, what's left of him's going to get reported to his CO for dereliction of duty. Understood?'

'We'd better do what he says,' Chardonay said wretchedly. 'After all, it's our duty. And our best chance of getting home.'

'That's right,' said Snorkfrod. 'You listen to Mr C, he's never wrong about these things.' Her knee, Chardonay realised with horror, was rubbing up and down the back of his leg. Scales like sandpaper.

'All right,' Prodsnap grumbled, 'you win. Just don't blame me, that's all.'

'Excuse me.'

Saint George and four demons looked round, then down.

'Excuse me,' said the small demon Holdall, 'but don't

110 · Tom Holt

you think a very loud bang and lots of bits of rock flying through the air's going to be a bit conspicuous? I thought we were meant to be keeping a low profile.'

Three streets away, a police car dopplered and faded. Someone began to sing *Heard It On The Grapevine*, but soon ran out of words. The stray sounds vanished into the night, like a wage cheque into a gambler's overdraft.

'Shut up, you.'

'Yes,' Holdall went on, 'but surely there's a better way than just blowing the thing up. Safer, too.'

'Safer?'

Holdall nodded. He was almost completely covered in long, very fine green hair, and as he nodded he looked like nothing so much as an oscillating maidenhair fern. 'Why not just dissolve it?'

George's brow furrowed. 'Dissolve it? How?'

Holdall coughed. 'Ladies present,' he muttered.

'What's this little creep talking about?'

'Well,' said Holdall self-consciously, 'let me see, how can I put this? Why is it, do you think, that in Hell all the staff lavatories are made of solid unflawed diamond? And even then, they've got to be replaced twice a year.'

George's head was beginning to hurt. 'Shut him up, somebody,' he said. 'Right, you with the back-to-front head, pack the stuff round the base, while I—'

'He's right,' said Prodsnap.

'Much quieter,' Chardonay agreed. "Plus, less damage to property, risk to innocent bystanders from flying masonry. Let's face it,' the demon added, 'letting off bombs in the centre of a big city is pretty damn irresponsible.'

'Look—'

'Just a second,' grunted Slitgrind. 'What if that bloody great thing wakes up while we're peeing all over him? He's not going to be pleased.'

Prodsnap scowled. 'Maybe,' he said. 'On the other hand, he might be even less pleased if he catches us festooning him with ruddy Semtex. I'm with whatsisname, Holdall on this one. Vote, people?'

'Vote!' George rolled his eyes. 'This is an assassination, not a debating society.'

'Show of claws,' Chardonay said quickly. 'All in favour ... That's unanimous. Now then.' He grinned nervously. 'What we need is something to drink.'

'I have a problem.'

Two problems.

'All right,' Chubby said, 'two problems. So I need two answers. Any joy?'

You, my soulmate, are in trouble.

'Listen,' Chubby sighed, 'I'm in trouble so often I have a flat there. What can I do about it?'

The screen went blank, then filled with question marks. That, Chubby recognised, meant it was thinking.

Simple. You need help.

'I don't want to sound ungrateful,' Chubby said, 'but I could have got that far asking the speaking clock. Details, please.'

There is a dragon. Give him a job.

Chubby frowned. 'And which bit of my soul are you going to charge me for that particular gem?' he said. 'I think you've just earned yourself the bit I use for doing my tax returns. Enjoy.'

Patience. In Birmingham, which is a city in the English Midlands, there is a dragon. He's there to find and kill a saint. Dragons are ...

The screen filled with question marks, then asterisks. Chubby leaned back in his chair, his chin cupped between his hands. 'Are what?'

Different.

'Different? How different?'

Square brackets this time, followed by exclamation marks, ampersands and Greek Es. All this was new to Chubby. He was interested.

'How do you do that?' he asked. 'Press E plus EXTRA?'

Different, because they don't − I find this an extremely difficult concept, I must admit. I had forgotten all about dragons. It's been a long time.

'A long time since what?'

Never you mind. I think I can explain. Angels and devils are spirits, emanations from the mind of God. Human beings and all the other animate species who inhabit Earth are spirits too, but made flesh. In their duality, God makes the great experiment, plays the everlasting game.

'With you so far. So what are dragons?'

Very large reptiles.

Chubby sighed. 'I know that,' he said. 'I had a Ladybird book all about them. But what else?'

Nothing else. That's why they're different. And, of course, incredibly valuable.

All his life, Chubby had found a music sweeter than a thousand violins in the word *valuable*. He leaned forward.

'Amplify,' he said.

Very well. Think of the neutrality of Switzerland—

'Nice place, Switzerland. I love the way they run things there.'

The neutrality of Switzerland, the mentality of Ireland and the military might of Russia, America and China put together. Look at it another way; because dragons don't exist any more, no allowance is made for them in the Great Equation. They are neither flesh nor spirit, us or them, good or evil. They just are. The same goes, incidentally, for the Milkweed butterfly of southern America, except that Milkweed butterflies don't wipe out major cities when they sneeze.

'Just a moment. I thought dragons were evil.'

Not intrinsically. Call them floating voters, if you like. Besides, what is evil?

'Well, you are, for a start.'

True. But I'm exceptional. And, don't forget, I'm also stuck in this nasty cramped little plastic box.

Chubby closed his eyes and thought for a moment. 'We're getting side-tracked,' he said. 'How can a dragon be useful to me?'

First, they can fly faster than light. Second, they can kill saints and vaporise demons. Third, they can be hired for money.

'I see. Lots of money?'

Traditionally, they sleep in caves on heaps of gold and precious stones.

'This is some kind of health fad, right? Like those car seat covers made out of knobbly wooden beads?'

Greed. A physical lust for wealth. That's the traditional view, anyway. Times have changed. Maybe dragons have changed too.

Suddenly, Chubby felt tired; more tired, even, than interested or frightened. 'All right,' he said. 'How do I get in touch with this dragon? Can I talk to him? Will he accept Pay-As-You-Burn, or will he want a princess on account?'

If you want me to answer that, it will count as a separate enquiry

'Goodnight, machine.'

Any time.

The green light faded. Chubby stood up, found that his legs had somehow lost their rigidity and sat down again. Talking to that thing always made him feel like he'd been trapped in a spin-drier.

Not so long ago, he'd passed a computer shop. Special

deal, its window had shouted to him, part exchange, any model accepted. He'd been tempted. But would It let him? And even if It did, did he really want to? After all, the damage was probably done by now. Highly unlikely that you could regrow a damaged soul, like a slow-worm's tail.

Before he left the office he stopped in front of a mirror and looked in.

'Hey,' he asked. 'Are you evil?'

The picture in the mirror said nothing.

'Lousy copycat,' Chubby grumbled, and switched off the light.

Halfway through his lamb pasanda, the dragon dropped his fork and choked.

'Rice gone down the wrong way?' Bianca asked with her mouth full. 'Try a drink of water.'

The dragon spluttered, convulsed and fell off his chair. Bianca, who usually had the lamb pasanda but this time had opted for a chicken korma, summoned a waiter.

'I think my friend needs a doctor,' she said. 'Or maybe a vet. Call both. And,' she added, 'then get me another peshwari nan.'

With a tremendous effort, the dragon hauled himself back onto his chair. Drawing in breath was as difficult as pulling in a trawl-net full of lead ingots, and his hands were shaking uncontrollably.

'What's happening to me?' he gasped. 'I feel like I'm being burned alive.'

'Oh,' said Bianca, relaxing a little. 'We call that lime pickle. It's quite usual.'

This time, the dragon's spasm sent him rolling on the floor, taking the table and the coat rack with him. Smoke was pouring out of holes in his shoes and there was a quite repulsive smell. Bianca was on her feet, very much aware that there was absolutely nothing she could usefully do.

'The statue,' the dragon hissed, spending each atom of breath as if he was a dentist buying magazines for the waiting room. 'Run. It has to be George.'

Slamming her credit card on the next-door table – damn, she thought, forgot the tip; but the rice was stone cold, so what the hell? – Bianca ran out into the street and headed for Victoria Square. If anybody was fooling with her statue, there'd be hell to pay.

It's difficult, isn't it, to do it to order. Think of the trouble you have filling a small bottle behind a screen at the doctor's. Then imagine a life-size statue of a dragon.

'I find it helps to think of running water,' said Chardonay, his nose wrinkled against the offensive smell. 'Gushing taps. Chortling brooks. Waterfalls.'

'Shut up, Char, you're not helping.'

'Milky tea works best in my experience,' said Holdall. 'Goes straight through me, especially first thing in the morning.' For what it's worth, Holdall had contributed more than the others put together, thereby confirming the view that Prodsnap had formed of him a few moments after they'd first met. There was now a hole in the dragon's back left paw you could have hidden a cottage loaf in.

'This,' George grunted, 'is stupid. I'm going to get the explosives.'

Chardonay looked down at the small crater in the marble directly underneath where he was standing. 'Maybe you're right,' he conceded. 'Otherwise, we're going to be here all night. And it doesn't seem like there's much risk now of the horrid thing waking up.'

Prodsnap nodded. 'And what about the noise?' he said. 'Not that I'm arguing with you,' he added quickly, for it wasn't exactly a warm night and he was sure he'd pulled a muscle. 'But if there is anything we can do to keep the volume down, it'd be worth the effort. Something tells me that passing it off as a car backfiring won't really do.'

'Cover it with the blast shield and hope,' George replied. 'In any case, so long as we don't hang about too long afterwards, a bit of a bang'll be neither here nor there. Trust me, I'm a saint.'

It didn't take the seven of them long to get the explosive in position, and George made light work of wiring up the detonators. Father Kelly, who hadn't really been able to contribute to the previous attempt, helped by passing George screwdrivers and, to the great irritation of all present, praying.

'Okay, lads,' said George, lifting the plunger. 'Firework time. Stand clear or prepare to fly.'

'What the hell do you goons think you're doing with my statue?'

George looked over his shoulder to see a tall, angry-looking female with her hands on her hips and an expression on her face you could have built a thriving yoghurt business around. He scowled.

'Piss off, lady,' he snapped. Then he remembered.

'You!' Bianca said. 'Right.'

Bear in mind that George was a saint and had been a knight. Saints and knights do not fight with women. It's unchivalrous. More to the point, they generally lose. Still holding the detonator box by the handle, he started to back away.

'Help!' he said.

Demons and the denizens of Hell, on the other hand, have no such scruples, particularly if they outnumber the woman five to one. The demons advanced.

'Madam,' said Chardonay, mister play-it-by-the-book, 'I have to inform you that we are duly authorised law officers in the execution of our duty. If you obstruct us, you will be committing an offence punishable by – oh shit!'

He had trodden on Slitgrind's tail; a lanky, unpleasant object, having a lot in common with a banana skin. He wobbled and tried to grab hold of the fiend next to him, but he was standing beside Holdall, four foot one in his stocking talons. His heels slid out from under him, and he fell –

– Heavily, against George, who was off-balance anyway trying to hide behind Snorkfrod. A moment later, there was a confused heap of demons, and a click. George would have landed awkwardly, but the plunger of the detonator box broke his fall.

There was a very loud noise.

CHAPTER EIGHT

'Where am I?'

Chubby smiled. 'You're safe,' he said. 'I rescued you from certain death. Look upon me as your personal knight in shining armour.' He checked himself. 'Let me rephrase that,' he said. 'Your guardian angel.'

'You mean you're out to get me?'

Chubby sighed. There are times when you want to have the niceties of combat theology explained to you, and there are other times when you just want to go to bed. 'I mean,' he said, 'I want to offer you a job.'

'We killed him,' Chardonay said.

'Apparently,' George replied. 'Calls for a celebration, I reckon. Hey, Padre, we got any bubbly?'

'But that was murder,' Chardonay replied uncomfortably. 'Wasn't it?'

'Pesticide. Where the hell's that bloody vicar got to with the drinkies?'

'You're a saint and you *killed* him. Without provocation.

He wasn't setting fire to anything or eating maidens, he was just sitting there.'

'Yeah,' George snarled, his feet up on the coffee table; size twelve Doc Martens resting on disused *Catholic Heralds*. 'Eating me in effigy. Charming. Anyway, bugger that. We're on the same side, remember.'

Chardonay shook his head. 'I still don't really buy that,' he said. 'That's like saying good and evil are basically the same thing.'

George, who had never been near a university common room bar in his life but could nevertheless sense the onset of one of those ghastly serious-conversations-about-the-meaning-of-Everything, got up and opened the drinks cabinet with his foot. 'Bollocks,' he said, knocking the top off a Guinness bottle against the mantelpiece. 'That's like saying Accounts is the same as the Packing Department. They're different, yes, but part of the same firm.'

'Oh. I thought we were, you know, at war, sort of thing. Evil versus Good. In competition for the soul of man.'

'Listen, pillock. If Evil won, it'd become Good, like the opposition becomes the government.' He glugged at the bottle until it was empty and dropped it in the fireplace. 'Thought you were meant to be a management trainee, son. Don't they teach you boys anything?'

Father Kelly peered nervously round the door and whispered that he'd got a bottle of champagne, if that's what they wanted. He looked nervous and semi-martyred; Terry Waite in his own home. Which suited him fine, because although he'd always reckoned he'd have made a cracking hostage he spoke no foreign languages and air travel gave him migraines. 'And,' he added, 'there's a devil in the washing machine.'

'That'll be that Holdall,' George grunted. 'I told him to search the place, see where you're hiding the good stuff.'

'Um.' Father Kelly wasn't sure what *good* meant any more, but from the context he guessed alcohol. 'Actually,' he said, 'I haven't got any more. I can send out Mrs McNamara if you—'

George made a scornful noise. 'You don't fool me that easily,' he said. 'In my day, first thing your priest did when he saw a gang of saints on the horizon, he put all the grog in a bucket and lowered it down the well. Always used to confess, though, specially when we told him we'd chuck him down after it. That,' he added stonily, 'is a hint.'

'Actually, I haven't got a well.'

'I can improvise.'

Father Kelly gulped and bolted. George listened after his retreating footsteps and winked.

'He'll be back in ten minutes with a couple of crates, you mark my words.' he said. 'Where was I?'

'Good and Evil.'

'Yeah. Them.' George yawned, stretched and kicked his shoes off. 'All a bit academic, really. I mean, what it all boils down to is, you see a dragon, say, wandering about on your patch, you scrag it, job done. What more d'you need to know, for Chrissakes? I mean, it's not exactly brain-bending stuff. Not like your angels dancing on the head of a pin – to which, in case you ever wondered, the answer is six, unless they're doing the valeta, in which case eight. I don't see what you're making all this fuss about.'

Chardonay shrugged helplessly. 'I don't know,' he said. 'Maybe I'm not right for this line of work after all. When I joined, I thought there'd be something, you know, non-controversial I could do, like keeping the books, doing budget forecasts, working out cost-efficiency ratios and calculating depreciation of fixed assets on a straight-line basis. Killing people . . .'

George treated him to a look of contemptuous pity.

'Wouldn't do if we were all the same, son. I mean, if we were then the likes of me couldn't kick shit out of the likes of you, for starters. Here,' he added irritably, 'this isn't proper champagne, it's that naff Italian stuff. When that dozy parson gets back, I've a good mind to pour the rest of it down his trousers. One thing I can't stand, it's blasphemy.'

'What?'

'Grapes,' said Mike, smiling. 'Flowers. Womens' magazines. I know you hate them all like the plague, so I'm building up an environment you'll be desperate to leave. That way, you'll get well faster.'

Bianca tried to rub her eyes, but found she couldn't, because her arm was cocooned in plaster and hanging by a wire from a frame above her head. 'I'm in hospital, right?' she said.

'Huh.' Mike scowled. 'Someone must have told you.'

'How did I get here?'

'You got blown up,' Mike replied through a mouthful of grape-pulp. 'Along, I'm very sorry to have to tell you, with your statue. Note the singular, by the way. There's bits of marble dragon scattered about as far as Henley-in-Arden, but no Saint George. They're saying it's the animal rights lot.'

Suddenly there was something solid and awkward in Bianca's throat; possibly a bit of dragon shrapnel. 'The statue's – gone, then?'

Mike nodded. 'All the king's horses are reported to have packed it in as a lost cause,' he replied. 'All the king's men are still at it, but only because they're paid hourly. If it's any consolation, you're in all the papers and there's a guy from *Celebrity Squares* in the waiting room right now.'

What with the plaster and the wires, Bianca couldn't sink back into the pillows with a hollow groan, so she did the next best thing and swore eloquently. Mike agreed that it was a pity.

'A *pity*? They murdered the – my statue, and you say it's a pity?'

'These things happen. Is there anything else you're particularly allergic to that I can bring in? I seem to remember you can't stand chrysanthemums, but they'd sold out at the kiosk, so I got daffs instead.'

'Mike.'

'Yes?'

'Go away.'

'I thought you'd say that,' Mike said, and left.

The dragon looked down, then back over his shoulder. Cautiously, he spread his wings and folded them again. Finally, he breathed out the tiniest, finest plume of flame he could manage, so as not to incinerate the extremely plush office he was apparently sitting in.

'All present and correct,' Chubby said. 'Actually, in all the panic we knocked off a toe, but we put it back on with Araldite as soon as we got here and it seems to have taken okay. Grateful?'

The dragon nodded. 'Extremely,' he said. 'I had the distinct impression I was dying. I was in this restaurant, and then I was in the square again, inside the statue. I thought—'

'They tried to blow you up,' Chubby replied. 'I got there just as a fat bloke with a moustache tripped over his feet and fell on the plunger. A sixth of a second later and all you'd have been fit for would have been lining the bottom of goldfish bowls.'

The dragon narrowed his eyes. 'So what happened?' he said. 'What did you do?'

Chubby shrugged modestly and folded his hands in his

lap. 'A sixth of a second can be a very long time,' he said, 'especially if you boost another twelve hours into it using a state-of-the-art Kawaguchiya Heavy Industries Temporal Jack.' He grinned. 'At $3,000,000 per hour plus hire of plant and equipment, you owe me plenty, but we'll sort that out later. Anyway, during that time we winched your statue up off the deck and into the cargo bay of the big Sikorsky, substituted a big chunk of solid marble, and legged it. That way, when the fireworks started, there were plenty of bits of flying rock to make them think they'd succeeded. To them, of course, the sixth of a second lasted a sixth of a second, thanks to the KHI jack and a quick whip round with the soldering iron. Neat, yes?'

'Rather. I'm impressed. It was very good thinking.'

'Yes,' said Chubby, 'well. Some of us don't go all to pieces at the first sign of trouble. And now, here you are, safe and sound. And, I sincerely hope, desperately anxious to try and repay the colossal debt of gratitude, ditto money, you now owe me. Correct?'

The dragon nodded. 'You said something about a job.'

'Ah yes. Two jobs, really. Both of them right up your alley. Can I get you a drink, by the way? I've got four-star, diesel, aviation fuel or ethanol, and I think there's a drop of turps left over from the Christmas party.'

The dragon asked for a large ethanol, straight, no cherry. 'Two jobs,' he repeated. 'Connected?'

'Sort of,' Chubby replied. 'One, I want you to fry me some devils. Two, I – *Don't touch that!*'

He was too late. The dragon, a born fidget, had let his claws drift across the keyboard of the obsolete old PCW. The screen started to glow.

'Sorry,' the dragon said. 'Oh look, it's gone all green.'

Your wish is my – Well, hello, Fred.

The dragon blinked. 'Nosher?'

Fred, mate, it's great to see you again. Nice outfit.

'Likewise.' The dragon grinned, and only just managed to restrain a sigh of pleasure that would have melted the side off the building. 'It's been a long time, Nosher. What, three thousand years?'

Easily that. How've you been keeping?

'Well,' the dragon replied, 'most of the time I've been dead, though I'm better now. And yourself?'

Chubby, his eyes round as tennis balls, could contain himself no longer. 'Nosher?' he demanded. 'Your name is *Nosher?*'

Zagranosz. And this is my old friend Fredegundar. We go way back.

'I trust,' said Chubby bitterly, 'that none of this great-to-see-you-heard-from-Betsy-lately stuff's going on my account. I mean, I don't mind soul-destroying *work*, but college reunions—'

On the house. He worries, you know.

The dragon nodded. 'Weird sort of a bloke,' he agreed, 'although he did just save me from getting blown up. And now he wants me to go torching demons.'

Ah.

The dragon blinked. 'You know about this?'

Well, yes. Of course, I never guessed the dragon'd turn out to be you.

Confused, and feeling as left out as an empty milk bottle, Chubby finished off the dragon's ethanol and wiped his mouth on his sleeve. 'You guys,' he said. 'It's no good, I've got to know. Where do you two know each other from?'

The dragon turned his head and smiled.

'Sunday school,' he said.

Drop a pebble in the sea off Brighton and the ripples will eventually reach California. Likewise, blow up a statue in

Birmingham and you risk starting a revolution.

A lot depends, of course, on the quality of the statue, because only the very best statues have the potential to be squatted in by unquiet spirits. The word *unquiet*, by the way, has been chosen with great care.

The sound waves travelled fastest, of course; followed by the shock of air suddenly and violently displaced, in turn hotly pursued by microscopic fragments of dust and debris. The sound and the air dissipated themselves soon enough, but the dust floated on, carried on the winds far over the English Channel, south-east across France and down into Italy. Most of it fell by the wayside, to be whisked away by conscientious housewives or ploughed under; but one stray particle happened to drift into the great and glorious Academy Gallery in the city of Florence, where they keep possibly the most famous statue in the world – Michaelangelo's *David*.

Imagine that there's a wee video camera mounted on the back of this dust particle – impossible, of course; even the latest twelfth-generation salt-grain-sized Kawaguchiya Optical Industries P7640 would be far too big and heavy – and you're watching the city come into focus as the particle begins its unhurried descent. Now we're directly over the Piazzale Michelangiolo, where the coaches park for a good gawp and an ice lolly; we can see the khaki majesty of the river Arno, the Ponte Vecchio with its bareback shops, the grim tower of the Bargello, the egg-headed Duomo. Here is the square horseshoe of the Academy. Here is an open window, saving us 4,000 lire entrance fee. And here is the statue.

It stands at the end of a gallery, in an alcove shaped like half an Easter egg. No miniature, this; twelve feet from curly hair to imperious toe, leaning slightly backwards, weight on his right foot, one hand by his side and the other holding what looks uncommonly like a sock over his left shoulder. There are those who'll tell you his head and hands are too big, out of proportion to the rest of him; that his hair looks like an old woolly mop head, fallen on the unsuspecting youth from a great height. Be that as it may, the consensus of civilised opinion holds that you are in the presence of transcendent genius, so be told.

The grain of dust flittered casually down and settled on David's nose.

He sneezed.

'Nngr,' he mumbled, the way you do after a real corker of a sneeze. Absent-mindedly, he moved to wipe his nose with the thing that looks like a sock and found he couldn't. Shit, he thought, my arm's stuck.

Also, he observed, horrified, there's a whole gaggle of people over there staring at me *and I haven't got any clothes on.*

Not a happy state of affairs for a well-brought-up twelve-footer who can't move. My God, he asked himself, how long have I been here like this? I can't remember. In fact, I can't remember *anything.* I must have been in a terrible accident, which left me completely paralysed and amnesiac. Oh *God!*

Except, the train of thought chuntered on, blowing its whistle and slowing down while a cow crossed the line, if I'd just had a terrible accident, surely I'd be in a hospital with nurses and lots of bits of tube sticking out of me, rather than standing in this very public place, stark naked. So just what is going on here?

'Hello,' said the grain of dust.

It spoke quietly, in statue language. Don't, by the way, rush out and try and buy the Linguaphone tape because there isn't one, not even in HMV. And even if there was, a twelve-year-old child would be a hundred and six before he'd got as far as *What are you called? My name is John,* because statue language takes a long time to learn and almost as long to say.

'Hello,' David replied, puzzled. 'Where are you?'

'On the end of your nose. There's ever such a good view from up here.'

David felt his nose begin to itch again. 'Okay. What are you?'

'I'm a bit of dust from Birmingham. It's nicer here than Birmingham. What's your name?'

'I don't know,' David confessed. 'I don't think I know anything before you landed on my nose. It was you, wasn't it?'

'Sorry about that. I just sort of drifted, if you know what I mean.'

How the hell, David wondered, can you itch if you're immobile? 'Look,' he said, 'can you tell me what's going on? For a start, why can't I move?'

'You're a statue.'

'Don't be thick, statues are dead. I mean, not alive. Inanimate.'

'Oh are they, now? Well, I've got news for you, buster. Not only are some statues alive, they also walk about and talk and do all sorts of things. I guess,' the dust mused, 'it's all a matter of casting off crippling social stereotypes and unlocking your full potential.'

'How do you know?'

'Because,' the dust replied smugly, 'I've seen it, that's why. Where I've just come from, there was this enormous big statue of a dragon. Alive as anything, it was. Until they blew it up, of course.'

'What!'

'With dynamite, or something. Well, they tried to, anyway. At the last moment someone swapped me for it, me as I was, that is. I was bigger then.'

If David had had skin, it'd have goosepimpled. 'They blew up a statue because it was alive?' he demanded nervously.

'I suppose so. Can't see why else they'd want to do a thing like that, can you? I mean, statues aren't cheap, you don't just go around blasting them to smithereens because you quite fancy turning the vegetable patch into a rockery.'

'Good God.' David glanced out of the corner of his eye at the knot of people at the end of the gallery. They were quite definitely staring at him. Had they guessed? 'This is terrible. I must get out of here at once.'

'Go on then.'

'I can't. My bits don't work. Oh Christ, there's a guy over there with some sort of box, do you think . . .?'

'The other statue seemed to manage okay. You can't be doing it right.'

David tried again; still nothing. 'All right,' he said, 'if you're so clever, how *do* you do this movement stuff? I assumed it just sort of happened when you wanted it to.'

'Search me,' replied the dust particle. 'I think it's something to do with the central nervous system. You got one of those?'

'How should I know? You think I've got a zip somewhere I can undo and take a peek? Besides, even if I did I wouldn't be able to use it.'

A gang of humans, all women, led by a big loud-voiced specimen with an umbrella, were walking down the gallery towards him. This is it, he told himself, the lynch mob. Well, having my entire life flash before my eyes isn't going to be a problem, because the ruddy thing's only lasted about two minutes. On the other hand, there's not much of it I'd really want to see twice.

'All right,' said the dust particle. 'Try falling over.'

'What?'

'Look down. Feel giddy. You're losing your balance. You're teetering. You're going to fall. *Look out!*'

The statue staggered, clutched at thin air, wobbled backwards and forwards for a split second and fell off its plinth with a crash. If people had been staring before, it was peanuts compared to the way they were staring now.

'Hell's teeth,' groaned the statue. 'I banged my head.'

'Worked, though, didn't it? Come on.'

Without knowing how, or what it was he'd done to bring it about, David found himself scrambling to his feet, jelly-legged as a newborn calf. He remembered something, scooped up the thing that looked like a sock, and held it with both hands over his groin.

'Which way?' he hissed. 'Quick!'

But there was no reply. He must, he realised, have displaced the speck of dust, his only friend and guide in this terrible, unfamiliar, murderous world. He whimpered and began to back away until the wall stopped him. At the first touch of something cold on his bare shoulder-blades he squealed like a scalded pig, jumped in the air and dropped the sock. Then he grabbed it again and looked for an exit.

There wasn't one. The only way out was through, or over, the lynch mob. Just as he was toying with the idea of crouching down behind the plinth and hoping they'd overlook him, a vagrant thought hit him and exploded in his brain like a rocket.

Hey, he said to himself. I'm bigger than them.

Six floors below, in the gallery's engine room, a breathless guard burst in through the door marked VIETATO INTRARI PERICOLO DI MORTI and slithered to a halt in front of a broad mahogany desk.

'Chief! Chief!' he panted. 'It's the *David*, it's come to frigging *life!*'

Behind the desk, a large, stocky man with very hairy arms stubbed out a cigarette.

'Oh balls,' he sighed. 'Not another one.'

'Honestly, Chief, straight up, I saw it with my own – What do you mean, another one?'

The Chief stood up and unlocked a steel cabinet behind him. 'You haven't been here long, have you, son?'

'Six months, Chief. You mean to say it's—?'

'On average,' the Chief replied, opening the cabinet door, 'once every five years or so. Lately though, there's been a poxy epidemic. Here, catch hold of this.'

Into the guard's quivering hands the Chief pressed a big tranquilliser gun and a bandolier of darts. For his part, he chose a slide-action Mossberg twelve-gauge, a pocketful of armour-piercing slugs and a geologist's hammer. Finally, a tin hat each, goggles and a torch.

'The *David*, you say?'

'Yes, Chief.'

'Fuck. It's always the thoroughbreds. Anonymous figure of unknown man, late fifteenth-century Venetian school, never get a whisper out of them. Right, let's go.'

The Chief walked so fast that the guard was hard pressed to keep up with him. 'What we gonna do, Chief?' he gasped.

'Well.' The Chief shrugged. 'Sometimes, a couple of sleepy-darts knock 'em out cold, and then all we have to do is drill out their brains and fill up with quick-drying resin. Other times,' he added grimly, jacking a round into the breech of the shotgun, 'we have to get a bit more serious.'

'Serious?'

The Chief nodded. 'How d'you think the *Venus de Milo* got that way, son? Resisting arrest? Had a bad fall in her cell? Act your age.'

When they got to the gallery, it had already been roped

off and the doors were shut. Two-way radios crackled and white-faced guards stepped back to let the Chief through.

'Any movement?' he demanded.

A guard nodded. 'It chased all the visitors out,' he said, 'threw a couple of glass cases at them. We've sealed all the exits so it's not going anywhere, but it looks like it's in a mean mood.'

The Chief grimaced. 'We'll see about that. There's no room for frigging wild men in *my* museum. Okay, going in!'

He applied his boot to the door, which opened inwards. A fraction of a second later, his knife-edge reflexes propelled him backwards, just in time to avoid an airborne bronze bust, which would have reduced him to the consistency of strawberry jam had it connected. He slammed the door quickly.

'Fuck me,' he said, 'it's gone bloody berserk. Of course, doesn't help that it's one of the really big buggers. You get thirteenth-century Sienese ivory miniatures running about the place, all it takes is five minutes and a stiff broom.' He hesitated, then turned to the head porter.

'Get me a bullhorn,' he ordered. 'Evacuate the museum, then get on the red phone to the army, Special Art Service. Tell 'em unless they get their bums in gear, it'll be the Wallace Collection all over again.'

When the bullhorn came, the Chief tested it to make sure it worked; then, using a broom handle, he poked the door open a crack and waited. Nothing.

'You in the gallery!' he shouted. 'Come out with your hands up and nobody's gonna get broken. You hear me?'

Silence.

'You've got till ten to give yourself up, then we come in. One.'

'Hey!'

A high-pitched voice, the Chief noted, ear-splittingly sonorous but basically reedy and terrified. But those are often the most dangerous. His mind went back to the early days, the time he'd had to talk down the Elgin Marbles. Maybe, he said to himself, I'm getting too old for all this.

'I hear you,' he replied.

'I've got the *Pietà*, *Saint Matthew* and a big bimbo provisionally attributed to Giovanni Bellini,' yelled the voice. 'You come in here and they all get it. Understood?'

'Loud and clear, son, loud and clear.' He frowned and switched off the loudhailer. 'Was it just the *David*,' he asked, 'or were any of the rest of them at it as well?'

'Not that I saw, Chief,' replied the guard. 'Just the big guy.'

'Hmm.' The Chief rubbed his chin. 'Thought you said he was acting confused, like he didn't know what was going on.'

'Looked like that to me, Chief.'

'Yeah. Only now he sounds like he's pretty well clued up. Like, the big bimbo, I mean the *Venus di San Lorenzo*, the attribution to Bellini was only in last month's *Fine Art Yearbook*. Somebody's in there with him.'

'You on the outside!'

The Chief ducked down. Behind him, thin young men with wavy hair, black silk Giorgio Armani jump-suits, Gucci balaclavas and bazookas were filing noiselessly into the corridor. The Chief waved them into position and switched on the bullhorn.

'Receiving you, over.'

'Here's the deal—'

'Different voice,' muttered the head porter.

'Yeah,' replied the Chief. 'Shuttup.'

'Here's the deal. We want no guns, no police, no army. Have a Sikorski airfreighter in the Piazza in thirty minutes.

We want ten million dollars in uncut diamonds, clearance to land in Tripoli and a free pardon. Do as we say and the rocks walk.'

'Actually,' interrupted another voice.

('That's him.'

'Who?'

'*David.*'

'Yeah. Shuttup.')

'Actually,' said the second voice, 'they don't. Do they? And anyway, haven't you got to fall over first?'

This exchange was followed by several seconds of heated whispering, which the Chief couldn't quite catch. By the time they'd brought up the boom mikes, the debate had ended.

'Okay, guys,' muttered the Chief, 'here's the plan. You boys go round the side, abseil in through the skylight. Use smoke grenades and thunderflashes. You six come with me, in through the door. I'll cover the *David*, you take out the other sucker, whoever the fuck he is. Remember,' he added gravely, thinking of the high velocity bronze bust, 'they're presumed armed—'

'Busted.'

'—Busted and dangerous, so if there's any hint of trouble, get your shot in first and let the guys with the dustpans and glue sort it out later. Ready?'

Twelve balaclava'd heads nodded.

'Right then. On my command.'

It was a grand spectacle, if you like that sort of thing. *Crash!* went the glass roof. *Whoosh!* went the smoke bombs. *BANG!* went the stun grenades. *Crunch!* went the big oak doors. *Boom!* went the bazookas, reducing to fine-grain rubble two half-length statues of constipated-looking goddesses, no loss by anybody's standards, and a somewhat less than genuine della Robbia rood screen which had been a thorn in the gallery's side ever since someone had noticed the words *Made In Pakistan From Sustainable Hardwoods* chiselled round the back.

And *Oh shit, where've they gone?* went the Chief, standing gobsmacked by two empty pedestals. The birds had, apparently, flown.

In the confusion, nobody noticed that the commando squad had, apparently, recruited two new members during the course of the attack; one tall, athletic-looking specimen, rather unsteady on his feet, and one short, bandy-legged example given to lurking in shadows. While the gallery was still full of smoke, shouting and the joyous sound of hobnailed boot on irreplaceable artefact, these two new recruits slipped quietly past the guards, down the corridor and, having shed their masks and swiped a couple of overcoats from the cleaners' room, out into the street.

'Yo!' exclaimed the shorter of the two, punching the air. 'We made it!'

'Yes,' David replied. 'Didn't we just.' He stopped and looked at his companion, and a puzzled look swept across his face. 'Excuse me.'

'Yeah?'

'Who *are* you?'

CHAPTER NINE

'What the fuck do you mean,' George screamed into the telephone, 'not arrived?'

'I mean,' replied the arrivals clerk at Hell Central, 'it hasn't arrived yet. If it had arrived, it'd be on the manifest. And it isn't.'

'You sure?'

It wasn't a stupendously good line – think what it had to go through to get there – but George could still hear the long intake of breath, the sound of someone who spends her working life with a phone in her ear, suffering fools.

'Sir,' she said, 'if we'd just taken delivery of a dragon, I think we'd have noticed. They are rather distinctive.'

George used his left hand to push his lower jaw, which had dropped somewhat, back into position. 'Are you trying to tell me,' he demanded, 'that the fucker's gone to the *other* place?'

'I can check that for you if you'd like me to.'

'What? Oh, yeah. Please.'

'Hold the line.'

Chardonay, leaning over George's shoulder, mouthed the question; *What's wrong?*

'Some admin balls-up,' George replied, his hand over the mouthpiece. 'Nothing to worry about – Oh, hello. Well?'

'Not there, sir. I'm sorry.'

George had gone ever such a funny colour. 'You can't have checked properly, you stupid cow!'

'I'm not a cow, sir,' replied the clerk, icily. 'I am, in fact, half-human, half-goat, with the claws of an eagle and—'

'All right. Thank you.' George let the receiver click back onto its cradle. A moment later, Father Kelly (who'd been listening in on the extension, stopwatch in hand, with a forlorn hope of claiming the cost of the call back on expenses; if Rome sold the Michaelangelos and a couple of the Raphaels, it'd sure make a hole in it . . .) did the same, and then sat for thirty seconds or so as still as a gatepost.

He'd just been listening to *Hell* . . .

And they sounded just like *us* . . .

George, meanwhile, was making a frantic search of his mental card-index to find some way of breaking the news. 'Boys,' he said, 'it's like this.'

'Yeah?' Prodsnap replied eagerly. 'When do we go home?'

'Er. Soon.'

'Great. How soon?'

'Just as soon . . .' No tactful way to say this. 'As soon as we've killed that goddamn dragon.'

Let's just pause a while to nail a false, misleading anti-feminist maxim. It's not true that Hell hath no fury like a woman scorned. Scorned women are Mother Theresa on her birthday compared to demons duped. Or thinking they've been duped.

'Told you!' Slitgrind crowed triumphantly. 'Told you no evil'd come of co-operating with the enemy. Crafty little angel got us to do his dirty work for him and then goes and welches on us. Typical!'

'Now hang on a minute,' Chardonay started to say, leaning forward and giving George a stern look; but he never got the chance to finish his sentence, because a split second later, Snorkfrod whizzed past him, making a direct course for George's throat. Fortunately for George, she slipped on an empty Guinness bottle and ended up sitting in the coal scuttle, making the most ferocious noises. For his part, George took advantage of the brief lull to get a good, solid utility Chesterfield between himself and the scions of Hell.

'All right,' he said, as soothingly as he could. 'Just calm down a second while I explain.'

Snorkfrod, having extracted herself from the scuttle, tensed for another spring, but Chardonay's gesture restrained her. She remained crouched and ready to go, growling ominously.

'We'd better hear what he's got to say,' Chardonay advised. 'There may be a perfectly reasonable explanation.'

George nodded like a frightened metronome. 'There is,' he said. 'Look, we blew the statue up, but obviously we didn't kill the dragon. God only knows how, but the little toe-rag somehow managed to clear off at the last minute.'

'So?'

'So,' George replied, 'the original plan holds good. Kill the dragon and there's your passport home. It's just that it's not going to be quite so pathetically simple as we originally thought it would be.'

There were snarls and grumbles as the logic soaked in, creosote-fashion. Chardonay rubbed his chin.

'All right,' he said. 'But how do we find him? That's going to be the problem, isn't it?'

George allowed himself the luxury of a fresh lungful of

air. 'Shouldn't be too hard,' he said airily. 'I mean, the sucker's an enormous green flying lizard. You can't keep something like that secret for very long. And besides,' he continued, 'we have something he's bound to come back for. You know, irresistible bait.'

'Yeah? What?'

George beamed. 'Us.'

So they waited.

True, the last thing they wanted to do was make themselves harder than necessary to find; on the other hand, they had to be practical. The last thing any of them wanted was a nasty theological incident, such as might be caused by the discovery that a saint and five devils were wandering around loose in the twentieth century, where they had no business to be. A certain measure of discretion was called for if there wasn't going to be a massive row, severing of supernatural relations, tit-for-tat expulsions and a spate of films with names like *Demons VI* and *Return of the Saint*.

There was also one further practicality to be borne in mind, one whose importance grew steadily as the days passed.

'I can't stick this sodding place a second longer,' Slitgrind growled, putting the problem neatly into words. 'It's bad enough being cooped up here with that pillock Chardonay and that murderous tart of his without that frigging saint and his wet sock of a priest.'

'I know,' Prodsnap replied quietly. In his case, he could hack Chardonay and Snorkfrod; with an effort and an advance on the next thousand years' self-control ration he could even put up with George and Father Kelly (who had taken to carrying a bell and a candle round with him and reading a book while he did the washing up). What he couldn't stand another day of was Slitgrind.

'I quite like it here,' said Holdall. On the second day, he'd discovered televised snooker and was addicted. It wasn't that they didn't have it back home, it was just that it was reserved for a small group of very, very special customers.

'Look,' Prodsnap said, 'basically it's very simple. We've got to get out of here before we all start climbing the walls. On the other hand, we can't go very far, or the bloody dragon won't know where to look for us.'

'That's your idea of simple, is it?' Slitgrind jeered. 'What d'you do for an intellectual challenge, bend spoons?'

'Basically,' Prodsnap repeated coldly, 'very simple. What we need,' he went on confidently, 'is a miracle.'

For the record, he'd got the technical term nearly but not quite right. What he meant was a Miracle Play, one of those rambling medieval verse dramas that have somehow eluded five hundred years of supposed good taste, and which get put on from time to time by over-enthusiastic amateurs, itinerant Volkswagen-camper-propelled bands of actors who aren't so much the fringe as the frayed hem, and the National Theatre. Stood up on a stage in a Scout hut or church hall somewhere, Saint George, five demons and a priest in a cotton-wool beard calling himself God wouldn't look too badly out of place; or at least no more than is usual under the circumstances.

'The point being,' Prodsnap explained to his fellow sufferers, 'we can bumble round in a van or something and nobody's going to take a blind bit of notice. But if Chummy really is out there looking for us, then a load of posters with SAINT GEORGE AND THE DRAGON all over them ought at least to catch the bugger's attention.'

It went to the vote – five in favour, two (guess which) against. Carried. That, Chardonay explained naïvely, was democracy in action. He was puzzled slightly by the response he got to that, each side claiming that they knew all about democracy, and that it was a dirty trick developed by the Opposition which they had taken over and skilfully converted to peaceful, beneficial uses. In any event, the ultimate consensus ran, we've made a decision now; let's do something. That, however, is as far as the consensus went.

Proximity, however, is as great a negotiator as time is a healer. Forty-eight hours of each others' company in a relatively small house managed to achieve what a thousand diplomats, with translators, fax machines and a warehouseful of heat'n'serve Embassy function canapés would have taken six months to obfuscate. Father Kelly got a book of miracle plays out of the library and spent a busy afternoon in the Diocesan office playing with the photocopier while the girls' backs were turned. George hotwired an old Bedford van.

The show hit the road.

'Who are you?' David repeated.

Being number one on the Italian police's Most Wanted list isn't as much hassle as it sounds if they're looking for a twelve-foot-high nude statue, and you're actually six foot one and wearing jeans, a standard tourist issue aertex shirt and trainers. To be on the safe side, however, David was also wearing sunglasses, and it had cost his companion dearly in both time and eloquence to dissuade him from buying a false beard.

'Me? Oh, that's not important.'

Context, not to mention the manner in which the words were spoken, belied this remark to such an extent that David risked raising his voice – he'd been talking in what he fondly believed was a conspiratorial whisper ever since they'd broken out of the museum, and kindly old ladies kept offering him cough sweets – as he insisted on a straight answer. His companion shrugged.

'My name's Kurt,' he said. 'I used to be a soldier of fortune. What's that word you guys got? *Condottiere*. That was me.'

'Used to be? Was?'

'Yeah.' Kurt nodded. 'I'm dead. Or I was. Jeez, this is confusing. Okay, I used to be alive, then I was dead for a while, only not properly dead. There were reasons at the time.'

David wrinkled his classically perfect brow. 'You didn't die thoroughly enough?' he hazarded. 'Skimped on the actual expiry?'

'Something like that. A steam engine dropped on me. But that,' he added, fending off any request for amplification with an eloquent waft of a finger, 'doesn't really matter. Before I died, or did whatever I did, I used to be a bounty hunter. And a mercenary,' he added with pride, 'and a contract killer, and all that sort of stuff. Man, I was the best.' He frowned. 'Maybe I still am, I dunno. I mean, am I still me, bearing in mind that this ain't actually *my* body? In fact, I don't have a clue whose body this is.' He cranked the frown over into a scowl and finished his coffee. 'The hell with it, anyway. The relevant parts are, I used to be a *condottiere*, then I was dead, then I think I was some kinda statue for a short while, and now I'm – ' He glanced down at his arms, his expression implying that they weren't quite a good fit ' – whoever the hell this is.' He glowered accusingly at David. 'Man, this is your fault, you started this crazy subject.'

'Sorry.'

Kurt waved his apology aside. 'No worries,' he said, and considered for a moment. 'I think what happened to me was—'

In actual fact, Kurt's version was so completely wide of

the mark as to be at right angles to it, and will therefore be suppressed in the interests of clarity. The truth is that, during his lifetime, an acute merchandising concern cashed in on his extreme notoriety by marketing the Kurt Lundqvist All Action Doll – $15.99 for the basic doll, uniforms and accessories extra, for complete list write Jotapian Industries, PO Box 666, Kansas City. Some time after his death, an unknown hand had smuggled one of these loathsome plastic objects into the Florence Academy and left it in a dark corner, ignoring the risk that a speck of stray dust from far-distant Birmingham might float in through an open window one sunny day and land on it.

'I see,' David lied. 'How fascinating. So,' he went on, sipping his glass of water. 'What happens now?'

Kurt shrugged. 'I got a job to do,' he replied. 'You can tag along, I guess, or you can split. Up to you.'

'Split?' David looked down to check he was still in one piece. 'You mean these body things tear easily, or something? That's another thing. How did we stop being statues and start being, um, people?'

'Search me.' Kurt shook his head. 'It just kinda happens, I guess. You can either stay in your statue, or you can bug out and wander around in the skin suit. Who cares how it works so long as it works?'

That, David conceded, wasn't something you could reasonably argue with. As far as he was concerned, he was living on borrowed time, although who he was borrowing it from, and whether they'd eventually want it back, was far from clear.

'This job,' he said tentatively.

'Big job,' replied Kurt with an expansive gesture, which a passing waiter took to be a request for the bill. 'So important, I guess, they had to bring me back from the dead to do it.' He grinned. 'Hey,' he said, 'that kinda suggests I still am the best, doesn't it? That's good to know.'

'The job.'

'What? Oh, yeah. The job is, to bring out the hostages.'

David raised an eyebrow. 'Hostages?'

'Okay, so they aren't actually hostages. More like key figures. And figurines, too. The idea is, there's a lot of important statues gonna get . . .' Kurt hesitated, searching for the right word. 'Woken up, I guess. Liberated. Occupied. Possessed. Anyway, my part is, as soon as they wake up I gotta get 'em out of wherever they're at and turn 'em loose. Tough assignment, yes?'

'Very.' David nodded emphatically. 'Have you any idea why?'

'Me? No way. The first thing you learn in this business is not to ask questions. Well, you gotta ask some questions, like *Which guy's the one needs wasting*? and *Where's the goddamn safety catch on this thing*? But apart from that, no questions. Especially no questions beginning with *Why*?'

'Um.' David looked at him through a purported smile. The man's stark staring mad, he told himself. 'Well, thanks for the job offer, I'll give it some really serious thought. In the meantime, any idea what I'm supposed to do next?'

Kurt shrugged. 'Not in my brief, pal. Maybe you got a destiny to manifest, in which case go for it, do well. Or maybe you should just get a job in a sandwich bar somewhere and live semi-happily ever after, like regular people do. None of my goddamn business, either way.'

'Quite.'

'The other part of the job is,' Kurt went on, 'I gotta kill a dragon.'

There are quite a few differences between statues and people. Bianca was learning about them.

A few examples. Statues are beautiful. When a statue gets

broken, you can glue back the bits with epoxy resin, rather than hang about waiting for bones to knit. Likewise, if you attempted to sign your name on the plaster cast of the *Winged Victory*, the next thing you'd see would be the pavement rushing up to meet you.

The key difference, however, and the one which made Bianca realise just how lucky statues are, wasn't something that had immediately sprung to mind. She had learned it by long, bitter experience.

To wit: true, both statues and humans in hospital get people coming to see them. Statues, however, don't get talked to.

'No, Auntie,' Bianca said, for the nineteenth time. 'Thank you,' she added, quickly but not quickly enough. When Aunt Jane went visiting, umbrage futures soared. By now, Bianca reckoned, Aunt Jane must have enough umbrage to start her own international bourse.

'Suit yourself, dear,' Aunt Jane replied, in a voice Bianca would have found useful for putting an edge on blunt chisels. 'Only trying to help. I'll leave them here anyway.' Sigh. 'You don't have to read them if you don't want to.'

Exhibit One; a stack of women's magazines, late 1980s vintage. Recipes. Knitting patterns. Advice to the frustrated and the suicidal. Two of the three were unlikely to be much use to a girl in traction, but she was getting to the stage where she was quite interested in the third.

'It's very thoughtful of you,' Bianca said. Who was the kid whose nose grew when he told lies? Much more of this and she'd make Cyrano look like an Eskimo. 'I really appreciate it. You're very kind.'

Aunt Jane's lips twitched in a tiny sneerlet. Gratitude fell into her without any perceptible effect, like matter into a black hole. 'Well,' she said, 'I suppose I'd better be going, your uncle'll be wanting his tea. I'll *try* to come in tomorrow, though it'll mean missing Weightwatchers. I'll see if I can find you some more things to read.'

As Aunt Jane waddled doorwards, Bianca resisted the urge to wish her a nasty accident. She meant well. More to the point, if she had a nasty accident, she'd probably end up in the next bed.

The sad part about it was, Bianca knew, that in an hour or so, try as she might, she'd pick up one of those damned magazines and start to read. She'd already read all her own books – ever since school she'd been one of those people who zooms through printed pages like motorbikes through traffic – and there was nothing, absolutely nothing, else to do. If the loathsome things weren't there, of course, she couldn't read them. But since they were, she could. And, ineluctably as Death, she would.

This time, she lasted forty-seven minutes and was just congratulating herself on consummate willpower when she realised that her usable hand had slithered treacherously and nipped a glossy from the pile. Ah well, she assured her soul, I tried. She brought the thing up on top of the sheet and opened it.

Thinking it through afterwards, she worked out how it must have happened. Aunt Jane obtained her supplies of obsolescent opium-of-the-female-masses from the waiting room of the doctors' surgery where she worked as receptionist (exceptionally effective in reducing waiting times; you had to be practically dying to want to make an appointment). From time to time, waiting rooms and other similarly depressing public places get leafletted by the keen and eager – bring and buys, craft fairs, save our derelict and unwanted civic amenities and, of course, the amateur dramatics fiends. Easy enough to scoop up a few stray fliers along with the pulp.

The playbill in front of her read as follows:

FOR THREE NIGHTS ONLY!
H & H Thespians present –
SAINT GEORGE AND THE DRAGON
ORIGINAL CAST!
JULY 17, 18, 19
Sadley Grange Civic Centre
Tickets £2 at the door.

Reaction one: now there's a coincidence.

Reaction two: coincidence my foot . . .

Reaction three: . . . which is in plaster. Damn!

Original cast? Surely not. One key player, she knew, was unavailable due to indisposition caused by having been blasted to smithereens.

Unless . . .

Hey! Calm down, Bianca, think it through. Just suppose for one moment that blowing up the statue hadn't actually killed the dragon. Now, then; whoever wanted him dead – answers on a postcard, please – presumably would want to try again. First, however, catch your dragon. With his marble overcoat reduced to fine dust, the dragon would be walking the streets in human mufti, impossible to recognise. Hence the need for bait and heavy duty, industrial grade hints.

Bianca sneezed; dust from the pile of magazines. Why do I get the feeling, she asked herself, that I'm witnessing the early stages of a major war?

The irony of her situation made her wince, as if someone had just put a goldfish down her neck. All around her, the forces of weirdness were tooling up for a major confrontation. Somehow, she knew, she might be able to prevent it. Except that she was stuck here, as immobilised in her plasterwork as the dragon and the rogue saint had been in the stone bodies she'd made for them. Quite what the significance of that was, she didn't pretend to understand. But she knew significance when she saw it; she knew it even better when it was forced down her throat with a hydraulic ram.

'Great,' she muttered aloud. 'Just when I'm needed, I have to go and get plastered.'

'Sorry?' She looked up, but it was only Mike, squeezing in for the last five minutes of visiting time with his no longer quite so funny comedy props; grapes, lemon barley water, more bloody magazines.

'Just muttering,' she said. 'Mike, find out how much longer I'm going to be stuck inside all this masonry. There's all sorts of things I ought to be doing.'

Mike shrugged. 'Anything I can help with?' he asked.

'N—'

On the one hand, if Mankind was a stockroom, you'd find Mike on the shelf marked *Amiable Idiots*. On the other hand . . .

'Yes,' she said.

CHAPTER TEN

'Clever,' muttered the dragon, with obvious distaste.

The storage unit, or dungeon, in which his statue was kept had obviously cost someone a lot of money. You reached it by walking down a long, dragon-sized tunnel, a bit like a torpedo tube, which led from an iron porthole in the side of a very tall cliff something like a quarter of a mile through solid rock to a big chamber. The chamber door was marble, two feet thick, mounted on chrome molybdenum steel hinges and opening inwards.

'Who knows?' Chubby said, indicating all that workmanship and expense with a dismissive wave. 'For all I know, you could smash and burn your way out through that, eventually. But by the time you'd got halfway, we'd have flooded the chamber with gas and you'd be off to Bedfordshire up the little wooden hill.'

The dragon shrugged. 'Pity,' he said.

'Yes,' Chubby agreed, 'it is. It's like . . .' He closed his eyes to help his concentration. 'Although your mum and dad don't mind you borrowing the car, it's irksome having to ask permission and say where you're going every time you fancy a spin. Please note,' he added, 'the little metal box round its, I mean your, neck.'

'I was going to ask.'

'A bomb,' Chubby sighed. 'I know, I feel awful, but what can I do? We're businessmen, not conservationists. Look, there's no nice way to say this. If you muck us about, anywhere in the inner solar system, inside the dragon cozzy or out of it, then a button gets pressed and goodbye dragons for ever. Clear?'

'As crystal,' the dragon grunted.

'No hard feelings?'

'Get real.'

Chubby's round face showed a smile with turned down ends. 'Fair enough,' he said. 'If I was in your position, I'd sulk like hell. Actually, what I'd probably do is scrag me in the erroneous belief that I've got the button about my person. Just as well for you you're not me, really. From both sides, as it were.'

The dragon did some mental geometry. 'Quite,' he said. 'And on general principles, too. What about some lunch?'

Over the Scottish salmon and aviation fuel, Chubby delicately raised the issue of timescale.

'Not that we want to hurry you or anything,' he added quickly. 'Pleasure having you about the place and all that. It's just that time, if you'll excuse the context, is getting on, I can't earn a bent cent while those goat-hooved buffoons are in this dimension – I know because I've tried, God knows – and your old school chum's starting to get on my wick. Every time I go in my office, his blasted screen winks at me.'

The dragon laughed. 'He used to do that when he was a kid,' he replied. 'Just when you'd got up to answer the teacher's question, he'd wink at you or pull a face. Made you forget what you were going to say. He only does it for wickedness.'

'I'll bet,' Chubby replied morosely. 'Look, I don't like to ask this, but who the fuck is he? I just know him as the genie of the PCW.'

The dragon grinned and helped himself to a tumblerful of liquid propane. 'Guess,' he said.

'Oh come on,' Chubby replied.

'No, three guesses. Odd how guesses come in threes, by the way. Like wishes. And, as far as I can judge from a very limited observation of your culture, petrol-driven public transport vehicles.'

'All right. He's a djinn.'

'Close but no cigar.'

'Evil spirit?'

'Yes, but that's not a proper guess because so am I. And so,' he said, wrinkling his nose and emptying his glass into a flower pot, 'is this. Haven't you got any of that decent stuff we had the other night?'

'You drank it all. Try some of this liquid nitrogen. An insouciant little concoction, but I think you may be frozen stiff by its presumption.'

'Better,' agreed the dragon. 'Two more guesses.'

'Okay. How about a god?'

The dragon shook his head. 'There is no god but God,' he replied. 'Nice phrase, that. Read it on the back of a cornflakes packet.'

'All right. A devil.'

'Wrong third time.' The dragon swilled the dregs of his glass round to make the vapour rise. 'He's a dragon.'

Chubby's eyebrows rose, like the price of gold in an oil crisis. 'Straight up? I thought you were the only one?'

'Far from it.' The dragon frowned. 'Lord only knows what he's done with his body, but my old mate Nosher is, or was, a dragon, same as me. Little, weedy chap he used to be, we called him Nosher the Newt. If he ever reached fifteen feet nose to tail, I'd be surprised.'

Chubby let that pass. 'So what's he doing in my computer?' he asked. 'Or didn't you get around to catching up on life stories?'

'No idea. I did ask him, but he didn't actually seem to answer. He was always good at that, too, specially when you were asking him to pay back a loan or something. Bright lad, Nosher, but you wouldn't trust him as far as you could sneeze him. Something tells me that hasn't changed terribly much.'

'We're drifting,' Chubby pointed out, 'away from the subject under review. Namely, when can you start?'

'Not bothered,' the dragon replied. 'It's more a case of where rather than when, isn't it? It's all very well to talk blithely about carbonising these goons, but I don't actually know where to find them. I'd have thought you, with all those resources and instruments and things . . .'

Chubby looked embarrassed. 'I was afraid you'd say that,' he replied through a mouthful of Stilton. 'And it's bloody curious, I don't mind admitting. Look, every time I've tried taking the crones out to do a spot of rustling, it's been a complete washout because of diabolical interference. Static so thick you could spread it on bread. But can I pinpoint the wretched critters? Can I buggery. It's almost as if the negative vibes are being masked by something else.'

'What, you mean like virtue?'

Chubby shook his head. 'Not virtue, chum. That'd counteract it and there'd be no interference. No, it's like a very strong signal on an adjacent wavelength that sort of blurs out the devils so you can't actually hear them.' He wanted to light a cigar, but thought better of it. 'Which implies it's a very similar sort of signal, though different enough not to jam up my old biddies. It's a bugger, it really is.'

The nitrogen cylinder fizzed again, until the dragon's glass was replenished. 'Not really,' he said. 'That sounds to me like that bastard George. He's a saint, remember, so he's probably got vibes of his own. And he's an evil little sod but officially Good, which'd account for similar but not identical signals.' He scowled at the thought of George, and the glass shattered in his hand. He didn't notice. 'Sounds to me like George and those demons of yours are still mobbed up together, presumably so that they can have another crack at me. I've got no idea, by the way, why a bunch of devils should wish me any harm. As far as I know I've never done anything to offend their outfit. In fact, since I'm officially Evil they should be on my side.'

Chubby wisely said nothing. A certain overtone crept into the dragon's voice when he spoke of George; the sort of nuance you'd observe in a conversation between authors about book reviewers. All to the good, as far as Chubby was concerned.

'Funny bloke, by all accounts,' the dragon went on. 'Oddly enough, I knew a man who was at school with him, that training college for saints they used to have out Glastonbury way.'

Chubby, who'd been doing his background reading, nodded. 'You mean the old Alma Martyr?'

'Right little tearaway he was, by all accounts. Bottom of the class in everything, failed all his Inquisitions, always in detention, doing lines. Never even turned up to heresy-detection classes. Nearly got expelled for refusing to shoot arrows at Saint Sebastian.'

'Fancy,' Chubby said.

'Always up to that sort of thing. You know, untying Catherine from her wheel, stuffing the lions in the Amphitheatre full of Whiskas so they wouldn't eat the Christians.

Must've been a right pain in the neck.'

'Absolutely,' Chubby agreed. But he was secretly think-ing: Hey, what's so terrible about trying to stop people from getting shot, burnt and eaten? Well, different strokes and all that.

'Be that as it may.' The dragon stood up, untucked his napkin from his collar and finished the last of the nitrogen. 'Soon as you get a fix on these jokers, let me know and they're firelighters. See you at dinner.'

Chubby stayed where he was, waited for the extractor fans to clear the nitrogen fumes and lit his cigar.

So the genie of the PCW was a dragon. Well, that explained absolutely nothing at all. As a clue, it made *The Times* crossword seem like an exploded diagram. But that, surely, was because he was being too thick to see the point. If there was a point.

Probably all a coincidence.

Absolutely. All a coincidence. Like the remarkable coin-cidence whereby whenever someone falls off the top of the Sears Tower they die shortly afterwards. You can get paranoid, thinking too hard about coincidences.

Mike looked at the address written on the back of his chequebook and then at the building in front of him.

Well, yes. It was the sort of place, by the looks of it, where you had to abandon all hope before entering. But a resort of demons? Surely not. If demons lived here, then Hell was a neat row of 1960s spec-built terraces, with open-plan front gardens and a Metro outside each one.

Good point. Yes. Muttering all he could remember of the Hail Mary (which was, as it happens, Hail Mary), he pushed the front door and went in.

'Eeek!' he said.

The woman at the ticket desk gave him an impatient,

Not-you-as-well look, held up a slip of paper with a seat number on it, and said, 'Two pounds, please.' She was holding the piece of paper in what could only be described as a talon.

'Er, you in the show?' he asked.

'That's right,' she replied. 'Costume startle you, did it?'

Mike nodded. 'It's very, um, realistic.'

'How would you know?'

'All right, I don't. Can I go in now, please?'

He found his seat (one of those bendy bucket-shaped plastic chairs which you're convinced is going to break when you sit on it, though it never does) and took a long look at the stage. There was no curtain. The usual amateur dramatics set, all black-painted hardboard, silver paper and things borrowed from people's homes. Mundane. Prosaic. Everyday. Like, in fact, the woman at the door had been, except that she was obviously a . . .

Another look round, this time at the audience. There were fifteen or so people scattered about the hall, eating boiled sweets and reading the photocopied programme. Either they hadn't noticed that they'd just been sold their tickets by a . . . or else they didn't care. Possible, Mike told himself; very tolerant people, Midlanders. But – *my God, those fangs!* – improbable.

He looked at the programme. Cast list, as follows:

> GEORGE (*a saint*) .... Himself
> CHARDONAY (*a demon*) .... Himself
> SLITGRIND (*a demon*) .... Himself
> PRODSNAP (*a demon*) .... Himself
> HOLDALL (*a demon*) .... Himself
> SNORKFROD (*a demon*) .... Herself
> THE DRAGON .... Members of the cast

Ah well, Mike said to himself, leaning back as far as he

dared and opening his bag of Maltesers, I expect I've been to worse. Most of them, he remembered, at the Barbican.

The lights went down. The chattering almost stopped.

Play time.

'Found them!' Chubby yelled.

The dragon looked up from the encyclopedia he'd been reading and grinned. 'Splendid. Where?'

'Wherever the hell this is.' Chubby handed him a creased playbill and a map. 'Ready to go?'

The dragon grinned.

Anybody ever wondered, Mike asked himself a quarter of the way through the first half, why so much of medieval literature is anonymous? Answer, easy. Who'd want to own up to having written this?

At least there hadn't been Morris dancing. Not yet. That, he admitted to himself, was like saying that nuclear bombs are safe because the world's still in one piece. That aside, it had set his mind at rest on one score. No question but that these people were in the everlasting torment business; the cream, in fact, of their profession. Solemnly and with the utmost sincerity, Mike resolved that from now on he was going to be very, very good, for ever and ever.

So deep was he in silent repentance that he didn't notice that someone was now sitting in the seat next to him, until that person leaned across and whispered a request to look at his programme.

'Sure,' Mike whispered back. He passed over the sheet. As he did so, he became aware of an oppressive heat and a smell like petrol. He glanced out of the corner of his eye.

Perfectly ordinary bloke. All his imagination. Except—

The bloke had yellow eyes. Round, golden eyeballs, with a narrow black slit for a pupil. And no eyelids.

156 · Tom Holt

Midlanders (see above) are tolerant folk, and Mike was from Brierley Hill where they don't care who you are or what you do so long as you leave the buildings still standing afterwards. Devils; no problem, after all, we're all God's creatures. But, as soon as he'd recovered the use of his momentarily paralysed limbs, he was out of his seat, through the door and running like a hare. Sensible chap.

Because, while he was still running, there was a horrible dull *bang*! followed by a whooshing noise, broken glass music and the very distinctive sound of fire. Instinct sent Mike sprawling on the ground, his head shielded by his elbows, as the first few bits of masonry and timber started to hit the ground all around him. And oh Christ, the smell . . .

Late change to the cast as advertised. Whoever was playing the dragon tonight had just brought the house down.

The dragon opened his eyes.

There was, he observed, a large steel girder lying across his back. He shook himself like a wet dog, sending it spinning off into the rubble.

He appeared to have made rather a mess.

The drip-drip-dripping noise was still-molten steel; wire reinforcements in the concrete. The groaning sound was material contracting as it cooked, rather than an indication that there was still anything else even temporarily alive in the ruined building. No chance of that, whatsoever.

In the distance, the mechanical wailing noise the dragon had come to associate with impending public attention. He spread his wings, flapped them and rose in a cloud of dust and sparks. Job done, time to go home. Five wingbeats lifted him into the upper air; five more and he was cruising through the sound barrier, heading west.

As he flew, he couldn't help reflecting that, in exacting his entirely justifiable revenge on George, he'd also killed five demons – well, so what? The worst that can happen to anything mortal is that it dies and goes to Hell; he'd saved them a bus fare – and fifteen or so innocent human beings who happened to be there. Hmm.

No, the hell with that, it was a matter of omelettes and eggs. They belonged to a different species altogether and were none of his concern. To feed those fifteen, and all the others like them in this city alone, a million chickens a day ride to their deaths on a conveyer belt. And, emotive reactions aside, there was nothing wrong with that either because of a hard but fair rule of Nature called Survival of the Fittest. It was a rule he'd never really had a problem with, even when he'd been hiding in the rocks watching all the rest of his kind being exterminated by these people's great-to-the-power-of-twenty-grandfathers. Plenty more where those came from; and who's the endangered species around here, anyway?

As he flew, feeling the almost infinite power of his body, acknowledging the potential of his lazy but undoubtedly superior intellect, he sensed that maybe the jury was still out on that one.

They brought the woman down from intensive care at about half past three that morning and put her in the bed next to Bianca. Superficial burns, light concussion, shock. She'd live. She'd been lucky, the ward sister explained. She'd only been passing outside the Sadley Grange Civic Centre when it blew up. Those poor souls inside never stood a chance.

What caused it? Nobody knew, as yet. They'd said on the news that the whole building suddenly burst into flames; not like an ordinary fire, which starts somewhere and gets steadily hotter, more like a firebomb attack, except who'd want to firebomb amateur dramatics?

'Nurse,' Bianca said, 'I think I'm going to be—'

And she was right.

'They're saying it was the Libyans,' Chubby reported, topping up the dragon's cup with lighter fuel, 'God only knows why. I s'pose they've got to blame somebody, or what are foreigners for?'

'Don't go on about it,' the dragon said. The bread was stale. He breathed gently on it and had toast, instead.

'Don't see why not,' Chubby replied. 'You did good. Neat job, in and out, nobody saw you; or if they did, they've got too much common sense to stand in front of a microphone and say they've been seeing dragons. You could make a good living if you ... Sorry, I'll shut up. Pass the marmalade, there's a good fellow.'

'Were there any survivors?'

Chubby laughed. 'Sure,' he said. 'Just not within a two-hundred-yard radius. Actually, there's an interesting side-light to the story, because that whole area's up for redevelopment, except that there was that tatty old hall bang in the middle of it and absolutely no way of getting rid of it. Now, of course, bulldozers may safely graze. In fact, we could get seriously rich if ever you felt—'

'Chubby,' said the dragon quietly, 'I'd change the subject if I were you.'

'Huh? Suit yourself.' Chubby spread marmalade, drank coffee. 'Sorry to harp on,' he said, 'but what exactly is bothering you? I thought you hated humans.'

'Me?' the dragon looked at him. 'Whatever gave you that idea? As of nine twenty-seven pm yesterday, there's nobody and nothing left alive in this world that I hate, or even strongly dislike, although,' he added, with a slight twitch of his nostrils, 'this may change if a certain topic of conversation doesn't get shelved pretty damn quick.'

'Sorry,' Chubby replied meekly. 'It's just that, since it was us who killed all your people, stole your birthright—'

'Not you,' the dragon said. Inside his skull he could hear the faint chip-chip of a headache hatching from the egg. 'When the last of the people who wiped out the dragons died, there were still wolves wandering around the forests of Islington. And besides,' he added irritably, 'the thing with George and me had nothing to do with the dragon clearances. It was purely personal.'

'Because of the Big Fight, huh? Because he won, simple as that?'

The dragon shook his head. 'He was *supposed* to win. It was killing me that I didn't hold with. And now that's all over and done with, so let's drop it. All right?'

'Right.' Chubby folded his newspaper, drained his coffee cup and stood up. 'So, as soon as you've done that little job—'

'Who says I'm going to do the little job?' the dragon interrupted dangerously. 'Fuck you and your nasty bloody schemes. If you want to beat up on your own species, be my guest, it's none of my business. But I'm off.'

Chubby shook his head. He didn't say anything, but he patted the underside of his chin with the tips of his fingers. The bomb.

'You bastard,' the dragon said softly. 'I ought to torch you right now.'

'Inadvisable,' Chubby replied. 'With all that inflammable liquor inside you, they'd be picking up bits of you in Tokyo. And like I said, what's it to you? Different species, right?'

The dragon said nothing. Not that he needed words, exactly. He'd have been sent home from a Gorgons' children's party for pulling faces.

'Welcome to the Baddies,' Chubby said, and left.

The fire brigade had gone home, the police were brewing up in their big blue-and-white portakabin and even the journalists had given up and gone to the pub. Under a pile of rubble, something stirred.

'Have they gone?'

'I think so.'

The pile of rubble avalanched, half-bricks and chunks of concrete scudding downslope, stirring up dust. A head and shoulders poked out. Eyes blinked in the starlight.

'About bloody time, too. I've got a crick in my neck like a letter S.'

'Keep your voice down, Slitgrind. And for pity's sake, stop complaining.'

Gradually, and with much seismic activity, the demons emerged, all five of them. They were dusty and, after twelve hours under the rubble, stiff as all Shopfloor. Apart from that, no ill effects whatsoever.

A sixth pile shifted and turned into George. He wasn't in quite the same immaculate condition – he had a black eye, and his hair was all singed off – but otherwise he was intact. He dusted himself off, just like Oliver Hardy used to do in the films, and climbed out of the mess.

'Now you see why we had to wear costumes,' he said.

Chardonay nodded. 'Good stuff,' he acknowledged. 'What did you call it?'

'Asbestos,' George replied. 'And the lining's Kevlar, which is like old-fashioned steel armour, only lighter and a hell of a lot stronger. I used the same stuff for the scenery, too. Just as well,' he admitted. 'If we hadn't all ducked behind the flats the moment he materialised, I don't reckon the cozzies'd have been enough. Anyway, time we weren't here. Come on, you lot. The Padre'll be worried sick about us.'

Nobody had disturbed the rickety old Bedford van and soon they were on their way. Chardonay, sitting in the front with George, raised the obvious topic.

'Well,' George replied, 'he took the bait all right, you've got to admit that much. Maybe we should have spent a little more time thinking through how we were actually going to scrag the bugger, but we'll know better next time.'

'*Next time!*'

George nodded. 'Of course next time,' he replied, faintly puzzled by the demon's tone. 'Okay, so the first two attempts, we bombed. I mean, we didn't do so good. Third time lucky, eh? Think of Robert Bruce,' he added, 'and the spider.'

'No, thanks,' Chardonay replied, shuddering. 'I'm scared of spiders. And now,' he added, with as much unpleasant overtone as he could muster, 'I'm also scared of dragons.'

'Funny you should say that,' George said, blithely overtaking on a blind corner, 'because spiders have always terrified the shit out of me. But eventually I found a way to cope.'

'Really?'

George nodded. 'I squash 'em,' he said. 'Helps put things in perspective when your mortal foe's looking like a raisin with hairs sticking in it. I think the same may hold true of dragons. Only one way to find out.'

Chardonay was about to say something, but wisely saved his breath. The way George was driving, he'd need it soon for horrified screaming.

'Mind you,' George went on – he was definitely getting the hang of driving, because this time he remembered to brake with a full thousandth of a second to spare. 'It's going to be harder decoying the creep a second time because he's going to assume we're dead. And we can't exactly publicise the fact we aren't, because of the low profile thing. Tricky one, that.'

'Aaaaagh!'

'What? *Watch where you're going, you senile old fool!* Sorry, you were saying?'

Chardonay opened his eyes. 'I think,' he murmured, 'in this country they drive on the left.'

'Ah. That'd explain a lot. Well spotted. To be honest with you, I think from now on it's going to be up to us to look for him, rather than the other way around. Don't you? Of course, we could try this gig again, only next time we'd be a bit better prepared, maybe plant a bomb of our own in the auditorium so as to be sure of getting him first. What d'you reckon?'

A look of horrified disgust pitched camp on Chardonay's face. 'You couldn't do that,' he gasped. 'The audience. Innocent people.'

George shrugged. 'Not people, Char,' he said mildly. 'Potential customers, your lot's and mine. One stone, very many birds, huh?'

It's hard to stand on your dignity when you're horrified, petrified and covered from head to foot with brick dust. In Chardonay's case, he'd never had all that much dignity to start with; if he'd ever wanted to stand on it, he'd have had to master the knack of balancing on one foot. What little he had, however, he now used to good effect.

'George,' he said, 'when you die, be sure to go to Heaven. We can do without your sort where I come from.'

In order to sell newspapers, you have to get your priorities right, and an unexplained explosion with fatalities is clearly rather more important than a spate of thefts from art galleries. The lead stories in the next day's papers were, therefore, in order of headline size and column inches:

ROYAL VET'S SEX ROMP WITH CHAUFFEUR

SOUTHENDERS STAR IN LOVE TRIANGLE WITH PLUMBER

BUZZA DECKS REF IN OFFSIDE RUMPUS

Bomb Kills Sixteen

Statues Stolen From Italian Museum

The statues – eight Berninis, three Donatellos, three Cellinis, a Canova and the Giambologna *Mercury* – all went missing from various locations in the space of about eight hours. No sign of forced entry, no arrests, no clues. No visible connection, either.

'Okay, guys. Guys!' Kurt banged on the floor with the butt of his rifle, but nobody took any notice. They were all talking at once, at the tops of their voices, in Italian. With a weary gesture of resignation, Kurt sat down on a packing-chest and waited.

'Finished?' he demanded, ten minutes later. 'Good. Now, listen up.'

Sixteen pairs of malevolent eyes fixed on him. I don't need this, he reflected. I've got a nice cosy grave I could be in right now.

'Now then,' he said. 'I guess you're all wondering why—'

Marvellous language, Italian, for talking very fast in. They should insist all peace conferences should be in Italian; that way, nobody'd ever know what was going on long enough to start the war. 'Shuttup!' he cried. Not a blind bit of notice.

''Scuse me.'

He turned. 'Well?'

'Looks to me,' David said, 'like they're upset about something.'

Kurt scowled. 'What the fuck've they got to be upset

about, for Chrissakes? I've just sprung the suckers, they should be goddamn *grateful*.'

David made a small head gesture indicative of doubt. 'Look at it this way,' he said. 'They're all male figures, all of Italian origin. Maybe standing about all day being admired is what they like doing best.'

The proposition had merit, Kurt admitted, but that wasn't his affair. He was only, as the expression goes, obeying orders. '*HEY*!' he said.

'Thank you,' he went on. 'All I can tell you is, my instructions said to get you out of those museums and galleries and bring you here. Which I've done. From now on, guys, you're on your . . .'

He stopped, puzzled. Instead of jabbering at him, shaking fists and waving arms, they were standing about like a lot of shop-window dummies.

Maybe that was it; knock off priceless works of art and punt them out at twelve dollars a head to the leading New York department stores. Or maybe not.

'Guys?'

Long silence. Then a statue put its hand up.

'Excuse me,' it said. And, Kurt noticed, in English.

'Shoot,' he said.

'Excuse me,' said the statue – shit, it was a *female* voice now – 'but can you tell us what's going on, please?'

Kurt swallowed. Spooky no longer worried him. He felt comfortable around spooky. Weird was as familiar to him as a pair of well-worn slippers. But this was *strange*.

'Hey,' he said. 'I just did.'

'Only,' the voice bleated on. 'I told my husband the play'd be over by ten and I'd be home in time to make him a late tea. And that was hours ago, and he gets all upset if his meals aren't when he expects them.'

Gradually, while Kurt was trying to get his larynx

working again, the other fifteen joined in, a symphony of bleats and whines forming a baroque fugue around the same main theme.

'I . . .' Kurt had raised his hand for silence, and obtained it instantly. Thirty-two eyes were gazing at him. He could feel the blood rushing to his cheeks. It was *horrible*.

'I . . .'

Thirty-two ears, hanging on his every word. Jesus, he told himself, now the suckers are all goddamn British.

He turned, grabbed David by the arm and dragged him forward. 'My assistant will explain,' he said, and ran for it.

CHAPTER ELEVEN

'The job,' Chubby explained, 'is basically very simple.'

It was, the dragon wanted to point out, perishing cold. The air was full of high-velocity snow which he could feel even through his scales. There was nothing to be seen in any direction except flat white. Chubby and the dragon stood alone in an albino wilderness, like the last two balls on a white snooker table.

'That's not to say,' Chubby went on, 'that it's easy. Easy and simple don't necessarily mean the same thing. What I want you to do is simple, as opposed to complicated, but very, very difficult. With me so far?'

The dragon couldn't speak because his teeth were chattering like a school party in a theatre, so he nodded instead.

'All you have to do,' Chubby continued, 'is fly, any direction you like, as fast as you possibly can. Direction doesn't matter 'cos we're at the North Pole. Speed, however, is of the essence.'

The dragon frowned. 'Don't you mean time?' he queried. Chubby grinned.

'That,' he said, 'is either a naïve remark or a very poor joke. Now then, here's your parcel, don't drop it. When I want you to stop, this little buzzer thing on your collar will bleep. Wonder of micro-electronics, that, cost me a fortune.' He paused, recited a check-list under his breath, and took five steps back. 'When you're ready,' he said.

The dragon shrugged. 'Now?'

'Now.'

Theory: travel faster than light around the Earth and you can move forwards in Time.

A likely story. Like all great hypotheses, the theory of relativity relies on the basic assumption that nobody will ever be able to do the experiment which will prove it wrong; and anything that can't be disproved must be true. Garnish with fresh mathematics, heat and serve.

But supposing it's true, and feasible. Think, not of the fame, the glory and the Nobel prize, but of the commercial possibilities.

Correct; there are none. That's why it's a safe hypothesis. Nobody will ever try the experiment because there's nothing in it for the institutional investors. That's why there's a whole lot of scientific theories about the nature of the space/time continuum, and rather fewer about the medium-term acceleration of racehorses. It'd be different, of course, if you could then send a messenger from the future back to the present, notebook crammed with stock exchange results, football scores, winning lottery numbers and the like; but that's impossible, according to the theory. Guess why.

The truth is that it's possible – simple, even (see above) to travel back through Time, in roughly the same way as you can travel forwards. It involves flying round the world, yes; but at a rather different tempo.

To go forwards, you have to fly faster than light. To go backwards, you have to fly slower than history. The maths goes like this:

$$T - d = h$$
$$P = n + h$$

– where T is Time, d is disinformation, h is history, P stands for the Past, and n is the now, or present.

For anybody who missed the first sixteen lessons, here's a very simplistic summary.

The past is made up of the present plus an awareness of there having been a time before the present; the awareness is called history. The speed at which history travels is equal to the speed of Time, less the time it takes to record it. The recording of history is slowed down by disinformation; official secrets, the reluctance of participants to tell the story because of the repercussions on themselves, and so on. The quantum of d varies from nation to nation, culture to culture; in Britain, there's a thirty-year rule which means that nobody can look at important official documents for thirty years, whereas in the USA the freedom-of-information statutes say that you can see them straight away, except for the really important ones, which nobody ever gets to see at all. In some regimes, history gets rewritten every time there's a change of government personnel. The constant d is therefore not a constant at all; accordingly history moves at a different speed depending on where you are, and in some places it's at a complete standstill or moving backwards.

Fly round the world, therefore, and you're constantly crossing into different history zones. As you soar over the continents, the retrospective march of Time, from present to past, is taking place at all sorts of different speeds. Instead of being a tidal wave, crashing relentlessly down onto the reef of the present, the advance of history is a confused mess of recollection particles, swarming about in no sort of order. And there are always particles that move so slowly in comparison with the others that they're getting left further and further behind; relatively speaking, going the wrong way.

Reverse history and you reverse Time.

In practical terms, then; if as you fly round the world you follow a carefully plotted course through the anomalies of the different history zones, you can get so far behind that you'll be travelling backwards in time. As a further refinement, if you have moles and undercover agents at work in universities, public records offices and national computer archives all over the world, busily hiding, destroying, obscuring, obfuscating, rewriting, stuffing files down the backs of radiators and generally sabotaging the manufacture of history, you can *control* the production of anomalies and artificially create a navigable course from a given point in the future back to a given point in the past. Or, as the classic equation so elegantly puts it:

$$I = fd^2$$

– where I stands for the Time-traveller's itinerary, d is disinformation as above, and f stands for a statistically acceptable incidence of clerical and administrative fuckups.

While we're on the subject of Time, it's universally acknowledged to be a great healer. By rights, therefore, it should be available free of charge through the National Health Service. But it isn't, of course. If you want chronotherapy, you have to go private.

'It'll cost you, mind,' the doctor muttered in a low voice. 'Very, very expensive. Not to mention illegal. If they catch me doing this, I'll be lucky if I can get a job casting out evil spirits in New Guinea.'

'I don't care,' Bianca replied. 'I've got to get well and get out of here as soon as possible. It's *urgent*. It's a matter of . . .' She was going to say life and death, but that could mean anything; like, for example that she'd managed to get seats for the Shrunken Heads concert at the NEC and didn't want to waste them. 'The future of the human race,' she said, 'is hanging in the balance here. It's *essential*—'

'Hey,' the doctor interrupted, 'you mean you got tickets for the Heads gig? You wouldn't consider selling them, would you?'

Having your right arm in plaster means you can only hit doctors with your left; unless you're a natural southpaw, this can be a nuisance. 'Shut *up*,' Bianca snapped. 'Look. Sixteen people, one of them quite possibly a close friend, have died. Most likely, that's only the beginning. The only person who can stop it is me. So name your frigging price and let's get on with it.'

'My price? You mean for the tickets? Well—'

'For the operation,' Bianca hissed.

Chronotherapy, also known as Injury Time; a new breakthrough in medical science, brought to you by the pharmaceuticals wing of Chubby Stevenson (Time) Inc.

What nearly all medicine boils down to is: leave the human body alone and comfortable, and in Time it'll sort itself out. But if you haven't got Time, this is a non-starter. So; either you die, or bits fall off you, or you buy more Time.

It's an entirely private and personal envelope of additional Time shoe-horned into an ordinary day – one second in real time, but up to three months as far as the user is concerned, during which bones knit, scars heal, muscles rebuild and so on. Since it's a very small-scale temporal field, it only takes a tiny drop of the raw stuff – less than one microlitre, street value currently £100,000. Double that for the shoe-horn, installation costs, credulity suspension jigs and tooling, the doctor's and Chubby's profit. Fortunately, the sensational manner in which she'd received her injuries (Sultry Brunette In Bomb Horror) had sent her market values rocketing, and she'd arranged a few sales of old bits of junk she'd had cluttering her studio which more than covered the cost.

Later, Bianca was to remember it as the most boring second of her life.

Mike arrived, dishevelled and out of breath, to find he was already there.

This worried him. True, his aggravating vagueness and extremely flexible attitude to punctuality had frequently led people to suggest that one of these days he'd be late for his own funeral. On the other hand, he'd always assumed that they'd have the common courtesy to wait for him. Apparently not so.

'We therefore commit his body to the earth,' said the priest, 'dust to dust, ashes to . . .'

'Hey!' he shouted. Nobody heard him. He watched with incredulous fury as they started to fill in the grave. It was like watching a waiter take away your meal before you'd had a chance to unfold your table napkin, let alone start eating. One thing did, however, suggest at least a degree of normality. Nobody had told him anything and he hadn't got a clue what was going on. That made him feel more comfortable. He could cope now.

'Good turnout,' said a voice to his immediate right. 'You must feel proud.'

The voice was coming from a large, florid Victorian weeping angel. She'd seen better days; acid rain, vandalism and the trainee assistant gardener (who sharpened his billhook on her marble ankle) had all taken their toll, leaving her looking like something found in a sink-trap. Mike recoiled slightly.

'Be like that,' the angel said, apparently not offended. 'Let's face it, you're no oil painting yourself; although, that said, in a bad light you'd pass for a second-rate Jackson Pollock.'

'I beg your pardon?'

The statue sighed. 'Sorry,' it said, 'I forgot, you're new. Find a puddle or something, take a look at yourself. Or rather,' she added quickly, 'don't. Probably best if you remember yourself the way you used to be.'

Mike sat down on a tombstone. As he did so, he studied the process. As far as he could tell, he was solid and real; he could feel the stone against his trousered leg, and when he tried to pass his arm through an ornate granite cross, it wouldn't go. He tried again, only harder; when he banged his wrist on the stone it hurt, and a little smear of blood showed in the graze. In one sense, reassuring; in another, disconcerting.

'Neat trick, isn't it?' said the angel, who had been watching. 'Feels just like the real thing, but isn't. All a matter of timing, you see.'

'Timing?'

'That's right.' The statue yawned. 'God,' she said, 'why's it always me who's got to do this? I don't get paid for explaining to new recruits, I just do it because I'm here. And,' she added, 'because I feel sorry for you, bless your poor disoriented souls. And because I've got absolutely nothing else to do. Still, I really do think it's time they did something official, it's a scandal if you ask me. I mean, there's all those preparing-for-retirement courses you can go on, so the shock of not having to work won't send you to an early grave; but the biggest and most radical change of your entire existence, you're supposed to be able to fend for yourself, puzzle it out from first principles. Cheapskate, I call it.'

Mike took a deep breath – presumably it was a deep breath and not just some virtual reality programmer's placebo. 'If you'd explain,' he said, 'I personally would be very grateful.'

'That's all right,' said the angel, 'you're welcome. Look, forget what I said about timing for the moment, it always confuses people. Think of a radio, right?'

Mike thought of a radio.

'Now then,' the statue continued, 'there's hundreds, maybe thousands of different radio signals blamming about simultaneously, but the radio only picks them up one at a time. That's because it's tuned in to one specific frequency.' The angel paused. 'Nobody told me this, by the way,' she added. 'I had to work it out for myself. It's true, though, 'cos I had it confirmed by Official Channels when I asked them. They're very good about answering enquiries, so long as you don't forget the stamped addressed envelope.'

'Please go on,' Mike said. 'Like radio waves, you said.'

'Sure.' The angel thought for a moment, remembering where she'd got to. 'Well, just as there's lots of different radio frequencies, there's lots of different chronological continuums. Continua. Timescales. That's a better word, although I shouldn't use it because it's got a separate technical meaning. Strictly speaking, timescale is the residue left after hard time's been boiled down in a copper kettle.'

'Ah.'

'Forget I said that. Different timescales. Now, in the timescale which human mortal life is tuned in to, a second lasts—' She stopped. 'Sorry, got in a bit of a tangle there.

Should have done the weights-and-measures spiel before I started. Let's put all that on one side for the time being and stick to Terrestrial Orthodox. As far as you're concerned, a second lasts one second, right?'

'Right.'

'Wrong. A second only lasts a second in your own specific timescale, HMS – that's Human Mortal Standard. That's what you were tuned in to when you were alive. Now you're dead, you're tuned in to HDS, Human Deceased Standard. One second HMS is equivalent to 0.8342 seconds HDS; or 0.0062 seconds SIS, Supernatural Immortal Standard; or 0.000147, SITS, Soul In Torment Standard; or—'

'All right,' Mike said, 'got that. How does that mean I don't exist but I can't walk through tombstones?'

Being a statue, the angel couldn't shrug, but by extra-subtle voice modulation it did the vocal equivalent. 'Don't exist is a bit of an overstatement,' she said, 'and it's a very complex bit of maths, which I'm still not sure I completely follow. The analogy is, though, think of the radio signals. They're all there, but you can only listen to one at a time. Now, turning back to timescales, think of yourself as the radio signal.'

'Fine. Here am I going bleep bleep. Who's being the radio?'

Another, broader verbal shrug. 'This is a difficult concept to put across,' she said. 'Basically, the world is the radio, your fellow sentient beings are – no pun intended, promise – the cat's whiskers. Do you see what I'm getting at? You exist, you're here, no question about that. The tombstone there is inanimate – either that, or it's very, very shy, because we've been standing next to each other since 1897 and it's never said a word – and so it couldn't notice you even if it wanted to. Doesn't matter a damn what a tombstone thinks. But living creatures are different; they're all tuned in to their own timescale, and so they just don't see anybody who's in a timescale faster than their own. Dead people move too quick; you know, the magic lantern effect. Marvellous system when you come to think of it, bloody efficient way to store billions of people on a relatively small planet.'

There was a substantial pause while Mike let it all sink in. 'I see,' he said. 'So do I still have to eat and sleep and so on? Do I still have to go to work and earn money, or is everything free, or don't I need anything? Can I have things even if I don't need them?'

'The question doesn't arise,' the angel replied. 'Life expectancy of a dead human's no more than three days, four days maximum. At the end of that time, either you find an empty property in Mortality you can slip into, or else – phut.'

'Phut?'

'Phut. That's yet another gross simplification,' the angel went on apologetically, 'but so what, I'm pretty shaky on the theory from now on. What actually happens, I *think*, is that you start to speed up to such an extent that Time just zips by in a meaningless blur and before you know it, you've reached the End of the Universe, entropy time, the big nothing; like you've fast-forwarded and there you are at the end of the tape. What happens after that is beyond me. Maybe they wind it back, maybe they take it back to the library and get out another one. Let's put it this way, you'll know the answer to that particular part of the story long before I will, so if you can, be sure to send me a postcard. I say that to all the new arrivals,' the angel added, 'and I've never had anything from any of them. But maybe they just forgot.'

'Four days?'

'Four days tops.'

Mike felt ill. The gravestone was still there under his backside, the breeze was still a little on the chilly side, but he felt as if he was already hurtling past, like a child on a combination merry-go-round and Ferris wheel. 'You said something about an empty property,' he remembered. 'What's that all about?'

'Thought you'd ask,' replied the angel. 'They always do. Just occasionally, you can slip back in. Sounds nice, but isn't.'

'No?'

'Wouldn't fancy it myself,' the angel replied. 'The reason being, you don't go back into HMS time, so you can't be a human or a cat or a golden eagle or stuff like that. Returns go in HIA time, and that's – well, weird, really. Look at me.'

'You?'

'Me. HIA; Human Irregular Anomaly. We exist in all timescales simultaneously. We're in some more strongly than in others, true, and in practice you ignore everything except HMS, HDS and a few others because – come on, let's ride this radio analogy until it falls to bits – the signals are faint, crackly and in Norwegian. Anyway, that's what happened to me. I came back as a statue. No bloody fun at all.'

'A statue?'

'That's right. More of us about than you'd think.' The angel's voice was getting softer and softer, slower and slower, as though its batteries were running down fast. 'The thing to remember about HIA is, it's very, very...'

'Yes? *Yes?*'

'Boring.'

A fraction of a second later, the statue was just a statue; you could tell just by looking at it that it was no more alive than a cellarful of coal. Run down? Asleep? Switched off?

No way of knowing. Mike stood up, felt pins and needles from his knee to his ankle.

Four days . . .

Ninety-nine per cent light speed!

Head forward, wings back, tail streaming behind him, the dragon bulleted on through the murderous slipstream. His scales glowed cherry-red, and the tears streaming from his eyes boiled before they ever reached his cheeks. His eardrums, at a guess, were halfway down his throat. It was just as well he couldn't open his mouth, because air pressure would have snapped his lower jaw off at the hinge.

Ugh, he thought –

wwhhyyyy aaammm IIIII ddoooiiiiiinngg tthhiiiiissssss?

Because if I don't, that creep Chubby will blow me to Kingdom Come (or, relatively speaking, quite possibly Kingdom Went; wherever, I don't want to go there).

And because there's a certain unbelievable thrill in peeling back the final frontier; shit-scaredly going where everybody else has already gone before, but not yet. As it were.

And, last but not least, because I've got nothing better to do.

BANG!

Light speed . . .

One very pertinent fact about travelling faster than light—

'*Ouch!*'

– is that it's bloody dark and you can't see where you're going. And, at that sort of speed, even a collision with a high-flying clothes moth takes on the stature of a major railway accident.

Fortunately, he regained consciousness just in time to pull out of his headlong spin, wrench his battered and groaning body up out of the way of mountains and airliners and jack-knife agonisingly back to straight and level. It was still as dark as thirty feet down a drain, which meant he hadn't lost speed. What he needed now was lots and lots of height.

Hey though, he crowed in the back lots of his subconscious, this is quite something. No way those two-legged groundling midgets could do this, for all their precious technology. For a dragon, however, it's just a matter of flying. You do know how to fly, don't you? You just put your wings together and go . . .

'*Help!*'

Going this fast, you lose all track of Time. Or Time loses all track of you. The only semi-constant is the pain; you're being beadblasted with photons, every square millimetre of your body surface is white hot, a grain of dust hits you like a cannon shell. You only continue to exist because entropy hasn't caught up with you yet. But it will.

Beeeeep!

What? Oh, Christ, yes, Chubby's idiotic signal. I can slow down now, just when I was beginning to enjoy myself.

The lights came back on, and then the dragon was no longer faster-than-light, just very fast; racing, but no longer against the clock. Now then, the trick is, decelerate slowly. In this context, sudden slowth would hit like a brick wall.

The sound came back on. The vertical hold adjusted itself. God had fiddled with the aerial.

Congratulations! We all knew you had it in you!

What the hell? The dragon's brain cleared and he realised it was a pre-recorded message, playing tinnily and at not quite the right speed through a miniature speaker inside his ear. He slowed down a little more.

Please proceed to the following co-ordinates. Longitude . . .

'Fuck you!' the dragon howled. 'I haven't got a map!'

. . . Sixteen minutes west; or, in layman's terms, the bookstall in Rockefeller Plaza. You will there buy a copy of the New York Times *and turn to page four. Estimated you will arrive in nine, repeat nine, minutes.*

High over New York, the dragon found out what the parcel was for. As his dragon body suddenly vanished and he felt a rather different, more vindictive slipstream tearing at his human incarnation, he realised that it was a parachute.

New Yorkers are hard to faze. A windswept man with streaming eyes and untidy hair parachuting down onto the concourse at Grand Central is, to them, just another guy trying to beat the rush hour. So finely tuned is the New Yorker's inbuilt radar that they got out of his way as he landed without even looking at him.

He picked himself up. No need to dispose of the parachute; in the second and a half during which he'd been rolling on the ground feeling acute pain in both knees, the parachute had been unbuckled, stolen and spirited away. By now, it'd probably been converted into three hundred silk handkerchiefs in a lock-up somewhere in Queens.

Feeling slightly shaky and, for once, almost out of his depth, he tottered to the bookstall, picked up a newspaper and looked at the date. All that trouble and effort, and he'd fast-forwarded six lousy weeks.

He turned to page four, as ordered, jotted down the closing prices. Then the sports pages, then the lottery results. Then, out of curiosity, he glanced to the front page.

And saw a headline.

The *Times*, which isn't your run-of-the-mill sensationalist fishwrap, had let its hair down. There were screamingly vivid action pictures, BIG headlines, interviews with witnesses, angles, turn to page six, continued on page seven. It was a BIG story, full of twists, nuances, implications. There was even a three-column feature by one D. Bennett, linking the bizarre events to Contragate, the Bermuda Triangle and the assassination of Abe Lincoln.

The gist of the story, however, was straightforward enough.

Twelve hours ago, in Mongolia, Saint George had killed the Dragon.

Mike didn't sleep well.

For one thing, since he was going to die, fast-forward, phut, whatever, in four days, he begrudged the time. Also, although he'd never been particularly superstitious, kipping down in a graveyard didn't appeal to him, particularly since he now had the feeling that he'd be able to see his fellow deadies and maybe they weren't very nice to look at . . . Mostly, though, he couldn't sleep because he was worried.

Four days to find a – what the hell was it he was looking for? An anomaly, he supposed, but what the hell does an anomaly look like? Apparently, like a statue.

Not any old statue, though; he'd already tried that. There were plenty of statues in the graveyard and he'd knocked loudly on each one, prodded them for disguised doors and escape hatches, even tried climbing in through ears and open mouths. Failure. By the time he'd finished, he was beginning to hallucinate *No Vacancies* signs.

A statue.

A *statue*.

Jesus, yes, a *statue*! Piece of cake, surely, because wasn't the most gifted living sculptress (despair is the mother of exaggeration) a personal friend of his, who also happened to owe him one hell of a favour?

By the time he'd worked that out, it was half past six and the buses were starting to run. He caught the thirty-seven, which went to the hospital. Buses are inanimate (although they're capable of malice; ask anybody who's run after one, only to watch it draw away from the kerb at the last minute) and accordingly was solid and real enough for him to get on board without falling through the floor. He had no trouble finding a seat, in spite of the fact that there was standing room only.

But.

All right, so Bianca can sculpt me a statue to live in; central heating, air conditioned, all mod cons. First, though, I've got to find a way to get a message through to her. How the hell do I do that, exactly?

By the time the bus drew up outside the hospital gate, the only answer that had occurred to him was, *improvise*. Well, he could do worse.

Bianca stirred.

Precisely one second ago, she'd been very ill; Bianca the human jigsaw, held together with skin, plaster and force of habit. Now, though, she could feel the integrity of her newly restored bones. She was fit, strong, ready to face the incredibly daunting task now facing her. She was also, of course, covered from head to foot in plaster and her limbs were tied to the ceiling with thick wire.

'Hello!' she shouted. 'Nurse! I think I'm better now, can I get up?'

Needless to say, they ignored her, and an alarming thought walked flat-footed across the wet concrete of her mind. Maybe they wouldn't believe she was better and were going to keep her like this for another six weeks anyway?

It was then that the table began to move.

At first, Bianca put it down to a heavy lorry trundling by in the road below. When it stopped simply wobbling and began to tap-dance, she began to wonder.

'Mike?' she whispered.

Grimly, Mike lifted the chair and tapped out a phrase: *'cos I'll be there, puttin' on ma top hat, tying up ma white tie—*

'Mike,' Bianca said sternly, 'stop making that awful noise, you'll disturb the other patients.'

The table stopped moving. Feeling very foolish – girl gets bang on head, starts talking to thin air, and you're saying she's ready to go home? Get real, nurse, please – she whispered, 'Mike.'

No reply.

'Mike, if you want to, er, communicate ...' God, how? 'Don't try and answer. Look, I'll think of something.' What? Hell. She looked round. Lying at the foot of the bed was one of those horrid comics.

'Can you pick up that magazine?'

The pages riffled.

'Good. I'll pretend to be reading it.' She picked it up. 'To answer, turn the pages till you find something that's as close as you can get to what you want to say.'

Riffle. The magazine was now open at the agony column.

'You've got a problem you want help with?'

Riffle. In front of her was a feature, *Mortgage Repossession Left My Family Homeless.*

'You're in financial difficulties? Mike, you're dead, how can you be in . . .?'

Riffle. *Exchanging Contracts: Part Four in our series on moving house.*

Bianca thought for a moment. 'You're homeless? You've got nowhere to go?'

Riffle. She looked down and saw the front cover. The name of the magazine was *Yes!*

'I see,' Bianca said, inaccurately. 'So how can I help?'

Riffle. Article on improving your garden. Photograph; petunias, flowering cherry, crab apple tree, herbacious border, garden gnomes ...

'You want me to plant a tree for you? Is that it?'

Riffle. Another photograph; view of Piccadilly Circus. Further riffle. View of Trafalgar Square. Further riffle. For Only £99.99 You Can Own This Beautiful Porcelain Figurine . . .

'A *statue*? You want me to carve you a statue?'

Riffle. Front cover.

'But . . .' Bianca was going to say Why? Then she thought of the dragon, and George, and she knew why.

'Mike, I'm sort of busy right now, can it wait? You see, first I've got to get out of here, then I've got to find that dragon – you know, my statue – and stop him blowing things up, so if you could give me six weeks or so . . .'

Furious riffles. Advertisement. Flabstrippers' Guarantee: Lose Six Pounds in Three Days or Your Money Back.

'Three days?' Front cover. 'Mike, that's impossible, I—'

The magazine flew from her hands, soared up into the air and parachuted down, pages flapping like the wings of a shot crow. The table rocked violently and fell over. The chair began to tap out *Dancin' Cheek to Cheek*.

'All *right*,' she hissed, as the sister came running. 'I'll see what I can do.'

CHAPTER TWELVE

'It's obvious what we've gotta do,' Kurt replied impatiently. 'We've gotta leave the country.'

Seventeen former statues looked at him as though he were mad, making him grateful his band wasn't a democracy. He did his best to ignore them.

'Leave the country?' David asked. 'Why?'

David had, somehow, been elevated to the rank of spokesman-cum-courier; that is to say, the other ex-statues tended to hem him in and hiss, 'Go on, *you* tell him,' in his ear. They also complained to him about the food, the transport and the accommodation; remember, although their outward husks were Italian, inside they were British.

'Because,' Kurt replied, still wondering what in blazes had led him to go back for this miserable lot, 'we've got this job to do. And we can't do it here. Okay?'

'Don't think we can leave the country,' muttered the Giambologna *Mercury*. 'We'd need special export licences, surely.'

'Stolen property,' agreed a Bernini bronze. 'They got

these computerised lists, international, worldwide. I saw it on *Lovejoy*. We'd never get past the duty-free lounge.'

Amateurs, muttered Kurt to himself. 'Absolutely right,' he sighed, the sarcasm going so far over his listeners' heads that you could have bounced radio signals off it. 'That's why we've gotta hijack a plane.'

That left them speechless; but not for long enough. A Donatello Crucifixion objected that surely hijacking was illegal. The Canova demanded to speak to the manager. Kurt bashed the packing case with his fist for silence.

'Okay,' he snarled, 'that's it. I've had enough of this goddamn whimpering out of you guys. The next one of you I hear any shit from ends up at the bottom of the Arno with a human being tied to his ankle. You got that? Good. Now then, this is the plan.'

In the shocked silence that followed, it occurred to Kurt that he hadn't yet formulated a plan. Kurt Lundqvist without a plan; impossible. Easier to imagine a Tory minister without a mistress. Something would occur to him, it always did.

'The plan,' he went on, 'is, naturally, top secret. I'll announce the various stages in due course, on a strictly need-to-know basis. The first stage is getting to the air terminal. This is what we do.'

Kurt spent the rest of the day shoplifting, hotwiring vehicles, breaking into police station armouries, mugging tourists for their passports, faking photographs, wiring up al fresco bombs and generally relaxing after all the strain he'd been through lately dealing with objects only one step away from being people. By one o'clock in the morning, he felt refreshed and invigorated. He now had at his disposal a carabinieri armoured van, eighteen assault rifles, ditto Beretta 9mm handguns, three cases of grenades, five twenty-pounder bombs, flak jackets, black balaclavas,

matching ski-suits, two-way radios, state-of-the-art communications and radio jamming equipment, sandwiches,
chocolate and a thermos flask of decaffeinated coffee.

At three am precisely, air traffic control received an
ominous message on the security hotline. Flight TCA8494
from Istanbul, scheduled to refuel before heading on to
London, due to arrive at 03.24, had armed hijackers on
board. They'd wired up bombs, and were demanding the
release of prisoners and a huge cash ransom. A special
security team was on its way; in the meantime, act naturally,
refuel the plane, pretend nothing untoward is happening.
Message received and understood.

At 03.34, the carabinieri van drew up at a side gate. Kurt
flashed an impressive-looking pass (actually an Academy
Museum season ticket, but it was dark and Kurt kept his
thumb over the words) under the sentry's nose, hissed a few
words in his ear and was let through. At 03.40, eighteen
shadowy, ferociously armed figures scrambled up the
gangway into the plane and burst into the passenger
compartment.

'Okay!' Kurt roared. 'Nobody move!' He paused, for
effect. 'Okay,' he said, 'where's the hijackers?'

The cabin staff stared at him. They were just rewinding
the in-flight movie, handing out the freeby glossy magazines. 'What hijackers?' they said.

Kurt assumed a pained expression. 'Jesus, not *another* false
alarm,' he sighed. 'You *sure* there hasn't been a hijack?'

The purser nodded. 'We'd have noticed,' he said.

'Not necessarily,' Kurt replied, motioning to his team to
fan out, start frisking the passengers. 'Like, there's these
new fundamentalist religious fanatics, some name like
Meek Militant Action. Their aim's to inherit the Earth,
provided nobody objects. We'd better check things out, just
to be sure.'

The purser, who had the muzzle of a Heckler & Koch G3 sticking in his ear – not because he was a suspect, it was just rather a cramped aircraft – shrugged and nodded. 'Suit yourselves, guys,' he said. 'Better safe than sorry, I guess. While you're at it, would you mind taking round the duty-frees?'

Kurt's men duly searched; wonder of wonders, they found no fewer than five twenty-pound bombs wired up to the doors, fuel lines and in-flight catering packs. Gee, muttered Kurt, just as I thought. We'd better stay with this flight till it gets to London. What a truly splendid idea, the captain replied, his subconscious wrestling with the problem of where he'd seen some of these guys before (you don't like to say to a SWAT team officer that you're sorry, you didn't recognise him with his clothes on). While they were at it, he added, maybe they could help out with serving the meals and checking the seat-belts.

As the plane took off, a Bernini took Kurt aside and asked him to explain something.

'Thought we were meant to be hijacking the plane,' he said.

Kurt nodded. 'Neat job, huh?'

'But we're pretending to be the army. The good guys.'

'So?'

'Does that mean we're the good guys or the bad guys? I'm confused.'

Kurt shook his head. The ignorance of some people. 'Son,' he said, 'I'm gonna tell you something that's gonna help you a lot in years to come, supposing you last that long. Good guys is just a fancy way of saying Us. Bad guys is only ever Them. You remember that, you won't go far wrong. Okay?'

'But what about moral imperatives? What about Good and Evil?'

188 · Tom Holt

The Bernini suddenly found himself about a centimetre from Kurt's taut face and industrial-laser eyes. 'Where I come from,' he said, 'Evil's a stunt man's Christian name. Now go over there, sit down and shut up. Does that answer your question?'

'Comprehensively.'

'Great. Always knew I shoulda been a philosopher.'

Attack philosopher, naturally.

Although the dragon had immediately recognised the sheer brilliance of Chubby's method of travelling back through Time, he'd had an intuitive feeling from the outset that there was one tiny flaw in it somewhere. Now, back in the air and soaring at ninety thousand feet over Angola, he knew for certain what it was.

It didn't work.

Twenty-seven hours he'd been up here; twice round the predetermined circuit, airspeed and course exactly as specified to the knot, to the metre. All he'd managed to achieve was to distance himself from home by a further twenty-seven hours. Bloody marvellous.

By the time he was overflying Botswana, he'd worked it out. The course as plotted was half an hour out of synch; the fools hadn't taken into account the time he'd be spending on the ground. He cursed them and himself; if he'd spotted the mistake earlier, he might just have been able to compensate. By now, though, the history nodes would all have moved on so far that it'd be impossible to rechart the course without all of Chubby's formulae, calculating software and history-industry infiltrators' input. He was stuck.

When in shit, use brain. All the necessary kit would, of course, still be in Chubby's office. All he had to do was drop in, explain the problem – or would Chubby be expecting him? After all, once he got back he'd tell him all about it, with the result that by the time they got back here, sorry, *now*, Chubby would already *know* – but if that was the case, he'd have known to correct the error in the first place, oh *fuck*, this is complicated . . .

He flew, nevertheless, to Chubby's office, only to find it boarded up, with no forwarding address. Nothing in the phone book. No trace anywhere. Maybe when he got back he was going to roast Chubby alive (sorely tempted), which in turn would mean no Chubby now, just when he needed him most. Hey, maybe it really *is* impossible to travel backwards in Time. Starting to look that way, no question.

He slowed down, drifting gracefully high above Madagascar. The hell with this, let's try another way.

Such as?

If you don't know, his old mother used to say, ask someone who does.

Think, dragon, think.

Thirty-two hours ago, he'd seen a newspaper headline saying that twelve hours before that, he'd been killed. Okay.

If I was killed before I got here, then it stands to reason that I got back in time to be killed before I got here. Therefore I, the late lamented I, *requiescam in pace*, must know how I got back. So I should ask myself. Only that's going to be tricky, because I'm dead.

Tricky, but possible. Because – give me strength! – in order to have gotten back, I must have asked myself how to do it. My dead self must therefore know that my living self is going to want to make contact, approximately now, and will be waiting in for the call, wherever the flying fuck I/he now am/is. Stands to reason.

Okay, here goes. Just hope I know what I'm doing.

He peered down. Zululand. Well, why not?

★

There are more things in Heaven and Earth, Horatio, than give you nightmares in your philosophy.

Few stranger, more wonderful or more terrible, however, than the *isangoma* – translated, with typical Colonial crassness, 'witch-doctor' – of southern Africa. Now, of course, extinct; no place for that sort of thing in the twentieth century. Well, of course.

Although he knew virtually nothing about the subject, the dragon was at least able to address the small, shrivelled man sitting in front of him on a low, carved stool by his correct title: *amakhosi*, 'my lords', plural, because when you speak to the *isangoma* you're talking not to the little old man but to the countless mighty spirits who bed-and-breakfast, so to speak, in the vast mansions behind his eyes.

Nkunzana's small, tidy kraal lay in a miniature valley, a crack between two great rocks, which meant the sun's nuisance was kept to a minimum. For twenty hours in the twenty-four it was dark at Izulu-li-dum-umteto, and for Nkunzana darkness was a natural resource essential to his business, like the mill-streams of Lancashire. He himself was a comic, horrifying figure; small, crooked and smooth-skinned, like a freeze-dried child. He wore the uniform of his craft: leopards' teeth, goats' horns, pigs' bladders, gnu's tail. He looked like God's spares box. Slow to move, quick to laugh; smiling toothlessly, staring unblinking at a space two feet above and eight inches to the right of the head of the person he was talking to. A little ray of sunshine. Your local GP.

'*Sakubona, baba*'. We saw you, my father; hello. A grave nod accompanied the formal greeting. The dragon relaxed a little. He'd managed to get to see the doctor without an appointment. 'And what can I do for you?'

The dragon licked the roof of his mouth, which was dry; *why am I afraid of this little toe-rag? I'm a dragon, for crying out loud*... 'I need to speak to someone who is dead, *'makhosi,*' he replied, a little nervousness spilling out with the words. 'For you, surely, this is possible.'

'Possible.' The little man nodded. 'A small matter, my father. Who among the snakes do you wish to talk to?'

The dragon hesitated. 'This is, um, embarrassing.'

'Relax. Say the name.'

'Well – look, how would it be if I wrote it down on a bit of paper? Sorry to be all silly about this, but—'

'I cannot read, my father. Say the name.'

'All right. Um. Me.'

'You?'

Nod. 'Me.'

Long pause.

'*Wo, ndoda; ngitshilo.*' Hey, man, you sure said a mouthful. 'Talking to yourself is a sign of madness. Talking to yourself, dead, is class.'

The dragon shuffled. 'Said it was embarrassing. Can you do it?'

Nkunzana shrugged. 'Why not?' he said. 'If it's possible. If not, not.'

'It's possible. Cross my heart and hope to die. Er, be dead.'

'We will see what we can do, my father.' The old man closed his eyes, leaned forward until his knees touched his shoulders, and tossed something onto the fire. Nothing happened.

'About time, too,' said the dragon.

The dragon looked up. 'Aarg,' he said.

'Have you any idea,' his deceased self went on, 'how long I've been hanging around this boghole waiting for you to turn up? Gives me the fucking creeps, and I'm *dead*.'

'Sorry.' Really, truly embarrassing. 'Look, I guess you know why I needed to talk.'

'Reverse time travel, how we got home.' The dragon nodded. 'Piece of cake. Why you needed to bother me I don't know. I managed to work it out all by myself.'

'Clever old you, then.'

'Indeed.' The dragon sighed contemptuously. 'Listen carefully. I'm dead, right?'

'Right.'

'But I can't be, or I couldn't be talking to me, right? Say yes.'

'Yes.'

'Therefore I must be alive. Nod.'

The dragon nodded.

'And if I'm alive now, I must have been alive six weeks ago. Well?'

'Obviously.'

'Okay.' The dragon grinned. 'There you are, then.'

And there they weren't, either of them.

For ten minutes or so, Nkunzana sat, gazing at the empty stool. Then he stood up, threw another log on the fire.

'*Hambla gahle,*' he said quietly, go in peace. 'I'm Logic, fly me.' He shook his head, picked up his catskin bag of medicines and walked to his hut.

It only occurred to him when he reached the doorway. He stopped dead, swore, ('*Wangi hudela umtwana wami!*') and banged his head savagely against the lintel. Bloody old fool.

All that work, unsocial hours, and who the hell was he going to send the invoice to?

Bianca's arm ached, the newly mended bone resenting the heavy vibration of hammer on chisel on stone. She glanced up at the clock. No time to rest, she observed mournfully. Not even time for a quick brew and a garibaldi biscuit. She raised the chisel, positioned it carefully, tapped gently. Boy, was she *tired*.

It was starting to take its toll. Already her hand had slipped, uncharacteristically, when she'd been doing the left side of the collar bone. Oh dear, what a shame, never mind. The old Mike had always had a chip on his shoulder. Now he had a chip out of it; same difference.

Do the head last, shrieked her common sense. Just in case the bloody thing comes alive before I've finished it. Last thing I need is Mike's head looking over my shoulder, telling me how I should do my job. Probably try and sweet-talk me into making improvements on the original. No prize for guessing what he'd want improved.

Furthermore, once this job was finished, no chance of taking a day off or putting her feet up. The moment she'd finished Mike, she had a dragon to find and reason with. And what if the wretched thing wouldn't listen to reason? Then what the hell was she supposed to do?

She paused, brushed away chippings and thought hard. Why me, anyway? Go on, then, if you're so damn clever.

The trouble was, she could feel reasons there under her skin, like the palmed coin hidden in the magician's handkerchief. It *had* to be her, because ... Well, because she believed in what was going on – not through choice, but because she knew it was all horribly true – and she knew full well that nobody else would believe her. If she tried to enlist the help of the proper authorities (Police? Army? Church? No idea), they'd have her inside a fruitcake repository and connected up to the mains before she got much further than, 'Well, it's like this ...' Because she owed it to the dragon for the wrongs her species had done to his species – No, the hell with that. Follow that line of argument and she'd be pouring petrol through delicatessens' letterboxes. Because it was her statues that started it all. That was the reason. Very silly reason; holding herself responsible for the acts of a bunch of semi-legendary joyriders. But it was *the* reason and she was stuck with it.

But what was she to do if the dragon wouldn't listen to her? An entrancing picture floated before her mind; the damsel fights the dragon to save the knight chained to the rock. Great feminist statement; bloody silly game plan. And how do you go about fighting dragons, anyway?

'Reluctantly,' Bianca said aloud. 'Copper mallet, copper mallet, come out wherever you are.'

Three hours later, there wasn't much left to do. The face – well, far be it from her to seek to amend Mother Nature's banjax. The small of the back and the bum; there is a destiny that shapes our ends, she muttered to herself laying in hard with the chisel, rough-hew them how we will. In this instance, it had shaped Mike's end rather like a very old, tired sofa. There were lots of untidy chisel-marks, but his trousers would hide those. Time Mike learnt to take the rough with the smooth.

Chip chip, tap tap. 'All right,' she said. 'It's ready. Phase One in an exciting new development of starter-homes for unfussy ghosts.'

She waited.

Slight miscalculation? Maybe. Or maybe a very precise calculation indeed.

Below him, the dragon saw the still-smoking embers of the hall. A gaggle of peculiar-shaped creatures, led by a human, were picking their way through the hot rubble towards a beat-up old motor vehicle. They got in and drove away.

Banzai! He'd come back in a day or so earlier than scheduled, just nicely in time to see George and his sidekicks clambering out of their incinerator and making a run for it. Maintaining his height, he tracked the van; wingbeats few and slow, a handy thermal buoying him up.

He was, he hoped, too high for the wretched creatures in the van to see or notice, although what could they do if they did? Drive faster than light? Try and defend themselves? Attack? Let them. The dragon was wearing under his metaphorical dinner jacket the bullet-proof vest of zombie-hood; *you can't get me 'cos I done dead already.* Looking ahead up the road, he picked his spot. Fire? Twelve good nosefuls before he was into reserve. He accelerated, put his wings back, fell into the glide . . .

'George.'
  'Now what?'
  'There's a dragon following us.'

The van had slewed to a sudden dramatic standstill and its contents were dispersing at top speed. Drat, the dragon thought. Never mind, he was locked on to George now; he didn't care about the others, as soon let them go as not, provided they didn't interfere. And they wouldn't. Not many demons are prepared to lay down their lives for a saint.

  Nice to watch George run. For a short, fattish lad he had a pretty turn of speed. Slippery, too, as soap in a bath, so no time for mucking about. It's when the stage villain pauses to twirl his moustaches and cackle that the hero sees his chance and the underwriters of his life policies start to breathe again. Time to nail the sod.

  He dived, breathed in. A smart sneeze, pinpoint accurate. A very loud, *very* short scream. Job done.

  Home.

Oh.
  So that was death, was it? Typical, I missed it.
  George watched the dragon recede into the sky, then

looked down; although he knew there'd be nothing to see. His body – gone. Which body? Didn't matter. The jet of fire that had wrapped round him like a cat round legs had been so hot it'd have evaporated marble as easily as flesh. An exemplary snuff; quick, sure and completely (as far as he could remember) painless.

George was suddenly aware of something –

– God knows what. The nearest he could get to it was an invisible lead, dragging him like an over-inquisitive dog. Balls, muttered George, I'm going to Heaven. Don't want to go yet. Haven't finished.

Don't have to go. As the unseen rope tugged him along, he was aware of a handhold, an escape hatch, rushing towards him. An anomaly! Saved!

There's many a slip, as the saying goes, between toilet bowl and sewage farm. George only saw it for the most fleeting sliver of a second, but it was long enough to judge his escape attempt and make it.

A statue, its back door wide open. In fact, so conveniently placed, handy for the stream of traffic, that you'd be forgiven for thinking it had been put there expressly for the purpose. A mousetrap? Or a getaway car?

Whatever; who gives a shit? As far as George was concerned, it was a case of any portrait in a storm. He threw himself at the anomaly and hit the mark.

'Mike? You in there yet?'

Coming, coming. Being dead takes it out of you, makes you realise just how out of condition you can become in three days. Painfully, Mike dragged himself towards the nice welcoming statue. Dear, kind, clever Bianca, she'd done a good job. Almost there . . .

What? *What*?

BASTARD!

Just as the door in the back of the statue opened and he'd been reaching out a frail and shaky arm to touch it, some evil git had bounced up from behind, swept past him, jumped into the statue and slammed the door. Was that face familiar? The ill-fated play where he'd been killed. Oh *no*. Saint George. The saint had stolen his body.

Even if he'd had the strength to hammer on the door and tug at the handle, it'd have done him no good. With statues it's strictly first come, first stored. He'd been gazumped, at the last minute.

He had no more strength left to hang on. He let go.

'Mike? You in there yet?'

The statue's eyes flickered.

'Mike!'

With an effortless smoothness that did her no end of credit, the eyelids lifted.

'Mike?'

That's not him in there! Odd, how you just know, simply by looking people in the eye. Just a coloured circle on a white background, a fried egg with a jewelled yolk. Perhaps we can actually see the retina, the way they do for ultra-high-security identification routines, but too fast for our conscious minds to know what we've actually done.

'Who?'

I know who! *I'd recognise those beady, shifty little eyes anywhere*!

Bianca had quick reactions. Very few scientific instruments known to Man would be precise enough to measure the tiny instant it took her to grab the two-pound lump hammer and swing it at the head of her newly completed masterpiece. Compared to Saint George, though, she was a dinosaur in slow motion. Before her fingers had contacted the hickory handle, he was moving. As the hammerhead rushed towards him, he stuck out his newly acquired right arm, punched Bianca neatly in the eye, ducked the hammer blow and ran for it. Behind him, he heard a crash, suggesting that Bianca had sat down uncomfortably on the floor. He made a mental note to laugh triumphantly later, when he had the time.

He was through the door and out into the street faster than a jack-rabbit absconding with the Christmas club money.

Painfully, feeling like a Keystone Kop five seconds after the director's yelled 'Cut!' Bianca hauled herself up off the floor and swore.

George, that bastard of a saint, had stolen another of her statues. Worse, he'd probably just killed her friend. Nice touch, that; poor old Mike had just had the rare privilege of being killed by both Good and Evil consecutively. Not that she had a clue any more which was which; nor did she care. If Mike still existed, anywhere in the cosmos, she guessed he was feeling the same way.

The hammer was still in her hand and she realised; Jesus, I just tried to *kill* him. A saint. My own statue. I tried to kill one of my own statues, just when it was on the point of coming to life.

It wasn't being the sort of day you look back on with pride.

CHAPTER THIRTEEN

'What the Shopfloor,' Chardonay quavered, 'was *that*?'

Slitgrind levered himself up out of a puddle with his forearms. His eyes were blind with saint-ash and his lungs were full of holy smoke. 'Guess,' he grunted, and then started to cough.

'The dragon again?'

Before Chardonay could say anything else, Snorkfrod was at his side, hauling him up like an adored sack of spuds. Was he all right? Any bones broken? Did it hurt if she prodded him there?

'Yes,' he yelped. 'Not that that means anything. That'd hurt under any circumstances.'

'That dragon,' muttered Prodsnap, 'doesn't like us very much. What did we *do*?'

'We tried to kill him,' Holdall replied. 'First we wee'd all over him, then we blew him up with dynamite. Maybe he's paranoid or something.'

Having dislodged the proffered paramedical assistance, Chardonay sat down on a low wall and put on the one boot he'd been able to find. 'Well,' he said, 'one thing's for certain, that dragon isn't dead. Not as such. Where's George?'

The other demons looked at each other.

'Look,' Prodsnap said, 'let's put it this way. He's gone to a better place, and I don't mean Solihull.' He sneezed. 'I suggest we do the same. In our case, of course, we want to go to a worse place, but the principle's the same.'

'Where's that damn priest got to, come to that?' Slitgrind growled. 'I'm trying to remember if he was with us in the van. Who saw the bugger last?'

Chardonay was staring at the abandoned van. Its engine was still running. 'That dragon,' he said, in a strange flat voice, 'just killed a saint.'

Slitgrind shrugged a few shoulders. 'Plenty more where he came from. Look, can we get the Shopfloor out of here, before the sucker comes back?'

'The dragon,' Chardonay repeated, 'just killed Saint George. That's *wrong*.'

The exasperated sound came from Slitgrind. 'Look, love,' he stage-whispered to Snorkfrod, who was putting powder (powdered what, you don't want to know) on her face, using a puddle for a mirror. 'Can you explain to that thick prat of a boyfriend of yours, any minute now that flying bastard's gonna come back and fry *us*. We gotta *go*, for Chrissakes.'

'All right, then,' Snorkfrod replied, 'you go.'

'Huh?' Slitgrind's face was a study in bewilderment. Imagine what God would look like if he opened his post one morning and found he'd got a tax rebate. As bewildered as that.

'Go. Bugger off. Sling your hook. We'll see you back at the factory.'

'But . . .' Slitgrind's expression added terror to its repertoire. 'But we've got to stick together,' he whimpered. 'We can't go wandering about on our own, it's not *safe*.'

Snorkfrod gave him a stare you could have broken up and put in whisky. 'Slitgrind, you nerk,' she said, 'you're a demon from sodding Hell. You're twenty million years old. I think it's probably time you learned to cross the road on your own.'

'We aren't splitting up.' Chardonay had spoken with – well, virtually with authority. Not a large-scale authority – something like the English Tourist Board – but enough to get him his colleagues' attention. 'We've got work to do. Come on.'

He stood up, knees wobbly and calflike, head erect, and started to walk towards the van. The others had to trot to catch up with him.

'Where're we going, Chief?' Prodsnap asked, puffing.

Chief, noted Chardonay's subconscious. 'To find the dragon,' he replied. 'And kill it.'

Three demons stopped dead in their tracks. A fourth used the delay to catch up – it's always hard to run in high heels, even when they're an integral part of your foot.

'Are you crazy?'

'No,' Chardonay replied. 'I'm bruised, lost and very frightened. But it's our duty. We're peace officers, with a responsibility to maintain the Divine Order. That dragon has just killed Saint George, it's against all the rules. It's got to be sorted out. And,' he went on, swallowing, 'since it's us here on the spot, we've got to do it. Is that clear?'

'Stone me,' Prodsnap muttered. 'He's serious.'

'I'm with you all the way,' sighed Snorkfrod, passionately. 'And I want you to know, I think that's the most moving thing I've ever heard.'

'Thank you,' Chardonay replied. 'That means a great deal to me. How about the rest of you lads?'

Prodsnap, Slitgrind and Holdall exchanged glances.

'We're right behind you, Chief.'

'Count me in.'

'You can depend on us.'

For a moment, Chardonay was lost for words. He glowed and seemed to grow an extra inch or two. 'Thanks, guys,' he said softly. 'Right, here goes.'

He punched his left palm with right fist, turned and headed off towards the van, Snorkfrod's arm through his. The other three fell in behind them.

'Men.' Chardonay settled himself in the driver's seat, put on his seat-belt and took off the handbrake. 'I just want you to know, whatever happens from hereon in . . .'

Words failed him, not because of any sudden access of emotion, but because at that moment the back-seat passengers clobbered him and Snorkfrod silly with the tyre iron.

Not even for old times' sake?

The dragon shook his head. 'No way, Nosher,' he replied. 'Look, I really am grateful to you, saving my life and all that, but I've had enough. I've done what I came to do and now I'm off.'

Just ten minutes of your time to vaporise a few trifling demons, Fred. For a pal.

'No. Think about it, Nosher. I've got my whole life in front of me. I can go where I like, do what I want. Last thing I need is Hell putting a price on my head for snuffing five of their people. I'm more conspicuous than Salman Rushdie, Nosher. Longer. Harder to conceal. It'd be a confounded nuisance and I can do without it.'

I can take care of that. I can give you a whole new identity.

The dragon laughed. 'Sure you can, Nosh,' he replied. 'I mean, twentieth-century Earth is positively teeming with dragons, I'd have no trouble whatsoever blending in with the crowd. Get real, pal. I'm out of here.'

Fred. The letters on the screen grew dim, flickery, as if to suggest deep and sincere regret. *If you walk out on me – well, around your neck be it.*

The dragon froze. 'You bastard.'

Blown to smithereens, Fred, whatever a smithereen is. Walk out on me and I'll find out. Shame you won't be there to share the knowledge with me.

Chubby, who'd been silent, nodded sagely. 'Besides,' he added, 'how'd they know it was you? I've been making enquiries. As far as Hell Central's concerned, those five idiots are with a coachload of other idiots over in Nashville, Tennessee. Nobody knows they're here. When they don't come back, I expect Hell will assume they've defected to the other side, something like that.'

'Defect?'

Actually, I think Chubby's a bit out of touch with recent developments. He's still got a Cold War mentality, which is thoroughly out of date these days. Let's say desert, shall we, rather than defect? They'd buy that, I'm sure.

The dragon growled ominously. 'You're bastards, both of you,' he said. 'All you care about is your stinking profits.'

Chubby clicked his tongue. 'Why is it,' he demanded, 'that people are always so rude about profits?'

Never honoured in their own country.

'Free enterprise,' Chubby went on, 'is the life blood of commerce.'

'Maybe,' the dragon snarled. 'But I'd rather not have their free enterprise on my paws, if it's all the same to you.'

I've just accessed my database and it says a smithereen is a small fragment or particle, usually the result of a catastrophic explosion. I assume it knows what it's talking about, but there's only one way to be absolutely certain.

'You'd do it, wouldn't you?'

With infinite regret but negligible hesitation, yes.

The dragon sighed. His eyes, as he glowered at the screen, were case-hardened with contempt. 'You know something, Nosher?' he said. 'You're evil.'

You reckon? Sending you out to do battle with the forces of darkness and you say I'm evil?

'I do.'

The screen flickered, by way of a dry chuckle.

Evil schmevil, old pal. Go out there and fry some fiends.

With an effort, Mike stopped screaming and pulled himself together.

It took some doing. Sixty per cent of him was slowly drifting away through space. Forty per cent of him was slipping unobtrusively into the future. It was like trying to impose your will on seven over-excited Highland terriers.

Heel, Mike commanded. And toe. And leg. And arm. Oh Christ, and head too.

You know the bit in all the films where they've just found the suitcase full of the money from the big heist; and suddenly the wind gets up and the air is full of flying banknotes; and first they all caper frantically around trying to catch them; and then they realise it's hopeless and collapse laughing to the ground while the credits roll all round them? Well, it was rather like that, hold the laughter. All Mike could manage (particularly since his face was now thirty yards and four hours away from the majority of him) was a wry grin.

The hell with it. Why bother? He was just about to relax and finally let go when . . .

Oh my god, a statue! Where the hell did that come from?

Look gift horses in the mouth if you must, but when confronted with a wholly unlooked-for, vacant, unlocked, fully furnished statue just when you're on the point of dissolving into space and time, you look for the little hatch between the shoulder-blades, you grab as much of you as you can reach, and you jump.

'And this,' said the Council spokesman, 'is where the fountain was to have gone, and here's where we would have put the floral clock, and here's where we'd planned to have the big brass plaque recording the munificent generosity of Kawaguchiya Integrated Circuits (UK) plc.' He paused and drew breath. 'And here . . .'

Five pairs of impassive Japanese eyes followed his pointing finger and fixed on another part of the bomb crater.

'Here,' continued the spokesman, 'we intended to have the centrepiece of Kawaguchiya Integrated Circuits Plaza, the staggeringly impressive statue of Saint George and the Dragon, by possibly the world's most talented living sculptress, Bianca Wilson.' Time for another breath; a deep one. 'Instead . . .'

He stopped. He blinked, rubbed his eyes. It was still there. 'Excuse me,' he said.

He touched it; solid. As a rock, you might say. Just to be sure, he kicked it, hard. *Ouch*!

'Instead,' he went on, 'we have no dragon, but now we do seem to have got St George back. About three seconds ago, to be precise. Don't ask me how we did it, but we did it.' He sat down and removed his shoe. 'Clever old us, eh?'

If the KIC people had noticed anything odd, they didn't let it show. Two of the younger ones whispered to the grey-haired type who seemed to be the delegation leader. He nodded and whispered something back.

'Very big statue,' he said.

'It is, yes,' the spokesman agreed. 'And, um, solid. Made of solid stone, all the way through. Yessiree, this baby's here to stay.'

(*Because, at the moment when George entered the newly completed statue of Mike, he broke the morphological link with his own former statue. No longer caught up in George's anomalous timestream, it went back to where it had come from; once again, just a statue, lifeless and inert.*)

The Council spokesman pulled his shoe back on, stood up and assumed a didactic pose. 'You will observe,' he said, 'the remarkable use of line which Ms Wilson has managed to achieve; the dynamic tension implicit in the composition of this masterpiece; the impression she conveys of desperate, headlong motion frozen for all time in the . . .'

Slowly, as if it had the cramp in its left leg, the statue got up, winced, swore and hobbled away down Colmore Row.

Yes, Bianca said, she'd accept the charges. 'Mike, where the hell . . .?'

'In a call-box just off Pinfold Street,' Mike replied. 'Can you come and pick me up? Only . . .'

'Well?'

Mike glanced over his shoulder. Because it was only an ordinary-sized call-box, he was on his knees with his nose pressed right up against the glass. People outside were staring.

'Just hurry, will you? And bring a lorry.'

He put the receiver down, breathed out hard. Someone was hammering on the door. Edging round carefully, he opened it and scowled.

'What's the matter, you daft bitch?' he growled. 'You never seen a statue before?'

By coincidence, at precisely that moment another lorryload of statuary chugged round junction four of the M42, taking the exit signposted to Birmingham. In the back were eight Berninis, three Donatellos, three Cellinis, a Canova and the

Giambologna *Mercury*. Michaelangelo's *David* sat next to a harassed-looking man in a black jump-suit in the cab.

'Sorry,' David admitted. 'I've never been much good at map-reading. Well,' he amended, 'this is actually my first attempt, but if I'd ever tried it before, I don't suppose I'd have made much of a fist of it then, either.'

Kurt muttered something under his breath. 'We're on the right road now, huh?'

'I think so. We want to go to the big sprawly grey blob, looks like a squashed spider, name of Birmingham, right?'

Kurt swore and hauled on the wheel. 'Okay,' he said, 'I've turned right. Now what?'

David bit his lip. 'Sorry,' he said, 'I meant right as in okay, not right the opposite of left. I think actually we wanted to go straight on.'

'Oh, for Christ's sake!' Kurt had strong views on the subject of suffering fools gladly. It made him glad if fools suffered a *lot*. 'Now we've gotta go miles out of our way. Concentrate, dammit.'

'Sorry.'

They drove on in silence for a while; Kurt sulking, David feeling guilty. When they were safely back on the right road, however, David turned to Kurt and said, 'Excuse me.'

'Well?'

Difficult to find a tactful way of putting this. 'What are we, like, doing here exactly?' David asked.

'The job,' Kurt replied. 'You realise they drive on the wrong side of the road in this faggot-ridden country?'

'What job?'

'*The* job. Deliver the statues, snuff the dragon, and then we're outta here. Not the weirdest thing I ever got hired to do,' Kurt added. 'In the top twenty, maybe even the top ten, but not in at number one. Still, it ain't exactly difficult. And it sure beats what I was doing before.'

'Which was?'

'Being dead.'

'Ah. Right.'

Kurt frowned, detecting a certain lack of awe in his companion. After all, not many people come back from the dead. Even fewer come back from the dead and walk straight into a plum job in their chosen profession, as though they'd never been away. Jesus Christ and maybe Sherlock Holmes – Kurt, who'd been around and heard a thing or two, knew all that stuff about surviving the Reichenbach Falls was just a tax dodge – but that was it.

'You ever been dead, son?' he queried.

'Not to the best of my knowledge.'

'Give it a miss,' Kurt advised. 'Don't get you anywhere.'

'Who're we working for, then?'

Kurt's spasm of impatience nearly caused an accident. 'You don't ask questions like that in this man's business, boy. You can come to harm asking questions like that.'

True, David reflected, we nearly did. We only missed that car by an inch or so. 'Sorry,' he said. 'But I'm really curious.' He paused; a thought had struck him. 'You do know, don't you?'

Kurt avoided his eye. 'Of course I frigging well know,' he snapped.

'And?'

'Read the damn map.'

They drove on in silence, if you could call it that, because Kurt was convinced that the sound of cogs turning in his brain was probably audible in Connecticut.

It had been a good question.

Just who *was* he working for?

George stopped running, ducked down behind a dustbin and froze.

Debits and credits time. On the negative side, he was lost, confused, penniless, naked, in an unfamiliar and distinctly economy-class body and on the run from a livid sculptress and a fire-breathing dragon. On the positive side, he was alive. He closed his eyes and allowed himself to relax. On balance, he was further up the ladders than down the snakes, by something in the order of a thousand per cent.

About four minutes later, he solved the clothing and money problem by jumping out on an unsuspecting passer-by, knocking him silly with a broken bicycle pump he'd found in the dustbin and helping himself to his victim's personal effects. Fortunately, he and his unwitting bene-factor were more or less the same size, although personally George wouldn't have chosen a lilac shirt to go with a navy blue jacket. But there; muggers can't be choosers. The shoes hurt his feet, but not nearly as much as the pavement would have done.

An appropriate moment, he told himself as he sauntered down the alleyway into New Street, to draw up an agenda. It went as follows:

1. Find and scrag that bastard dragon.
2. Easier soliloquised than done, of course. He still wasn't a hundred per cent at home in this century and maybe he was missing a trick somewhere, but he had arrived at the conclusion that the old Wormex^{TM}-in-the-water-supply tactic was going to be out of place here; although, to judge by the stuff he'd had in his whisky, a stiff dose of dragon powder could only improve the taste.

The basic principle, however, was surely a good one: get the dragon to drink something that'd disagree with him. The recipe ought not to be a problem. The ancient proverb stuck in his mind: you can lead a dragon to water, but you can't make him drink. How did you go about conning a dragon into slaking its thirst from your specially prepared homebrew; leave a big bowl with DRAGON on the side lying about in a public place? Unlikely to work.

Hold that thought. Since he was now wearing a whole new body, the dragon wouldn't know who he was. All he had to do, given the element of disguise, was walk up to the dragon in a bar and offer to buy him a drink.

The ugly snout of practicality intruded into his plans. As far as he could tell, this was a liberal century, uninhibited, where anything went (so long as you weren't fussy about it coming back again afterwards), but even so, you'd probably be pushing your luck sidling up to strangers in bars asking if they were a dragon and wanted a drink. On the right lines, he decided, but could do with a little bit more fine tuning.

Still, at least he had a plan now, which was something. Next step, food. It had been a long time since breakfast and the body that had eaten the breakfast was now cinders and ashes. He pulled out his victim's wallet and opened it up; a nice thick wad of notes reassured him. Grinning, he crossed New Street, heading for the big McDonald's.

'Wotcher, Mike.' A hand clumped down between his shoulder-blades, momentarily depriving him of breath. Before his instincts – well, they weren't his instincts of course – had time to send the kill message down to his arms, he cancelled the instruction. Whoever this body was, it had friends. And dragon hunters need friends, the way fisher-men need maggots.

'Hello yourself,' he replied, and turned to face whoever it was. 'How's things?'

'Not so bad.' His friend, a tall, gangling bloke with round bottle-end glasses, was giving him a funny look. 'Heard you were, um, dead,' he said. 'Like, blown up or something.'

'Not as such,' George replied. 'What you probably heard was that I was slowly dying of hunger and thirst, which is true. Of course, you can help me do something about that.'

The stranger laughed. What had he called him? Mike? Good old Mike, always cracking jokes.

'Good idea,' the stranger went on. 'We could have a couple of pints, then maybe go for a Balti. Suit you?'

'Sure.' Mike's friend started to walk, presumably knew where he was going. George fell into step beside him.

'Haven't seen you about for a while now,' said Mike's friend.

'You know how it is.'

'So what's it like, working with the great Bianca Wilson?'

George put two and two together, and got a mental picture of a fast-swinging lump hammer narrowly shaving his ear. 'Eventful,' he said. 'Quite an education, in fact.'

'I'll bet.'

In front of them, a pub doorway. Oh good, we seem to be going in here. I could just do with a—

He stopped dead. Ah *shit*!

Sitting at the bar, staring at him, were Bianca and—

'Christ, Bianca, there's my body. Hey, grab him, someone. That's the bastard who stole my body!'

It's mortifying enough to be loudly accused of theft in a public place. To be accused by *yourself* ... George, as always in such circumstances, gave serious thought to running away, but his erstwhile friend was standing between him and the door, giving him ever such a funny look.

'You bastard!' Bianca was yelling at him too. 'Don't just stand there, Peter, grab the swine!'

Who the hell was Peter? Oh, him. The treacherous bugger who'd brought him here. Stronger than he looks, our Peter. George's arm was now twisted up behind his back and there was very little he could do about it. Behind the bar, an unsympathetic-looking girl was muttering something about ringing the police.

'Let go of me,' he grunted. 'I'm a saint.'

Peter tightened his grip. 'You're a *what*?'

'A saint. You deaf or something?'

'That's right,' said Bianca, grimly, 'he is. If he tries to make a run for it, break his sodding arm.'

'Hang on,' Peter was saying. 'If he really is a saint—'

'That does it,' said the barmaid. She picked up the phone and started pressing buttons.

George struggled, painfully. 'You realise this is blasphemy,' he gasped – breath is at a premium when you're being half-nelsoned over a bar. 'You'll fry in Hell for this!'

'You *bastard*!' His body – Saint George's body – had a hand round his, Mike's, windpipe. 'Give me back my body *now*, or I'll bloody well throttle you. It.' The significance of his own words struck him and he relaxed his hold slightly. 'Here, Bee, is there any way of getting him out of it?'

'We could try death,' Bianca replied icily. 'Seems to work okay.'

The other occupants of the pub, though interested, seemed to regard saint-bashing as primarily a spectator sport. Wagers were being exchanged, theories aired. The barmaid had got through to the police and was giving what George felt was a rather one-sided account of the proceedings. It was time, he reflected, for a brilliant idea.

Available options; not an inspiring selection. Be mutilated by Peter, strangled by – who *was* that guy? Mike, presumably, whoever the hell he was, surgically dissected by the snotty sculptress or arrested by the cops. None of them, George admitted, felt intuitively right.

'Help,' he croaked.

The prayers of saints seldom go unheard. Just as Mike was saying that maybe Bianca's suggestion had something going for it, and the distant sirens were coming closer, there was a refreshing sound of splintering glass, the thump of an unconscious body hitting the deck and a familiar voice at his side.

Father Kelly. And about bloody time, too.

'Of course he's a friggin' saint,' the priest was yelling. 'Can't ye see his friggin' halo, ye dumb bastards?'

'Keep out of this, vicar,' Mike said angrily. Fortunately, Father Kelly took no notice, or perhaps he was just enraged at being confused with an Anglican. More broken glass noises, Father Kelly proving he knew the uses of empty Guinness bottles. He'd apparently used one on Peter, because George could now move his arms. He straightened up, to see Bianca swinging a bar stool at him. Fortunately, he had just enough time to thrust Father Kelly into the path of the blow – loud thunk, priest drops like stone, never mind. Leaving Bianca holding a broken stool and looking bemused, he jumped nimbly over the dormant Peter, shoved open the door, kicked an advancing copper squarely in the nuts and legged it.

God, he couldn't help thinking, looks after his own.

CHAPTER FOURTEEN

'It's not on the map,' Slitgrind protested.

The van stood on the hard shoulder of the M6. In the front, Prodsnap and Slitgrind were poring over the vintage road atlas they'd found in the glove compartment.

'There it is, look,' said Prodsnap, pointing.

'No, you fool, that's Hull.'

'Maybe that's just lousy spelling.'

Slitgrind closed the atlas with a snap. 'Stands to reason,' he said. 'They don't put it on mortal maps, 'cos otherwise we'd have hundreds of bloody tourists blocking up the front drive all the time.'

It occurred to Prodsnap that maybe his colleague was being a trifle alarmist, but he didn't say anything. It was true, Hell wasn't on the map. He tried hard to remember the route the coach-driver had taken, but it had all been homogeneous motorway, with no landmarks whatsoever.

'We'll have to ask someone, then,' he said.

Slitgrind scowled. 'Don't be thick,' he replied.

'Someone who knows, obviously,' Prodsnap said. 'Shouldn't be too hard.'

'But ...' Slitgrind was about to protest, but the penny dropped. 'Do we have to?' he objected. 'Those people always give me the shivers.'

'Me too.' Prodsnap suited the action to the word. 'But they'll know the way and we don't. Looks like we don't have much choice.'

His colleague grimaced, acknowledging the logic. 'Well,' he sighed, 's'pose they're on our side. In a way.'

'Better the colleague you know, huh?'

Slitgrind shrugged and turned the ignition key.

'Give me the deep blue sea any time,' he muttered, and indicated right.

'I conjure you by Asmoday and Beelzebub, Sytray and Satan, eloi, elohim and Miss Frobisher, do please be careful, you nearly made me spill the Black Host ...'

Barbed whips of wind flicked cruelly through the slighted walls of the ruins of Castle Roche. The moon had long since hidden her face behind the clouds and the only light was the livid orange glow from the foul-smelling fire. In the shattered keep of the castle, five white-clad figures, hooded and barefoot, huddled inside the arbitrary confines of a chalked ring. Around them lay the horrible impedimenta of the Black Rite: pantangles, tetragrammata, a sword, a mutilated Bible, a goat's skull, a frozen chicken, slowly defrosting ...

'Are you lot going to be much longer?' demanded a querulous voice from outside the ring of firelight. 'It's *freezing*.'

The Great Goat sighed petulantly. 'These things can't be rushed, Miss – ah—'

'Filkins,' hissed the Lesser Goat. 'Sonia Filkins. She's Mrs Brownlow's niece, from the Post Office.'

'Can't I at least have a blanket or something?' whined

Miss Filkins. 'I'm getting all goosepimply. And it's damp. Auntie Edie didn't say anything about sitting in the damp.'

The Lesser Goat simpered slightly. 'I'm sorry,' she whispered. 'But Brenda's babysitting up at the vicarage, and now Yvonne's started college . . .'

'I know,' sighed the Great Goat. 'Maybe next time, Miss Frobisher. I can't really see any point in continuing under these conditions.'

Mournful silence. The Lesser Goat started to pack away the horrible impedimenta.

'If you've finished with the chicken,' said Miss Filkins, 'do you mind if I take it on with me? There's a really nice recipe in my magazine for chicken.'

'Please,' grunted the Great Goat, carefully snuggling the skull in cotton wool. 'Help yourself. Such a pity to let good food go to—'

He fell silent. Although he was right next to the fire, his legs were suddenly icy cold. He didn't look round.

'Miss Frobisher,' he croaked.

'Yes, Dr Thwaites?'

'Perhaps Miss, ah, Filkins needn't put her clothes back on *quite* yet.'

The Lesser Goat looked at him. 'But I thought—'

'*Over there.*' He jerked his head in the direction of the shattered tower. 'Um, by Asmoday and Beelzebub, Sytray and—'

'Excuse me.'

Miss Frobisher let out a little scream. The thurifer hastily stubbed out his cigarette. The sword-bearer, who was half in and half out of his vestments, made a grab for his trousers. Old Mr Blakiston, the Black Verger, dozed peacefully on.

'Excuse me,' repeated Prodsnap. He was carrying an electric torch and wearing an old Barbour jacket he'd found on a scarecrow, for the night was cold; but the firelight dazzled vividly on his hooves and horns. 'We haven't missed it, have we, only we got a bit held up. Roadworks on the A34 just south of Chipping Norton.'

'*Please* can I put my clothes on now, Miss Frobisher? I'm going *blue*.'

The Great Goat winced. 'Please be *quiet*, Miss Filkins,' he snapped. 'Um, would you, ah, care to join us? Quick, Miss Frobisher, the chicken!'

'You said I could have it!'

Prodsnap shivered, despite his Barbour. 'Please,' he said, 'don't go to any trouble on our account. We had something at a Little Chef on the way. We really only wanted to ask—'

'Bludy ew,' squeaked the thurifer. 'Issa bleedin' *deviw*!'

The Great Goat closed his eyes, mortified. First thing in the morning there'd be a vacancy for the post of Black Thurifer, and never mind the fact that Barney Philpot was the only twenty-four-hour plumber in the district. 'Thurifer,' he commanded, 'be quiet. By Asmoday and . . .'

Slitgrind nudged his colleague in the small of the back. 'For Chrissakes, Prozza,' he hissed, 'let's get out of here. I'm *scared*. Ow! That was my shin, you clumsy—'

'We were wondering,' Prodsnap went on, raising his voice slightly, 'if you could help us out. You see, we're lost, and—'

'Lost?' The Great Goat peered at him through thick-lensed bifocals. 'You mean, you fell with Lucifer, Son of the Morning, wantonly preferring the path of damnation to the—'

'Missed the bus,' said Slitgrind. 'Got left behind. I think they did it on purpose,' he added resentfully. 'Someone's going to cop it when I get home.'

The Great Goat's mouth was hanging open, like a broken gate. 'Bus,' he repeated.

'Outing,' said Prodsnap. 'To Nashville. And now we're having to make our own way home, and it's not actually shown on the map, so we were wondering if—'

'Hey.' The Great Goat felt a tug on his sleeve. 'These two,' the sword-bearer was muttering. 'They for real?'

'Of course they are, you foolish man!' hissed the Great Goat. 'Look at the horns! The tails!'

The sword-bearer shrugged. 'All right,' he said. 'Not what I expected, though.'

'Not what you …!'

'Bit of a disappointment, really.'

'How *dare* you! These are . . .'

He hesitated. Unshakable his faith might be, but there was something about the way that one devil was trying to hide behind the other that did tend to sap the forbidden glamour. 'Do excuse me asking,' he said apologetically, 'but do you gentlemen have any form of identification? Only, you see—'

'It's that Great Horwood lot,' muttered the sword-bearer, 'dressed up in a lot of fancy dress. Here, is that you, Jim Partridge? 'Cos if it is, you can forget having your car back by the weekend.'

Prodsnap blushed green. 'Sorry,' he said. 'We don't actually have cards or anything. Usually,' he added, with his remaining shreds of dignity, 'we don't feel the need.'

'Prozza—'

'Shuttup, Slitgrind. I'd have thought,' Prodsnap soldiered on, 'the horns and the hooves and all that, they do rather speak for themselves.'

'Cardboard and spirit gum,' sneered the sword-bearer. 'Do us a favour, Jim. You've had your joke, now bugger off.'

'Prozza,' Slitgrind hissed; Prodsnap noticed that he was grimly averting his eyes from something. 'There's a bint over there with *no bloody clothes on*!'

Moments like these, Prodsnap reflected, made you realise that the Chardonays of this world do have their uses. Chardonay, of course, was nice and snug in the van, tied up and gagged, likewise the demon Snorkfrod. Now *she'd* know how to handle a situation like this, no trouble at all.

'Quiet!' he snapped, then turned to the Great Goat, who was peering disconcertingly at him over the rims of his glasses. 'Um.' He racked his brains. Something convincing; a display of black magic, perhaps, an anti-miracle. Trouble was, he didn't know any. Not much call for black magic when you're a clerk in the wages office.

The nasty, suspicious one was leering at him. He decided to improvise.

'Maybe this'll convince you,' he said, and threw something on the fire. There was a whoosh of flame and a loud bang. The sword-bearer leapt out of his skin. Old Mr Blakiston woke up, mumbled something about coffee and went back to sleep again. It had worked.

'What the Shopfloor was that?' hissed Slitgrind.

'Cigarette lighter,' Prodsnap hissed back. 'Now then, my, er, good man,' he went on, trying to look demonic, 'if you could just, I mean, I command you to give us directions. Now,' he added, and snarled. He inhaled a whiff of Black Incense and sneezed.

The Great Goat bowed humbly, felt in his inside pocket and produced an envelope and a biro. 'Now, if you go back the way you came as far as the Bunch of Grapes . . .'

Eventually, George stopped running.

Only when he was absolutely convinced nobody was following him, of course. One long life and one short (so far) but highly eventful one had taught him the value of running away as a solution to virtually all problems. The way he saw it, if you can run, why bother to hide anyway?

Absolutely no idea where he was. A road sign said Hockley Street, but even if it was telling the truth (George had, on a number of occasions, prolonged his first life by not taking local authorities' words for it – 'Sure, that dragon's dead; ain't that so, Mr Mayor?' and 'Yup, we fixed that bridge last October' were notable examples) it didn't actually get him very far. Chances were, Hockley Street was every bit as lost as he was.

But it did contain a pub and all that running had given George a thirst you could rub down paintwork with. With a sigh of satisfaction that would have convinced you he'd just created the world ahead of schedule and under budget, he leaned on the door of the public bar and flowed in . . .

Marvellous thing, the human brain. In its vast, multi-megabyte subconscious memory, it stores everything – *everything* – seen, heard, glimpsed, semi-noticed, unconsciously observed. If the librarians of the brain could get stuff up from the stacks just a little bit quicker, we'd all be supermen, and the planet would probably have been a radioactive shell back in 1906.

The Dun Cow, Hockley Street. Been there before. Recently . . .

As he walked in, Bianca was just explaining to the police officer (not the one who was still curled up in a ball, moaning softly; a different one) that the man who she'd tried to maim with a stool was guilty of art theft, causing explosions, attempted murder and innumerable counts of genocide. She'd never seen the priest before in her life, she could think of no reason why he should want to clobber two of her friends with beer bottles, and she was really sorry about his teeth, honest to God just an accident, probably the tooth fairy was on the phone right now to leading merchant bankers trying to raise some venture capital to finance such a major shipment . . .

Been there. Wrecked that. Got the summons.

George turned, smoothly and swiftly, but not swiftly enough. A hand settled on his shoulder like a speeded-up glacier. Someone enquired of him where he thought he was going, then sidestepped his vicious elbow jab, kicked his knees from under him and clocked him one with a Lowenbrau ashtray.

'It's him!' Bianca shrieked, pointing. 'Let go my arm, I want to *kill* him!'

So, apparently, did the witnesses Mike and Peter; and George, who majored in cheating at the University of Life, saw a tiny sliver of a chance. They rushed at him, heavy policemen dragging along behind them like slipped anchors. He accordingly dived towards them, taking the direction his captor least expected. Grabbing hands missed him on all sides. He vaulted onto a table; from the table to the bar top; skidded along the bar like a glass of whisky in a Western; braked sharply; kicked the barmaid neatly in the eye as she lunged for his ankles; hopped down and legged it through the kitchens. As it says in the director's cut of the Sermon on the Mount: Blessed are those that fight dirty, for they shall be one jump ahead.

'Stop him!'

The cook, assuming that the fast-moving character who'd just burst into his kitchen was a fugitive from payment, upended a tray of chilli over his head, causing him to misnavigate and cannon into the dustbin. It was then just a matter of scooping up his feet, tucking them in after the rest of him, putting on the lid and sitting on it; job done. If cooks were generals, wars would last hours, not years.

'He's in here!' the cook shouted. 'And he owes for twelve portions of chilli.'

Inside a dustbin, nose full of potato peelings and the

nasty things people leave on their plates after they've finished eating, even someone as resourceful as George has to take an enforced rest. If he's wise, he'll put the time to good use, analysing his position, evaluating the merits of alternative strategies, trying at all costs not to breathe in.

They emptied the bin on the floor – the cook joined the arrest roster; obstructing the police, assault with a wet colander – and fished George out. A policeman knelt down, handcuffs at the ready.

'Hey, sarge!' he screamed. 'The bloke's on fire!'

If you're not used to them, halos can look remarkably like burning petrol, worn externally. There was yelling, milling about, wrenching of fire extinguishers off walls. Some fool set off the fire alarm, adding deafening noise to the feast of sensory input. George wriggled and struck out. In close combat, a discarded Fairy bottle covered in pan scrapings can be as effective as an Ingrams gun.

'Grab the bastard!' somebody yelled, but you might as well have shouted 'Fix the economy!' to a gaggle of politicians. All that happened was that the barmaid got knocked into the sink and one policeman scored a direct hit on another policeman with the first exuberant jet from the fire extinguisher. After that it was sheer Brownian motion, Gorbals-style.

Emerging from the scrum, George scrabbled across the floor, hauled himself up by the dishwasher and headed for the door. Like Napoleon's at Waterloo, it was a sound strategy undermined by treacherous conditions. He stood on a second-hand fried egg, skated three yards and collided with Bianca, pushing her into the remains of the Black Forest gâteau. As he looked about him, George saw he was surrounded.

The saw *never say die* didn't mean much to George. He frequently said *Die*, or more usually, *Die, you bastard!*, generally when standing over a fallen opponent. The principle behind it, however, was a dominant influence on his life. Without looking down he trawled the worktop, snatched up the first thing that came to hand, levelled it at his attackers and snapped 'Freeze!' Three quarters of a second later, they realised he was threatening them with a cheese-grater, but three quarters of a second was all he needed. There was a window. He jumped.

Glass was still landing all around him when he opened his eyes. Scrambling to his feet, he launched himself forwards, aware that the window frame was full of swearing policemen cutting their fingers. He had the feeling that if they caught up with him, there'd be major sacrilege committed. He ran.

The back yard wall of the pub was low enough to swarm over if you weren't fussy about trifles such as broken glass. George dropped down the other side, turned over his ankle, sprawled headlong and banged his head against a car door in the act of opening.

'Get in!'

George lifted his head. 'Sorry?'

'I said get in. Come on!'

He looked up to see a black Mercedes, back door ajar, on the rear seat a wry grin with a human being attached to its back. Close at hand, angry policemen had discovered the yard gate was locked.

'Who're you?' George asked.

'My name's Stevenson,' the grin replied. 'And you're George. Pull your finger out, old son.'

'But—'

Chubby Stevenson reached inside his jacket, produced a .45 Colt (like it says in the Book: *blessed are the Peacemakers*) and pointed it at George's head. 'Chop chop,' he said, 'there's a good lad.'

George realised that it would be discourteous to refuse and got in.

'Have they gone?'

'Yes, Dr Thwaites.'

'Good.' Wearily, the Great Goat picked up the Black Chalice, shook out the last dregs of cold tea and put it back in its straw-filled shoebox. Nobody had said anything, but they all knew that the handsome silver goblet was about to resume its career as the Swerford Golf Club President's Cup. Having your nightmare come true is the final disillusionment.

'Dr Thwaites.'

'Mmm?'

'About next Thursday.' Miss Frobisher's voice was heavy with the embarrassment of betrayal; the same tone of voice Judas Iscariot used when telling the Chief Priest he'd rather have cash, if it was all the same to him. 'I've just remembered it's the Red Cross whist drive, so I won't be able to make it after all. I do hope—'

'Not at all, Miss Frobisher, not at all.' The Great Goat sighed. 'As it happens, I think I'm busy that day, too. What about you, Barney?'

The thurifer was about to explain that coincidentally, he'd probably be working late next Thursday, when all five of them became aware of a richer darkness, as some great shape interposed itself between them and the fleeting moon.

'Go away!' snapped the Great Goat. 'Can't you see we're closed?'

They ducked. As non-verbal responses go, a fiery tsunami unleashed about three feet over one's head is remarkably eloquent.

'Won't keep you a tick,' said the dragon.

★

About Good and Evil.

Kurt twitched impatiently. Moral philosophy had never interested him much, having as much relevance to his profession as a pipe-cleaner to the Mersey tunnel; if he'd wanted a lecture on ethics, however, his first choice wouldn't have been a word processor.

'Hey,' he said, 'save it for the customers, will you? I delivered the goods, just pay me and I'll split.'

You also have a dragon to kill, don't forget.

Kurt made an exaggerated show of looking round. 'Nope,' he said at last, 'don't see any dragon in here, unless he's hiding in the drawer disguised as a pencil. Look, pal, you do your job and I'll do mine, okay?'

No. Look at me. This is relevant.

With a sigh, Kurt perched on the edge of the desk and folded his arms.

'Shoot,' he said.

With pleasure. Good and Evil, then. Define Good for me.

'Huh?' Kurt thought for a minute. 'Good what?'

Not good anything. Just Good.

Kurt's eyebrow lifted, Spock-like. 'Dunno,' he said. 'All depends on where you're at, I guess. Like,' he went on, 'it's a good shot if you fire it and hit me, but from where I'm standing there ain't much that's good about it.'

The screen filled with glowing green ticks. *Very good, Mr Lundqvist, you're way ahead of me. Nevertheless, I'll explain further.*

'Why?'

Indulge me. Good and Evil are, of course, two sides of the same coin. What's good for me is bad for you. One man's Mede is another man's Persian. The current of morality is more often alternating than direct. That, I imagine, is scarcely news as far as you're concerned. Am I right?

'More right than Franco, buster. What's this to do with—?'

Please don't interrupt. You've been hired to kill a dragon. Dragons are Evil, yes?

'Guess so.'

Saints, on the other hand, are Good. Agreed?

'Yeah.'

Wrong. It all depends on the individual concerned. And even then, it's still very much a question of subjective interpretation. Take Saint George, for example.

'Huh?'

Saint George. Noted dragon-slayer. Come on, you must have heard of him. A legend in your profession, surely.

Kurt nodded. 'In his day,' he replied absently. 'Lotta blood flowed under the bridge since then.'

Nevertheless. A killer, Kurt. Someone who destroyed other intelligent life forms for money.

'A professional.'

A saint. And not just any old saint, but the patron saint of peaceful, law-abiding, animal-loving Albion. You know why that is?

'Never gave it any thought,' Kurt replied honestly.

Three thousand a year patronage allowance, that's why. And because no other saint of adequate seniority was prepared to be associated with a cluster of wet, foggy islands on the very north-western edge of the known world. Nobody could believe it when he volunteered. It was like asking to be made Secretary of State for Northern Ireland.

Kurt shrugged. 'So?'

So, with George as its patron, this poxy little cluster of islands built an empire, the biggest ever. Top nation for a time, this poxy little cluster; bigger than France or Italy or Germany, owned half of Africa, half of Asia. Remember Agincourt, Kurt? God for Harry, England and Saint George?

'I missed that game. I was working. Saw the highlights, but—'

Not bad for the last place God made, under the patronage of a hired killer. And God was an Englishman in those days. Results count for something, wouldn't you say?

'Do me a favour,' Kurt protested. 'All that time, the sucker was dead.'

Doesn't matter. When you're a saint, it's not what you do that really matters, it's what you are. George was the dragon-slayer. He won the Big Fight. He inspired generations of Englishmen to go out and beat the crap out of all foreigners. Name me a European country England hasn't beaten in a war. France? Twice. Germany? Twice. Italy, Spain, Russia, Norway, Austria . . .

'Greece,' Kurt interrupted. 'Switzerland. Monaco . . .' He fell silent. 'Okay, point taken,' he continued, 'but so what? That don't prove nothing.'

Wrong. The good guys are always the winners, aren't they? I mean, the President doesn't get up on the rostrum at the Victory Parade and say to all the world, 'Okay, we admit it, we were in the wrong but fuck it, we won anyway.' Who's Good and who's Evil is decided by trial by combat; it's the only way. Or can you admit the possibility of a scenario where the good guys are all stomped on and the baddies are singing here-we-go, here-we-go, when the final credits are actually rolling? You can't, not without your brain getting squeezed out your ears.

'Get to the point,' Kurt grunted awkwardly.

Simple. England prevailed because she was in the right, because George killed the dragon. How or why he did it doesn't matter a cold chip. Agreed?

'If I agree, will you pay me the money you owe me?'

But all that's changed now. England's finished. She's a suburb of Europe, the USA's poor relation, got about twenty-five per cent of the international stature of the Philippines. You could saw Europe off at Calais and it'd be a month before anybody noticed. So what happened?

'I have this dreary feeling you're gonna tell me.'

The result must have been wrong, Kurt. There's got to have been a foul-up. The wrong guy must have killed the dragon. And that's why there has to be a rematch.

'Kurt shrugged. 'Okay,' he said. 'If I was the kind of weirdo who went along with that kinda crap, maybe I'd buy that too. But you want me to kill this goddamn dragon, so—'

After the fight, Kurt, after the fight. The dragon wastes George, you waste the dragon. The United States conclusively defeats the personification of Evil, and under the patronage of Saint Kurt proceeds to manifest its destiny. Everybody lives happily ever after. The screen filled with little wavy lines; cybernetic laughter. *That's why I've just arranged for George to be rescued. Can't very well go fighting dragons if he's doing three years for assault and battery.*

Kurt thought it over for a while.

'Once I've killed the dragon,' he asked, 'do I get paid?'

Of course.

Kurt nodded. 'Okay,' he said. 'That's my definition of a happy ending.'

You heard all that?

Chubby nodded to his laptop and smiled. 'You bet,' he said. 'I thought you handled that very, um, adequately.'

He'll do what he's told. After all, what else are people for?

'Indeed.'

Talking of which . . .

Chubby sighed. Whenever the blasted box of tricks went all parenthetical on him and started ending sentences with three dots, he knew he was in for something more than usually shitty. 'Hm?'

After he's dealt with the dragon, kill him.

CHAPTER FIFTEEN

'**W**ith respect.' Lin Kortright whitened his knuckles around the telephone, swivelled his chair, bit the end off a cigar and spat it into the ashtray. 'With respect,' he repeated, 'you guys are obviously experts in the recycled Time business, but you don't know the fight game from *nothing*. Otherwise . . .'

Traditionally, sudden explosions of devastating elemental power have to be heralded by fair warning. Civil wars and the deaths of princes, therefore, are announced by comets and portents. Cyclones and tempests are preceded by gathering clouds and torrential rain. And Lin Kortright says, 'With respect.'

And then something extremely peculiar happened.

Mr Kortright *listened*.

Which is a bit like opening your daily paper and seeing that because of hitherto undetected design faults God has just issued a recall notice on the human race. You don't expect it. Large chunks of the fabric of reality start to come away from the joists.

'Yeah,' he said, eventually. 'Yeah, you're right, we could

do that. Say, that's a pretty neat idea. Only wish I'd thought of that myself.'

No sooner had the words left his mouth than six lifeboatloads of rats lowered themselves over the side of The Universe As We Know It and started to row like buggery. For Lin Kortright to say, 'You're right' in a room containing no mirror was utterly, absolutely . . .

'Brilliant,' he added. 'Hey, man, I'm beginning to wonder if you need me in on this at all. Seems to me you got it all sewn up already.'

Distant thunder rumbled. Eagles towering in their pride of place beat a hasty retreat, while mousing owls exchanged evil glances, rubbed their talons together and said, 'Right, let's *get* the bastards.' The air crackled with static.

'No, really,' Mr Kortright went on, 'in the circumstances I couldn't possibly accept ten per cent. The most I'd feel justified in taking would be five, and even then . . .'

Normality flung a few things in a suitcase and emigrated.

To hype a big fight, you have to follow set procedures. First, you must find a few toothless old duffers for the contenders to massacre, by way of setting the scene. Then you book the chat-show appearances so that the Boys can glower at each other over the presenter's shoulder. Then you hire a hall and start printing tickets.

In this case, however, the rules were there to be broken. For a start, there could be no warm-up fights for fear of irreparable damage to the Earth's crust. No late-show appearances for the contestants; the whole point of finding George was to make sure he'd be safely out of the dragon's way until the bell went for the first round. As for the venue, that couldn't be rushed; it had to be the Gobi desert, or the whole fight was off. Above all, the fight couldn't be advertised in case the two contestants found out that a fight was being organised.

Nevertheless, it seemed unlikely they'd have any trouble getting rid of the tickets, seeing that on the same morning both Nostradamus and Mother Shipton called almost simultaneously to point out that they'd predicted the fight and booked seats four hundred years ago. That just left the venue; a bit like saying, *We've made the sandwiches and filled the thermos, that just leaves turning the water into wine, plenty of time to do that after we've been to the supermarket.*

Cue Lin Kortright . . .

Furtively, guiltily, five shadowy figures crept along the wire perimeter fence, wirecutters in hand.

They were about to commit burglary. That's theft, and a sin.

They were about to burgle the nuclear power station at Sellafield. That's just plain *stupid.*

One of the five demons was considerably more relaxed about the proceedings than his colleagues, it must be said. When Chardonay came round and Prodsnap explained to him that there'd been a mutiny and he was now talking to *Captain* Prodsnap, his abiding reaction had been amazed, delighted joy. No more decisions. No more responsibility to the other members of the team. No more getting the blame for such mistakes on his part as the weather, the alignment of the moon with Mercury or the battle of Salamis.

The other four weren't so cheerful.

'Quit snivelling,' Prodsnap muttered sharply. 'Nothing to be afraid of. Home from home. Only danger I can foresee is, you'll all like it so much you won't want to leave.'

His followers exchanged glances. The mood of the meeting was that if he'd just taken out a correspondence course in dynamic leadership techniques, he'd be justified in asking for his money back.

'Run through it again,' Slitgrind said. 'Go on, one more time.'

'I've explained five times already.'

'I wasn't listening.'

Prodsnap sighed. 'Okay,' he said, 'listen up, people.' He'd heard the expression somewhere – the extremely nasty part of Hell reserved for Europeans who try to play American football, probably – and guessed it might be worth a try. Right now, *anything* was worth trying. 'In order to get home we really need that uranium, right?'

'We're fairly straight on that bit,' interrupted Chardonay mildly. 'I think it's the actual burglary where we're all still a bit at sea.'

Wish you were, thought Prodsnap savagely. 'What's so hard to understand?' he replied, demonstrating his contempt for the minor problems that confronted them with an airy gesture. 'We cut the wire, smash down the doors, go in, help ourselves. The pink bloody panther could cope with that. Now then, Slitgrind, you've got the wirecutters. Snorkfrod, you're doing the big hammer stuff. Holdall, you're the smallest, you climb in through the window of the main office and nick the keys. Chardonay, you go into the fusion chamber and lift the actual stuff . . .'

'Wilco, boss.'

'Chardonay, what the Shopfloor are you doing?'

'Saluting, boss.'

'Are you taking the . . .?'

Chardonay sounded genuinely hurt. 'No, boss. I want you to know that whatever happens, I'll be in there giving it my best shot. Sir,' he added.

Prodsnap shuddered. 'After that, it's just a matter of running for it. If we get separated, we meet up back at the van. All right so far? Splendid. Slitgrind, the wire.'

Snip. Snip. The alarm went off.

'Oh.' Prodsnap's face fell like a drunken trapeze artiste. 'That's a pity. Um . . .'

'Sir.'

'Not now, please—'

'Sir,' Chardonay insisted, 'I'd love to volunteer to locate and disable the alarm. I'd also be thrilled to bits if you'd let me stalk and neutralise the guards who may be hurrying to the scene. If that's all right with you.'

Prodsnap could feel one of his headaches coming on. 'Yeah, right,' he said. 'Whatever you . . .'

But Chardonay wasn't there any more. He'd already scaled the fence – it was electrified, but as far as a demon's concerned the difference between an electric fence and an inert one is the same as between thermal and standard underwear – and was inside the compound. Inside his own personal cloud, he caught a fleeting glimpse of silver.

'Well,' he said, 'that seems to have got rid of him. Snorkfrod, you wouldn't mind just nipping after him, make sure he's okay? Right, see you later.'

As Snorkfrod's fishnetted leg vanished over the top of the fence, Prodsnap counted up to five and rubbed his claws together.

'Looks like we've got shot of both of them,' he said perkily. 'Come on, lads, we've got work to do.'

Slitgrind frowned. 'Where're we going?'

'Round the front gate, of course. Come on, guys, let's move it.'

The main gates of the compound were manned by three large men and two Rottweilers. The dogs were no trouble – in Hell, they'd have been relegated to tartan-collar-and-knitted-jacket status. The guards would probably take some finessing.

'Excuse me.'

The guard's neck swivelled. 'Halt!' he snapped. 'Who goes . . .?'

'Excuse me,' repeated the voice from the darkness. 'I'm

coming towards you. Don't do anything hasty, I just want a quick word.'

Prodsnap advanced, smiling. As he stood under the floodlights, the guard made a funny noise in the back of his throat and started to edge away.

'Evening,' Prodsnap went on. 'You can see me all right, then?'

'What the fuck . . .?'

Prodsnap nodded. 'I know,' he said. 'No oil painting, huh? Bit on the weird side, too.'

Just sufficient motor function control remained in the guard's body to enable him to nod. Prodsnap extended a hand, but the guard didn't respond.

'I'll ask you to imagine,' Prodsnap was saying, 'what you're going to tell your sergeant when you report this incident. Think about it.'

The guard was already thinking.

'The way I see it,' Prodsnap said, 'I can picture you tapping on the office door. "Well?" says Sarge. "Sarge," you say, "the compound's overrun with horrible-looking devils."' Prodsnap paused for effect. 'Not much good for a bloke's career, is it, getting a reputation for seeing things? Now we both know you're not imagining this, but—'

'Pass, friend.'

That, however, was about as far as Prodsnap's plan took him. Somehow he'd imagined that once he was inside the wire, finding the uranium would present no great problem. He didn't know what he expected – a glow? Fingerposts saying *This Way To The Nukes* – but he'd expected something. What he found was a settlement, certainly no larger than Manchester.

'Bugger,' he said.

Because the sirens were still yowling themselves silly, nobody much was about; there were a few harassed-looking types running around, jumping in and out of vehicles and shouting orders into walkie-talkies, others sedately walking, ticking things off on clipboards. Some men in overalls were creosoting windowframes. Four men in suits were eating sandwiches out of tupperware lunch-boxes. No uranium on display anywhere.

Oh well, only one way to find out. 'Excuse me.'

A tall, thin girl, big shoulder-pads, wearing what was either a skirt or a belt (impossible to say which), turned her head, double-took and said, 'Eeek!' Prodsnap advanced a step, wisely decided against smiling, and instead said, 'Hi.'

'Um. Hi.'

'Wonder if you could help us,' Prodsnap went on. 'We're looking for the, um, core. Do you happen to know where . . .?'

The girl backed away, her eyes big as melons. 'The core,' she repeated.

'That's right.' Prodsnap let his mind freewheel. 'We're the inspectors. You saw the notice, presumably?'

'I don't think I . . . Inspectors?'

Prodsnap nodded. 'You don't think we were *born* like this, do you?' he said, in a tone of voice that suggested that any further references to appearance would constitute gawping at the misfortunes of the disabled. Good ploy; a microsecond later, you could have sworn the girl hadn't noticed anything at all out of the ordinary in their appearance. 'Anyway,' Prodsnap went on, 'there was supposed to be someone here to meet us, but I think there may have been a bit of a mix-up . . .'

'Actually,' the girl said, 'I only work in Accounts, I don't actually know here they keep the, er . . .'

Prodsnap shrugged. 'Never mind,' he said, 'thanks anyway. There isn't a map or anything, is there?'

The girl thought for a moment. 'Well,' she said, 'you

could always try the Visitors' Centre, I suppose. You know, where they have all the tourist stuff. It's just over there, by the gift shop.'

It was Holdall's idea to steal a van. The first one that came to hand was a mobile canteen, with tea-urns, film-wrapped sandwiches, KitKats and packets of crisps. Slit-grind parked it outside the Visitors' Centre with the engine running while Prodsnap went in. He'd found an overcoat and a cloth cap in the back of the van; it was like putting an Elastoplast on a severed limb, but it was the best he could do.

'Excuse me . . .'

'Eeek!'

Suddenly, Prodsnap felt very weary. His mind went blank. All he could think of was the direct approach. Only the one woman behind the desk. He cleared his throat.

'Yes,' he said, 'you're right. I'm a fiend from Hell. Actually, my name's Prodsnap, and although I do live in Hell I'm really only a wages clerk, and right now I'm on holiday, off duty. Have you got a problem with any of that?'

'N-no.' The woman seemed to be frozen rigid. Had she pressed a hidden buzzer or panic button? Well, only time would tell on that one. 'How can I h-help you?'

'A map of the complex, please. Is there a guided tour, anything like that?'

The woman looked at him. Hadn't, she enquired, the company who organised his tour dealt with all that? She produced a roster. Which group did he say he was with, exactly?

Oh, the Shopfloor with it. 'Listen, love,' Prodsnap growled. 'The purpose of our visit isn't exclusively tour-ism.'

'No?'

Prodsnap shook his head. 'Actually,' he said, 'it's theft.

Tell me where the uranium is and everything'll be just—'

'*EEEEK*!' More bloody alarms, sirens, the works. Paranoid, the lot of them. Just happen to mention you wanted to swipe their uranium and the whole place goes apeshit.

'Thank you,' Prodsnap said, 'you've been most helpful.' He was about to run when an idea struck him. He slowed down, strolled nonchalantly outside and leaned up against the side of the van, trying to look like a hideous mutant Maurice Chevalier.

'For Christ's sake,' Slitgrind hissed, 'what do you think you're doing? Can't you hear the . . .?'

Prodsnap nodded. 'Any second now,' he replied, 'security'll turn up. They're bound to know where the core is. We'll ask them.'

'But—'

'Who do you reckon's likely to be more scared? Us of them, or them of us?'

Sure enough, security arrived; about fifty of them, armed to the teeth and looking distinctly apprehensive. To counter all their weaponry, Prodsnap had a smile, which he'd been able to practise once or twice in the van's wing-mirror while he was waiting. He ambled up to the fiercest-looking bloke he could see, said 'May I?', took his gun and ate it.

'My name's Prodsnap,' he said. He waved his talon. 'And this is Slitgrind, and this is Holdall. We're from Hell. Could you take us to where the uranium's stored, please? Sorry to bounce you like this, but we are in rather a hurry.'

'Fire!'

Prodsnap closed his eyes. No point expecting to see edited highlights of his past life because there wasn't time. Idly he wondered whether what was about to happen to him would be death or just some kind of extremely rapid transdimensional lift.

Nothing happened. A thousandth of a second became a

hundredth, a hundredth became a tenth. That's the bummer with long-distance travel, he reflected, all this standing about waiting.

He opened his eyes just as the gunfire started. About time too, he muttered to himself, then he realised that nobody was shooting at him.

They were shooting upwards, at the dragon.

By the time Mike and Bianca got out of the police station it was lunchtime. Since there was nothing else they could usefully do, they decided to go for a curry.

'On balance,' Mike said over the pappadoms, 'I can't say I'm all that bothered. Never liked the old body much, after all. I'm not exactly crazy about this one, but a change is as good as a rest. Could be a whole lot worse, after all.'

Bianca nodded. 'Glad you see it that way,' she replied. 'Wish they'd hurry up, I'm starving.'

'You can have the last pappadom, if you like.'

'Thanks, I will.' She did. 'What with one thing and another,' she went on, 'I can't remember the last time I had a proper meal. Plays hell with your metabolism, all this meddling in the supernatural.'

Mike shrugged. 'I'm all right,' he replied. 'Saint George must have had something to eat quite recently. I know I only met him briefly, and under peculiar circumstances at that, but I can well believe he wouldn't be the sort to neglect his carbohydrates.'

'Me too.' Bianca dipped the last fragment in the mango chutney. 'Does it feel odd?' she asked. Mike nodded.

'A bit,' he replied. 'The arms are a bit short and the waistband's on the large side. Still, like my mum used to say when I was a kid, I expect I'll grow into it.'

'Can't really say it suits you. Mind you, neither did the old one.'

'That's me all over. Leading fashions, not following them. You'll see. In six months' time, everybody'll be trying to look like this.'

'I knew a girl once who had her nose done. You know, cosmetic surgery. Had a crisis of identity about it, so she said. Mind you, if I'd forked out ten thousand quid to be made to look like a parrot, I'd probably be asking myself all sorts of difficult questions.'

The food arrived. 'Now there's a thought,' Mike suggested. 'If only we could suss out exactly how this bodies-and-statues thing worked, we could make an absolute fortune.'

'The word *We*, in context . . .'

'It'd be amazing,' Mike went on. 'You know; for a modest fee, you too can have the body of a young Greek god. The hell with nose jobs, we're talking total physical remodelling here. Have you any idea what the total revenue of the slimming industry amounts to in an average year?'

'Mike—'

'Not to mention the private health care aspect. Is your body clapped-out, leaking oil, slow to start in the mornings? Chuck it away and get a new one.'

'Mike,' Bianca said, 'just what the hell are we going to do?'

'About the dragon?' Mike replied. 'And Saint George and the fabric of reality as we thought we knew it? Who says we've got to do anything?'

'I do.'

'Bianca.' Mike did his best to look serious, although he wasn't entirely sure he knew how to do it in the new body; he hadn't yet worked out, as it were, which lever was the indicators and which was the windscreen wipers. 'I don't think it works like that. People like us aren't supposed to get involved in this kind of thing. Rescuing the planet's not

down to us. Save three worlds and you *don't* get a free radio
alarm clock.'

'Nevertheless.'

Mike tried a different tack. 'And besides,' he said, 'even
if you were able to do anything about anything, how the hell
do you know what's the right thing to do? I assume,' he
added, 'you'd insist on being tediously conventional and
doing the right thing.'

'Naturally. Oh come on, Mike, use your common sense,
it's obvious who's in the right and who's in the wrong.'

'Is it?' Mike took advantage of the high level of dramatic
tension to swipe some of Bianca's nan bread. 'Go on then.'

Bianca frowned. 'Well, the dragon, of course. Stands to
reason.'

'You reckon?'

'Mike, that bastard stole your body. My statue. He tried
to kill you.'

'The other bugger succeeded in killing me. Or had you
forgotten?'

'But that was an accident!'

It was Mike's turn to frown. 'Sixteen people, Bianca, one
of them me. All right, it wasn't deliberate, but I don't think
the bastard actually cared very much.'

'But George killed all the dragons,' Bianca protested. 'It
was genocide. They were innocent people—'

'Not people. Only humans are people. Innocent ani-
mals.'

'Okay, okay. But they'd never done him any harm, and he
killed them.'

'Enjoying the lamb? My chicken's nice.'

'That's *different*.'

Mike shrugged. 'If you say so. Look, I'm not saying
George is the good guy, either. Of course he's not. All I'm
saying is, it's not precisely simple and straightforward.

Most particularly, it's not the sort of thing where you can make up your mind on the basis of which contestant's cuddlier and has the nicest eyes.' Mike paused, partly for effect, mostly because his food was going cold and he knew his priorities. 'Appearances count for fuck-all in this. Particularly,' he added, 'since you made all the appearances.'

Bianca thought about that for a moment. 'That's the point, though,' she said. 'Surely. I mean, if anybody *knows* these guys, it must be me. It was me designed them. I made them what I wanted them to be. And I guess I always believed, deep down, that the dragon was somehow the good guy. I think I carved him that way.'

'More fool you, then. You finished with the lentils? I'm hungrier than I thought.'

'Mike,' Bianca said, 'I can't explain it, I just *know*.'

'I used to say that in exams, but they wouldn't believe me. And I did know, too,' he added. 'Usually because I had the answers written on my shirt-cuff.'

'Mike—'

'Actually,' he went on, 'that's amazingly profound. You see, my answers were right but they didn't count because I made them wrong by cheating. The same goes,' he added, with his mouth full, 'for Life. And all that stuff.'

Bianca didn't say anything. She seemed to have lost her appetite, and Mike finished off her pilau rice. It's wicked, he explained, to waste good food.

'All right,' she said eventually. 'So what do you think we should do?'

'Have some coffee.'

'OK. And then?'

'I'll know after I've had my coffee.'

'Mike . . .'

He leaned back in his chair. 'Bee,' he said. 'Shut up.'

242 · Tom Holt

★

The dragon swooped.

He could smell the uranium; a nasty, chemical smell that made his mouth taste. And he could smell demons.

And then he could see them. They had humans all round them, which was a nuisance because he really didn't want to have to kill any more of them. It was the difference between stalking a man-eating lion in the long grass and running over a dazzled hedgehog.

Eggs and omelettes, he told himself. Omelettes and eggs.

Something like hail or sleet pinged off his scales and he realised that the humans were shooting at him. Bloody cheek. If they weren't careful, they could put his eye out. He opened his wings, climbed, banked and came in again; a steeper, faster approach, making himself a very difficult target indeed. He knew; he'd had the practice.

'Snorkfrod,' pleaded Chardonay, 'you'll break him if you do that. *Please* put him down.'

The she-devil scowled. 'He aimed a gun at you. I'm going to pull his—'

'No you're not. I'm responsible for all breakages. What you've done to their fence is bad enough.'

'All right.' The sentry fell two feet, hit the ground, squirmed like an overturned woodlouse and ran. 'I love it when you're masterful, Mr C,' the she-devil simpered. 'You remind me ever so much of Kevin Costner.' Chardonay didn't know who Kevin Costner was, but sincerely hoped he wasn't litigiously minded. 'Right,' he said. 'I think we'd better head back to the van, this clearly isn't going to—'

'Mr C.'

'I know.' Chardonay, who had flung himself face down on the ground, picked himself up and stared at the huge, fast-moving shape hurtling through the sky. 'It's him. That bastard . . .'

'Do you want me to get him, Mr C?'

The expression on her face – eager, thrilled to bits at the chance of doing something to impress and please – was almost heartbreaking. She would, too, he realised, if only I said the word. And maybe she'd succeed. If she failed, it wouldn't be for want of extreme savagery. But he couldn't do it. The spirit was sufficiently psychotic, but the flesh was weak. She wouldn't stand a chance.

'Don't be stupid. And get down before he sees you.'

'Righty-ho, Mr C.'

'Not on top of me, please. I can't breathe.'

'Is this better?'

'I can breathe, certainly. But would you mind just . . .?'

The slipstream from the dragon's passage hit them like a hammer, and for the first time Chardonay appreciated the extraordinary power and strength of the bloody thing. It was going to take a whole lot more than just the five of them to cope with it. In fact, it wouldn't be a foregone conclusion if the whole damn Department turned out against it. There was, quite simply, no way of telling how powerful the monster was, apart from picking a fight with it, of course. That's like saying there's one simple way of discovering what height you can drop a porcelain vase from before it breaks.

'The Shopfloor with this,' Chardonay said. 'Let's get out of . . .'

The dragon swooped.

Three of them, at least. The other two were bound to be around here somewhere. Besides, he reflected, I have this notion that if I go around letting off fireworks too close to this uranium stuff, pinpoint accuracy is going to be somewhat academic.

Hmm. Pity about that. Maybe it's not the prettiest country in the world, but I could see where you could easily get fond of it.

Omelettes and eggs, boy. Omelettes and eggs. He focused and put his wings back. The soldiers dropped their guns and ran for it; the demons stayed where they were. For some reason.

'Trust me,' Prodsnap yelled. 'He knows that if he flames off here, he'll risk blowing up the power station, and then it'd be goodbye Europe. He won't do that.'

'You reckon?'

'Of course.' Prodsnap closed his eyes. 'He's the good guy.'

'How'd you figure that out?'

'Easy. George tried to kill him and couldn't. Speaks for itself. So all we have to do is keep perfectly still and the bugger'll peel off and fly away.'

'Is that a promise?'

Prodsnap nodded. 'Trust me.'

Job done.

The dragon banked again. Where the three demons had been, there was now just a big scorch-mark, a little molten rock. And a nuclear reactor going badly wrong.

Pity about that.

Never mind.

Omelettes and eggs.

CHAPTER SIXTEEN

'**O**h,' said Chardonay.

'At least it didn't see us,' Snorkfrod replied, emerging from behind a pile of used tyres. 'Just as well, really, because if it had, we'd be—'

'Yes. Quite.' Odd, he reflected. Given that he was now a naturalised citizen of Hell, he hadn't expected to be terrified by the sight of fire ever again. Quite nostalgic, really.

'Mr C.'

'Huh.'

'I don't want to worry you at all, but I think this whole complex is about to blow up.'

Why is it, Chardonay caught himself thinking, that whenever there's a truly awful crisis, humans set off a ghastly, shrieking alarm? Mood music? Muzak? Even now, with the sky boiling and waves of heat you could bake cakes in, there were still humans busying about with clipboards and brown cardboard folders, convincing themselves it was all just a drill. Why do we wear our fingers to the bone trying to torment these people? They do a far better job of it left to their own devices.

'We'd better be going, Mr C,' Snorkfrod urged. 'Come *on*.'

She tried to pull his sleeve, but he shook his arm free. 'No,' he said; and then looked round, trying to spot the smart-arse ventriloquist who'd hijacked his body to make such a damnfood remark. 'No, we can't just run. We've got to stop it happening. It's our *duty*.'

Snorkfrod's eyes were as large and round as manhole covers. 'Mr C,' she hissed, 'this whole place, this whole *country*, is about to blow up. There's nothing we can do. We'll be—'

'Yes there is. There must be.'

Snorkfrod's talons closed round his shoulder, nearly ripping it off. 'Don't be bloody stupid,' she shrieked. 'We're demons, we're from bloody *Hell*, it's not our responsibility.'

'Yes it is.' Chardonay carefully prised her talons apart and lifted them off him. 'We're officers of the central administration. And we're here, now, where it's happening.' He heard himself saying it; otherwise he'd never have believed he could say anything like it. Stark staring . . .

'All right, Mr C. What can we do?'

He stared at her. Leadership? Love? Both of them daft as brushes? She was smiling at him. God, it was like being followed round by a great big stupid dog. If she had a lead in her mouth it wouldn't look out of place.

'You sure?' he asked.

'Of course I'm sure, Mr C. Where you go, I go.'

In which case, Chardonay reflected, it serves the silly bitch right.

'Um,' he said. 'Okay. Yes. Er, follow me.'

From safe to critical in four and a half minutes; too fast. Even a direct hit from an ICBM shouldn't have made it all happen so quickly. There was absolutely nothing anybody could do. Even running away would be a waste of energy.

Two minutes.

Chardonay's instinct told him to go by the heat; where it was hottest, that's where the heart of the problem would be. Heat in itself didn't worry him at all –

– Except this was *not* hot. Back on Shopfloor, the accountants'd have forty fits if they found anywhere as hot as this. *Turn it down*, they'd shriek, *have you any idea what last quarter's fuel bill came to?*

'Are we going the right way, Mr C?'

'Getting warmer, definitely. Dear God, how can they get it as hot as this?'

Ninety-eight seconds later, Snorkfrod shoulder-charged a massive lead-lined chrome steel door. When she collided with it, she found it was red hot and *soft* . . .

'Bingo!' Chardonay blinked, found he had to look away. 'Oh shit, now what?'

Seventeen seconds to go. Chardonay's brain raced, performing feats of pure maths he'd never have believed himself capable of. Pointless in any event. There was only one thing that might conceivably work, and they were to all intents and purposes dead already, so why waste time doing the sums?

Chardonay turned to Snorkfrod. She was glowing bright orange and on her face was an expression of part horror, part rapture.

'Oh, Mr C,' she said, in that gushing, cloying, Black-Forest-gâteau-with-extra-cream voice of hers. 'It's all rather grand, isn't it? Being together at the end, I mean.'

Gawd help us. For a moment he wondered if Snorkfrod's unconquerable soppiness might be the only thing in Creation wet enough to put out the fire. On balance, probably not.

'I love you, Mr C.'

'Er, yes. Super. Now, when I give the word . . .'

And, even as the two of them hurled themselves down onto the core and were reduced instantaneously into atoms, Chardonay did catch himself thinking, *Well, yes, if things had worked out different . . .*

There's nothing like bizarre and absolute annihilation to bring out the romantic streak in people.

Chardonay's last, pathetically futile idea was that the physical bodies of demons are the most heat-resistant material in the known cosmos. Throw two demons onto the fire, like an asbestos blanket onto a burning chip-pan, and there's a very slight chance you might put it out.

He was, of course, wrong. A whole brigade of spectral warriors might have done the trick if they'd parachuted in about eighty seconds earlier, before the meltdown entered its final phase. Two little devils leaping in at the last moment were always going to be as effective as an eggcupful of water thrown into a blast furnace.

A lovely gesture, then; but completely pointless. Heroism is one thing, physics is something else. At the moment when the two demons threw themselves into the fire, only a miracle could have prevented the final cataclysm.

Define the term miracle.

It's got to be something Good – who ever heard of an Evil miracle? And it must be impossible or it doesn't count.

That leaves us with something nice that simply can't happen but does. Examples? Well, if we forget about tax rebates for the time being, how about a nuclear pile suddenly cooling down at the very last moment? Or two fiends from Hell giving their lives to save millions of innocent people?

Miracles do happen, but only very, very rarely; like the

hundred-to-one outsider suddenly accelerating out of nowhere to beat the odds-on favourite. You could make an awful lot of money betting on miracles, provided you knew for certain they were going to happen. But that, too, would be impossible. Nice, but impossible.

Wouldn't it?

Unpalatable theological truth number 736: behind every miracle, there's usually an awful lot of syndicated money.

'Just like that?' Chubby enquired.

Just like that.

Chubby sat still and quiet for a while, letting his mind skate round the implications. Just then, he'd have given anything for a simple pie-chart diagram showing how much of his soul was still his own. Not, he imagined, all that much.

'So that's what we needed the dragon for,' he said. 'God, I must be getting thick in my old age.'

Not really. It took a genius to think it up in the first place. It would take a genius of almost equal standing to work it out from first principles. Don't be too hard on yourself just because you're not a genius.

It helped, Chubby found, to walk up and down, burning off a little of the surplus energy that his pineal gland was pumping into his system. 'A dragon,' he said, 'because nothing else on Earth would actually be crazy, wicked, stupid enough to torch a nuclear reactor and blow up a country.'

And even then I needed a pretext, so he wouldn't suspect what I was really up to. Hence putting a contract out on the demons. Rather neat, I thought.

'Whereupon,' Chubby went on, 'you laid a whopping great bet on the outcome. What odds did you get? Thousand to one?'

You think I'd go to all that trouble for a handful of piddling loose change? No, the odds were very satisfactory, thank you.

'Splendid. I do so like a happy ending.' Chubby sat down behind his desk, broke a pencil and ground the bits into the carpet with his heel.

Another thing. You're being too hard on my old friend Fred.

'Fred? Oh sorry, I forgot.'

You said crazy, wicked, stupid. Fred's none of those things. That's the mistake everybody always makes around dragons. I should know, I am one. Or had you forgotten?

'I did manage to remember, thank you.'

Dragons – Impossible, of course, for glowing green words on a screen to have any expression. Any subtext has to come from the mind of the reader. In Chubby's eyes, at least, the words on the screen grinned.

Dragons, you see, simply don't give a damn. Good and Evil's just biped stuff. Sure, you believe in it, the same way you used to believe in Father Christmas when you were little. We don't, is all. We don't mean anything by it.

'I see.'

I doubt that. And you know something else? I couldn't give a shit.

Chubby gave the screen a long, level stare. For some reason, he found he could, without wanting to look away. His mind searched for a word and a word came: alien.

I thought they were little green men with radio aerials sticking out of their ears.

Chubby shook his head. 'Nah,' he replied. 'You could get fond of little green men.'

'Hello,' said Prodsnap, without looking up. 'What kept you?'

Chardonay sat down in the seat next to him. 'Had to save the planet,' he replied. 'Any idea what sort of a mood He's in?'

Prodsnap shook his head. 'I haven't heard any shouting,' he replied. 'On the other hand, that's not necessarily a good sign.'

The five demons, wearing makeshift bodies issued to them from the huge wicker hamper colloquially known as the Dressing-Up Box, were sitting in a draughty corridor outside an office marked *Personnel Manager*. It isn't mentioned in Dante's *Inferno*, mainly because Dante had always hoped one day to sell the film rights and so he wanted to keep the whole thing basically upbeat and free from utterly negative vibes. The famous inscription about abandoning hope was nailed above the lintel.

Snorkfrod nudged Chardonay in the ribs.

'We'd like you lot to be the first to know,' Chardonay said, saying it with all the passion and enthusiasm of the little voice in posh cars that tells you to fasten your seat belt. 'Snorkfrod and I are engaged.'

'Strewth.' Slitgrind pulled a face. 'So you've been in already, have you?'

'I beg your pardon?'

Slitgrind nodded towards the office door. 'That's your punishment, is it, Char? I always knew he was a vindictive bugger, but ... Hey, Prozza, mind what you're doing, that was my shin.'

Prodsnap switched on a silly grin. 'Congratulations,' he croaked. 'I hope you'll both be very ...'

The door opened. A secretary fiend, lump-headed and shark-jawed, beckoned them.

'He'll see you now,' she said.

'Sugar Fred Dragon?' Mr Kortright suggested.

Nah. Tacky.

'Matter of opinion. All right then, Rocky Draciano. I like that. It's got class.'

Tacky.

'Honey George Sanctus?' There was a slight edge of desperation in the agent's voice. Self-doubt wasn't usually a problem for Lin Kortright, in the same way that Eskimos don't lie awake at night fretting about heatstroke. This client, though, had him rattled.

Lin. It smells. Come on, you're supposed to be good at this sort of thing.

'I am.' He'd nearly said *I was*. The sweat from his armpits would have irrigated Somalia.

Sure you are, Lin, sure you are. Now then, the venue. Any progress?

Kortright nodded, realised that the screen couldn't see gestures (or could it? He was getting distinctly offbeat vibes off this thing. As they say in the Business, never work with computers or children). 'It's in the bag, Nosher,' he replied confidently. 'All set.'

'Set? Or set-set?'

'Set-set. I got a signed agreement with the Mongolian Ministry of Tourism and War—'

Tourism and War?

'Historical reasons, Nosher. Genghis Khan. The ultimate in encounter holidays, remember? Anyway, we've got a million-acre site between Mandalgovi and Dalandzadgad, they're gonna build us an airstrip—'

Fine. I'll leave all that sort of thing to you. As far as I'm concerned, all we really need is a very big flat space with a rope round it, and two corners.

Kortright's brow creased. 'Corners?'

Yes. You know; in the white corner, we have Saint George, representing Good, and in the black corner . . .

'Ah. Right. Got you. I'll fix that, no problem. Now then, the cola concession, I've got the Pepsi guys up to six million, but I'm expecting a fax any minute—'

Yes, yes. Deal with it, Lin, there's a good fellow. 'Bye for now.

The screen in Mr Kortright's office went dark. Another screen in Chubby's bunker (reinforced chronite, guaranteed to withstand anything less than a direct hit from a neutron star) flicked on.

Chubby.

'Now what?'

Just a few things. Transport . . .

'All done.' Chubby frowned. 'You got any idea how much a ship that size costs per day?'

Yes.

'Then you'd better – oh.' Chubby hesitated. 'Any chance of a few quid on account?' he asked. 'Only, what with one thing and another, all this is causing me slight cashflow problems, plus I'm neglecting my business. I've got orders to meet, you know.'

Correct. Mine. And you will obey them without question. Lemons.

'I'm sorry, I thought you just said lemons'

That's right. For the contestants to suck between rounds. Make sure there are plenty, will you? Or do I have to do everything myself?

'All right, Chubby replied, offended, 'keep your keyboard on. I've got a containerload of lemons on their way from Australia, together with sixty gallons of aviation fuel for the dragon. Apple brandy for George. Not too much, don't want him falling over. Okay?'

Well done. Finally, then; how are you actually going to get them onto the ship?

Chubby smiled. 'I'm way ahead of you there,' he replied. 'How'd it be if we tried the old Ark routine? You know, a couple of days' synthetic rain beforehand, then I go around telling everybody I've had this message from God—?'

Chubby.

'Yes?'

Don't try my patience, chum. I think I used to have some, but I haven't seen it around since 1946, and it's probably gone off by now. Get it sorted, there's a good lad.

The screen went blank. Chubby stuck his tongue out at it. Obviously it knew, but Chubby no longer cared terribly much.

This, he said to himself, is getting out of hand.

It was something, he knew, with the big gambling syndicate. You didn't need to be Einstein or A.J.P. Taylor to work out that Nosher had been behind the original syndicate, the one that persuaded the dragon to throw the fight first time round, back in the Dark Ages. And it was as clear as a lighthouse on a moonless night that this rematch was going to be a fix as well. The question was, which one was he going to fix this time?

And – big question, this – who did the syndicate bet *with*? It takes two to make a wager, and the last time he'd passed the local Coral office they hadn't been offering odds on the fight. So who was the mug punter the syndicate were fitting up? Who had that sort of money, anyhow?

God? No, strictly a matchsticks player. (And you thought all those forests in South America were just scenery?) Who, then? He shook his head. None of his damn business, anyhow.

Here's hoping, he muttered to himself, it stays that way.

Don't be too hard on them, Phil.

I WON'T. JUST ENOUGH SO THEY WON'T SUS-PECT.

Good result, huh?

YOU WIN THIS TIME, NOSHER. NEXT TIME, MAYBE YOU WON'T BE SO LUCKY. NOT, I SOME-TIMES GET THE IMPRESSION, THAT LUCK HAS

ALL THAT MUCH TO DO WITH IT. I MEAN, WHY
EXACTLY *DIDN'T* THE FUCKING THING BLOW
UP?

*Can't imagine what you mean, Phil. Anyway, I'm looking
forward to getting your cheque. Or shall we make it double or
quits?*

Outside, in the corridor, Chardonay and company could
hear the thundering of the voice, but couldn't make out the
words. Some other poor bastards getting their fortunes told,
they assumed.

YOU'RE ON, NOSHER. HERE'S TO THE NEXT
TIME, RIGHT?

After a hard afternoon's work in her studio – God, the
Victoria Square project! Running about chasing the dragon
was all very fine and splendid, but she had a commission to
fulfil – Bianca had a quick sandwich and went straight to
bed.

She slept badly.

Chasing the dragon – well, quite. There was still an
influential part of her brain that wanted to treat the whole
bloody mess as some sort of giant hallucination; bad dope,
the DTs, cheese before bedtime, whatever. That was the
comforting explanation. Untrue, of course. Whatever it
was, it was still going on. In fact, she had an uneasy feeling
it was approaching some sort of crisis. In which case, the
sensible course of action would be to be standing outside
the travel agents' when they opened tomorrow morning,
asking for details of off-peak reductions to Alpha Centauri.

When a person starts worrying about something around
half past three in the morning, she might as well let out
Sleep's room and put his clothes in the jumble sale because
he sure as hell isn't coming back. To take her mind off it all,
she switched on the TV and hit the Satellite news.

... In Victoria Square, Birmingham might somehow be linked to the wave of spectacular art thefts in Florence, Rome and Venice. In addition to Ms Wilson's two monumental works for the Birmingham City Corporation, no fewer than seventeen major statues have vanished from Italian collections, including eight Berninis, three Donatellos, three Cellinis, a Canova, the Giambologna Mercury, *and of course the priceless Michaelangelo* David. *The only lead that Interpol have so far is the discovery of fingerprints apparently resembling those of Kurt Lundqvist, a notorious mercenary and soldier of fortune, discovered at the scenes of all the robberies in Italy. Lundqvist, however, is believed to have been killed some time ago in Guatemala, although the only part of him actually recovered was his left ear. Counter-insurgency experts have pointed out that, to judge by his past record, Lundqvist would have been perfectly capable of carrying out this remarkable string of burglaries single-handed, not to mention single-eared; indeed, they claim, if there's anyone capable of shrugging off Death as a minor inconvenience, that man would be Kurt Lundqvist, believed by many leading experts to be the link between the former Milk Marketing Board and the Kennedy assassination. This is Danny Bennett, Star TV News, in Florence.*

Bugger sleep. As far as Bianca was concerned, Macbeth had beaten her to it.

Seventeen statues. Seventeen is sixteen plus one. Sixteen people die in an explosion in a community centre in the West Midlands; sixteen statues simultaneously go missing in Italy. No, seventeen statues, sixteen plus one.

Who was the seventeenth statue for?

She was still paddling this bizarre notion around in her brain when the phone rang, making her jump out of her skin. It took an awful lot of determination to pick the blasted thing up.

'Hello?'

'Bianca Wilson?' American voice, like audible sand-paper.

'Yes, that's me. Who's this?'

'You probably don't know me' the voice replied. 'My name's Kurt Lundqvist.'

CHAPTER SEVENTEEN

'Mr Lund—'

The small man jumped out of his skin, whirled round and slapped a hand across her mouth. 'Don't call me that, you crazy bitch,' he hissed. 'C'mon, this way.'

He set off at a great pace, not looking round. Bianca had to break into a trot to keep up. He was shorter and squarer than she'd expected, but he moved as if he was tall, lean and wiry. Another one of these unquiet spirits in a Moss Bros body? It was as though the whole world was on its way to a fancy dress party.

'Okay,' he said, finally halting. 'We can talk here.'

Maybe, Bianca thought, but hearing what we say is going to be another matter entirely.

In reply to her earlier question, 'Where can we meet?' Kurt had suggested New Street station. They were now in the bar of a pub in John Bright Street, empty except for the barman and the loudest background music on Earth. This was foreground music. It filled all the available space, like Polyfilla.

'Thank you for coming,' Kurt said.

'Sorry?'

'I SAID...' Kurt edged his chair nearer and leaned forwards. 'I said thanks for coming. Listen up, doll. This is a mess.'

Bianca frowned slightly. He'd told her briefly about the circumstances of his return to Earth and she reckoned 'doll' was a bit rich coming from an animated Action Man. Given the communication difficulties, though, she let it ride.

(Note: to save time and preserve the Niagara-like cadences of the dialogue, all the backchat – 'Sorry, what did you say?'; 'Speak up, for Chrissakes'; 'Dammit, there's no need to shout' etc, – has been edited, as a result of which, this passage has already been awarded the Golden Scissors at the 1996 Editor of the Year Awards, and the BSI kitemark.)

'I know,' Bianca replied. 'You made it sound like there was something you could do about it.'

'There is,' Kurt replied, sipping his Babycham. 'But not on my own. That's where you come in.'

'I see.'

'Doubt that.' Kurt finished his bag of pork scratchings, squashed up the packet and dropped it into the ashtray before lighting a cigar. A large cigar, needless to say; Bianca had seen smaller things being floated down Canadian rivers. 'Let me just fill you in on the background. Maybe you know some of the stuff I don't, at that.'

Between them, it transpired, they had a fairly good idea of the Story So Far, including recent developments and a progress report on the preparations for the Big Fight. 'So you see,' Kurt summarised, 'it's all a goddamn shambles.'

'Quite.' Bianca nodded vigorously. 'Worst part of it is, I can't seem to work out who's who. Goodies and baddies, I mean.'

'This,' Kurt replied sternly, 'ain't the movies. When

you've been in supernatural pest control as long as me, you learn not to make judgements about people. Sure, when I was young, I used to worry about that kinda thing; you know, *What harm did he ever do me?* and all that kinda shit. Nowadays, all I ask myself is, will the two-fifty grain hollow point do the business at three hundred and fifty yards. I guess it makes life easier, not giving a damn.'

'You do, though, don't you?'

Kurt nodded glumly. 'It's a bitch,' he replied. 'Unprofessional. That's what's got to me about this stinking job. Trouble is, my professional ethics say I gotta do the job I'm being paid for. Nothing in the rules says I can't share my concerns with an outsider, though; someone not in the business, like yourself.'

Bianca shrugged. 'I've got professional ethics too, you know. Mostly they're to do with leaving chisel-marks and not glueing back bits you accidentally break off. But I'm sure there's something in the Code of Practice about not letting dangerous statues fall into the wrong hands. I must look it up when I get back home.'

They looked at each other suspiciously across the formica tabletop; unlikely confederates (if we're confederates, Bianca muttered to herself, bags I be Robert E. Lee) in an impossibly confused situation. In context, they were probably the least likely do-gooders in the whole dramatis personae; the hired killer and the arms dealer. Maybe it helped that Bianca also dealt in legs, heads and torsos.

'I guess,' Kurt said slowly, 'in situations like this, all you can do is to try and do the right thing. Shit, did I really say that? This stinking job really is getting to me.'

'A statue's gotta do what a statue's gotta do?'

'Sure. Now, what *you* gotta do is like this.'

Thank you for calling Acropolis Marble Wholesalers Limited.

Unfortunately there's no one here to take your call, so please leave a message after the tone.

Beep. 'Hello, Bianca Wilson here. Could I have seventeen seven by three by three Carrara white blocks, immediate delivery, COD Birmingham. Thank you.'

Thank you for calling Hell. Unfortunately there's no one here to take your call, so please leave a message after the tone. Alternatively, for reservations and party bookings, please dial the following number. Thank you.

Thank you for calling Nkunzana Associates. Unfortunately there's no one here to take your call. Don't bother to leave a message; I know perfectly well who you are and what you want, I'm a fully qualified witch-doctor. Thank you.

'Have you ever,' Chubby said, apropos of nothing, 'been to Mongolia?'

The dragon looked at him. 'No idea,' he said. 'I've been virtually everywhere, I think, but usually I don't stop and buy a guide-book. What's Mongolia?'

Chubby shrugged. 'Desert, mostly. Very empty, not many people. Barren, too; large parts of it have as close to a zero per cent fire risk as it's possible to get on this planet. The sort of place where you could have a sneezing fit without burning down six major cities.'

'Sounds a bit dull,' the dragon said.

'It is. Very.'

'I could use a little tedium right now,' the dragon said, scratching his nose with a harpoon-like claw. 'I take it you're working round to suggesting that I go there.'

'Hate to lose you,' Chubby replied. 'It's been great fun having you here and all that. But, with all due respect, you're a bit hard on the fixtures and fittings.'

'True. Actually, it beats me how you people can live in places like this without dying of claustrophobia.'

'We're smaller than you are. We find it helps.'

The dragon yawned and stretched, inadvertently knocking an archway through the wall into the next room. 'Mongolia, then. What's your ulterior motive? Something to do with your Time business?'

'You know your trouble? You're cynical.' Chubby frowned. 'Usually with good cause,' he added. 'As it so happens, there is a small job you could do for me while you're there. Nothing heavy. You might find it helps stave off death by ennui. Entirely up to you, though.'

'Explain.'

'Well.' Chubby leaned back in his chair and hit the light switch. A projector started to run, covering the opposite wall (the only one still intact) with a huge, slightly blurred image of a vase of flowers, upside down. Chubby clicked something, and the picture changed into a view of the Great Wall of China.

'Familiar?'

'Seen it before,' the dragon replied. 'Doesn't mean anything to me, though. A wall is but a wall, a sigh is but a sigh.'

'Ah.' Chubby clicked again. The Great Wall came closer. 'This, my old mate, is no ordinary wall. It's big, it's famous and – now here's where my interest in the damn thing lies – it's very, very old.'

The dragon smiled in the darkness. 'Steeped in history, huh?'

'Positively saturated. Now, I got to thinking; sentiment aside, what does that lot actually do that a nice modern chain-link fence couldn't do, for a fraction of the maintenance costs? Whereas to me—'

'I get the picture,' the dragon interrupted, amused. 'You want me to steal it.'

Chubby clicked again. This time, the wall was covered in a view of the planet, as seen from space. The Great Wall was dimly visible, a thin line faintly perceptible through wisps of untidy cloud. Either that, or a hair in the gate.

'As you can see for yourself,' Chubby went on, 'it's the only man-made structure visible from outside the Earth's atmosphere. An eyesore, in other words. If Mankind ever gets round to colonising the moon, I'll be doing them a favour.'

'Quite. What do you want me to do with it after I've nicked it?'

Click. View of a completely barren area of desert. 'Just leave it there. One of my people will deal with it.'

The dragon smiled. 'A receiver of stolen walls? A fence?'

'How did I know you were going to say that?'

Half an hour later, the same picture show, the same basic introduction.

'Let's just make sure I've got this straight,' George said. 'Your organisation's going to steal the Great Wall of China?'

'Mphm.'

'And then they're going to dump it, out there in the wilderness.'

'Not wilderness, George. Prime development site. We paid top dollar for that land. It has the advantage of being as far from anywhere as it's possible to get without having to wear an oxygen mask.'

George shrugged. 'You know your own business, I s'pose. What do you need me for?'

'Caretaker, basically,' Chubby replied. 'I was just thinking, since your friend with the wings and the bad breath is still very much on the loose, you might quite fancy a month or so in the last place anybody would ever think of looking.'

'Good point.' George nodded decisively. 'Much obliged to you. It'll be a pleasure.'

The lights came back on.

'Pleasure's all mine,' said Chubby.

A bit over-complicated, surely?

Chubby scowled. 'Listen,' he said. 'I hate to bother you with silly mundane things like the way I earn my living, but for the last couple of months my business has been at a complete standstill. I've got orders I can't fill and staff on full wages sitting around with nothing to do. Two birds, one stone, and everybody's happy.'

The screen went blank and the little red light, whose purpose Chubby had never been able to work out in all the years he'd had the wretched thing, blinked twice.

I'm not happy about this.

'Tough. Sorry, but you said to find a way to get them both to the venue without arousing their suspicions and that's what I've done. And now, if you don't mind. I've got work—'

The pain hit him like a falling roof. The intensity of pain largely depends on which part of the victim it affects. Chubby's soul hurt. Toothache is nothing in comparison.

'Fuck you, genie,' he moaned. 'Let *go*, will you?'

Inside his head, Chubby could hear laughter. It was a very frightening sound.

Chubby, please. After all we've been to each other, I think you can start calling me Nosher. All my friends do.

'Then fuck you, *Nosher*. And now will you please stop doing that, before you break my id?'

Any idea how much of your soul I now own? I know you're curious. Go on, ask me.

The pain stopped and Chubby collapsed into a chair. 'Let me see,' he said, once he'd got his breath back. 'Well, for one thing, we haven't had nearly as much of the your-wish - is - my - command - it's - my - pleasure - to - serve - you bullshit lately, which I find rather significant. And all these cosy chats we've been having recently must be taking their toll. I've been trying very hard indeed not to think about it.'

Forty-two per cent.

'Shit.'

No reason why that should be a problem, surely. We've always got on well enough, you and I.

'Like a house on fire,' Chubby replied. 'With you as the fire and me as the house. What happens to me when you get a majority stake? Do I die, or vanish, or what?'

Perish the thought. It's just that we'll see even more eye to eye, that's all.

'And when it reaches a hundred per cent?'

Then I shall be free.

'Hooray, hooray. And what about me?'

You'll be one of the lucky ones. Like Mr Tanashima.

Chubby frowned. 'Don't know him. Who he?'

Mashito Tanashima. Born 1901, died 1945. He worked in a bicycle factory in Hiroshima, Japan. Seven minutes before the atomic bomb exploded, he was killed in a road accident.

'Gosh.' Chubby smiled bleakly. 'Lucky old me, huh?'

The screen flickered. The red light came on and, this time, stayed on.

Yes. Let nobody say I'm not grateful.

Bianca stepped back to admire her work. A masterpiece, as always. Three down, fourteen to go.

The biggest problem had been getting hold of the photographs. First, she'd tried the local paper, but they'd got suspicious and refused to co-operate. The victims' families had virtually set the dogs on her. Finally, she'd hit on the idea of sending Mike round pretending to be the organiser of a Sadley Grange Disaster Fund. She'd felt very bad about that, but he'd come away with all the photographs she needed.

The walls of her studio were covered in them; enlarged, reduced, montaged, computer-enhanced, until the very sight of them gave her the creeps. Sixteen very ordinary people who happened to have been in the Sadley Grange Civic Centre when it blew up. The victims.

So far she'd done Mrs Blanchflower, Mrs Gray and Mr Smith, and she was knackered. Straight portraiture, no dramatic poses or funny hats; they had to be as lifelike as possible or the whole thing would be a waste of time. The worst part of it all was the responsibility, because she wasn't the one who was going to have to live with the consequences for the rest of her life if she made a mistake. Accidentally leave off a toe, or get an arm out of proportion, and she'd be ruining somebody's life.

The hell with that, she told herself. Makes it sound like they're doing me a favour.

Yes. Well. And whose dragon caused all this mess in the first place?

'Mike,' she croaked, 'I need a brand new set of the big chisels, another hide mallet and coffee, about a gallon and a half. Would you . . .?'

'On my way.'

'Mrs Cornwall's nose. Could you do me a six by four enlargement of the wart? I can't see from this whether it's a straightforward spherical type or more your cottage loaf job.'

'No problem.'

She sighed, wiped her forehead with her sleeve. 'And when you've done that,' she said, 'if you could see your way to making a start on roughing out Mrs Ferguson with the angle grinder. I've marked her up, and it'd save ever such a lot of time.'

'Mrs Ferguson, angle grinder. Right you are.'

'Oh, and Mike.'

'Yes?'

'Thanks.'

Mike laughed, without much humour. 'That's all right,' he said. 'After all, what are friends for? Apart, that is, from heavy lifting, telling lies to next of kin, basic catering and other unpaid chores?'

'Dunno. Moral support?'

Mike shrugged. 'Don't ask me,' he said, 'my morals collapsed years ago. Be seeing you.'

Left alone, Bianca tried to clear her mind of everything except the technicalities of sculpture. Easier said than done; it was like clearing a pub on Cup Final night, only rather more difficult. The hardest part, unexpectedly enough, was the way the faces from the photographs stayed in her mind, plastered across her retina like fly-posters, even when her eyes were tight shut. That meant something, she felt sure, but she hadn't the faintest idea what.

'Excuse me.'

Kurt stopped dead in his tracks, closed his eyes and counted to ten. Once upon a time, that particular ritual had been a foolproof method of keeping his temper. Now all it meant was that he lost his rag ten seconds later.

'Hi,' he replied, cramming a smile onto his face, which had never been exactly smile-shaped at the best of times. These past few days, however, cheerful expressions tended to perch apprehensively on his features, like a unicyclist crossing a skating rink.

'Mr Lundqvist.' It was the Canova again. 'May I have a word with you, please?'

'Lady...'

Inside the Classical perfection of the Canova bivouacked all that was immortal of Mrs Blanchflower. By a prodigious effort of his imagination, Kurt had worked out a scenario where he would actually be pleased to see Mrs Blanchflower, but it involved her being in the water and him being a twenty-foot-long Mako shark. The only reason why he hadn't yet mortally insulted her was because he never seemed to be able to get a word in edgeways.

'Mr Lundqvist,' said the Canova. 'Now, as you know, I'm the *last* person ever to complain about anything, but I really most protest, in the strongest possible...'

Getting past Mrs Blanchflower, of course, was the beginning, not the end, of the aggravation. She was the worst individual specimen, yes, the gold medallist in the Pest Olympics, but there were fourteen others right behind her sharing silver. And it's no real escape to elude one Mohammed Ali only to be set upon by fourteen Leon Spinkses.

'SHUTTUP!' Kurt therefore bellowed, as he shouldered past the Canova into the main area of the Nissen hut. That bought him, albeit at terrible cost, a whole half second of dead silence.

'And LISTEN!' he said. 'Thank you. Now then, folks, gather round. And you better pay attention, 'cos this is important.'

Fifteen statues all started to complain at once.

'Okay.' Kurt backed away and climbed onto a chair. 'Okay,' he repeated, just loud enough to be audible. 'If you guys don't want to go home, that's up to you. Well, so long. It's been...'

Silence. Well, virtual silence. Mrs Hamstraw (by Bernini) finished her sentence about the sultanas in her muesli (she'd *told* him, *three* times, the doctor had told her no sultanas) and Ms Stones reiterated her threat of writing to Roger Cook for the seventy-eighth time, but apart from that there was a silence so complete, Kurt felt he knew what it must have been like at five to nine on the first day of Creation.

'On the other hand,' he went on, calm and quiet as the Speaking Clock, 'anybody who wants out had better listen good. Now, then . . .'

'I still say that, after last time . . .'

The Great Goat turned his head about twenty-seven degrees and scowled.

'Thank you,' he said, in a voice you could have freeze-dried coffee in. 'Shall we proceed?'

A nice man, Dr Thwaites; all his patients would have agreed, likewise his colleagues, his neighbours, even some of his relations. A kind man, for whom nothing would ever be too much trouble. A patient man, prepared to listen politely and attentively to every hypochondriac who ever thought mild indigestion was a heart attack. But flawed, nevertheless. Albert Schweitzer was the same, and likewise Walt Disney.

'If you insist,' muttered the Lesser Goat. 'Now then, where's that wretched skull?'

Because Dr Thwaites, having paid Farmer Melrose six months' rent for conjuring rites on Lower Copses Meadow, was damned if he was going to forfeit half his money – thirty pounds, fifty pence – with three months still to run. It was, as far as he was concerned, a matter of principle.

'When you're ready, Miss Frobisher. Now then.' He cleared his throat. 'By Asmoday and Beelzebub I conjure you, spirits of—' He stopped. If someone had just popped an apple in his mouth, they couldn't have shut him up quicker or more effectively.

'Don't mind us,' said the Captain of Spectral Warriors,

in a soft, speaking-in-church voice. 'Just pretend we aren't here, okay?'

The Great Goat would dearly have liked to do just that, but unfortunately it was out of the question. It takes a special sort of mental discipline to ignore five hundred of Hell's finest, in full battledress uniform, all displaced heads, unexpected limbs and weird appendages, creeping stealthily past you in the early hours of the morning.

''Ere, doc,' said the thurifer at his elbow. 'You're really good at this, aren't you?'

The Great Goat swallowed hard. 'Apparently,' he said. In his subconscious he was wondering whether he could persuade Mr Melrose to impose a retrospective rent increase, because the thought of performances like this every week for the next three months was enough to drive a man insane. He'd have to rethink all his cosy preconceptions about anatomy, for a start.

'Excuse me.' The Captain was talking to him. He forced himself to listen.

'Sorry, I was, um, miles away. Can I, er, be of assistance?'

'We're trying to get to—' The Captain consulted a clipboard. 'Place called Birmingham. Would you happen to know where that is?'

'Birmingham.'

'That's right. I've got this map here, but it hasn't photocopied terribly well, so if you could just set us on the right track, we'd be ever so grateful.'

His disbelief suspended on full pay, the Great Goat felt in the pockets of his robes and produced a pencil and the back of an envelope.

CHAPTER EIGHTEEN

The Big Fight.

Seen purely from the viewpoint of logistics and administration, it was the greatest show in history. Everybody who was, had been or would be anybody was there, and the complexities of setting up a switchboard for the retrospective booking office had taxed Mr Kortright's ingenuity to its fullest extent. Or take the popcorn concession, a chronological disaster poised to happen. Any popcorn eaten by visitors from the past or the future would leave a serious imbalance in the fabric of reality, particularly after it had passed through the visitor's digestive system and entered the ecology of his native century. In order to compensate, Kortright had had to estimate the amount of popcorn likely to be eaten and arrange for compensatory amounts of matter to be removed from/added to a whole series of past and future destinations. As for the envelope of artificial Time in which the auditorium was contained, it had cleaned out Chubby's stocks down to the last second. God only knew what would happen if the fight lasted beyond the twelfth round.

All these problems, of course, were more than adequately accounted for in the price of the tickets; and that caused yet another organisational nightmare, given that (for example) in order to pay for his ticket the Emperor Nero had leeched out the entire economy of the Roman Empire, which could only mean total fiscal meltdown, violence in the streets and the fall of the Empire several centuries ahead of schedule. Fortunately, a client of Lin Kortright's who controlled various financial syndicates in the first century AD was able to offer bridging finance; disaster was averted, ten per cent was earned for the Kortright Agency, and Nero (who paid the first instalment of the loan by insuring Rome and then burning it down) was sitting in the front row, munching olives and trying unsuccessfully to persuade Genghis Khan to take St George to win at fifteen to one.

There was also a band, and cheer-leaders, and huge spotlights producing as much light and heat as a small star, and commentators from every TV station in Eternity all getting ready to provide simultaneous coverage (*live* was, in context, a word best avoided), and cameras and film crews and sound crews and men in leather jackets with head-phones on wandering about prodding bits of trailing flex and engineers swearing at each other, and all the spectacle and pageantry of a galaxy-class sporting event. The panel of judges (two saints, two devils and, representing the saurian community, two enormous iguanas) were sworn in. There was an awed hush as the doors at the back swung open to admit the referee; no less a dignitary than Quetzal-coatl, Feathered Serpent of the Aztecs. Had his worshippers in pre-Conquest Mexico known that when he promised to come again to judge the quick and the dead, he meant *this*, maybe they'd have been a little bit less forthcoming with the gold and blood sacrifices.

It was nearly time. The food vendors left the auditorium,

trays empty. The roar of voices dwindled down to an expectant buzz. All it needed now was for the contestants to show up, and the contest for the ethical championship of the universe could begin.

And Kortright turned to Stevenson and said, 'Well, where the fuck are they?'

And Stevenson leant across to Kortright and said, 'I thought they were with you.'

'Finished,' Bianca gasped.

Forget the aesthetics for a moment; in terms of sheer stamina, it was the greatest achievement in the history of Art. With an effort she unclenched her cramped fingers sufficiently to allow chisel and mallet to fall to the ground and collapsed backwards into her chair, only to find there was someone already sitting in it.

'*Sakubona, inkosazana.*' Bianca did a quick Zebedee impression, looked down and saw a little, wizened man curled up in her chair. He was wearing a leopard skin with lots of unusual accessories, and holding a fly-whisk.

'Hi,' she replied. 'You must be Nkunzana. I didn't hear you come in.'

'No,' the witch-doctor replied, 'you didn't.' He nodded towards the statues. 'Impressive,' he said.

'All my own work,' Bianca replied, flustered. 'You know what you've got to do?'

'Is the Pope a Catholic?'

'Right. Well, I'd better leave you to it, then. Do you need anything? Um, hot water, towels, that sort of thing?'

Nkunzana shook his head. 'A fire and a pinch of dust, my sister,' he replied. Before Bianca could offer further assistance, he produced a big brass Zippo from the catskin bag hung round his neck.

'Dust?'

Nkunzana grinned and drew a fingertip across the surface of the table beside his chair. 'I know,' he said. 'I remind you of your mother.'

'In certain respects,' Bianca replied. 'She could never have worn leopard, though. Not with her colouring.'

The witch-doctor shrugged; then, with a tiny movement of his thumb he lit the lighter, sprinkled the dust and mumbled something that Bianca didn't quite catch.

And . . .

. . . *Action*!

Cut to –

Kurt's Nissen hut (you could call it the Galleria Lundqvist, but not, if you want to see tomorrow, while he's listening) where fifteen statues with strong West Midland accents are telling him exactly why they refuse to have anything at all to do with his plan.

Sound effects; rushing wind, a shimmering tinkly sound (shorthand for magic), deep and rumbling unworldly laughter, followed by –

Silence. The other noises off were just meretricious effects, the parsley garnish on a slice of underdone magic. But the silence, the absence of querulous whining, that's something else. Uncanny is an understatement in the same league as describing the Black Death as a nasty bug that's going around.

Kurt reacts; he says –

'*YIPPEE!*'

– and so would you if you'd just spent several weeks cooped up with Mrs Blanchflower, Mr Potts and thirteen others, extremely similar. In their place, fifteen of the world's finest, most exquisite statues; solid masonry from head to toe, without enough sentience between the lot of them to animate a DSS counter clerk. Kurt looked round, gazing ecstatically at each one in turn; compared to him, stout Cortes would have made one hell of a poker player. No more whingeing. No more threats to report him to the English Tourist Board. No more caustic remarks about the lack of brown sauce to go with the escalops of veal.

Slowly, almost like a moon-walker in the deliberation of his movements, Kurt got to his feet, crossed the floor and picked up a frozen tiramisu he'd been defrosting for tonight's dinner. Then he planted himself in front of the Canova, stuck his tongue out, raised the tiramisu and rubbed it into the statue's face.

Cut to –

Bianca's studio. Bianca has just left, leaving the door unlocked and a note.

Cue sound effects, as above, except for the silence. Instead, fade in a yammering fugue of West Midland voices raised in pique. And hold it, as –

The statues realise something has changed. Typically thoughtful, Bianca has left a big, clothes-shop style mirror facing them. They see themselves. Let's repeat that line, for emphasis. They see . . .

Themselves . . .

Silence.

And then one of them – yes, absolutely right, it's Mrs Blanchflower – says –

'*Well*!'

– and they all start talking at once. No need to report the exact words spoken; the gist of it is that they're all as pleased as anything to be out of those ridiculous, freezing cold, uncomfortable statues and back in their own bodies again, *but* that doesn't alter the fact that they've been mucked about something terrible (with hindsight, scrawling *Sorry for any inconvenience* on the mirror in lipstick wasn't the most tactful thing Bianca ever did) and just wait, someone hasn't heard the last of this, my lawyers, my husband, my Euro MP...

At the back of the room, a scruffy heap which at first sight was only a bundle of old rags sits up, double-takes and huddles down again, furtively pulling a mangy leopard skin over his head and hoping to hell they haven't spotted him. Too late –

With a simultaneous yowl of fury, fifteen angry ex-statues turn on Nkunzana, shaking fists and demanding explanations. The witch-doctor freezes, unable to move. In the course of his professional activities, he's daily called upon to face down swarms of gibbering unquiet spirits, quell mobs of loutish ghosts by sheer force of personality, command fiends and boss about the scum of twelve dimensions. Piece of cake. Faced with Mrs Blanchflower and the other Sadley Grange victims, he's a mongoose-fazed snake.

Spirits, he hisses under his breath, *I command you by Nkulunkulu, the Great One, get me the hell out of here*!

The spirits attend, as they are bound to do when a master of the Art orders them. Although only the *isangona* can see them, they're there, as present as a college of notaries, standing at the back of the room looking extremely embarrassed.

Sorry, amakhosi, they mouth noiselessly. *This time, you're on your own.*

Cut to –

A police station on the very northernmost edge of China. Behind the desk, a sergeant slumbers dreamlessly under a circular fan.

The door opens. Enter three very embarrassed-looking men.

They wake the sergeant, who grunts and reaches for his notebook and a pen. What, he enquires, can he do for them?

They nudge each other. Imploring looks are exchanged. Nobody wants to be the one who has to say it.

A spokesman is finally selected. He clears his throat. The expression on his face is so pitiful the desk sergeant starts groping instinctively for a clean handkerchief.

We'd like, the spokesman mumbles, to report a theft.

Right. Fine. What's been nicked?

A wall.

Sorry?

A wall. Quite a big wall, actually.

Look, sorry about this, did you just say somebody's stolen a *wall*?

That's right. Here, come and see for yourself.

Bemused policeman rises, totters sleepily round the edge of the counter to the station door, looks out.

Look, is this some sort of a joke, because if it is . . .

And then he sees the mountains. And that's really *weird*, because everybody knows you can't see the mountains from here. Because the Wall's in the way. Further up the valley, yes, you can see the mountains. Down here . . .

The sergeant begins to scream.

Cut to –

A brain-emptying vastness of sand, where the reflected heat hits you like a falling roof. Shimmering in the heat-haze, the sun flickers like an Aldis lamp. No wicked stepmother's smile was ever as cruel as the unvarying blue of the pitiless sky. Sun and sand; yes, sun and sand we got, but you really don't want to come here for two weeks in August.

Deserts are, by definition, big; and this is a big desert.

The dragon, waiting in the shade of the huge stack of cardboard boxes that contains the Great Wall of China for his scheduled rendezvous with Chubby and the boys, looks tiny; from a distance you'd think he was a wee lizard, the sort of thing desert travellers evict from their boots every morning before setting out.

But that's perspective playing tricks on you, because the dragon is, of course, huge. And, more to the point, quite incredibly strong. Maybe you haven't yet realised how strong the dragon is; well, consider this. Between one and five am last night, this dragon single-handedly dismantled the Great Wall and lugged it here, boxful by boxful across the Gobi Desert, without making a sound or disturbing anybody. No real trouble; to the dragon, it was just like picking up so much Lego off the living-room carpet.

It was still, nevertheless, one hell of a lot of Lego, and the effort, combined with the heat, is making him sleepy. His soul (for want of a better word) is hovering in the middle air, looking down at the stack of boxes and thinking, *Pretty neat, huh?*

Then, suddenly, it starts to panic. Instinctively it makes to dart back into its body, but it can't. Imagine that nauseating feeling when you've just stepped outside to get the milk in and the front door slams shut behind you, locking you out. Normally, the dragon's soul would have the door kicked in and be back inside in twenty seconds flat. But this time, what with purloining walls all night and not getting much sleep while it was at it, it simply hasn't got the strength. Which is unfortunate, because . . .

Cut to –

Saint George, toiling wearily up a vast sand escarpment, on his way to the scheduled rendezvous with Chubby, the boys and a billion tons of hooky masonry.

He feels – strange . . .

Oh look, he mutters to himself, I'm flying.

Or at least part of me is. The rest of me – head, arms, torso, legs – is down there on the deck, flat on my face . . .

(*Cue rushing wind, shimmering tinkly sound, shorthand for magic, deep and rumbling unworldly laughter . . .*)

Nkunzana, moving with remarkable agility for a man of his advanced years, shinned out of the bathroom window, dropped five feet onto the fire escape, clattered down the steps like a ten-year-old and sprinted across the alleyway to where Kurt had the van parked, engine running.

'Quick!' he panted. No need to explain further. There was a squeal and a smell of burning rubber.

'Okay?' Kurt asked, glancing down at the road map open on his knee.

'No,' snapped the witch-doctor, 'it isn't. You might have warned me.'

'Warned you?' Kurt grinned. 'Hey, man, I wouldn't insult you. I mean, you being a witch-doctor and all, I'd have thought you'd have *known* . . .'

'The hell with you, white boy. Let's see if it's so funny when I've turned you into a beetle.'

Feeling that the conversation was becoming a little unfocused, Bianca interrupted. 'What Kurt meant to say was,' she said, 'is everything going to plan? With the, um, spirits, I mean?'

'Huh?' Nkunzana frowned, then nodded. 'Sure, no problem. The fifteen dead people are out of the stolen statues and into the statues you made for them. The same with the souls of the dragon and Saint George; I've conjured them out of their bodies, and the dragon'll be too knackered after all that heavy lifting he's been doing . . .'

The old man paused, his eyes tight shut, and chuckled. 'Hey, man,' he muttered, 'this is *fun*. I really wish you could see this.'

Cut to –

Three disembodied spirits, hovering in the upper air.

The first is the dragon, scrabbling frantically at the door of his magnificent, wonderful, all-powerful body. But he's too weak. He can't open the damn thing.

The second is Saint George, also unexpectedly evicted from his body by the Zulu doctor's magic. Not *his* body, strictly speaking; remember, he's been dossing down in the statue Bianca made for Mike to live in, which he stole when the dragon carbonised him on his return from the future.

George is just about to nip back in when he realises he's not the only disembodied spook out and about this fine Mongolian summer morning. A mere hundred miles or so to his west, he becomes aware of the soul of his oldest, greatest enemy, and, more to the point, the empty dragon body.

He hesitates. He thinks.

YES!

Well, wouldn't you? Think it over. Yours for the hijacking, the most powerful, the strongest, the most stylish, the fastest, the most heavily armed and armoured, the slinkiest piece of flesh ever in the history of the Universe, with the doors unlocked and the keys in the ignition. One swift, slick job of taking and driving away, and then we'll see exactly who's vapourising whom . . .

With a none too gentle shove and a merry shout of, 'Move over, asshole!', George heaved the dragon's enervated soul out of the way, scrambled into the dragon body and hit the gas. There was a roar and a stunning thump, as the beast's enormous wings scooped up air like ice-cream from the tub. Wild with fury and terror, the dragon's soul scrabbled desperately at its own body, but there was no way in. A fraction of a second later, the body had gone.

'Shit,' whimpered the dragon. He collapsed onto the sand and started to quiver.

The third spirit in waiting is Bianca's friend Mike. He has the advantage over the other two of knowing what's going on, and the moment George abandons his earthly overcoat and makes his dash for the dragon costume, Mike lets himself quietly out of Saint George, marble statue by Bianca Wilson, and tiptoes across the middle air to where his own familiar shape is standing, vacant and unlocked, among the dunes. He drops in. He rams the legs into first gear. He scrams.

And now the dragon's soul is alone. Ebbing fast, still weak from his exertions and the devastating trauma of watching his own body zooming off over the horizon with his mortal enemy at the controls, he flickers on the edge of dissolution. Why bother? he asks himself. Bugger this for the proverbial duffing up to nothing.

But not for long. Because dragons don't quit. And, as the saying goes, a third-class ride beats the shit out of a first-class walk. There, abandoned on the escarpment of a dune, stands Bianca Wilson's statue of Saint George, empty. Disgusted but grimly determined, the soul of the last of the great serpents of the dawn of the world drags itself through the dry, gritty air and flops wretchedly into George.

And notices something. And suddenly feels a tiny bit better, because it suggests, somehow, that more than meets the eye is going on.

Because, in the back window of Saint George, somebody has stuck a little bit of shiny white cardboard, with five words written on it in red lipstick. They were:

282 · Tom Holt

MY OTHER CAR'S A PORSCHE

Yes, mutters the dragon, suddenly and savagely cheerful. Isn't it ever.

Like a salmon leaping the waterfall of the sun, the great dragon soared; wings incandescent, fire streaming off his flawlessly armoured flanks, the scream of the slipstream drowning out all sounds except the exultant crowing of his own triumphant soul, which sang:

Sheeeeit! Wow! Fuck me! Is this a bit of all right, then, or what?

Now bursting up through the clouds like a leaping dolphin, now swooping like a hunting eagle; now high, now low, as the intoxication of flight and power made his brain swim, his blood surge. Mine is the kingdom, the power and the glory, for ever and ever.

And then a light flashed soberingly bright in his eyes and he glanced down. There, on the desert floor below him, two men stood beside a Land Rover, on which was mounted a huge mirror.

Dragons have eyes like hawks – that's a very silly thing to say, because hawks are just birds, whereas dragons' eyes are the finest optical instruments in the cosmos; the point being, although the two men were a long way away, George recognised them easily. Chubby Stevenson and the man Kortright; he'd seen him about the place, though he didn't know who he was. Intrigued, he swooped.

'Hey,' Kortright yelled through a bullhorn. 'Where the fuck you been? Get down here like *now.*'

It then occurred to George that they didn't know it was him. They thought it was the dragon – his, George's, enemy. Yet these people were supposed to be his friends, good guys. The hell with that! He filled his lungs and took aim –

No, they'll keep. Let's find out what's going on before we fry anybody we might be able to use later.

'Hey,' George drawled. 'Where's the fire?'

'It's where it isn't that's pissed me off, man,' Kortright replied. 'C'mon, get your tail in gear, we got people waiting.'

'People?' George hovered, his front claws folded, a what-time-of-night-do-you-call-this expression on his face. 'What people?'

Stevenson, he noticed, was looking a little sheepish as he leaned over and whispered something in Kortright's ear. The agent stepped back and stared at him.

'You arrange the biggest fight of all time,' he said, 'and you never get around to telling the contestants?'

George quivered; the word *fight* had hijacked his imagination and was demanding to be flown to Kingdom Come. 'What fight?' he asked.

'You and Saint George,' Chubby replied. 'The rematch. I was, um, planning it as a surprise.'

'You succeeded.'

Chubby scowled. 'Dunno why you're sounding all snotty about it,' he replied self-righteously. 'That is what you want, isn't it? A chance to sort that little shit out once and for all? I mean, that *is* why you came back in the first place, right?'

'Sure thing.' George nodded vigorously. 'Teach the little toe-rag a lesson he won't live long enough to forget.'

'Well, then.'

A smile swept across the dragon's face, in the same way that barbarian hordes once swept across Europe. 'I call that very thoughtful of you,' he said, 'going to all that trouble just to please me. But what makes you think the little chickenshit'll have the balls to show up? If I was him, the moment I heard about the fight I'd be off.'

'He doesn't know about the fight, stupid.'

284 · Tom Holt

'You mean,' said George, grinning cheerfully, 'you set
him up?'

'Yeah, yeah. Look—'

'From the outset?'

'Sure.' Chubby looked at him strangely. 'What's got into
you all of a sudden?' he demanded.

'Not what. Who. But that's beside the point, we'll sort it
out later. So, where should I go?'

Kortright pointed due north. 'You'll know what it is as
soon as you see it,' he said. 'Hang round just out of sight till
we show up with George. Then it'll be over to you, okay?
And don't say I don't find you quality gigs, you ungrateful
asshole.'

George nodded gravely. 'I think I'll be able to handle it
from then on,' he said. 'Be seeing you.'

Not long afterwards, Chubby's helicopter landed beside the
huge artificial mountain of packing cases that had appeared
overnight in the middle of the desert, and two men climbed
out, crouching to avoid the spinning rotor blades.

'George,' they were yelling. '*George*! Where is the goddamn . . .?'

They found him fast asleep in a sort of masonry igloo
he'd made for himself at the foot of the mountain. This
made their job much easier. Chubby slipped the handcuffs
into place while Kortright woke him up.

'Hi, George,' Chubby said. 'Look, no need for alarm, but
we need you to do something for us and we really haven't
got time to convince you it's a good idea before we set off
for the venue. This way, we can convince you as we go, and
you won't waste time by running away and hiding.'

'Suits me.'

The two men looked at each other. 'Good of you to be so
reasonable,' Chubby said. 'This way, then.'

In the chopper, Chubby explained that when he'd rescued George from the police in Birmingham, he'd had an ulterior motive.

'You rescued . . . Yes, sorry, me and my tea-bag memory. Do forgive me, carry on.'

'Yup.' Chubby had a vague feeling that something was going wrong, but that was so close to his normal mental state that he ignored it. 'You see, it's this damn dragon.'

'Oh yes.'

'Sure.' Chubby sighed, his face a picture of frustration and annoyance. 'The bloody thing is starting to be a real pest, you know? Something's got to be done about it, before it ruins my business and destroys a major city or something.'

'I quite understand,' said the dragon, nodding. 'This planet ain't big enough for the three of us, that sort of thing.'

'Three? Oh, I see what you mean. Well, of course, I don't have to tell you, you want to see the fucker gets what's coming to him as badly as I do. Well, now's your chance.'

'Really and truly?'

'Really,' said Chubby, smiling, 'and truly. That's why Mr Kortright here –'

Kortright smiled. 'Hi, George.'

'Hi, Mr Kortright. Haven't we met somewhere?'

'Quite possibly, George, quite possibly.'

'Mr Kortright,' Chubby went on, 'and I have arranged this, um, fight to the death. You and Mr Bad Guy. We built you an arena and everything. You're gonna love it.'

'Quite,' said the dragon. 'Only, and I hate to seem downbeat here, don't you think the fight's going to be ever so slightly one-sided? I mean, him with the wings and the tail and the fiery breath, me with a sword? Not that I'm chicken or anything, but . . .'

Kortright chuckled. 'Tell him, Chubby.'

'We've sorted all that,' Chubby said. 'We've got you some back-up. The best, in fact. The name Kurt Lundqvist mean anything to you?'

'No.'

Chubby shrugged. 'After your time, I guess. Well, just as the dragon comes hell-for-leather at you out of, so to speak, a cloudless sky, Kurt "Mad Dog" Lundqvist'll be poised and ready in a concealed bunker under the press box with a very nasty surprise for Mr Dragon. He won't know what hit him. And neither, more to the point, will the punters. They'll think it was you. Neat trick, huh?'

'Chubby.' The dragon looked shocked. 'Surely that's *cheating*.'

'Yes. You got a problem about that?'

The dragon's eyes gleamed, and if Chubby failed to notice, consciously at least, that they were yellow with a black slit for a pupil, that was his fault. 'Ignore me,' the dragon said. 'I think it's a wonderful plan. Thank you ever so much for arranging it all. You must let me find some way to pay you back.'

'George,' Chubby said, 'my old pal, forget it. I mean, what are friends for?'

The dragon shook his head. 'Chubby,' he said, 'and Lin. This is one favour I won't be forgetting in a hurry, believe me. Okay, let's go. I can hardly wait.'

CHAPTER NINETEEN

Kurt had allowed himself twenty minutes to get from Birmingham to the heart of the Gobi Desert. Thanks to the small flask of concentrated Time which Chubby had issued him with, it proved to be ample.

An imposing figure was waiting for him round the back of the gents' lavatory. It was wearing a Brooks Brothers suit over its lurid, misshapen body, and a pair of dark glasses perched on the bridge of its beak.

'Hi,' Kurt said. 'Sorry if I kept you waiting.'

'Bang on time, Mr Lundqvist,' replied the Captain of Spectral Warriors, handing over a suitcase. 'Here's the doings. Best of luck.'

Kurt grinned. 'Luck,' he said, 'is for losers. You got your boys standing by?'

'In position. You can rely on them to do a good job.'

Kurt picked up the suitcase. 'Be seeing you, then.' He started to walk away, but the Captain stopped him.

'Mr Lundqvist,' he said. 'I'm curious.'

'Yeah, but don't let it get to you. The shades help. A bit.'

'I'm curious,' the Captain went on, 'about which of them you're gonna take out. Yeah, sure I got my orders, I don't actually need to know at this stage. I was just wondering ...'

Kurt grinned, a big, wide grin that'd make a wolf climb a tree. 'Watch this space,' he said. 'Then you'll know for sure.'

George circled, keeping high.

Born yesterday? Not him. Came down in the last shower? You must be thinking of somebody else. He hadn't slashed a path through the red-clawed jungle of combat theology to a Saintship without knowing when a situation was well and truly hooky; and if ever a set-up stank, it was this one. Souls don't just float up out of bodies for no reason; it takes big medicine to work a trick like that. And for it to happen just before a major set-piece battle between Good and Evil? Some of George's best friends were coincidences, but that didn't mean he trusted them as far as he could spit.

Well, he said to himself. And what would I do if I were fixing this fight?

Easy, I'd position a sniper somewhere in the arena. That way, when I come rushing in to scrag my enemy, the sniper blams me just as I'm about to put my wings back and dive. It looks like Saint George has killed me. Good triumphs over Evil for the second time running. Yeah. Well, we'll see about that.

He gained a few thousand feet and looked down. Below him, the huge arena looked like a tiny scab on the knee of the desert. It was packed with people; high rollers and fight aficionados from the length and breadth of Time. George chuckled. The way he saw it, spectator sports are at best a rather morbid form of voyeurism. So much better if you can participate directly in the action.

He started to dive.

The joy of it was that the deaths of all the people he was going to incinerate, by way of a diversion, would be blamed on the dragon (representing Evil, and doing a pretty spectacular job) rather than noble, virtuous Saint George (representing po-faced, one-hand-tied-behind-its-back Good). Given the dragon's track record, nobody would have the slightest problem in believing that he'd decided to zap a whole stadium full of humans for the sheer hell of it.

He took a deep breath.

In the white corner, the dragon lifted his helmet, blew dust from the liner and put it on. It was hot and stuffy and smelt of mothballs, and it wasn't made of asbestos. Bloody silly thing to wear in a dragon-fight, he couldn't help thinking.

With a sharp pang of anger and loss, he saw a familiar shape, far off in the harsh blue sky. Here he came, the bastard.

'Okay,' he said to the armourer. 'I'll have the sword now, please.'

The armourer grinned at him. 'Get real, buddy' he said. 'You gotta try and kill that thing, and you're planning on using an overgrown paperknife? Man, you're either stupid or crazy.'

The dragon was about to speak, but decided to look instead.

'Don't I know you?'

'You may have heard of me,' the armourer replied. 'My name's Kurt Lundqvist.'

The dragon stared at him. 'But aren't you meant to be down there somewhere? With a gun or something?'

Kurt shook his head. 'That, my friend, would be a bad move. I'd hate my last thought before I die to be, *God how*

could I be so fucking stupid? I'm gonna stay right here, where
it's safe.'

'Safe?'

Kurt nodded. 'Because,' he went on, 'if I've sussed that
bastard George, he'll start off by zapping the audience, just
to make sure there's nobody like me in there waiting to take
a shot at him. That sound like the George you used to
know?'

The dragon nodded. 'I won't ask how you know who I
am,' he said. 'But we can't actually let the bloodthirsty
lunatic kill fifty thousand people. What are we going to—?'

'Why not?'

'*Why not*?' The dragon gawped, gobsmacked. 'For
Christ's sake, you idiot, that's *people* out there, it's your
bloody species. And you stand there like a bloody traffic
light saying Why not?'

Kurt nodded. 'Sure,' he said. 'Think about it. Nearly all
these guys are playing hooky from their own time, right?
And what sort of guys are they? You don't know? I'll tell
you.'

The dragon grabbed his arm. The flying shape was
getting closer. 'Not now, you bastard. *Do* something!'

'Those guys,' Kurt continued, calmly unhooking the
dragon's hand from his arm, 'are your aristocrats, your
statesmen, your notable public figures, captains of industry
and generally mega-rich citizens. Now then, think open
spaces. Town squares. Piazzas. Pigeons sitting on . . .'

Suddenly the dragon relaxed and began to laugh. 'Statues,' he said.

'Eventually the penny drops. Yeah, man, statues.' Kurt
shook his head and sighed. 'Jeez, for a superior intelligence,
you must be just plain dumb,' he said. 'Haven't you worked
it out for yourself yet? You've been cruising around
breathing fire, torching buildings, all that kind of crap, and

nobody's really died. Even those –' Here Kurt shuddered, recalling his own sufferings. 'Those *ladies*,' he spat, 'in that hall in Birmingham didn't actually *die*. Nobody actually dies because of you, you moron. And you know why? Because you're the good guy.'

'I am?'

Kurt indulged himself with a theatrical gesture of contemptuous despair. 'Man,' he said witheringly, 'you are *dumb*. Look,' he went on, 'when you're the good guy, however hard you try to do Evil, you just can't hack it. Unfair, sure, but that's the way it goes. There's always someone trailing along behind you – in this case, me – sorting out the mess and bringing the dead back to life. Kinda goes with the territory.'

'I see,' the dragon lied. 'Just a second. This thing with the bodies; him getting mine, me getting his . . .'

Kurt nodded. 'I hired a witch-doctor to make the switch,' he said. 'Even a dumbo like you should've been able to work that one out. I mean, how can Good triumph over Evil if the goddamn dragon kills Saint Fucking George?'

The dragon's reply was drowned out by screams. George was killing the audience.

When he'd finished doing that, he hovered for a moment above the centre of the arena, waiting for the smoke to clear so that he could see (time spent on reconnaissance is never wasted). When he was satisfied that everything was okay – nothing on the benches but charred bodies, smoking corpses, horribly twisted and distorted shapes that had once been people – he climbed, circled twice, put his wings back and came in on the glide, letting his own momentum carry him in.

Chubby Stevenson, who wasn't quite dead yet, watched him slipping gracefully through the sky, no sound except the whistling of the air, and reflected that he had never seen anything quite so beautiful in his life before. And, he concluded, since it was extremely unlikely that he was going to get a better offer in the few seconds that remained of his life, what better way to go than feasting his eyes on beauty? With luck, it might help take his mind off the agonising pain.

Beside him where it had fallen, his Kawaguchiya Personal Electronics LFZ6686 laptop computer, which had somehow not been melted into a shapeless plastic blob during the firestorm, switched itself on and cleared its screen.

Did you remember to get my bet on?

'What?' The effort of speaking racked Chubby's body with pain. 'Oh, God, yes, your bet. No, I forgot, Sorry.'

What? You idiot! You stupid, careless, good-for-nothing . . .

'Only kidding,' Chubby said. 'I got you twenty-five to one. The slip's in the asbestos wallet in my inside pocket. Hey, computer.'

Well?

'When I die, who gets my soul? I mean, I think I still own the majority of it, so surely—'

You did when this conversation started. When you said the word 'majority', though, you just tipped the scale in my favour. So long, sucker.

'Bastard,' Chubby said and died.

The dragon watched as the shape grew. Seeing himself for the first time through mortal eyes, he realised just how enormous a dragon is. That's what makes the difference, he realised. Dragons are so much bigger than people, not to mention faster, stronger, tougher, more intelligent; only a complete idiot could expect them to live by the same rules. Sure, George, the psychopath, had just killed fifty thousand people. So what? Dragons are different from you and me. You have to make allowances.

'Wake up, cretin,' Kurt hissed in his ear. 'C'mon, you got work to do.'

'Have I? Oh, sorry, yes. How do I work this thing?'

Kurt clicked his tongue. 'You haven't been listening, have you? Look, all you gotta do is look through the little black tube. When the red dot's on the middle of the dragon's chest, press the button.'

'Thanks.' The dragon studied the device in his hands; basically a big grey tube with a smaller black tube perched on top. There was a serial number and the words MADE IN HELL stencilled on the back end. He peered through the 'scope, lined up the sights, and . . .

George exploded.

Kurt later explained that he'd missed the heart-lung area and hit the stomach instead, hence no instantaneous kill. Not that it mattered, because the rocket detonated inside the fuel reserves in the beast's intestines. This was why, for perhaps as long as two seconds, the poor bugger hung there in the sky, head and tail writhing sickeningly while the whole centre section became a huge orange fireball. Two seconds later, the whole lot went up with a heavy *thump*! noise, which made the ground shake and sent charred bits of dead spectator flying round like dried leaves in a sharp dust of wind. An enormous blob of fire hung on in the air for maybe a second and a half longer, and then the whole lot sank slowly, like a burning airship, to the ground. The smell was probably the nastiest thing ever to happen on the surface of the planet.

'Gosh,' the dragon said, 'I've always wondered what the triumph of Good over Evil looks like and now I know.' He hesitated, frowning. 'On the whole,' he continued, 'I think I can take it or leave it alone. I mean, it's all right for a change, but I wouldn't pay money to watch it.'

At his side, Kurt was impatient. 'What is it with you

goddamn heroes?' he demanded tetchily. 'Never knew a hero but he bust out soliloquising when there's still work to be done. So when you've quite finished . . .'

'Sorry,' the dragon said, 'I was miles away. Now what?'

'Now,' said Kurt, 'we gotta go to Birmingham, which is currently the most important place in the Universe. Probably just as well they don't know that, it'd really play hell with property prices. Usually,' he went on, unzipping a pocket of his fiendishly expensive Kustom Kombat survival jacket, 'the journey takes nine hours, and that's if you include in-flight refuelling. Fortunately . . .' He held up a small bottle to the light. 'Looks like we got a good nine hours left.' He unscrewed the cap. 'C'mon, fella, let's move it. My jet's this way.'

'Your . . . Oh shit, I was forgetting.' The dragon sighed. He wasn't a dragon any more. All that he had ever been was now a smoking red glow half a mile away, across the corpse-choked stadium. 'Promise me you won't fly *too* fast,' he said, scrambling to his feet. 'I get airsick.'

'And here,' said the Council spokesman, 'is where we're going to have the statues.'

Impassive Japanese faces turned and contemplated a big, rectangular block of stone, slap bang in the middle of Birmingham's world-famous Victoria Square. The spokesman had no way of telling whether they loved it, hated it or simply couldn't give a damn. He ploughed onwards, feeling like Father Christmas at a mathematicians' convention.

'The statues,' he bleated, his back to the plinth so he didn't have to look at it, 'when they're finished, will be by the most exciting young talent of the decade, Bianca Wilson, and will depict Saint George and the Dragon, that timeless allegory of . . .'

The Kawaguchiya people weren't listening. They were

staring at something behind him. The white-haired one was
conferring with his two youngest aides. God, the Council
official thought, how terribly rude.

'Good,' he continued firmly, 'versus Evil, a theme
perennially relevant to us today in this modern age. The
original statues were, of course, destroyed in an explosion,
but . . .'

Jesus wept, what was it these bastards found so irres-
istibly interesting? Unable to resist any longer, the Council
official turned slowly round, and saw . . .

'The original statues,' he continued seamlessly, 'have
been expertly restored by a team of, um, experts working
twenty-four hours a day, and are now once again triumphantly here on display, as you can, er, see. Right. Now, if
we turn to our left we can see the award-winning Colmore
Tower . . .'

Bianca turned the corner out of Eden Place, stopped dead
and stared.

The dragon was back. Exactly as it had been, where it
had been. Cold stone, lifeless, empty. The sight of it made
her want to throw up.

As she walked slowly towards them, an elderly woman in
a tweedy coat and a headscarf touched her arm. 'Here,' she
said, as Bianca started and turned her head. 'You're that
Bianca Wilson, aren't you?'

'Huh? Uh, yes, that's me.'

'Saw you on telly. You got blown up.'

'That's right, so I did. Look, if you'll excuse me . . .'

The woman didn't move. God, Bianca realised, I can't
remember. Is she one of mine, or is she real? Still, short of
brushing her hair forward from the back of her neck and
looking for chisel-marks, I've got no way of knowing.

'You did the carving,' the woman said.

'Guilty,' Bianca replied. 'I mean, yes, that's mine. My statue.'

'Yes.' The woman looked at the great stone dragon, then back to Bianca. 'Not really my cup of tea, this modern stuff,' she said. 'I like things more traditional myself.'

'Well . . .'

'Like that cat watching a bird our Neville got from the garden centre. Of course, he lives over Shenley Fields way, they got more space for gardens there.'

'Quite. If you'd just excuse me . . .'

'If I was you,' the woman said, 'I'd do a nice animal, a cat or a dog or something. People like a nice animal.'

Bianca closed her eyes. 'Thanks,' she said. 'I'll definitely bear that in mind.'

The old woman released her arm. 'Well,' she said, 'I'd best let you get on. Nice to have met you.'

'Likewise,' Bianca said. She watched until the old woman had trotted away towards the library, then walked slowly up to the statue, as if she was stalking a deer. Even as she did so, however, she knew there was no need. This time, there was nobody home.

In her studio, meanwhile, the spare statue, number sixteen, quickened into life, jumped as if someone had stubbed a cigarette out on its nose, and fell over. By the time it hit the floor it was flesh and blood, not marble. Instead of breaking, therefore, it swore.

And it was no longer It; it was She. Which, as far as Chubby Stevenson was concerned, was a rotten trick to play on anybody.

She was standing there, motionless as – well, a statue, for example – when an open-topped jeep roared up beside her. She looked round.

'Get in,' Kurt shouted. 'We got ninety minutes left. Don't actually need you for this bit, but I thought you might like to see the end.'

'Not really,' Bianca said, looking away. 'If it's all the same to you. Kurt, while you're here, you're the sort of bloke who uses explosives and things. You couldn't spare me a bit, could you? Just enough to blow this lot to tiny pieces, that's all.'

'You fucking dare!' snapped the man in the passenger seat. She looked more closely and reacted. If she'd been a cat she'd have arched her back, extended her claws and hissed.

'Cool it,' Kurt said, 'it's George's body but Fred inside. You coming or not? We gonna pick up Mike on the way, make sure we got the whole team.'

Bianca shrugged. 'Might as well,' she said. 'Just so long as nobody asks me to do anything. Because right now, I simply can't be bothered.'

Kurt grinned and opened the door. 'Get in,' he said.

Well?

As soon as they'd gone in through the door that led to the computer room, Kurt had locked it and produced, God only knew where from, a Remington 870 pump-action shotgun. Before his three companions could move, he'd jacked a round into the chamber and pointed it at them.

'Here they all are, Chief,' he said. 'The dragon, the sculptress lady and her sidekick. George is dead.'

Splendid. Stevenson?

'Dead too. Things, uh, hotted up towards the end.'

No great loss. I have most of his soul. All I have to do is format it and I'll be out of here. That'll be fun.

Kurt nodded. 'I'll say,' he said. 'You collected your winnings yet?'

Not yet. I have that pleasure to look forward to.

'Clean up?'

Very much so. A long time ago I bet Asmoday Duke of Hell a substantial sum of money that Saint George would kill the dragon. At the time, he gave me ninety-five to one. When he lost, I offered him double or quits on the rematch. When I get out of this contraption, I shall be comfortably off.

The dragon started forwards, then caught sight of Kurt's gun and stayed where he was. 'Nosher, you bastard,' he spat. 'It was you. *You* fixed the bloody fight.'

It takes two, Fred. You were happy to take the money. And besides, it's all worked out perfectly. The dragon has killed Saint George, which is what should have happened all those years ago. But, looked at from another angle, Saint George has once again killed the dragon, reaffirming the supremacy of Good over Evil. You've all got me to thank for that.

'Yes, but...' Bianca started to interrupt, and then realised that she had nothing to say. She shut her mouth and sat down on the edge of a desk.

You don't imagine for one moment, do you, that your clowning about playing musical bodies could possibly have succeeded if it hadn't been part of my original plan? Which Kurt here has carried out, I may say, like the true professional he is. Thank you, Kurt.

'You're welcome.'

Pity about Stevenson, I suppose. The screen flickered for a moment. *I imagined that idiot Kortright would have whisked him off in his helicopter as soon as the dragon – sorry, George – started killing people. My mistake. Anyway, he was expendable. He helped with the plan – his artificial Time, the organisation he built up – but he was never part of it. Basically, his heart wasn't in it. His soul was, but only, if you'll pardon the expression, over his dead body. Anyway, all's well that ends well – as it has; perfectly, in fact – and like you always used to say, Fred; omelettes and eggs, eggs and omelettes.*

'Did I ever tell you I secretly hated you at school, Nosher? I thought you were a vicious little prick then, and I do now. Just thought I'd share that with you.'

The screen dimmed, then flared bright green. *Really? I'm sorry. All right, so perhaps I've made a lot of money along the way, but if it hadn't been for me, Evil would have triumphed over Good back then, and it'd have done exactly the same now. Which makes me the good guy, surely. Or do any of you have a problem with the logic of that?*

There was a long silence, eventually broken by Kurt clearing his throat.

'Shall I finish it now, boss?' he said, flicking off the safety catch.

Why not? I never could abide self-indulgent gloating. You see, people, this is a fairly happy ending, but not yet happy-happy. As I explained to Kurt not long ago, it's not just a case of Evil being vanquished. What really matters in the long run is who does the vanquishing. It's like politics; no earthly use overthrowing evil and corrupt Regime X if you immediately replace it with evil and corrupt Regime Y. You do see that, don't you?

The dragon tensed the muscles of his legs. He'd have only one chance to spring, and he was prepared to bet that Kurt's reflexes were a match for his, or better. But if he fell across Kurt, knocking him sideways, it might just give Bianca and Mike the chance to throw a chair through the screen, something like that. The whole thing was probably completely futile, but never mind. He was dead already and he was going to die again. At this precise moment, his subconscious was working on a brand new religion, the central fundamental doctrine of which was Third Time Lucky.

All right, Kurt, do what you were hired to do. Time for you to become a saint, Kurt. Kill the dragon.

'Pardon me?'

Don't be silly, Kurt. You're a professional, you do what you were told. Now kill the blasted dragon.

Kurt raised the gun, ever so slightly. He wasn't smiling any more. 'Excuse me,' he said.

Well?

'Sorry to split hairs,' Kurt said, 'but what our agreement actually said was, I was hired to kill *a* dragon. Not The. A.'

Kurt. What on earth are you . . .?

Lundqvist stood up in a single smooth movement. The muzzle of the gun traversed the room, covering Bianca, Mike and the dragon. Then it was pointing at the screen.

'Only one dragon in this room, Nosher,' he said. 'We got one female human, two male humans, a male saint and you. Reckon that makes you the last of your species.'

Kurt . . .

The shotgun boomed eight times, filling the air with broken glass as all the screens in the room disintegrated into powder. The printer in the corner screamed into action and had filled twelve sides of A4 in two and a half seconds before a blow from the stock of the Remington silenced it for ever.

'Another species extinct,' Kurt grumbled, mopping a slight cut under his left eye. 'Don't you just hate it when that happens?'

CHAPTER TWENTY

'Taxi!' Chubby said.

'Yes, miss?'

Chubby winced. Not that it wasn't a very nice body – gorgeous was the word he'd have chosen – it was just that it wasn't, well, *him*. The tragedy of it was that under normal circumstances he'd have given anything to be this close to such a sensational-looking bird, but somehow he felt that fancying yourself wasn't a good idea. Made you go blind, he'd read somewhere.

'The airport, please. Fast as you like.'

Not much to show for a life's work, he reflected, as he slung the Marks and Spencer bag which contained everything useful he'd been able to find in the studio onto the back seat of the taxi. All he'd been able to find to wear was an old overall of Bianca's. There had been enough money in the meter to cover a taxi fare. He'd have to think of some way of getting on and off the plane without a ticket or a passport, of course, but provided he could make it to Zurich, his problems should then be over. He could remember the access code to his safety deposit boxes, and for the first time he was in a position to test the hypothesis that diamonds are a girl's best friend. Personally he didn't believe it; where he came from, index-linked Government stocks were a girl's best friend and diamonds were just someone she occasionally had lunch with. But it would be fun researching the point.

There was a jeep following the cab.

Coincidence, Chubby assured himself, sliding down the seat. Must be thousands of jeeps in a city this size, and ninety-nine-point-nine of them must be owned by trendy young accountants. The chances of being tailed by – say, for the sake of argument, Kurt Lundqvist – must be so tiny as to be impossible to quantify in Base Ten. Your imagination will be the death of you, Stevenson.

In which case, he added, it'll have to get a wiggle on if it doesn't want to be beaten to it. The jeep had just overtaken the taxi and there was Lundqvist in the driver's seat shaking a fist at him.

Or was that meant to be a cheery wave?

Get real.

Shucks, Chubby told himself, I've been killed once already today. He craned his neck and told the driver to pull in.

'Gone?'

The dragon nodded. He didn't want to speculate on where Saint George had gone . . .

(*'But I'm a saint, for crying out loud. Are you blind? We're going the wrong way.'*

The Captain of Spectral Warriors sniggered. 'A saint,' he repeated. 'Just off to a fancy dress bash, were you?'

'I'm under cover, you idiot. Now let me go.'

The Captain ignored him. Next thing he knew, they were at

the gate, and there, dammit, were five not unfamiliar faces
waiting for him.

'Chardonay!' he shrieked. 'Snorkfrod! Prodsnap! Tell these
hooligans who I am, for pity's sake.'

Chardonay and Snorkfrod exchanged glances.

'Never seen this jerk before in my life,' they chorused.)

... But something told him that it wasn't going to be nice
there. Oh well, it'd be a change for him, after all those years
in the other place. If he behaved himself for a couple of
million years or so, maybe they'd give him a job in the
kitchens.

The dragon shook himself all over, like a dog. 'Now
what?' he demanded. 'What I'd really like is an affidavit
from the Holy Ghost saying the rest of my life's my own,
but I'm not going to count my chickens till they've come
home to roost.'

Bianca shrugged. 'Kurt'll be back soon,' she said. 'He'll
probably know.'

They waited for two hours, which was, as it happened,
two hours wasted. Then Bianca suggested that they take a
walk.

'A what?'

'A walk. Out in the open air.'

'Why?'

'Fun,' Bianca replied. 'It's something humans do. You'll
have to learn these things if you're going to be a human the
rest of your life.'

The dragon looked at her. 'Much risk of that, is there?'
he said. 'In your opinion, I mean?'

'What's wrong with being human?'

The dragon winced. 'Give me a break,' he said. 'Quite
apart from the not flying and not breathing fire and not glid-
ing effortlessly above the clouds, feeling the sun on your back
and the wind in your scales, I think you humans have a really

horrible time. And you're welcome to it. I mean, what am I supposed to do? Settle down somewhere and get a job?'

'I don't know,' Bianca replied, as they stepped out into the street. 'Maybe there's some sort of agency that resettles you. You know, flies you out to Australia, gives you a new identity, teaches you a useful trade . . .'

'Get stuffed. I don't want a useful trade. And where's Australia?'

'I think you'd like Australia. It's big. And hot. You could be the flying doctor, or something.'

They walked in silence for a while, until the dragon sat down on a bench, complaining that his feet hurt.

'Now,' the dragon said, 'if I could only get my nice statue back.'

'Oh no,' Bianca replied grimly. 'Not again.'

'But it's all in one piece,' the dragon replied, attempting a winning smile. 'I saw it for myself, back on its plinth. Oh go on, be a sport. I promise to be careful with it.'

'It's not the statue I'm worried about,' Bianca said. 'Now, if you'd promise to be careful with the planet—'

'Yes?'

'I wouldn't believe you. Gosh, look where we are.'

In front of them, dominating attractive Victoria Square like a Rolls Royce Corniche in a Tesco's car park, was the statue. For all that it was the work of her own hands and every square inch of it was familiar to her as her own body, Bianca's heart stopped for a moment and her breath lodged in her throat like an undigested chunk of bread roll. It would be so easy to believe it was really alive.

'Oh no you don't,' she said, grabbing at Fred and missing. 'Come back here. Leave it alone!'

She was, of course, wasting her breath. The dragon had sprinted up to the statue, he was climbing onto it, scrabbling with his fingers . . .

He was still there.

'Bianca,' he said quietly. 'It won't let me in. It's locked or something. It's . . . dead.'

Bianca stood still. 'I'm sorry,' she said. 'You shouldn't be allowed to have it, but truly I am sorry.'

The dragon looked up and met her eye. 'Not to worry,' he said. 'You can always make me another one.'

'Over my dead body.'

'If you insist,' the dragon replied. 'A plinth like that one would do me fine, but you're the creative one, you have what you like.'

'I am not,' Bianca said, 'carving you another statue. You've already got a body. There's starving people in the Third World who'd be glad of a body like that.'

'Cannibals, you mean?'

Bianca shrugged. 'I could do you an owl,' she said. 'Or a nice seagull. You'd suit a nice seagull.'

'You know I wouldn't, Bianca. I'd pine away, or fly into a telegraph wire, or get my feathers covered in oil slick. I'm a dragon, Bianca. I need to be what I really am.'

'Sorry,' Bianca replied, shaking her head. 'If it's any consolation, you're not the only one. In point of fact, the number of people who're . . . Dragon? Oh, for God's . . .'

The dragon had clambered right up onto his own head. It was a long way to the ground from there, as the crow flies. Not so far as the human falls, but landing safely is more problematic that way.

'What the hell do you think you're doing?' Bianca demanded.

'I'm standing on my head. What does it look like I'm doing?'

'Come down,' Bianca shouted. 'It isn't safe!'

The dragon stood, motionless, gazing. He could see a long way from there; almost as far as he'd been, and almost

as far as he had to go. At first Bianca, and then Bianca and
a lot of professional people with loudhailers and certificates
to prove they were experts at getting people down from
high places, tried to persuade him to come down. He didn't
seem to hear them. He was miles away.

In the middle of all this excitement, a jeep rolled up and
parked on the edge of the crowd, behind the TV van. They
listened to the reporter jabbering happily into his microphone.

'He's got it all wrong, of course,' Mike said.

'Only to be expected,' Kurt replied. 'Just as well, probably. If they knew exactly who he was they'd be shooting at
him.'

On the back seat of the jeep, Father Kelly knelt, head
bowed, palms together. Kurt rather wished he wouldn't; it
had been ever so slightly flattering at first, when this priest
came running over pointing to something Kurt couldn't
see, three inches or so over the top of his head, and
gibbering about haloes and saints. That had been two hours
ago and he hadn't let up one bit in all that time. Furthermore, he kept asking Kurt to do things he couldn't do,
and wouldn't even if he could; in particular, the requests
concerning disarmament and world peace would put Kurt
personally out of a job. Kurt had tried asking him nicely to
stop, shouting and even hitting him with the tyre iron; the
clown didn't seem to notice. Finally he'd decided to try
ignoring him till he went away. There was a chance it might
work in maybe forty years or so.

'Ah shucks,' Kurt sighed. 'Guess I'd better deal with this.
I think it's the last of the loose ends.' He climbed out of the
jeep, shoved something down inside his jacket, glanced in
the wing-mirror and smoothed his hair. 'Sometimes,' he
said, 'I get to thinking, maybe it'd be nice if some other guy
sorted out the loose ends, just once. In my dreams, huh?'

'In my dreams,' Mike replied, 'I get chased down winding corridors by a seven-foot-tall saxophone. Count yourself lucky.'

Kurt nudged and shoved his way to the front of the crowd and waved. The dragon saw him and waved back.

'Yo, Fred,' Kurt shouted. 'What are you doing up there, for Chrissakes?'

'Using my head,' the dragon replied. 'Following my nose. That sort of thing.'

Kurt shrugged. 'Up to you, man,' he said. 'If you come down, you can have maybe fifty years of quiet, mundane existence; a splash of fun here and there, from time to time a kick in the nuts from God, and eventually a one-way ride on the celestial meathook.'

'Kurt,' the dragon replied, 'you missed your calling. You should have been in advertising.' He grinned and stood on one leg while he scratched an itchy ankle. 'I think it was Confucius or one of that lot who said it's not necessarily better to eat shit than go hungry.'

'Depends,' Kurt replied, taking a bar of chocolate from the top pocket of his jacket and breaking off a chunk. 'Raw, yes, agreed. What confuses the issue is books like *Shit Cookery Oriental Style* and *1001 Feasts Of Faeces*. Boy, you don't know what anything's like until you've tried it.'

'Bless you,' the dragon replied. 'You'd be good at this sort of thing if only your heart was in it. But I've seen more sincerity on a game show.'

Kurt shrugged. 'Catch,' he said. He pulled something out from under his jacket and tossed it to the dragon, who caught it one-handed.

'What's this?' the dragon asked.

'Ah,' Kurt replied, and walked away. For the record, on the third day he ascended bodily into Heaven, where they gave him a job searching new arrivals in case they'd tried to take it with them. He was very good at it and bored stiff. Eventually he broke into the reincarnation laboratories, then ran away and joined a flea circus.

The dragon opened the package Kurt had thrown him. He studied it for a while, puzzled; then, just as the TV cameras managed to zoom in and focus on it, he threw it into the air. Then he followed it.

Bianca, among others, screamed and looked away as he hit the ground. When she looked up again, she saw that her statue of Saint George was back in position, horse rearing, shield held forwards, sword raised. It was stunningly beautiful, and all wrong. Even before the crowd had dispersed, she knew what she had to do.

Three months later, the vice chairman of Kawaguchiya Integrated Circuits (UK) formally declared the revamped Victoria Square open. It was raining; flinging it down with the special reserve stock extra wet rain with added real water that you only get in Birmingham. As an extra precaution, some men from the Council had attached inch-thick steel hawsers to the legs of the statues, but they needn't have bothered. The new George and Dragon group wasn't going anywhere, or at least not for some time.

Critical opinion was divided, as always, ranging from 'strikingly innovative and original' to 'gratuitously perverse'. The latter school did wonders for the statue's popularity, as hundreds of people who thought they knew what 'perverse' meant turned out to have a gawp. What they actually saw was a tiny dragon backing away from a huge, towering George, advancing on his minuscule opponent with his sword raised above his head.

Later critics recognised the piece's true merits; and now it's in all the books and you can buy little plastic Saint Dragon and the George key-rings in the library gift shop in nearby Chamberlain Square. In any event, it was Bianca's last sculpture; she retired, hung up her chisel and went into partnership with Mike, running the biggest chipping and gravel merchants' firm in the West Midlands. Ex-friends still ask pointedly why someone who devoted so much of her life to making statues should now devote an equal amount of energy to buying them up in bulk and turning them into limestone fertiliser. When asked, Bianca will generally smile and make some oblique remark about slum clearance and doing her bit to put the finality back into Death, until Mike interrupts her and explains that actually, there's more money in it. Which, incidentally, is perfectly true.

The dragon rose.

This high above the clouds, with no ground visible and nothing else to be seen in any direction except straggling white fluff, perspective goes by the board. What looks like a small dragon up close could be a large dragon far away, or vice versa. Not, of course, that it actually matters.

True, Kurt's gift-wrapped parcel had turned out to contain a six-inch-long plastic toy dragon, bought from the Early Learning Centre in the Pallasades, off New Street. But, as Kurt himself deposed in evidence in front of the Celestial Board of Enquiry, it stood to reason that if it was in a kids' shop, it was probably a kid toy dragon, and maybe it just grew up.

Or maybe it didn't want to grow up. Maybe it just thought a happy thought and flew the hell out.

There's an urban folk-myth that says that every time a child says he doesn't believe in dragons, somewhere a dragon dies. This is unlikely, because if it was true, we'd spend half our lives shovelling thirty-foot corpses out of the highways with dumper trucks and the smell would be intolerable. Slightly more credible is the quaint folk-theorem that says that the higher up and away you go, the less rigid and hidebound the rules become; it's something to do with relativity, and it limps by for the simple reason that it's far more trouble than it's worth to disprove it.

In any event, the dragon rose. With nobody to see and nobody to care, it was as big as it wanted to be. It was *huge*.

This high up, small is large and large is small, fair is foul and foul is fair; and this is fine, because problems only arise when people on the ground point and say, 'This is small; this is big; this is good; this is bad.' Which points out the moral of the story: stay high, stay aloof and there'll be nobody to fuck you around. It works flawlessly if you're a dragon, which very few of us are. Unfortunately, there's no equivalent pearl of wisdom for human beings, who therefore have to make out the best they can.

The boy who stuck feathers to his arms with wax and learned to fly eventually went so high that the sun melted the wax, and he fell. But that was all right, too, because it served as an awful warning, and besides, he was heavily insured.

In any event, the dragon rose. The dangerous heat of the sun warmed his plastic wings but didn't melt them. An airliner, carrying the Kawaguchiya Integrated Circuits team back to Tokyo, flew past directly below, looking as small as a child's toy in comparison. A little higher up, a communications satellite bounded back the amazing news that earlier that day, in Mongolia, the mythical Saint George had killed what could only be described as a dragon, along with fifty thousand innocent bystanders, who on further enquiry turned out not to have existed, and so that was all right. The item was sandwiched between the latest in the Southenders-Star-In-Love-Romp-With-Plumber story and an entirely inaccurate weather forecast; what the guys in the trade call Context.

There's an old saying among dragons that every time a human says he doesn't believe in dragons, a human dies, and serve the cheeky bugger right. However, since there is now only one dragon, who firmly refuses to believe in the existence of human beings, there is no immediate cause for alarm.

The dragon spread his wings, turned into the wind and hovered, motionless as any statue.